"PLAY IT AGAIN," A STRANGE MALE VOICE SAID.

Gillian wavered on the threshold, clutching the doorjamb.

"You have heard it three times," another voice said. Female, with crisp, clipped consonants. "She gives away nothing. She could be two acres away, she could be two thousand. This machine will not help us find her."

Gillian wiped her palms on her skirt and crept towards the living room.

"Play it again," the man insisted. "Listen *behind* her. There must be a shift of earth or a rattle of gravel—"

"Not if she is on one of those tarred plains. There will only be the shift and rattle of candy wrappers."

"If that's what it takes to track her down."

Gillian pressed herself against the wall. Call the cops from KC's or confront these people—how dangerous were they? She crept toward the living room to get a peek.

A sudden weariness broke in the man's voice. "What if she refuses to come back? What if she refuses the rites?"

Gillian stopped midstep.

"We will kill her," the woman said. "That is what we promised her."

THE
SEVENTH
HEART

MARINA FITCH

ACE BOOKS, NEW YORK

This book is an Ace original edition,
and has never been previously published.

THE SEVENTH HEART

An Ace Book / published by arrangement with
the author

PRINTING HISTORY
Ace edition / June 1997

The Putnam Berkley World Wide Web site address is
http://www.berkley.com

Make sure to check out *PB Plug*,
the science fiction/fantasy newsletter, at
http://www.pbplug.com

ISBN: 0-441-00451-2

ACE®
Ace Books are published by The Berkley Publishing Group,
200 Madison Avenue, New York, NY 10016.
ACE and the "A" design are trademarks
belonging to Charter Communications, Inc.

PRINTED IN THE UNITED STATES OF AMERICA

10 9 8 7 6 5 4 3 2 1

To Tom, Joan, James, Bill, Cindy, and Georgina,
for the night we spent together on
October 17, 1989.

With special thanks to Katie Musitelli,
speech therapist extraordinaire.
And, always, to Mark Budz.

THE
SEVENTH
HEART

ONE

THE CRICKETS STOPPED CHIRPING.

Gillian felt along the kitchen counter. Her hand brushed the flashlight like a leaf snagging a spiderweb. A rumble hummed in the distance, deepening as it rolled toward her. She grabbed the flashlight and ran for the doorway.

"Melanie!" she shouted. "Another one!"

Elbows braced against the door frame, Gillian pitched forward with the first lurch of the aftershock. She dropped the flashlight and grasped the frame as the kitchen floor rippled and bucked. A shatter of glass tinkled above the rattling pans and the aftershock's deep-throated growl. A burst of fragrance: sugary, fruity—Melanie's homemade blackberry jam. Amazing the jar hadn't fallen during the initial earthquake a half hour ago.

The floor slammed to a stop. Gillian strained to hear. The crickets started to chirp.

In broad daylight. Well, early evening.

Gillian let go of the doorjamb. She squatted to pick up the flashlight, cradling it to her chest, and surveyed the L-shaped kitchen. Metal and wood floated among a sea of glass, china, olives, mustard, smoked chicken, peeled garlic—the entire contents of the refrigerator—and Melanie's blackberry jam.

Head crushed, a small rabbit saltshaker bled salt into a

swirl of mustard. Gillian pinched a plug of salt and tossed it over her shoulder. It pinged off a pan behind her. She rose slowly, flexing her toes in the hot, knee-high rubber boots.

Picking her way toward the living room, she shuffled through the ankle-deep debris. Glass and china scraped and crunched under her feet. "Melanie!" she called.

She paused to listen. Melanie had gone to the linen closet to get blankets . . . there was nothing in the hall that could fall on her—nothing that hadn't fallen already. Gillian waded into the living room.

If the kitchen was a sea of glass and food, the living room was a sea of books, splintered wood, and ceramic. Gillian scratched her nose with the flashlight. A pine bookshelf had draped itself over the green sofa, its back broken, and spewed books onto the floor. "There's a sick image," she muttered.

Somehow the other pine bookshelf had managed to remain standing. *Standing.* Its books rose in a steep, frozen wave, ready to break if set in motion. Gillian crept past the bookshelf. The thing'd probably kill her if it landed on her—

A bang reverberated through the house. Gillian yelped, scrambling away from the bookshelf. She tripped and sat down in a tangle of spider plant, potting soil, and ceramic.

Nothing moved.

Melanie's voice echoed in the entry. "Gillian?"

Gillian exhaled, slow and long. "In the living room."

Melanie leaned into the room, her short blond hair matted with dust. A smudge of dirt striped her freckled nose, making it look even flatter than it was. "I've staked us a place away from the trees," she said. "Already got the blankets there. The park's filling up fast. Nobody wants to sleep indoors tonight."

Gillian eyed the standing bookshelf, then pulled herself to her feet. "Why doesn't that surprise me?"

Melanie smiled. "That woman two down, the one with the barking rat? She's got a radio set up on a picnic table. Says if anyone's got batteries, it'd be a help. Oh, and

Hiram's got one of the barbecues going. Gonna make a stone soup out of the perishables.''

"Well, we've got a lovely smoked-chicken-and-glass salad," Gillian said, wiping a dirty hand across her thigh. "We might have some canned stuff."

A pile of books slid to one side. Gillian jumped, ready to run, then relaxed. A tiny aftershock, probably not even worth a number.

Hadn't even broken the crickets' rhythm.

Melanie's smile faded. "What have I done?"

Gillian cocked her head. "Mel?"

Melanie's face hardened. She placed her arms on her hips, thrusting her chest forward. But the light in her blue eyes receded like the moon sinking below the surface of the sea.

She cleared her throat. "Hiram says we gotta save the cans for later. Don't know what state the market's in. Come on. I'll show you camp."

Camp. Gillian shook her head and waded out of the living room toward Melanie. It almost sounded like fun. Almost.

She stepped outside into the early evening. The air hung hot and still, clinging to her like a balloon to a wall. So hot—too hot for early November. Indian summer had come and gone and here was this weird weather—Gillian wet her lips. *Earthquake weather.*

The crickets stopped chirping. Melanie and Gillian grabbed each other's arms as a small aftershock rolled through. This one only rattled the windows, shaking loose a brick from the barrier around KC's house next door. The brick snapped a branch off the rosemary Melanie planted to hide the retaining wall.

The crickets began singing again.

Gillian waited till her heartbeat slowed before releasing Melanie. "Is KC back?" she asked.

"Nobody's seen him," Melanie said. She did not let go.

Gillian clenched her teeth. God, she hoped he wasn't under a house somewhere checking the insulation or whatever it was energy consultants did under houses. Her back molars ached. *Don't think like that, Gilly. The earthquake hit at five-thirty. He never works past four-thirty.*

But it had to be after six now. . . .

And Nora—what about Nora? It was Wednesday, the one day Nora left the store in Debbie's questionable hands. Gillian forced herself to unclench her jaw. No power, no gas, no water, no phones—she couldn't even call her older sister to be sure she was all right.

Gillian clamped her jaw again. Nora was all right. She had to be—

Melanie jerked her arm. "Come on," she said, leading Gillian across the brown lawn toward Linnet Park.

Blankets and sleeping bags quilted the park's drought-parched grass. A block long and two deep, the park offered little more than hay, a volleyball pit, a metal play structure, picnic tables, and four concrete barbecues. Scrawny maples butted up against the yards of the houses bordering the park on two sides. More of an afterthought than any real attempt at landscaping. A park had to have trees, right?

The last of the yellow maple leaves hung motionless. Gillian looked away.

Thirty or more people clustered around the picnic tables near one of the barbecues, children pressed against their parents like chicks around hens. Smoke hung over them, unable to drift away in the torpid air. At the barbecue, Hiram jabbed at the charcoals with a fireplace poker, then squinted into one of three soup kettles. His white hair dripped down the sides of his face, damp with steam. His bow tie hung undone around his neck. He said something. No one responded. Everyone was too busy listening to Mrs. Timako's radio.

"How big was it?" Melanie asked, wedging into the crowd. She stood on her toes. "They know yet?"

The man beside her, the guy four doors down, glared at her. Mrs. Timako said, "They're not sure, dear, but they think it might have been a seven. Maybe bigger. That last aftershock, the big one, may have been a six."

Gillian blinked. A seven. Like the Loma Prieta quake five years ago.

"—have asked people to stay away from the downtown area unless they are working with the emergency crews," the radio announcer said. He sounded amazingly calm. "Rio Santo police have asked that people refrain from using Highway Nineteen through the mountains. One-oh-one has also suffered some damage along the north coastal access—"

A shrill wail rose from the blanket in Mrs. Timako's lap. A tiny black-and-white face peeped from the folds. The whole blanket trembled as the Chihuahua whimpered and whined.

Mrs. Timako leaned down and kissed the dog's head. The net of tiny wrinkles around her mouth and eyes made her blue-black pageboy's authenticity suspect. "Hush, Frankie. The worst is over. Mommy promises."

"Did everyone get bowls and utensils?" Hiram said. "You'll want to get them now before it gets dark."

The Chihuahua barked and dug its way out of the blanket.

Melanie dropped to her heels. "Bowls. I forgot—"

Thunder growled toward them. Gillian reached for Melanie as the ground bucked and twisted. The first jolt flung Melanie to the grass, the man next to her toppling beside her. The second whacked Hiram against the barbecue. Gillian scooted her feet wide apart, knees bent, trying to ride out the wave of earth swelling beneath her feet. Fissures, she thought, cracks. With the earth straining to tear itself apart, why weren't there cracks?

Someone screamed. The ground shivered to a stop.

A woman laughed nervously. "That was at least a six-point-five—"

The explosion knocked Gillian to her knees. She sat back as a seething fireball rose above the roofs several blocks away then slowly blackened into a pillar of smoke. How many blocks away? Five? Six? How long before the fire reached Linnet Park?

Gillian raked her fingers through the tinder-dry grass,

half rising in a sprinter's crouch. She could run from the fire, try to escape the same death that had consumed Mom and Dad—

Sirens shrieked in the distance. Gillian hugged herself. The Chihuahua stood in front of her, trembling like glass wind chimes in a gale.

THE FIRST STAR WINKED THROUGH THE SMOKE. GILLIAN wished for an end to the aftershocks, then glanced across the park at KC's house. Still not home. She hoped he was only caught in traffic. She tugged at the grass in front of her, letting the dried blades slip between her fingers.

A flashlight beam stopped in front of KC's house as Hiram and Lily Gerber rechecked the gas and water mains. After that explosion two hours ago everyone was double-checking.

Gillian rested her forehead on her bent knees. If someone had double-checked Mom and Dad's house four years ago, would it have made any difference? Would they have found . . . ?

Gillian closed her eyes. She'd never known what had sparked the house in the Saratoga hills, consuming it like a dried Christmas tree. She hadn't wanted to know. Nora knew, down to the last detail, but the little Gillian had been told was already too much. In unguarded moments she imagined her parents melting like candles pleated with blood. Around them the house, the only home she'd known in her twenty-eight years—the only home she'd *ever* know—disintegrated into smoke.

Without photographs, she couldn't even picture the house. She could recite its physical attributes: three bedrooms, a living room with a picture window overlooking the Santa Clara Valley, a plank exterior painted pale, watered teal. But imagining it detail by detail . . . she drew a blank, saw only a huge black pit at the base of a hill dotted with old fruit trees.

Home no longer existed—not the house, not her parents. There was no place to touch all that she *was*, to absorb the strength of her history. No place to feel completely safe and whole and refreshed. Not like home. Not like her parents. In the roaring flare of that fire she'd lost the touchstones of her life. She'd become rootless and adrift . . . except for Nora. Nora was her one bit of home.

"Please, Nora, be all right," Gillian prayed.

She pushed herself to her feet. Something, there must be something she could do. She needed to make herself useful instead of wallowing in this slippery panic.

The crickets stopped and the Chihuahua started up. She bent her knees. A small aftershock rolled through. She willed her heartbeat to slow down, then walked over to the picnic tables and Melanie.

Kerosene and battery-powered lanterns ringed the picnic area. Gillian avoided the kerosene lanterns and joined Melanie. Light pooled over Melanie's "massage" table. The guy down the street, Jake Rubio, lay shirtless and glistening, murmuring with each press of Melanie's fingers. Gillian smiled. Melanie, easing the tension from the shoulders of the same guy she cursed every morning at five when the alarm on his truck went off. Well, sometimes compassion had no limits. After all, Melanie's first postearthquake "patient" *had* been Mrs. Timako's "barking rat."

Melanie had reached for the terrified Chihuahua before the sirens hissed into silence. "Poor little thing," she'd said. "Don't worry, Mrs. Timako. This is my bread and butter."

She'd answered Gillian's look with a whispered, "Hey, I did a golden retriever once. Sort of. Besides, they have muscles, right?"

She hadn't stopped massaging muscles since. Except to gulp down a bowl of Hiram's stone soup.

Gillian leaned against the table near Jake Rubio's head. "Need any help?"

"Naw." Melanie brushed her fingers along the man's spine, then raised her hands and shook them. "There. Stay away from aftershocks. I don't want all my hard work to come to squat."

Jake sighed, his eyelids fluttering open. "Marry me."

"Not till you get rid of that truck alarm." Melanie sat down on the bench. Kneading her right wrist, she looked at Gillian. "How're you doing? You want to be next?"

Gillian shook her head. "No. I need something useful to do, but I can't think of anything. I just keep waiting for the next aftershock. They're like hiccups. Just when I decide the next one isn't coming and relax—*bang!* There it is."

"Yeah, no kidding. Like giving up on somebody late . . ." Melanie's voice trailed off.

Gillian frowned. "Mel?"

"There she is," a booming voice announced. "She's a speech therapist. Now you go tell her what's happened."

Gillian turned slowly. The blond woman from the corner, Ms. Jansen, shoved her equally blond, eight-year-old daughter toward Gillian. The child pinched her lower lip, pulling it forward in an exaggerated pout, then released it.

"Go on," the mother said, prodding the girl forward. "Tell Ms. Wheatley what happened."

Poor child was terrified. "Gillian's fine," Gillian said, crouching in front of the girl. "What's your name?"

The pupils widened, eclipsing the irises. The girl pinched her lip again.

"Go on," Ms. Jansen said.

The girl released her lip. "Buh-buh-buh-buh." The girl pressed her lips shut. Tears swam in her brown eyes. "Buh-buh-buh-beth . . ."

"Beth Ellen," Ms. Jansen said. She hissed through gritted teeth. "We spent *years* getting rid of that stutter and now it's back. I just can't believe it!"

Gillian stared at the woman. "A lot of children—a lot of people—revert to old behavior patterns during times of trauma. It's normal—"

"Trauma!" Ms. Jansen huffed and folded her arms over her chest. "Trauma, indeed. The earthquake's over, we survived. Our house isn't even damaged. Where's the trauma in that?"

And some people, Gillian thought, turn to denial. She placed her hand gently on the girl's shoulders. "Beth Ellen,'' she began, but the crickets stopped chirping. She pulled the child into her arms as a rumble swept toward them and the ground began to shake.

The girl clung to her, the small hands grasping handfuls of Gillian's shirt and hair. Gillian fought her own panic as the ground tilted and rocked. "We're okay, we're okay," she whispered over and over.

The ground quieted. Beth Ellen buried her face in Gillian's brown hair.

Gillian pried the child gently away, tipping Beth Ellen's chin up with a finger. She waited till the girl gazed directly into her eyes, then said, "It's scary, huh? Really scary. It feels like if you can't trust the earth, what can you trust?"

Beth Ellen bit her lip, then nodded.

Gillian smiled, then hugged her hard. "And you know what? It's okay to be scared. And right now it's okay to stutter. The worst is over, but sometimes the scared lasts a little longer."

Melanie squatted beside them. "Hey," she said, placing a hand on the girl's shoulder. "You know, I don't have anybody right now. How about a massage?"

"A ruh-ruh-real massage?" Beth Ellen said, her fingers letting go of Gillian's hair and shirt. "You're a ruh-ruh-real mas-mas—"

"You bet," Melanie said. "I usually do asthmatics and injured people and stuff, but I got a special massage for brave, scared little girls."

Melanie swung the girl into her arms and set her on the table. Ms. Jansen smiled sweetly at them, then turned on Gillian. "What should I do?" she said. "Her speech therapist told me she was cured. What should I do?"

Gillian stood. She straightened her shirt. "Be patient. And accept the fact that she's frightened."

Ms. Jansen rolled her eyes. "How can she be frightened? There's nothing to be afraid of!"

Gillian rubbed her chin. She did not want to be around when this woman's denial broke down. "Accept it."

Ms. Jansen huffed. "How long will it take?"

"Maybe a few weeks, maybe months." Gillian glanced

at the small body stretched out on the picnic table. Beth
Ellen's stuttering was caused by a tendency to concentrate
tension in the vocal cords, a speech impediment often trig-
gered by anxiety. Her own students would be a different
case. They had problems with articulation and language
development—problems unrelated to stress. Their hard-
won *R*s, *L*s, and *S*s wouldn't be shaken loose by the
trauma, but the students were going to need something
reassuring and affirming to bolster them. . . .

Gillian chafed her arms. "Accept it," she said.

The crickets stopped chirping.

GILLIAN WOKE WITH A START. SILENCE, THEN A LOW RUM-
ble, more like a hum on the lips than a growl in the back
of the throat. She flattened herself, clumps of grass poking
into her back, and stared up at the stars. The aftershock
rolled through, jerking and tossing her. The stars blurred.
Across the park, someone cried out. Someone else responded with a shout. Groans and exhausted whimpers
filled in for the crickets.

Then the earth quieted. A child—Beth Ellen?—started
to cry. Gillian pulled her own blanket tighter, not because
she was cold, but to keep out the darkness. It was so dark,
so weirdly dark with only the stars. No porch lights, no
streetlights—Gillian never realized how much the city
glowed, the artificial light casting radiant shadows. The
sky was truly midnight blue, not the deep, amber-tinged
gray she took for granted.

Gillian rolled toward Melanie. Melanie's eyes reflected
the sparse starlight. "My nerves are shot," Melanie said.
"Every time I doze off, another one hits."

"Yeah," Gillian said. "Yeah."

Melanie's eyes closed.

Gillian shivered. How was Nora taking all of this? Was
she okay? She imagined Nora crushed beneath an avalanche of plaster, trapped in her own house . . . how well
did Victorians handle earthquakes? Would it still be standing? *Of course, Gilly, you idiot,* she chided herself. *That
damn house stood up to the San Francisco earthquake—*

and *the Loma Prieta one. It's Nora you need to worry about—*

Nora, twisted and bloodied, crawling across the pocked hardwood floors toward a gaping hole spitting flames—

She forced the image from her mind. She should have gone downtown, despite the radio's pleas to stay away. She imagined Nora's store, the carpet a mosaic of smashed glass shelves inlaid with earrings from Mexico, necklaces from the Zuni, brooches from England. Shards of Hopi and Italian pottery clutched at Peruvian woolens while stone animals from Kenya prowled amid a hundred other snarled, mangled treasures. Nora had spent the last two years building and shaping the inventory of The Happy Wanderer, and now it was—it had to be—gone. Gillian fisted and unfisted her hands. What could she have done? Gathered a few things between aftershocks? Swept up glass and ceramics? She hadn't even done that at her house. Guarded against looters—?

"Melanie," she said, grasping her housemate's shoulder. "Did you lock the door?"

Melanie's eyes opened. "What for? Nothing worth taking. Not anymore."

The living room, a stew of books, wood, and pottery chunks, the kitchen a tide of goo mined with glass—she hadn't even looked at her bedroom. "I guess you're right," Gillian said. "Sorry. I didn't mean to wake you."

Melanie snorted. "Who's asleep?"

A gut-churning rumble silenced the night chorus.

"Another one," Melanie said. "A big one."

They braced themselves, clutching each other's wrists. The aftershock swept through, tossing and dropping them through its peaks and troughs. For nearly a second they floated like spume above the earthen wave, then dropped like stones. After lifting and slamming them two more times, the aftershock seeped into the soil.

A sharp intake of breath punctuated the tremor. A raw, pervasive awareness sparked the air, but no one uttered a sound. Gillian's chest expanded with a trapped scream. Then someone said, "Six-point-two?"

Nervous laughter washed over the park. Gillian's scream escaped as a giggle. Beside her Melanie remained as rigid as a toothpick.

"My God," Melanie whispered, "what have I done?"

TWO

BETH ELLEN STUTTERED, GILLIAN HAD DREAMS.

Stress dreams, Nora called them. During tense times, Gillian woke herself talking to people who weren't there— usually Mom and Dad. The setting never changed: her old bedroom at home, with its blue walls and northern-constellation curtains. She was in bed, usually naked. Mom and Dad sat in vinyl kitchen chairs pulled up to the cherry footboard. At some point she always asked them to leave so she could get dressed. She woke herself either laughing or talking out loud.

Tonight, Dad smiled, patting her feet. "That boyfriend of yours is a real keeper, Gilly. Better hang on to him."

"Boyfriend?" Gillian said, struggling to wake. "I'm not seeing anyone—"

Mom and Dad exchanged winks. "KC, Pumpkin," Mom said.

"KC's just a friend," Gillian said. She felt along the blankets for her bathrobe. "Look, could you two please leave so I can get dressed? Go into the next room and I'll join you—"

Mom snorted. "Like I never bathed you."

Gillian gaped at her. "Mom, I'm twenty-eight—" she began.

And woke up.

Gillian blinked at the sky. Still that inky, midnight darkness salted with stars. A gentle aftershock shivered through. Melanie murmured in her sleep, turning over without waking. Gillian raised herself on one elbow and scanned the park. It'd be impossible to single out KC amid all those blanketed bodies. If he was even here. Probably at a friend's. And safe. Gillian lay back down.

KC as her boyfriend . . . she clicked her teeth. If her parents hadn't died—she and KC had just started dating, after living next door to each other for six months. "The boy next door—won't Dad love that one?" Nora had teased.

"Won't Mom?" Gillian had said.

But Mom and Dad never got to laugh about it.

Longing scraped Gillian, reopening fragile wounds; grief bled through her. This same grief had turned a budding romance into a solid friendship. Maybe she should be glad for that. She couldn't settle here. Rio Santo wasn't home—KC wasn't home. No place, nobody was. Except Nora.

Crickets harmonized cheerfully. Gillian tugged the blanket to her chin. Despite the heat, she felt safer with the blanket between her and the raw air.

"It won't happen again," Melanie whispered.

Gillian started to turn toward her, then relaxed. Just talking in her sleep.

"I know, I know," Melanie whispered. "Weeks—okay, months. Look, I promise, first thing in the morning. Just stop. Please."

Gillian frowned. Who was Melanie talking to?

"A major screwup," Melanie said. "I didn't think it mattered. But you gotta believe me. *It won't happen again.*"

The plea in Melanie's voice chilled Gillian. A rash of goose bumps pimpled her sweat-slick skin. Melanie was talking in her sleep, she had to be.

Minutes passed. Only the crickets spoke to the night. Exhaustion finally soothed Gillian's nerves. As she drifted into a light sleep she heard Melanie say one last time, "It won't. . . ."

• • •

THE GROUND STAMMERED. GILLIAN THRASHED AWAKE, flinging the blanket aside, then relaxed. A bird warbled, its song piling up in a rush of notes as if the bird feared being cut off. A bit cooler, the still air smelled faintly of damp straw. Gillian blinked at the deep gray sky. As even as felt, the color stretched above her without a hint of sunrise. Or cloud. Gillian scratched her nose with the side of her finger. Not surprising. The drought had been going for, what? Five years? The bird bolted through its song again.

Gillian closed her eyes.

Blankets and sleeping bags flapped around her. Gillian smiled. It reminded her of the time Mom had taken her camping at Lake Berryessa when she was nine while the "homebodies"—Dad and Nora—stayed home. She and Mom, the big adventurers, always going off to explore and then coming home . . .

As they sat around the campfire that night at Berryessa, watching the fire's shadows leap among the oak trees and making s'mores, something winged and black darted above them and disappeared. "Mom," Gillian said, "was that a bat?"

Mom skewered another marshmallow. "Yep."

"A vampire bat?"

Mom lowered her stick. "Who's been telling you about vampires?"

"Nora. She said they eat people."

Mom poked at the flames with her marshmallow. "No, Pumpkin, they do not eat people. Well, maybe if they're rabid. They suck the blood out of cattle, mostly."

Gillian lowered her s'more, the marshmallow adhering instantly to her shorts. "Do they live around here?"

Mom leaned over and hugged her. "No, they live in South America. And they're not going to come here. This is California. We have agricultural inspections."

The logic was lost on Gillian. That night she'd slept scrunched way down in her sleeping bag, without even her nose showing. And all night long she heard the ominous flapping of vampire bats circling the camp. What a relief to crawl out of her sleeping bag just before sunrise and see Mom roll over to that sinister flapping. . . .

The same flapping she heard now. Gillian sighed and turned to face Melanie.

Melanie's blanket lay in a tangled heap, sans Melanie. Gillian stretched and yawned. Must have gone to pee in one of those little ditches Jake Rubio dug behind the maples.

Gillian closed her eyes and dozed until an aftershock, probably a four, shuddered beneath her. She counted five seconds, then it was over. Predawn edged the sky with pale, grayish pink. Gillian rolled onto her side.

And froze, her stomach hardening around a ball of fear. A man crouched beside Melanie's still-abandoned blanket, his fingers probing the folds as if he hoped to find her. The man's skin, a buff, moist red, angled thinly over his wrists, his elbows, his cheekbones, the bridge of his long, tapered nose. His cheeks hollowed and swelled with a wordless sigh. He touched Melanie's dented pillow, then brought his fingers to his upper lip—to smell her or to taste her?

Gillian pressed herself flat to the ground, hoping the dried grass wouldn't rustle. Hoping the strange man wouldn't notice her. One scream and a parkful of people would come running—

Fear pinned her to the ground.

The man stroked his upper lip, then gazed out over the field of blanketed bodies. He frowned, anger furrowing the high forehead. He tilted his head back. His reddish, gray-brown curls spilled over the collar of his blue work shirt like roots reaching for better soil. Or water.

Gillian probed her dry mouth with her tongue. She tried to clear her throat without making a sound, but a soft rattle betrayed her. The stranger turned to her, the skin stretched so tight over his jaw it looked as if it would crack.

Gillian's heart stopped, then hammered wildly.

The man inhaled, his nostrils flaring. His gaze locked onto hers. Gillian scooted onto her elbows, ready to thrust herself to her feet, but found herself unable to look away.

Don't let him know how scared you are, she told herself. *Don't focus on the anger. Focus on his eyes.*

His eyes sparkled in the rosy morning light. She had never seen eyes those colors before: mossy, agate green shot with glimmering copper and flecks of clear, creek-water blue. Round like river stones, and as polished. Framed by rust-brown lashes, they stared at her unblinking. Gillian swallowed, tilting her chin a little. Then gasped.

Black rings circled deep, forest-green pupils.

Green.

Gillian pushed herself to her knees.

The skin around the eyes crinkled into a smile. The stranger's hand moved into Gillian's view, the fingers flexed to cup her cheek.

Gillian flinched. "Get away from me," she said, whipping her head side to side. Her own hair blinded her.

He caught her shoulders with large, meaty hands. Jerking backward, she slammed into his chest. She went limp with surprise—how did he get behind her? The large hands pulled her close, holding her like a broken shell cupping a yolk.

Gillian struck out with her fists. "Leave me alone!"

He rocked her to his chest. A firm, mountainous slope, it slanted to a soft belly. "Gillian, hey. Gilly, it's me."

KC.

Gillian took a deep breath, inhaling the familiar scent of English lavender. And sweat. She relaxed into KC's embrace and looked up. He frowned above her, his brown hair matted to his forehead, his lower lip thrust forward. His beard seemed to bristle with concern. "You okay?" he said.

Gillian rubbed a stray hair from her cheek. "God, KC, I thought—"

She clawed her way out of KC's arms and spun toward Melanie's tumbled blankets, but the strange man had disappeared.

Like Melanie.

THREE

"TWO MINUTES!" NORA CALLED. HEAPS OF RAVAGED CE-
ramics, glass, and textiles absorbed her voice, muffling it
in the dim store. Somewhere to Gillian's left KC grunted,
his flashlight creasing the darkness. Gillian scooted the picnic basket farther up her arm. Jewelry, stone animals, and
a miraculously intact cobalt vase rattled against the wicker.
Gillian wrinkled her nose. Sweat pooled in her rubber
boots, the gardening gloves itched, sandalwood, jasmine,
and musk clogged her lungs. The hard hat slid to one side,
folding her ear. Two minutes wasn't soon enough.

Stepping carefully over a jagged display case, she prodded the shadows with her flashlight. A sparkle of bright,
dewy aqua flashed from under a dented iron lantern. Gillian paused, the basket balanced on her hip. It might be an
earring. It was probably a piece of glass. Gillian scraped
her teeth across her lower lip. After two days of this she'd
have sworn they'd found everything worth salvaging, but
each foray into The Happy Wanderer uncovered new
spoils. She waded toward the glimmer.

"One minute!" Nora called.

b Gillian squatted beside the lantern, brushing it aside
with a gloved hand. The aqua flared brighter under the
direct beam. Gillian smiled, reaching for the gold-and-
aquamarine brooch. "Good eyes, Gilly," she said.

She set the brooch in the basket next to an obsidian coyote. The flashlight tracked to the right, raking broken tapers and twisted metal before illuminating a simple face of antler and turquoise: a Zuni altar doll, her coral-pink arms laden with crumbled turquoise and a small, kernel-shaped stone. With three turquoise circles for her eyes and mouth, she looked like she was singing. Or somehow offering the gift of communication.

Gillian glanced at Nora, outlined by the sunlit door, then shuffled through the debris. She'd wanted to buy the altar doll, but Nora refused. "Wait till I get another one," she said. "I'll *give* you this one. I just want people to see it."

Gillian strained toward the little figure, her fingers spread wide. Not quite. A little closer—

"Now," said a firm, male voice. "You and your crew have had fifteen minutes—"

"Fifteen minutes," Nora said. "Like the aftershocks are on a timetable. Gillian, KC! Time's up!"

Gillian squatted, creeping toward the doll. A shard of glass snagged her jeans just above the boot.

"Look, if we had our way, none of you would be allowed in here," the male voice said. "The whole thing could come down—"

"If you don't like it, talk to the city council. Gillian!" Nora shouted. "We're out of here!"

Gillian's fingers brushed the doll's feet. She pulled it into her palm. Calm welled up in her, a warmth and balance that grounded her.

"Gillian!" KC bellowed.

She stroked the doll's head. "Coming!"

"If you don't leave now we'll red-tag and it won't matter what the city council—"

"Yeah, by what authority?" Nora's voice bristled. "Gillian! Get your butt out here before this guy seals you in!"

"In a sec!" Gillian pushed herself to her feet, her palm scraping glass. She stuffed the doll into her pocket. Straddling hillocks of cloth and wood, glass and metal, she stumbled toward the light. Within feet of the door, Nora grabbed her by the arm and dragged her outside.

Gillian blinked at the bright sunlight. Nora released her arm and Gillian immediately removed the hard hat and nestled it in her basket. A slight breeze ruffled her hair. She raised her hand to shade her eyes.

Arms locked over his chest, a firefighter glared at Nora. His lean, dark face glistened with sweat under his hard hat. A thick roll of yellow disaster tape dangled from his white-knuckled fingers. "The city council has no right allowing you people in these buildings," he said, then turned to Gillian. "The next aftershock could drop the whole—hell in a hand basket! This is exactly what I'm talking about! Look at her leg—you people could get hurt in there!"

Gillian glanced at her thigh. A flap of denim gapped like a smile. She brushed at it with her hand. Blood streaked the cloth mouth. She hid her cut palm behind her back. "Old jeans," she said.

Nora grabbed the firefighter by the elbow and spun him toward her. "When can we go back in?"

"Shit, lady, I just got you *out*," he said. Shaking his head, he unfolded his arms and unrolled the tape. He stuck it to one side of the paneless window. Plaster crumbled under his hands. "Nothing's changed since yesterday. Fifteen minutes in, hour and a half wait, then fifteen minutes in." The firefighter stretched the tape across the door frame. "If I had my way . . ."

"If you had your way, I'd lose everything," Nora said. She picked up the picnic basket at her feet and swung it over her arm. She nudged Gillian with her elbow. "Come on. KC's already gone ahead to the Action."

Gillian followed her sister. Crippled buildings hunched over the narrow street, windows shattered. A plush turkey and a snowman peeked from one doorway, refugees from someone's window display. Molding dangled like torn scabs, strings of Christmas lights drooled to the sidewalks. Its rust-and-gold gingerbread stained gray with plaster dust, the Fredrico Building sagged heavily on thick wooden beams. Like crutches. Across the street, the old Palisade Hotel had also been shored up. Jagged scars crosshatched its face, huge scraps of plaster torn away to expose the skeletal frame underneath. Gillian stopped, her throat constricting. Four of the six mermaids that had beckoned from the Palisade's third-floor molding were gone. One of the survivors teetered headlessly over the sidewalk below.

The sidewalks. Gillian blinked, smearing a teary film over her eyes. The sidewalks and the street were fairly clean except for a brick here, a sheet of plaster there, an occasional spear of wood. Volunteers had cleared out as much of the debris as they could on Friday, the day after the earthquake. Armed with rakes, brooms, shovels, and dust masks, the volunteers loaded a fleet of pickups with broken trees and shrubs, glass, brick, and the flesh of injured buildings. After the last loads were hauled away, a local construction company fastened a bandage of cyclone fencing around the two-block-by-six-block wound.

Nora had been there, along with the other merchants and employees. Guilt twisted Gillian's stomach. She'd spent the day sweeping and salvaging what she could at the house.

Alone. God, she wished she knew where Melanie was.

A hand closed on her shoulder. Gillian turned. Nora held her breath, that smooth alabaster calm replaced by a haggard sense of loss. The corners of her mouth twitched, her eyelids drooped. As she stared at the old Palisade her hand tightened on Gillian's shoulder. Gillian wound her free arm around Nora's waist and pulled her close.

A low rumble sped beneath them. The buildings ground against each other, then were silent. Gillian and Nora reeled apart, grasping each other's shirts. "Three," Nora said. She hurried toward the Action, Gillian in tow.

YELLOW TAPE DRAPED THE FRONT OF THE ACTION CAFÉ, looping across the paneless picture windows and the black-and-white tile trim. The narrow, three-story building looked fairly stable; plaster and brick connected the office windows above the café, not cracks. Gillian sighed, grateful for any and all surviving buildings.

Plastic chairs and tables overflowed the sidewalk and marched halfway across the street in front of the Action. Shop owners, employees, and friends slumped at the tables, hands wrapped around paper cups. Teetering back in a stained, white chair, KC chatted with a man in gray sweats and T-shirt standing between a card table loaded with sandwiches and another table sagging under a Coleman stove warming two metal coffeepots. KC nodded to Gillian and Nora, then rocked forward so that all four chair legs touched the ground. "I was wondering where you two were," he said.

"Tea or coffee?" the man in gray said.

"Rich, you're a lifesaver," Nora said. "Coffee. How much for the sandwiches?"

Rich shrugged. He poured her a cup. "Nothing. The stuff's gonna go bad if the power doesn't come on soon. Might as well give it away. And you—tea or coffee?"

"Tea, herbal," Gillian said.

Nora reached for a sandwich. "What's the damage? Think they'll tear it down?"

"Naw, I don't think so," Rich said, handing Gillian her tea. "Place looks pretty solid. The fire marshal—"

Gillian peered through the windows into the ravaged café. Director's chairs surrounded white tables while posters of action stars—Keanu Reeves, Linda Hamilton, Arnold Schwarzenegger, Bruce Willis, Sigourney Weaver—papered the walls. Gillian scratched the side of her nose. She'd never been in the Action. Looking over the menu, a huge clapboard on the far wall over the grill, she knew why. Breakfast alone was enough to kill someone. The Die Hard omelette, three eggs fluffed with cream and stuffed with cream cheese, avocado, and chorizo. The Die Harder, the above omelette smothered in white sauce. Of course, the Sudden Impact waffle might be okay, if one had the presence of mind to scrape off the whipped butter and whipped cream, and avoided the two eggs, bacon, and sausage. Gillian took her tea and sat next to KC.

"—can't they just let us go in and get the stuff and get it over with?" said a woman wearing a gold bandanna.

"We've already lost seven people," the man at the next table said. He unfolded the lip of his paper cup. "That's why."

Gillian shivered and sipped her tea. Seven people—three on the freeway when a car went out of control, two in homes that collapsed, one struck by a falling tree, one in the store two down from Nora's. Gillian studied the beams shoring the buildings across the street. Considering how many people died in San Francisco and Oakland during the Loma Prieta earthquake, Rio Santo was lucky.

"Seem to be fewer aftershocks today," the woman in the gold bandanna said hopefully. "Maybe they'll be over soon."

Nora sniffed and sipped her coffee.

A woman in cammo ran a hand through her powdered hair. "Dream on. We won't see the last of these for at least six months. Maybe even a year."

As if on cue, a low growl surged toward them. The earth became a raging beast, thrashing and bucking. Nora slipped under the plastic table. She grasped Gillian's torn pant leg and tugged. Gillian dived under the table.

Two loud clangs smacked against the sidewalk. Rivulets of coffee and water shimmied toward Gillian and Nora, advancing and retreating with each jolt. All around them plaster groaned and wheezed. A crash echoed between the buildings. From under a nearby table someone offered a rushed Hail Mary.

The aftershock shuddered to a stop.

Gillian poked her head out from under the table. Everyone but KC and Rich crouched beneath the plastic furniture. Not that the tables offered any protection, but somehow the idea of having a shield, no matter how flimsy, was comforting. Gillian shoved a chair aside and crawled out from under the table.

KC stood in the middle of the street gazing toward the Palisade and the Fredrico. His lips disappeared in a thin fold. Rich stood beside him, shaking his head. "Shit," Rich said. "Shit."

"Something went down," the man with the mangled cup said.

Gillian wove through the tables and hurried to KC's side. He rested a hand on her shoulder. His scent, sweat and lavender, calmed her. At the far end of the street, dust hung in the air, a fog of plaster. Nora squeezed between KC and Rich.

"I'm sorry, Nora," KC said.

Nora stared, unblinking, at the cascade of brick and yellow tape trailing across the asphalt from The Happy Wanderer. She touched her throat. Her voice quavered slightly, at odds with its flatness of tone. "Well," she said. "I guess that's it. Anyone need another set of hands?"

MELANIE'S SILVER HONDA STILL WASN'T IN THE DRIVE-way.

Gillian stood on the top step, KC beside her, and peered down the street as if Melanie might drive up any minute. City-issue liquid amber trees and sycamores planted along both sides of the street chained their leafless arms. The houses, a hodgepodge of one- and two-story ranch, East Lake, and pseudo-Colonial styles, stood still and silent, several chimneys tilted to one side like jaunty top hats. A car growled around the corner—Gillian strained to see past the old trailer parked in Hiram's yard. A red Nissan shot by. Gillian struck the door with her fist.

KC caught her arm. "Gilly, you okay?"

Gillian forced her shoulders to relax. "Sure. My sister's shop just collapsed, my housemate's been missing for three days, my nerves are shot—but, hey."

KC gave her a sidearm hug. "Well, if *that's* all."

She looked up at him. "My house is a mess."

KC nodded. "That *is* a problem."

Gillian winked. "Yeah, but at least I'm only renting, home owner."

KC clutched at the front of his shirt and pretended to crumple. "Wounded by the truth."

"Hey, KC! Gillian!" Hiram waved from the sidewalk. The smile above his wilted bow tie was perky as ever.

"Spaghetti tonight, five-thirty. It may be the last dinner in the park. The radio said the power'll be on by tomorrow. They're going to wait on the gas till sometime next week."

"And the water?" KC asked.

"The water district is still testing for impurities." Hiram pursed his lips. "Ma Bell thinks she can get the phones up and running by Tuesday. Say, Gillian—any word on that housemate of yours?"

Gillian sighed. "Not yet. Well, I've got some things I want to get done before the sun goes down. See you two at five-thirty."

She unlocked the door and stalked into the living room. Pictures and short stacks of books lined the walls. The only thing still standing, besides the sofa and two easy chairs, was that one bookshelf. After removing the last of the books and knickknacks, she'd discovered the shelf's secret: Melanie had molly-bolted it to the wall. Why hadn't she bolted the other two? Gillian wondered. "Who knows?" she said aloud, then flopped down on the sofa.

She yanked her feet out of the slick rubber boots, gagging on the moldy, yeasty stench of damp socks. She stripped them off and tossed them toward the entry, then kicked the boots over near one of the fallen bookshelves.

Leaning her head on the back of the sofa, she stared at the ceiling. This disappearance, this wasn't like Melanie at all. Melanie was a homebody, like Nora and Dad.

No, even more of a homebody than Nora. Nora had moved here from Saratoga several years ago. Then, after Mom and Dad died, she started turning Rio Santo into home by buying a house, starting a business. Melanie had never left Rio Santo—not once in her twenty-seven years. Everyone in her family, for more than a century, had lived and died in Rio Santo. "My grandparents are dead, my parents are dead, everyone's dead but me," Melanie had said once. "Where am I gonna go? This town *is* my family."

Gillian frowned. "So where *did* you go?" she asked her absent friend.

A pile of books shifted with a soft shush.

Gillian pushed herself to her feet. Time to stop wasting daylight. What next . . . ? She'd cleaned the kitchen and the living room Friday after she'd ridden her bike across town to Nora's house—an adventure right there, with all the traffic lights down and half the streets blocked with abandoned cars. She'd found a note addressed to her pinned on Nora's door, assuring her that Nora was all right and had gone downtown to salvage what she could. Gillian had left a note of her own, then pedaled back here, stopping at Vine Hill Super to buy some canned goods. Apparently the owner thought the earthquake was the next best thing to winning the lottery. After prowling the dimly lit store, escorted by an employee with a flashlight, her nerves frayed by the hum of the generator, Gillian had come away with nothing. She hadn't been desperate enough to spend thirty dollars for a jar of peanut butter.

"Every road into town's blocked, doll," the store owner had said. He'd grinned at her around a sucker stick. "May not be any deliveries for days—weeks. What I got on my shelf's gold."

Gillian bristled just remembering him. "Ass," she muttered.

She brushed at the front of her dusty hair. Might as well check Melanie's room. She padded down the dim hall past the photographs that had fallen and now lined the baseboards like a gallery for cats, Chihuahuas, and small, flightless waterfowl. Stopping outside Melanie's door, she twisted the knob and went inside.

No cloud of scent greeted her—not like her own room. It would take forever for that rose oil to dissipate. . . .

Placing her hands on her hips, she surveyed the wreckage. The debris was only ankle-deep here. Melanie's two bookshelves, hip-high and made of oak, were squat enough to withstand the shaking. The contents were a different story. While a handful of the books still waited on the shelves, the rest floated across the floor, multicolored icebergs adrift on the pale blue carpet. A badger of Picasso marble crouched by the foot of the futon sofa bed.

More objects scattered between and under the books. Colored pens and bottled tinctures clustered around the legs of a half-collapsed card table. Gillian picked her way carefully to the window on the opposite wall, stepping over a stone mortar and pestle. She tugged open the sheer lace curtains.

A row of tiny potted herbs lined the sill, desperately in need of water. Gillian poked at the chamomile, releasing a puff of dust. She turned, resting her back against the sill. ''Where to begin?'' she murmured.

The closet. She nodded to herself then walked over to the French door and folded it open. The trunk with Melanie's clothes, her collection of sneakers, her broken tennis racket—Gillian smiled—her portable massage table. Melanie would be back. She never went anywhere for very long without that table.

Gillian shut the closet. She knelt, dredging the carpet for the odd, runelike coins Melanie collected and for colored stones. Lapis, amethyst, rose quartz, tiger's eye, carnelian—stones of all colors and shapes. Gillian held each to the window so that they glowed with the wan sunlight. She righted a monkey-pod salad bowl, dribbling the coins and stones into its steep basin. Pulling the bowl closer, she uncovered a medallion of unglazed ceramic.

Gillian crawled toward it. A face stared up at her, its thick, molten features crudely rendered. The medallion was ugly, but somehow beautiful. Gillian rose and carried it to the window. Light fell on the face, reflecting off the eyes. Gillian frowned, peering closely at the medallion. A dot of glaze—no, glass . . . no. Stone. Moss agate.

A shudder spasmed through her. Moss agate—why did that disturb her?

A surge of memory took Gillian's breath away. The strange man in the park, the one pawing through Melanie's blanket—he'd turned to look at her, his green eyes veined with copper and clear, creek-water blue. And those green pupils . . .

The floor rippled without warning. Dropping the medallion, Gillian sprang for the door. She grasped the door frame, bracing herself. The floor stilled.

Gillian waited. Safe—for now. She stepped out into the hallway and shut the door. Melanie could straighten the room herself when she came home.

The hall light flickered on.

FOUR

"WE GOT WATER YESTERDAY, WE GOT PHONES THIS MORN-ing," Jenna Pelligrini said. The first-grade teacher twisted a strand of long auburn hair around her finger. "Power, water, phones—what more do they want?"

Gillian gouged the lawn in front of Lowen Elementary with her heel. A tall man with a clipboard and an even taller woman rounded the cinderblock building that housed the principal's office. They stopped and faced the school. The woman pointed at the paper leaves taped to Gillian's window. "They want to be sure there's no structural damage," Gillian said.

"Structural damage!" Jenna snorted. The curl cascaded free. "As if anything could harm *these* monstrosities. I tell you, whoever designed these things should be forced to work in one."

Gillian nodded. The buildings *were* ugly. The rectangular wings of gray cinder block looked like shoe boxes, their dark roofs set at a gentle slope like lids gone askew. Metal shutters in faded mustard, salmon, and turquoise broke up the monotony of the walls like misplaced bar codes. Someone, probably Earl the custodian, had tried to soften the lines with rosemary, lavender, Peruvian lilies, and other drought-resistant plants. Tried.

She wondered if the school's hideousness added a little

to her reluctance each year to tell the district she was coming back. Just another place that didn't feel like home. . . .

"We need to get the kids back in school as soon as possible," Jenna said. "It's been a week, for God's sake. The sooner they can get back into the old routines, the safer they'll feel."

Gillian sighed. "Me, too. I'd like to believe there's more to life than waiting for the next aftershock—"

"Gillian!"

Gillian turned in time to catch the leaping girl. Gillian hugged her, touching noses with the kindergartner. "Hey, Lucinda," she said. "What pretty braids!"

Lucinda shook her head, the three braids waggling side to side. "Mommy did it. Her made me pretty. We comed to thee if thchool'th open."

Gillian set Lucinda down. "Not yet. Maybe tomorrow."

"And maybe yethterday or the day after?" Lucinda said.

"Tomorrow—"

"Ms. Wheatley?" a nasal voice asked.

Gillian looked up. A police officer stood a respectful distance away. Gillian's chest constricted. "Yes?" she managed.

The cop's face puckered. Wisps of ginger hair clutched the sides of his hat. "Ms. Wheatley, can I talk to you for a minute?"

Melanie, it was about Melanie. Gillian touched Lucinda's shoulder. "I have to talk to the officer, Lucinda. Hopefully I'll see you *tomorrow*. Okay?"

Lucinda nodded, gaping at the cop, then turned and ran to her mother. Jenna joined the two second-grade teachers, Marci Gomez and Tish Kimura, over by the curb. Marci tucked a few loose hairs beneath her red knit cap, then pointed to the school's roof. Tish shook her head, her full lips pursed.

Gillian walked over to the officer. "Yes?" she said.

He stepped back. "Do you know a Ms. Melanie Frost?"

Gillian's heart skipped a beat. "She's my housemate."

"Well, we found her car, a 1989 Honda Civic?" He

paused, searching Gillian's face. "Out by Eucalyptus Road. The neighbors say it's been there since the day after the quake."

Anger warmed Gillian's cheeks. "The car showed up Friday and you're just now checking it out? Today is Wednesday, for God's sake—"

It hit her like cold water. Wednesday. The day she and Melanie went out. . . .

The officer took another step back. "We've had more urgent matters to attend to."

Like an earthquake. Gillian rubbed her neck. "Sorry, I just—was there any sign of her?"

The cop relaxed a little. "No. Sorry, ma'am. We were hoping you might be able to help us locate her. See, the car was parked in someone's front yard and the guy was pretty upset."

Gillian smiled wryly. "Yeah, I'll bet."

"We've impounded the car." He took off his cap and ran his fingers through his tight curls. "Listen, when you see Ms. Frost, tell her she'll have to come down—"

Gillian nodded and murmured appropriately as the man rattled on. Eucalyptus Road was just outside the city limits . . . had Melanie left town without telling her? And without her car? This was crazy—Melanie had only left Rio Santo once in the three years Gillian had known her, to go camping for a week in the Sierras. She wouldn't just pick up and go—

"Thanks, ma'am," the officer said, placing his cap back on his head. He leaned closer. "Ms. Wheatley, are you all right?"

"Hmm?" She shook herself. "Oh, fine. I'll give Melanie the message—"

The screech of a bullhorn split the air. Gillian turned toward the school. The tall man handed the bullhorn to the taller woman, then held his clipboard over his crotch like a fig leaf.

Gillian sniffed. A bullhorn—to talk to thirty people?

The woman raised the bullhorn to her mouth. "The buildings are structurally sound," she boomed. "Classes will resume tomorrow. Staff may now enter the building.''

"Now that we're allowed in, I'm not sure I *want* to see my room," Jenna said, rejoining Gillian. "God, I'm sick of cleaning up."

"Yeah," Gillian said. Her stomach knotted around the uneasy feeling she'd be cleaning up for a long time.

GILLIAN SET THE BAGS OF GROCERIES ON THE TOP STEP, then dug in her skirt pocket for her house key. Thank God the roads had finally been cleared and reopened, allowing a few delivery trucks to trickle into town—the extortion of some store owners rivaled that of Woodstock II. For less than eighty bucks, she'd actually been able to buy pasta, carrots, squash, cheese, two jugs of water, and batteries. And four cans of fruit cocktail.

Gillian pulled the key from her pocket and slipped it into the lock. She wasn't sure why she'd bought the fruit cocktail; she didn't really like the stuff. But it had looked so inviting and familiar and . . . comforting, on the shelf. Whenever Mom had gone to visit her brother in Pennsylvania, Dad stocked up on fruit cocktail. Then, when she and Nora filled to bursting with missing Mom, Dad would place a card table under the peach tree nearest the house. He'd set it with a linen tablecloth, Mom's best silver, and two cut-crystal bowls. Then he'd open two cans of fruit cocktail and pour cool, syrupy fruit into each bowl. Before taking a bite, she and Nora would count all the cherries to see who had the most. . . .

Lowering her shaking hand, Gillian left the key in the lock. All these memories, hissing from her consciousness like air from a punctured tire. It was as if her past—every regret, every ghost, every lost comfort—had been released by the ruptured earth, leaving her dizzy with grief and longing.

Gillian counted to ten, reached for the key, and unlocked the door. She squatted to retrieve her groceries, freezing at the sound of Melanie's voice.

"—tell you," Melanie said. "I miss you. Life permitting, I'll call sometime—"

The answering machine. Gillian sprang to her feet. If she could grab the phone before Melanie hung up—

Click and dial tone.

"Play it again," a strange male voice said.

Gillian wavered on the threshold, clutching the door-jamb.

"You have heard it three times," another voice said. Female, with crisp, clipped consonants. "She gives away nothing. She could be two acres away, she could be two thousand. This machine will not help us find her."

Gillian wiped her palms on her skirt and crept toward the living room.

"Play it again," the man insisted. "Listen *behind* her. There must be a shift of earth or a rattle of gravel—"

"Not if she is on one of those tarred plains. There will be only the shift and rattle of candy wrappers."

"If that's what it takes to track her down."

Gillian pressed herself against the wall. Call the cops from KC's or confront these people—how dangerous were they? She crept toward the living room to get a peek.

A sudden weariness broke the man's voice. "What if she refuses to come back? What if she refuses the rites?"

Gillian stopped midstep.

"We will kill her," the woman said. "That is what we promised her. Do you feel a draft?"

Gillian backpedaled out the door, as quickly and as quietly as she could. Once outside, she bounded down the steps, darting across the withered lawn toward KC's. "Damn rosemary," she said, doubling back to the sidewalk to avoid the hedge.

She lunged up the steps and pounded on KC's door. She glanced at her door, expecting to see the intruders vaulting after her. They were nowhere in sight—yet. She pounded again. "KC, open up!"

KC opened the door. "Gillian, what is it? What's wrong?"

She squeezed past him into the entry. "Watch my door and be sure they don't leave."

KC gaped at her. "Gillian?"

"Don't stare at me, stare at my house," she said. "And be careful. They might be dangerous."

She dashed into the living room and stopped. Anything that could fall had been stacked or dismantled and tucked against the wall, including KC's telescope. She smiled crookedly. They had the same decorator, one E.Q. Sobering quickly, she looked around. "KC, where'd you leave the phone?" she called.

"By the kitchen door," he called back. "Stack of cookbooks."

Right on top of *The Mediterranean Diet Cookbook*. Gillian picked up the cordless phone and dialed. She flipped open the cookbook's cover. "Not another diet, KC," she said. "Uh, hello?"

As she explained the situation to the dispatcher Gillian watched the second hand on the clock leaning against the refrigerator. How long before the intruders stopped listening to Melanie's message and decided to ransack the house? she wondered. Maybe they'd already ransacked the house. . . .

"They're here *now*," Gillian told the dispatcher for the third time. "You've got to send—"

"Hey! Stop right there!" KC shouted.

"You've got to send someone now," Gillian said. "They're trying to escape!" Dropping the phone, she ran outside.

"Get away!" KC shouted, jogging along the rosemary. He waved his arms. "Get back!"

Doorknob in hand, Mrs. Timako stood frozen on Gillian's front step. The little Chihuahua cowered beside her, trembling and piddling all over Mrs. Timako's Converse All-Stars.

"Mrs. Timako!" Gillian called. "Get away from the door!"

Eyes wide, Mrs. Timako stared first at Gillian, then at KC. She pulled the door shut, then walked slowly down the steps, glancing over her shoulder. The Chihuahua skittered after her, tail between its legs.

As soon as Mrs. Timako was within reach, KC caught

her arm and reeled her to him. They sank behind the rosemary like archers behind a castle wall. The Chihuahua
crawled under the fragrant branches and disappeared. Gillian dropped to a crouch and scrambled to join them.
"This is crazy," she whispered. "If they've got a gun,
this hedge isn't going to do shit. Uh, sorry, Mrs. Timako."

"A gun?" Mrs. Timako's eyes narrowed. "Someone's
robbing you?"

"I, uh, don't know," Gillian said, alarmed by the
brightness of the older woman's eyes. She had to be at
least seventy—what if she had a heart attack? "I mean, as
far as I know they're just listening to my answering machine."

Mrs. Timako shot to her full height, face purpled with
fury. "Haven't we been through enough?" she shouted at
Gillian's house. She shook her fist. "You should be
ashamed!"

Gillian braced herself for a volley of gunfire. Nothing.
She and KC exchanged glances, then rose slowly. Something warm and wet tickled along Gillian's ankle. *Goddamn rat's peeing on me,* she thought, but when she
looked down, the terrified dog was licking her foot and
pleading with its bulging dark eyes.

"THEY PROBABLY RAN OUT THE BACK AND HOPPED THE
fence," KC said as the four of them crowded Gillian's
steps.

Gillian waved him quiet and pressed her ear to the door.
Not a sound.

Mrs. Timako set the Chihuahua on the step next to Gillian's groceries. "Honey, if these were the kind of bas-
tards"—Mrs. Timako smiled at Gillian's surprise—"who
would shoot an old lady and her dog, they'd have done it
by now. They may be armed, but they're not stupid. If
they shoot somebody, they're in for a world of grief."

Gillian pressed her lips together. TV logic. "Shouldn't
we wait for the police? We might disturb the evidence or
something."

"Most people arrive after the burglary and before the

police are called,'' KC said, reaching past her and opening the door. An odd smell wafted from the house: must, with a tang of crushed spearmint.

Mrs. Timako bent over and patted the Chihuahua's head. ''Frankie, stay right here and wait for Mommy.''

KC followed Gillian inside, then hurried past her toward the living room. ''I'll check the back door.''

Gillian and Mrs. Timako stood in the entry, listening. Only the shuffle of KC's feet. Mrs. Timako turned to each of the compass points in the entryway, then headed east down the hallway. ''Perhaps you and I should check the windows, dear,'' she said. ''See which ones have been forced.''

Gillian nodded. She had just placed her hand on Melanie's doorknob when KC trotted up to her. ''The back door is closed,'' he panted, ''and locked—from the inside.''

The hairs rose on the back of Gillian's neck. It was impossible to lock that sliding-glass door from the outside. ''Mrs. Timako,'' she called. ''Be careful. They might still be in the house.''

''Well, they're not in here,'' Mrs. Timako shouted from Gillian's room. ''My! Your room smells like a rose garden!''

''A perfume bottle broke,'' Gillian mumbled. She turned to KC. ''Check the kitchen, see if they're in—the garage! They might be in the garage!''

KC ran down the hall. ''Sure thing, Captain.''

Gillian turned again to Melanie's door.

The intruders were interested in Melanie—they might well be hiding in here. Or they may have searched the room for clues. Not that Gillian would be able to tell the difference between the effects of an aftershock or ransacking. She forced her shoulders back, wiped her hands on her skirt, counted to three. She thrust open the door—

No one.

She stepped tentatively into the room. It looked pretty much as she'd left it except that the bowl of coins and colored stones had tipped over. No breeze fluttered the curtains; the window remained shut. Gillian glanced at the closet. Ajar. She crept closer, then slid the door open wide—

No one.

Gillian exhaled and leaned her head against the wall. When her heart slowed, she backed out of the room.

Mrs. Timako joined her. "No one went out the bathroom window or yours."

"Or Melanie's," Gillian said.

KC met them in the entry. "No one in the garage. How long has the door to the backyard been nailed shut?"

"Since I moved in," Gillian said, her voice flattening.

KC shook his head. "How the hell did they get out of here?"

Mrs. Timako patted his arm. "That's for the police to figure out. I'm going. Too many bodies will only confuse things. Gillian, you're welcome to stay with me if you get nervous."

"Thanks, Mrs. Timako. I'll be all right." Gillian steeled herself. *I think.*

"If you change your mind," Mrs. Timako said, then stepped outside to an eruption of sharp, happy barks.

Gillian followed KC into the living room. They stared at the answering machine balanced on a stack of books. Crumbs of pungent damp soil led from the books to the sliding-glass door.

KC nodded toward the machine's blinking light. "Do you want to wait for the cops or do you want to listen to it now?"

"I hate to destroy any fingerprints," Gillian said. "Can you get me a tissue? Over there, by the bookshelf."

KC handed her a white tissue. Wrapping it carefully around her finger, she jabbed at the playback button. The machine whirred to life.

"Gillian, hi, it's Wednesday." An ache thinned Melanie's voice. "Sorry I won't be there for the 'Women at the Edge of Sanity' tour."

Gillian and KC inched closer together.

Melanie's voice regained its usual bravado. "I know this

really sucks on the rent and shit. Just sell my stuff. What's left of it. Should cover my rent for next month, give you a chance to get a housemate without taking just anybody. I can't tell you more 'cause I don't want you mixed up in this. Don't know what else to tell you. I miss you. Life permitting, I'll call sometime.''

Gillian hugged herself. "God, KC, what has she got herself into?"

The front door banged open. "Freeze!" someone shouted.

"Never mind her," KC said. "What have we gotten into?"

FIVE

"I COULDN'T BELIEVE THEY WANTED TO ARREST GIL-
LIAN," Mrs. Timako said. She scooted her milk crate away
from the garage door and closer to Nora. Leaning over to
press a price sticker onto a vase, she nearly crushed Frankie. The Chihuahua whimpered. "They claimed it was a
hoax, just because *they* couldn't find anything," Mrs. Timako confided.

"Just that trail of dirt," Gillian said, setting a box at
her sister's feet.

Mrs. Timako shook her head, her black pageboy bobbing. "They hadn't even analyzed the fingerprints."

Gillian picked up the vase. "Not a one."

Nora grunted, then looked up from pricing Melanie's
books. Her cheek ridged over her tongue, her eyes cool
and annoyed beneath a slight frown—the same expression
Dad used to wear when forced to hear the same story for
a third time.

Gillian carried the vase through the garage-sale maze.
The futon sofa bed stood to one side, three sets of sheets
and four pillows nestled against one arm. The small table,
an old orange armchair, and the portable massage table
lined the other side of the driveway. Boxes of stones,
coins, books, ceramics, and other odds and ends clustered
around and under the furniture. To the side, on the front

lawn, KC had lined up the bookshelves. On the other side, in the shadow of the rosemary, the old steamer trunk stood open, Melanie's clothes still neatly folded inside.

Gillian set the vase on the table. Those clothes wouldn't stay folded for long. Just wait till the first bargain hunters showed up.

"Hey, Gillian," Hiram said, edging past the sofa bed. He clutched a sheaf of lime-green papers to his chest. He peeled one off and handed it to her. "I'm organizing a boycott of all the markets that practiced graft and petty thievery while we were cut off from the outside world."

Gillian accepted the flyer. "You forgot Vine Hill Super."

"Vine Hill—but I've known Keith since he was a kid." Hiram's eyes narrowed. "And he was an opportunistic little bugger even then."

Gillian folded the paper and slid it into her back pocket. "Thirty dollars for a jar of peanut butter."

"I'll be sure to add him to the list," Hiram said, a razored edge to his voice. "Mrs. Timako, are you ready?"

Mrs. Timako scooped up Frankie and tottered to her feet. She patted Nora's arm as she marched past. Nora rolled her eyes heavenward, offering thanks to God, providence—whoever had answered her prayer for deliverance. Mom's expression.

Two cars pulled up in front of KC's. Gillian glanced at her watch. Seven. Right on time. "Sure, we're advertising nine," Nora had said, "but the pros'll be here for setup. Trust me—I know sales."

A man and a woman rushed the driveway, exchanging dirty looks across the sofa bed. Gillian smiled sweetly. "If you need any help . . ." she said, and made her way to the milk crate beside Nora.

A familiar white truck pulled up. KC got out carrying two pastry bags.

"What are you going to do about a housemate?" Nora said, penciling a price inside the cover of *A Modern Herbal, Vol. I.*

Gillian took the book and flipped through it. "The ad's coming out today."

"You know, Debbie—my employee," Nora said, flipping open the cover of *A Modern Herbal, Vol. II.* "Her house was flattened."

"No fruit slippers today, Nora," KC said, pulling up another milk crate. "I got you a blueberry cream-cheese Danish."

"Would've been my second choice," Nora said. She and KC divvied up the contents of the white bags.

Accepting a particularly splayed bear claw, Gillian pictured Debbie, a twenty-nine-year-old waif with trailing autumn-brown hair and blue eyes. "Willowy" described her to a tee—so did "dense." Ask her how much something cost at The Happy Wanderer and she'd say, "It's from Peru." Any question she was unsure of she generally answered, "Peru."

She'd once sold an Irish claddagh as a Peruvian wedding ring. Of course, Gillian had to wonder about the man who bought it. . . .

The man and woman circled the orange armchair.

KC handed Gillian a cup. "Hot chocolate," he said. He handed a second cup to Nora. "Latté."

Gillian lifted the lid and blinked at the sudden burst of peppermint. "Tea," she said.

KC swapped cups.

Nora picked up another book. "What is it with all these herbals? This is the eighth one I've priced."

"You should see the jars of herbs and stuff in the garage," KC said, sipping his tea. "A whole canning cupboard full."

"Why aren't you selling those?" Nora asked.

Three car doors slammed. The adversaries circling the orange armchair drew closer to their prize.

"Fifty dollars seems steep," the woman said, opening the negotiations.

"I told you," Gillian whispered to Nora.

Nora set the book aside and stood. "Chair like that will cost you six times that new."

The man snorted. "Where do *you* shop?"

"Besides, they don't make chairs that color anymore," Nora said.

KC nudged Gillian. "There's a reason for that."

Five new people invaded the driveway. Two women exclaimed and hugged a third, one of them asking her, "Are you back at work yet?" Meanwhile two men, dressed in identical black jeans and raspberry T-shirts, made a beeline for the orange chair. The taller one plopped down, snuggling into the worn cushions. "It's perfect!" he exclaimed.

"We'll take it," said the other, whipping out a roll of bills. "Who do I . . . ?"

Nora stepped forward. "Fifty dollars," she said, glancing coolly at the first woman. "I'll get your change—"

"Keep it, keep it!" the tall black-and-raspberry said. "Do you know how long it takes to break in a chair like this?"

"Ages," said his friend. "Simply ages."

The first man and woman paled, then turned in a panic as the newcomers swarmed over the driveway.

Nora sat down and handed Gillian three twenties. "It's too early to barter," she said.

The morning went quickly. So did the futon sofa bed, two lamps, the small table, and several books. The pros snarled at the price on the bookshelves, but Nora refused to come down. A little before noon, Lily Gerber snapped them up, recruiting KC, Jake Rubio, and his housemate, Denny, as muscle.

Gillian gave Nora a high five, then walked over to where Beth Ellen stirred the bowl of colored stones and old coins. A girl with a black ponytail knelt beside her, picking at the stones. A blue tiger's eye had been pushed to the side of the bowl, safe from the whirlpool created by Beth Ellen's finger.

Beth Ellen's hair had been French-braided with green and pink ribbons, at stylistic odds with her ragged cerulean sweat shirt. A snarling lion threatened to leap from Beth Ellen's chest.

Gillian crouched beside Beth Ellen. The other girl

scrambled away and began digging through a box of clothes. "Great sweatshirt," Gillian said.

Beth Ellen flashed Gillian a huge smile. "It's my favorite." She lowered her voice. "Mom hates it."

"Oh, well." Gillian nodded at the other girl. "Who's your friend?"

"Bibbie Leeds," Beth Ellen said. "She lives on the other side of the park. She's looking for Barbie clothes."

"I don't think Melanie had any Barbie clothes." Gillian picked up the tiger's eye. "See this one?"

Beth Ellen nodded.

Gillian placed the stone in Beth Ellen's hand. "If you carry this stone with you all the time, it'll help you when you get nervous or scared or too excited. You just hold it and roll it around in your hand and you won't stutter as much."

Beth Ellen's hand fisted around the tiger's eye. "Is it magic?"

Gillian smiled. "No. But you are. Sometimes you just need something to help you. No, no, put your money away. It's a gift."

Beth Ellen looked up. "Really?"

Gillian nodded.

Two women squeezed between them, forcing them apart. "Where were you when it hit?" one woman asked the other.

AN AFTERSHOCK ROLLED THROUGH JUST BEFORE NOON with a deep guttural rumble. The customers stopped, gazed warily at the vibrating telephone poles, then bent over Melanie's dwindling possessions as the earth stilled and lisped into silence. A man in a Greek fishing cap turned to KC. "D'you sleep through that four-point-six last night?" he said.

KC shook his head and went next door to make sandwiches.

"So, Gillian, how about it?" Nora said, straightening the box of herbals. "It would solve your problem and Debbie's."

Gillian could pretend she didn't understand . . . that
would only postpone the inevitable. "I don't know,
Nora—"

"Look, you already know her—"

"*That's* stretching it—"

"—so why take a chance on some yo-yo who wanders
in off the street?"

Gillian put her hands on her hips. "I'm advertising in
the paper, not on telephone poles."

Nora flared her nostrils.

Gillian sighed. "I need someone to help with the rent—"

"She has a job."

"Nora . . ."

"Rich is running the Action out of a trailer on Rowan.
I'm going to open next to him. She's got a job, Gillian."

And how many hours could Nora afford to give Debbie
and how much of Debbie's rent would Nora have to sub-
sidize? Nora's savings couldn't be very large—not enough
to float Debbie *and* get the shop going again. Never mind
that—how crazy would it make Gillian to live with a
woman who grinned blankly, chirping in mindless rapture
anytime anyone spoke to her?

Gillian shifted her weight. "Why doesn't she move in
with you? You've got that guest room—"

"I don't have room," Nora said flatly.

"Two ham sandwiches, one cheese," KC said, handing
the cheese sandwich to Gillian. He eased between Gillian
and Nora, cornering Nora by the garage. Gillian raised her
eyebrows in thanks and headed for the end of the driveway.

The first bite of sandwich stuck in Gillian's throat. Why
was she being such a jerk? The poor woman needed a
place to live—so make it temporary. Not like Gillian was
planning to renew her contract with the school district.
She'd be leaving this summer anyway—

Gillian stopped in mid-chew, stunned. She hadn't realized she'd made a decision. Was that really what she in-
tended to do? Pick up and go . . . ?

She looked up. A couple marched toward her, their foot-fall slapping the sidewalk in unison. The woman, her skin tanned a deep, even sienna, folded her arms over her chest and stopped, tossing her straw-white hair over her shoulder. The man stopped, too, cocking his head to one side. Gillian winced at the sunlight strobing off his sunglasses. When she recovered, the man had bowed his head so that his shaggy brick-red hair curtained his face. Like the woman, he had folded his arms, equally tanned but more of a cinnamon color. "Use the contractions I taught you," the man said in a harsh whisper. "You'll sound more human."

The woman glared at him and stalked toward Gillian.

Gillian retreated to the milk crates, her uneasiness growing as she watched them. Creepy people . . . the woman radiated anger like summer heat, the man ground his jaw like a millstone. Gillian nibbled her sandwich. These two couldn't leave too soon.

The couple crouched beside the box at the end of the driveway. Books, which had seen a lot of pawing but no buying. The woman lifted a book by one corner, scowled at it, then tossed it back in the box. The man said something in that same low voice. The woman's lip curled. The man sighed, a rumbling sound—3.1?—and crossed the driveway to the steamer trunk.

"But it's a historic landmark," KC said, sitting on the milk crate to Gillian's left.

Nora sat down beside him. "The guy I talked to, the one from the planning commission, says he doesn't see any way to save it."

The man sifted the clothes in Melanie's trunk, burying his face in one of her blouses.

KC sniffed. "But the city spent all that money reinforcing it four years ago—"

"Tear what down?" Gillian said absently. The woman pored over the bowl of coins and colored stones.

"The Seraphim Theater," KC said.

The man closed his eyes, nuzzling and brushing his lips

across Melanie's pink cotton sweater. Gillian wrinkled her nose. "That's sick," she said.

"Maybe so," Nora said, "but that's not going to stop them if they decide it's too dangerous."

The woman cried out, then dug furiously through the stones and coins. Gillian set her sandwich on the unoccupied milk crate and crept toward the woman.

The man looked over at the woman. She gestured to him, her arm swaying like a tree branch. He rushed to join her, bending over the bowl. He sifted the coins and stones, handing the woman three or four coins before sitting on the driveway. He sorted through the bowl quickly, handing three more coins to the woman. She smiled, cheeks craggy with sudden hollows.

"Those—those aren't for sale," Gillian stammered.

"The hell they're not," Nora said, rising. She whispered through gritted teeth, "What are *you* going to do with them?"

The man and woman stared at Gillian. The woman's gaze, cold and black, staked Gillian's fear and held her.

Gillian wavered, helpless as a carrot on a stick. "I, uh, I thought you were looking at something else. Sorry."

The man and the woman exchanged looks. "What did you think we were looking at?" he said.

"I, uh." Gillian ran her tongue along the back of her teeth. "Well, those, but I forgot I'd sorted out the ones I wanted."

The man's eyebrows shot above the rim of the sunglasses. He jerked toward the woman. She shook her head. "We've them all," she said.

The man relaxed. Bowing his head slightly to Gillian, he scooted over to where the woman dug through a box of ceramics and incense.

KC whispered in Gillian's ear, "I don't like them."

"Me neither," she said.

"Customers," Nora said, and went to join the couple. She smiled at the woman. "Are you looking for anything in particular?"

The woman frowned, sizing Nora up. She dismissed

Nora with a toss of the head. She picked up a porcelain
vase and examined it.

Nora's smile collapsed from the inside. "If I can help
with anything, just let me know," she said in her best sales
voice.

"I *really* don't like them," KC said.

The man smiled at Nora, then went back to ravage the
trunk again. He fingered and sniffed most of Melanie's
clothes, then turned to Nora. "Do you have any shoes?"
he asked.

Want to smell my rubber boots? Gillian thought.

"They were too worn," Nora said. "We tossed them."

The man's shoulders sagged. "We'll never find her,"
he told the woman. She held up the mortar and pestle. He
brightened.

A chill invaded Gillian. Find her? Melanie? Gillian's
memory played back the voices discussing the answering
machine. This woman's voice seemed lower, but the way
she clipped her consonants was exactly the same . . . but
the man—sure, he shared a similar timbre with the male
intruder, but he shadowed his *S*s with a gentle slur, like
the ghost of a Castilian *C*. He also spoke more rapidly
than the other man. That could be nerves. Gillian watched
them closely.

They studied everything with excruciating care. The
man removed everything from the trunk, then felt along
the sides, rapping here and there as if looking for some
hidden compartment. The woman emptied every box, setting aside the Zuni badger and two candlesticks. Whenever
another customer got too close, she curled her upper lip
and bared her teeth. The other customers gave her a wide
berth.

Finally the strange couple reunited by the rosemary
hedge. Gillian knelt by the steamer trunk, within hearing,
and folded the clothes draped over the sides of the trunk
and heaped on the lawn. Blanched grass clung to sleeves
and collars.

"I can't find it," the man said.

The woman inhaled with a hiss. "She must have it with her."

"That won't do us any good if we can't find her."

The two fell silent. Gillian folded a turquoise sweatshirt and set it on top of a muslin blouse. Her neck prickled. She looked up slowly. They were staring at her.

Gillian sat back. "Yes?"

"Is this all?" the woman said.

"This is all I'm selling," Gillian said, standing.

"But is this all she left behind?" the man pressed.

"There's a cupboard full of herbs, but I don't feel right . . ." Gillian's breath caught. "How did you know she left?"

The man looked down at his hands. The woman folded her arms over her chest and tried to look bored. Tried. A twitch around the eyes gave her away. "We overheard you telling someone that your friend left and asked you to sell her things," she said. "We just wondered if there's anything else."

Gillian studied them. It was possible they'd overheard her telling one of the neighbors. It was also possible they'd heard it from Melanie herself via tape. . . .

"There's nothing else," Gillian said.

The man and woman looked at each other. The woman nodded. The man stepped toward Gillian, holding out the coins, a velvet pouch, the stone badger, and two candlesticks. He gestured toward the woman, who held two more candlesticks and the mortar and pestle. "We'd like to buy these," he said.

Gillian eyed them coolly. "Sure," she said. *Price them high. Get rid of these creeps.* "Seventy-seven dollars."

"Seventy-seven?" the man said, his eyebrows shooting above the sunglasses' frames again.

"If you don't want them, someone else will," Gillian said.

The man gurgled and shook his head. The woman unfolded her arms. "You'll pay her," she said.

The man set his treasures at his feet, then reached into his jacket pocket and pulled out a plastic bag. Bills and coins clung to the plastic, held in place by a thin film of rust. Crumbs of dirt clung to the bills.

He opened the bag and started handing her the soggy money without counting it. Fives, twenties, he paid no attention to the denominations, but instead to her face, as if using her expression to gauge how much money he'd given her. When he had handed her all the bills this way—seventy-two dollars—he began handing her the coins. Gillian's damp palms itched with disgust. Slimy *and* gritty, the coins stuck to her skin. After handing her four quarters, three dimes, one nickel, and seven extremely foul pennies, he looked up at her expectantly.

Gillian cupped the money in her hands. With bills and coins like this, $73.42 was plenty. "Great, great. Thanks. Do you need a bag or anything?"

"No, thank you," the woman said.

The man stuffed the plastic bag back in his pocket, then squatted and scooped up his prizes. He stood, nodding to the woman. They walked away. At the end of the driveway, the man turned to Gillian.

He smiled.

Chill bumps carpeted her arms until the couple turned the corner and disappeared. Throughout the day Gillian caught herself glancing at the corner, afraid they'd come back.

SIX

KC WAVED AS GILLIAN PULLED INTO HER DRIVEWAY AFTER work. He walked over to the rosemary hedge and waited until she got out of her car. "What you got there?" he said.

"Blocks and little people," Gillian said. Bag cradled in one arm, water jug in the other, she bumped her car door shut with her hip. She walked across the crispy lawn to join him. "The kids have trouble focusing, especially after the big ones, like that five this morning. Thought I'd let them play for the next couple of weeks, until they start to feel safe again."

KC peeked in the bag, then looked at her sideways. "Aren't blocks a little young for most of your kids?"

Gillian set the jug and the bag at her feet and arched her back. Vertebrae crackled. "I have a fourth grader who's making houses out of my flash cards. Then he and two other kids drum on the table, harder and harder, until they knock the house down. The whole time they're shouting, 'Earthquake, earthquake!' Blocks just seemed like a natural."

"Geez."

"Yeah." Gillian ground a fist into the small of her back. "They've all regressed a little. They're scared. God, KC, it breaks my heart. Roz, the school psychologist, keeps telling us, 'The kids know what they need to help them cope with this. Listen to them.' ''

A rumble heralded a gentle swell. Gillian planted her feet and rode it out. The panic drained from her one heartbeat at a time. "I wish I knew what *I* needed," she said. "Do you suppose we grow out of knowing?"

KC motioned for her to turn around. He rubbed her shoulders. "No, we just complicate our needs with sociopolitical agendas."

Gillian laughed. "Where'd you hear that?"

"On the radio. Lot of shows are being replaced by on-air disaster counseling." His fingers wore down her tension. "And which agenda is confusing your natural healing instincts?"

"Nora's."

"Ah, yes—the Debbie proposal. And what does your heart tell you?"

"Well, Dr. KC, my heart tells me I'll feel like a jerk for not opening my home and heart to this needy soul." Gillian hummed low in her throat. "That's perfect. Thanks. Anyway, *I* keep telling myself it doesn't have to be permanent, let her stay till she gets something else. But you know how hard it's going to be to say, 'Gosh, two months already? So, when are you moving?' ''

KC's hands lingered on her shoulders. "Why doesn't Nora take her in?"

Gillian squatted from under KC's hands and picked up the bag and the water. She took a step back before facing him. "No room—she says. Anyway, I can't afford it and Nora can't afford it."

A residue of hope lingered in his eyes. Gillian hugged the bag to her chest. They'd spent too much time together again, let each other get too close. Allowed promises unspoken and unkept to flare momentarily from that past spark. *A little distance,* she thought, *and we'll be friends again. Just friends.*

She pushed him away with a torrent of words. "Besides, my gut feeling is that it would be a big mistake. It just doesn't feel right." Gillian ran her toe along the bottom of the hedge, cheeks aflame with the twining of the spoken and the unspoken conversations. She separated them. "It's the saintly thing to do, take in someone in need. A helping hand, and all that. But I have this weird feeling. . . ." She looked up. "I ran into Debbie outside the toy store today. I tried to talk to her. . . ."

Understanding tempered KC's gray eyes. "Tried?"

Gillian made a face. "I can't live with that woman."

He shrugged. "Then don't. Listen, why don't you come over for dinner? I'm making linguine with feta and olives. . . ."

Distance, Gilly, she warned herself. Distance, but how much? "Tempting, very tempting. Can I let you know in an hour?"

"Just show up. Six-thirty." He nodded at the water jug. "You're in charge of the libations."

Gillian ran her tongue along the inside of her cheek. "Careful or I'll bring dessert—fruit cocktail."

KC blinked. "Fruit cocktail?"

Gillian grinned and strode toward her house. "Got a case of it in the trunk," she said.

Blocks for her students, fruit cocktail for herself—she'd even bought a tiny stuffed lion for Beth Ellen. A twinge of sadness passed through her—what comfort could she offer KC?

THE MESSAGE LIGHT BLINKED FURIOUSLY. NOT UNEXpected. The phone had been ringing nonstop since the ad came out Sunday. The only surprise was that the phone wasn't ringing now.

Gillian set the bag on the kitchen table, then poured herself a glass of water. Grabbing a pen and a pad of paper, she returned to the living room and hit the play button. Fifteen names and phone numbers echoed off the bare walls.

Including Nora's.

"I can't believe you still have that ad in the paper," Nora said. "Debbie's a nice person. I don't know what you've got against her. Come on, Gillian, help me out.

When I get the shop up and running I'm going to need her. She's reliable and down-to-earth, which is more than you can say about Melanie.''

Gillian glared at the answering machine. Melanie *was* reliable—in her own way. And her feet were firmly planted compared to Debbie's.

Gillian scribbled down the last three names and numbers without really listening. Sure, Debbie was nice. That wasn't the point. The point was—well, it was . . .

Gillian had run into Debbie at the (undamaged) shopping mall and invited her to join her for tea at the book café. It started out pleasantly enough. Gillian ordered Red Zinger, Debbie did the same, making some giggly comment about great minds. But at the table she reached for the sugar, noticed that Gillian hadn't, reached for the honey, again noticed Gillian hadn't, then sat very still, staring into the red depths of her tea. A confused, woeful look pinched her narrow features, shrinking her forehead to half its size. She took one sip.

One. She spent the rest of the time playing with the tea bag.

Gillian made some attempts at conversation with the usual get-acquainted, idiot questions: where are you from, what do you do for fun, where were you when the earthquake hit? Gillian hated herself for not being more original, but there was nothing about Debbie to hint at anything more intriguing. At least Gillian didn't ask her her sign. After each question, answered briefly with a giggle and shrug, Debbie stared at Gillian and shoved the tea bag to the bottom of her cup with her spoon.

Then a small aftershock coughed through the book café. Debbie jerked to attention. ''Earthworms have seven hearts, you know,'' she said. ''Think how many heart attacks you could have with seven hearts. I mean, before you died.''

Gillian lowered her cup and stared. Debbie's tittery nervousness had disappeared, replaced by an intense earnestness. ''Did, uh, someone you love die of a heart attack?'' Gillian asked.

"No, no," Debbie said, shaking her head emphatically. "But just think. Most people are good for two, maybe three heart attacks. So you'd get at least fourteen, maybe twenty-one."

Gillian drained her cup. If she hadn't seen Debbie do this before, often to customers who had asked about an item's price or availability, she'd have thought it was post-traumatic stress. Like that teacher at school, Paul Kestrel, who refused to open the shutters in his classroom since the earthquake. An old fear of windows, he said, from his civil-rights days in Mississippi. Something about being seen by snipers. Gillian herself found that her wandering mind strayed home, just as the house exploded into flame with Mom and Dad waving from the upper windows. But Debbie had been like this before the earthquake. . . .

The doorbell and the phone rang at the same time. Gillian hesitated. The answering machine could handle the phone. She went to the door and opened it.

Blood drained from her face in a chilling rush. The strange man smiled at her, his eyes still shrouded by sunglasses despite the gathering dusk. "Hello," he said.

Gillian held the door between them. "Hello."

"I, uh, realize the sale is over—"

"Two days ago," Gillian said.

"Yes." The man touched the right stem of his glasses, then lowered his hand. "There's something . . ."

He pressed his lips together, and looked down at his feet—his bare feet. A chill laced the air; the cement step had to be cold enough to leech the heat right out of him.

Wariness spread through Gillian like a rash. Bare feet, sunglasses at dusk, moldy money . . . the man was odd. Never mind his references to Melanie—

Gillian started to shut the door. "I've sold or given everything away."

The man caught the door with his hand. "Please. I knew Melanie and there was something, a ceramic, that she used to wear."

A ceramic . . . ? Gillian leaned against the door. She couldn't budge it. "Maybe she took it with her. Now, if you'll excuse me, I have a friend in the kitchen I need to get back to," she lied.

The man's shoulders slumped, but he hung onto the door. "She might have," he murmured. Then he rallied. "But I have a feeling she didn't. That it's still here. If I describe it to you—"

"Look," Gillian said, pressing all her weight against the door. "I don't know who you are or what you want, but if you don't leave now—"

"If I could just see what's left—"

"There's nothing left," Gillian said. A low hum invaded her mind. Nerves. "Just a cabinet full of herbs. Now, if you'd be so kind—"

"Please," the man said. He leaned more heavily on the door. The smell of freshly turned earth reached Gillian. Freshly turned earth and the sharp tang of bruised mint.

Gillian's pulse pounded at her temples. The hum swelled to a growl. "You were—" she began. *In my house.* His voice had the right timbre, but again, that hinted Castilian *C*—

"It's just a small thing," he pleaded. He made a broken circle with the thumb and forefinger of his right hand. "About this big. A face, with stone eyes."

Gillian wedged her shoulder against the door. The door rattled between them. "I want you to leave *now*," she said.

The man's eyebrows rose above the sunglasses. "You *have* seen it, haven't you? Where? Where is it?"

The panel of pebbled glass beside the door rattled. Gillian gripped the knob more firmly, terror rising in her to the same slow tempo as the aftershock.

The man spun to face Linnet Park. Stepping back without releasing the door, he listened to the rumble deepening around them. "I can stop this," he said, turning to Gillian. "If you give me the ceramic face, I can stop this."

The house groaned. Glass rattled and shattered behind Gillian.

"It's not here," Gillian said. "I don't know where it is. I haven't seen it since I first went through her room."

Two rigid faults rose along the man's jaw. "Don't play

with me," he said, his voice honed to an edge. "This isn't an aftershock. It'll probably be worse than the original earthquake. *Where is the ceramic face?*"

"I don't know!" Gillian shouted.

The earthquake hit with stunning force, slamming Gillian backward into the wall with the door and the strange man on top of her, then hurling her sideways to the floor. The pebbled glass vibrated above her like a tuning fork. Gillian snatched at the trim, trying to pull herself to her feet and away from the glass, but the floor roiled beneath her, tossing her wall to wall. Gaze fixed on the trembling glass, she reached out to catch hold of anything and found the stranger's damp hand. Another vicious jolt whipped her to the left, her hand sliding free of his.

His fingers locked around her wrist. With a snap, he jerked her onto the doorstep, then dragged her out into the yard. The pebbled glass exploded in a shower of topaz splinters. Gillian curled into a ball, her shoulders tensed and waiting for the house to collapse on top of her.

The strange man shielded her body with his own. The scent of mint and mulch clogged her throat, but his solidness calmed her.

Then the earth stilled.

Gillian curled a little tighter, just for a second, then wriggled from under the strange man. He helped her to her knees. Brushing hair and dried grass from her face, he searched her eyes. "Are you all right?" he said.

Gillian licked her lips, then spat out crumbs of dirt. "I think so." She looked up at him. "Are you—" The words died on her lips.

His sunglasses had fallen off and even in the dim light, Gillian could see his eyes. The shape of the face, the coloring, the soft features, everything else was different—except the eyes. The irises, a lacework of moss, blue, and rust, surrounded pupils of forest green ringed with black.

Gillian backed away. "You were at the park, the morning after the earthquake. But your face was different, more like—like rock. Now it's—it's—"

"Like clay," the man said. "Gillian, I don't want to

scare you, but I need all the objects Melanie used so I can ease her pain. She's lost in it, striking out blindly. I don't know how much longer we can hold her back.''

''Whose pain?'' Gillian said, inching away. ''Melanie's? What have you done to Melanie?''

The man reached for her. ''We haven't done anything—''

Gillian scrambled out of reach. ''You broke into my house, didn't you? To try to find Melanie. Because—'' Gillian clamped her jaw shut. *Because you promised to kill her.*

''Gillian,'' someone called. ''Are you all right?''

Gillian swung toward the voice. Hiram and Mrs. Timako crouched beside the gas main in front of Mrs. Timako's. ''What do you think, Gillian?'' Mrs. Timako said. ''Another seven?''

More and more people ventured from their houses. A sense of security surged through Gillian. Safety in numbers. This guy wouldn't try anything in front of all these people. ''At least a seven, Mrs. Timako,'' she said, turning smugly to the strange man.

But he had vanished, as if he had melted into the earth—or as if it had swallowed him whole.

SEVEN

GILLIAN SURVEYED THE EMPTY ROOM, TRYING TO SEE IT
as a prospective housemate might. It looked so bleak without Melanie's things. Maybe a little sunlight would
brighten the room, make it more welcoming. She pulled
back the curtains—and groaned. She'd forgotten about the
herbs. Collapsed over the sides of their pots, the plants
brushed the sill with their brittle leaves and crippled tendrils.

Gillian ran a hand through her hair. At least this would
be an easier fix than the broken window in the living room.
She still had a few minutes before the first applicant,
Holly, arrived.

"Trust people, Gilly," she muttered. "Dead herbs
aren't going to drive anyone away. No one in Rio Santo
has running water—who's going to waste it on a plant?"

She collected two of the small pots, tucking one into
the crook of her elbow, then grabbed the powdered chamomile. A circle of ceramic slapped to the sill.

Gillian set down the chamomile, then picked up the medallion. The ceramic face stared back at her with its glittering eyes. Agate eyes, like the stranger's. She traced the
loopy nose and gently curved lips, then pressed her fingers
over the eyes to shut them.

A hard knot formed in her throat. The stranger would

be back. She was as sure of this as she was of the earth beneath—she rubbed the hollow of her throat with the medallion. She was as sure of this as she was that the sun would rise next morning. Somewhere.

She uncovered the eyes. She could give the stranger the ceramic and get rid of him. Or—she tensed. Or she could bargain with it for Melanie's life. . . .

A knock echoed from the entry.

Holly or the stranger?

Gillian slipped the medallion into her shirt pocket and stalked out of the room. She swept her hand over the light switch, then smiled wryly. The second earthquake had knocked out power, water, and gas, closed the schools . . . and she was still trying to turn off the lights, just like Dad taught her.

Dad, his skin peeled away layer by layer by fingers of flame. . . .

Gillian hurried to the entry.

A short, broad-shouldered woman with a spray of blond curls stood on the doorstep, her hands outstretched toward the house. Her fingers hovered inches from the wooden trim. "Oh, wow," she murmured.

Gillian watched the woman's hands follow the door frame in each direction. "Hello . . . Holly?"

"Yeah," the woman said breathlessly. Her left hand skimmed the cardboard replacing the pebbled glass. "The reading I'm getting off this place . . . some heavy shit going down. Listen, these house chakras are really muddy. If I was you, I'd move. Like, today."

"I guess you don't want to see the room?" Gillian said.

Holly looked at Gillian for the first time. Her eyes widened at the sight of the dead herbs. "I wouldn't set foot in this house. Come with me," she said, reaching for Gillian. "Save yourself."

"I . . . think I'll manage," Gillian said. She eased the door shut.

Gillian took the dead herbs to the kitchen. Had the earthquakes pushed this woman over the edge or was she already there? Gillian wrinkled her nose. Probably already there.

"Come on, Gilly, be kind," she said, setting the herbs in the sink. Holly was probably just trying to cope like everyone else. Paul Kestrel still hid from phantom snipers even he knew weren't there, Vern Horowski and Marci Gomez burst into tears—daily—in the staff room. Melanie ran away. . . .

Gillian smiled crookedly and shut off the empty tap. And she tried to water plants without water.

Pulling the medallion out of her pocket, she turned it over in her hand. No one had signed the ceramic or made any identifying mark. Not that she expected to find Melanie's name; Melanie only made coiled or pinched things.

Gillian traced the medallion's rough edge. That's where they met, in a ceramics class. Got such a kick out of each other, they declared themselves housemates and moved in here.

And stopped taking ceramics. Gillian turned the medallion over. Melanie kept her bag of clay, dragging it into the backyard every now and then to make pinch pots or roll the clay into snakes. When the clay dried out, she'd dump it in a big yellow bucket and reclaim it, submerging it in water till it became pliable again. But she refused to fire anything. Said it trapped the soul of the clay.

Gillian rubbed the bridge of her nose. She'd forgotten about that. Suddenly that Sunday, six months ago, made sense. The Sunday Melanie had loaded the yellow bucket into the trunk of her car. . . .

"Taking your clay on an outing?" Gillian had asked, following Melanie outside.

Melanie slammed the trunk. "Taking it to the river to set it free."

Gillian stared at her. "You're canceling our weekly brunch to dump a bucket of clay in the river? Why don't we just meet afterward?"

Melanie gave her the look—mouth pinched shut, cheeks hollowed, eyebrows raised. "Once in four years isn't gonna hurt us."

Then she got in the car and drove off. . . .

Gillian got out an old piece of foil and wrapped the medallion carefully, then placed it in an old margarine tub. Snapping the lid in place, she hid the tub in the back of the refrigerator, behind a box of baking soda.

She glanced at the clock. Twenty minutes before the next prospective housemate arrived. She went to the cupboard and got out a can of fruit cocktail.

PROSPECTIVE HOUSEMATE NUMBER THREE, A TALL, conga-shaped woman named Gigi, snapped her gum and glanced at the sheet of clear plastic stretched over the former living-room window. "Tough luck," she said, shaking her mane of red frizz. "So, you got a well?"

Gillian frowned. "Excuse me?"

"You got a well?" Gigi repeated. She blew a bubble, then inhaled the gum back into her mouth. "You know, water. On the radio, on the way over, they were saying what with the drought and the quakes and all, they're going to start rationing again. No way I'm taking anything without a well."

"No, just the water district." Gillian forced her shoulders to relax. *So she's not Melanie,* Gillian told herself. *None of them have been Melanie, none of them are going to be Melanie, so forget finding another Melanie.* "Would you like to see the room?" she asked.

Gigi shrugged. "Sure, why not?"

Gillian could think of a lot of reasons, none of them having to do with wells. "It's back this way—"

The phone rang. Gillian glanced at it. With the electricity out, the answering machine wasn't working—

"Go ahead," Gigi said. "I'll show myself around."

"First door on the right," Gillian said. She sprinted for the phone, snatching it mid-ring. "Hello?"

"Gillian, you should see this trailer!" Nora said. "Debbie's done a great job fixing it up."

Gillian hugged herself with her free arm. "That's wonderful. Listen, I'm in the middle of something. Can I call you back?"

"Not really. I'm on a pay phone." Nora lowered her voice. "Debbie and I are almost done here. Why don't I bring her by so she can see the room?"

"It's nice," Gigi shouted from the entry, "but I'm looking for a well. Don't get off. I'll let myself out."

Gillian swiveled toward the entry. "Uh, wait—Nora, can you call me back in five—"

"Naw, don't bother," Gigi said. "Nice place, but it's not home, you know?"

Gillian sighed. She knew.

"Gillian, who is that?" Nora said.

"It's—hang on," Gillian said. But the front door had already banged shut behind Gigi. Gillian raised the phone to her ear. "Nora?"

"You're interviewing people, aren't you?" Nora's voice dropped to subzero. "I can't believe you. I ask you for one little favor—"

"Nora, I don't want to talk about this right now—"

"You're interviewing people, you can interview Debbie. I'll bring her by in an hour."

Gillian locked her jaw. "Don't, Nora. Look, I told you—Debbie can't afford the room, I can't afford the room, *you* can't afford the room. How many years did you work your tail off at that law office to earn the money to open The Happy Wanderer? I'm not going to help you throw all that away—"

"The woman has no place to go—"

"She must have someplace to go. Where is she staying now?"

"—find something soon, she may have to move back to Redding and stay with her parents." Nora paused. "She's staying with a friend but she has to be out by the end of the month because he's moving out of state."

Gillian rubbed the bridge of her nose. Him and half the town. "Why can't she stay with you?"

"I can't believe you're being so unreasonable. Look, I'll bring her by on the way home. We'll be there in an hour."

"I won't be here in an hour."

"Where will you be?"

Anywhere but showing Debbie the room. "I have to run some errands. I'll talk to you later."

"Gillian—"

"I'll talk to you," Gillian said, "later."

Gillian hung up and sat on the floor. She rested her head on her knees. Why was she being such a jerk? All Debbie wanted was a place to live; she wasn't looking for companionship. Gillian raised her head and looked at the bookcase molly-bolted to the wall. No, Debbie wasn't looking for companionship, but maybe she was.

She missed Melanie. She missed the little things: Melanie's specially blended teas, the dried papaya she set beside Gillian's mug every morning, her mud-crusted hiking boots in the entry. Wednesday evenings on the town—the "Women on the Edge of Sanity Tours," Melanie called them—for dinner, dancing, movies, whatever. Brunch every Sunday. Gillian sighed. The way Melanie made room in her life to absorb Gillian's extra time whenever KC started dating. The way Melanie suddenly discovered some new passion of her own whenever Gillian met someone or KC stopped dating. The pleasure it gave Gillian to open up her life the same way when Melanie needed it. . . .

Gillian rested her chin on her knees. She'd been so lucky. Thank God she'd known it.

Gillian looked around the dismantled living room. Not a trace of Melanie remained except the molly bolt. She should have kept something besides the herbs and a handful of colored stones. What had she been thinking? She smeared a tear across her cheek.

Someone knocked at the door. Gillian pushed herself to her feet, then pulled the list from her pocket: *2:30—Janice.*

Janice knocked again. Gillian wiped her cheek, then went to answer the door.

A short wisp of a woman waited on the step, her face turned toward the park. Her dark, downy hair rose like dandelion fluff—or pine needles. Clothed in a T-shirt and jeans, her body curved like a twelve-year-old girl's. Then the woman turned. Soft crow's-feet highlighted her gray eyes; a dimple added a dash of wry humor to her narrow face. "You must be Gillian," she said.

Gillian savored the clear resonance of the woman's voice. "And you must be Janice," she said.

The dimple deepened. "Canice."

"Oh, sorry. I must have written it down wrong." Gillian smiled and backed out of the doorway. "Come on in."

Canice stepped inside. "I'm a little early—"

A low growl shook the house. The aftershock threw Gillian against the closet door. Canice grasped her arms and steadied her, somehow absorbing most of the jolt. *Like a shock absorber,* Gillian thought, watching the blurred outline of the house tremble around them. Then the world grew still. Canice released her.

Gillian exhaled with a hiss. "Five."

"At least," Canice said.

Gillian tried to shut the front door. It refused. She left it ajar. She led Canice to the living room. "I don't think I'll ever arrange the furniture in quite the same way again," she said.

Canice laughed. "No kidding! Nothing heavy on a top shelf, everything bolted to the walls or floor, no pictures over the bed—nothing *near* the bed."

Gillian nodded. "Condiments and syrups in plastic bottles."

"That or childproof cabinets." Canice shook her head, then walked across the room and touched the bookshelf. She turned. "Tell me about yourself," she said.

Gillian blinked. "About myself?"

Canice's face warmed with an open, breeze of a smile. "The house feels good, but it's not the house I'll be living with."

CANICE SAT CROSS-LEGGED BENEATH MELANIE'S WINDOW. Her eyes danced. "Let me get this straight—your roommate's growing dope in the flower box outside your dorm window and *you* get sent to a counselor for taking No Doz?"

"That's not all," Gillian said, leaning forward, fingers

fanned along the carpet. "A flu had taken the campus hostage, so most of the counselors were out sick. The dean was so worried about me, he sent me to the only therapist not spending office hours in the bathroom—the speech therapist. She wasn't sure what to do with me, so we talked about her job. After two sessions with her I changed my major."

"Ask not what you can do for Fate," Canice said.

Gillian grinned. "She was helping people. I wanted to help people. And that's how I got into speech therapy."

"So just how does a speech therapist help people?"

Gillian puffed her cheeks and blew. "Simple or complicated?"

"Simple."

"By helping some people regain language, helping others decipher language's complexities . . . and helping others overcome obstacles to expression—stuttering or lisping, things like that." Gillian cocked her head. "How about you? How did you get into midwifery?"

"How did I get into it?" Canice gazed at the ceiling, her lower lip caught between her teeth. "I've always been a caretaker, sort of watching over people. And it occurred to me, who better to watch over than someone entering life?"

A loud knock and a bang echoed from the entry. Gillian scrambled to her feet. The next applicant—already? She frowned. "Has it really been half an hour?"

Canice stood. "Forty-five minutes. I was early."

Gillian headed for the front door. Canice followed.

"Well, what do you think, Nugget?" a man's voice said.

A sneer colored the young woman's response. "God, Daddy, what a dump. You couldn't pay me."

Gillian and Canice stopped.

"I am getting sick and tired of hearing you say that," the man said, his voice tight with controlled anger. "You are going to *look* at this one."

Gillian questioned Canice with a glance. Canice said, "Tomorrow?"

Gillian smiled. "Perfect."

When she got to the door, Gillian sobered. "I'm sorry," she told the scowling man and his sour-faced daughter. "The room's been rented."

EIGHT

"NOT SPEAKING? THIS CLOSE TO THANKSGIVING?" MOM shook her head sadly. "Promise me you'll call Nora and apologize."

Dad leaned forward, elbows on knees. The kitchen chair squeaked. "Please, honey?" Dad said.

"Nora was the one who threw me out of her house and told me she never wanted to speak to me again," Gillian said. She felt along the bed for her bathrobe. "It's up to her this time."

"Oh, Pumpkin," Mom said. "Nora's stubborn. Like your father. You're going to have to make the first move, you know that."

"I always have to make the first move," Gillian muttered. Her fingers snagged the lush terry robe. "Tell you what—go into the next room and let me get dressed. I'll join you in a minute—"

Gillian woke, the collar of her bathrobe knotted in her fist. She sat up and rubbed the side of her face with her hand. Stress dream. No surprise there. What could be more stressful than two earthquakes, countless aftershocks, a missing housemate, and an angry sister crammed into nineteen days?

She squinted at the clock. Two forty-six. The alarm was set for five-thirty. Gillian lay down and closed her eyes.

"You can't have her," Mom said. "I won't allow it."

Gillian groaned. God, not one of those lingering dreams. She needed sleep—she had to be at the school by eight. She burrowed under the covers. She jerked once and started to doze. . . .

"Once she understands," Dad said, "she'll choose to help us."

Gillian rolled over.

"She's not right for you," Mom said. "If you use her, you might kill her."

"Damn it," Gillian mumbled, flopping onto her back. A decent night's sleep, was that too much to ask for? What were those relaxation techniques Melanie taught her? Clench toes, hold, relax.

"Using her is our last resort," Dad said. "We need her to help us find the face."

Flex feet, hold, relax.

"Leave her alone. You should be searching for Melanie, not frightening Gillian."

Flex ankles—Melanie?

Gillian sat up a little. The woman—her voice was wrong. That wasn't Mom. And the man—she listened, waiting in the darkness.

"We can't feel Melanie anywhere," he said. "She may be acres away, beyond the mountains, hiding in one of those concrete buildings."

And that wasn't Dad. Gillian backed against the headboard. Maybe this wasn't a dream—

"You should have known she'd run," the woman said. "When did she stop performing the rites? Four months ago?"

"Six."

"*Six?* Why didn't you act sooner?"

Gillian peered across the dim, still room. The voices seemed to be coming from over by the door . . .

"We didn't think she'd run," the man said.

. . . or outside the door. Maybe Canice had a friend over—

The woman hissed. "You knew from the moment she

was born her spirit was weak. And her faith. She stopped believing in high school. If she hadn't gotten involved with those pagans and started dabbling in herb lore, she'd have gone a long time ago.''

Gillian frowned. The voice was wrong for Canice—too breathy and lacking that wonderful resonance. A stress dream. It had to be.

"Why didn't you send Melanie a warning?" the woman said. "Some small display of anger and discomfort? Why an earthquake?"

"I didn't send it," the man said. "And what was I supposed to do? Trapped under the foundations of that house . . .''

A ribbon of sweat trickled down Gillian's cheek. She was too awake, too aware to be dreaming. But this conversation was so strange. . . .

"Someone should have gone to her," the woman said softly. "What will you do if you find her?"

"Convince her to come back."

"And if she refuses?"

Gillian pushed the covers aside and pulled on her robe. After what seemed ages, the woman said, "You can't be serious."

Weariness weighted the man's voice. "The madness has already set in. She is fragmented with the pain. Some have withdrawn. Others are lashing out in anger. Others are striking out in fear. Some are crazed with agony. Some, like Petra, seek revenge.''

"And you seek reconciliation."

"I seek an end to the pain. If I can't persuade Melanie, I'll find someone else.''

Gillian dropped to her feet. She padded silently to the door.

"Stay away from her," the woman said. "She's not what you're looking for. She's language—"

"If she is, then she's also prayer—"

"Stay away from her."

Gillian placed her hand on the knob.

"Let me use her once—" the man said.

Gillian jerked the door open. The voices evaporated without a hiss or a sigh. The hall was empty.

GILLIAN SLAPPED AT THE ALARM CLOCK, THEN ROLLED onto her back, exhausted. God, what a night. She'd finally fallen asleep around four. She rubbed her eyes. The second dream had seemed so real, but skewed somehow and seeded with false information. Melanie wasn't a pagan—not while Gillian knew her. And all that talk about language and prayer, and being trapped under foundations. . . .

She sat up a little and frowned. Something the man said nagged at her, something about "acres away, beyond the mountains." It reminded her of something—or someone. She shuddered involuntarily.

An aftershock shattered the quiet, rattling the windows and dumping a basket of jewelry. The bed moonwalked toward the middle of the room. Gillian snatched at her bathrobe, ready to dash for the door. Then the floor settled and the world grew still. Shoulders hunched, Gillian got out of bed and stepped into her slippers. She padded down the hall.

A light beckoned from the kitchen, its bright fingers reaching for her across the living-room carpet. She followed the light to the heart of its glow, shuffling to a stop beside the kitchen table.

Canice turned from the stove, kettle in hand. "Good morning. I'm making tea."

"You read my mind," Gillian said, sinking into a chair.

"No, I heard your alarm." Canice set two mugs on the table next to a white bag. "I got up to use the bathroom last night. You were talking in your sleep. You okay?"

Gillian rested her neck on the back of the chair. "A little stressed. That fight with Nora . . ."

Canice sat down. She nudged one cup closer to Gillian. "This'll help."

Gillian straightened. She hesitated, then reached for the cup. Steam danced above the dark tea. "Thanks. What is it?"

"Something to help you relax," Canice said.

Gillian sniffed the fragrant liquid. It smelled good, minty, but Melanie had used mint to disguise a lot of things, like that infusion of nettles, parsley, and yellow dock—Gillian's gag reflex spasmed. She eyed the mug suspiciously. "What's in it?"

"Peppermint, cinnamon, chamomile, lemon grass, catnip, tilia flowers, hops," Canice said. "I found them in Melanie's herb cabinet."

Gillian braced herself and took a tiny sip. The sweet, warm liquid dribbled onto her tongue. Gillian smiled. "Wonderful. What's in the bag?"

Canice laughed. She picked up her own mug. "You always ask this many questions in the morning?"

"You've only been here a week," Gillian said. "Once I get used to you, I'll just grunt at you in the morning."

Canice sipped her tea. "*That's* something to look forward to."

"Hmmm."

Canice grinned and pushed the bag toward Gillian. "It's for you. I forgot to give it to you last night."

Gillian opened the bag, releasing a soothing burst of chamomile. She reached in and pulled out a bar of homemade soap. She held it to her nose, drinking in the delicate scent. "It smells so fresh. Thanks."

"It's one of my favorites," Canice said. "I wanted to share it with you." She tapped the bag. "There's more."

Gillian raised her eyebrows. Reaching into the bag, she pulled out a tiny, unlabeled vial.

"To replace the rose oil that got spilled during the earthquake," Canice said. "I thought you might want to try something new."

Gillian swallowed. "You're so thoughtful."

Canice watched her intently. "Go on, open it."

Gillian undid the stopper. A warm, untamed scent overwhelmed those of the soap and the tea. Gillian inhaled deeply. Lilac, rose, and hints of unknown flowers blended with cedar and spruce, the floral sweetness tempered by the spicy wood.

"Wow." Gillian applied a little to each wrist and

sniffed. "I like it. I've never smelled anything like it before."

Canice relaxed, visibly relieved. She smiled. "I blended it for you."

NINE

GILLIAN SQUEEZED BETWEEN THE NARROW TABLES BOWED under ceramics and jewelry, amazed at how much the trailer actually held. She caught up to her sister near the trailer's one tiny window. "Nora, please," she said. "Can't we talk this thing out?"

Nora swung to face her, hands on hips. "What is there to talk about? I asked you for a favor—a simple favor. How often do I ask you for help?"

"You don't ask," Gillian said. *You expect.*

"And the one time I do—" Nora turned and strode to the far end of the trailer.

Gillian leaned against the nearest table. Her cheekbones burned with the anger simmering inside her. She thought about the dream last night. How often had Mom given her that same advice—"Make the first move, Gillian"? Gillian had made the first move the time Nora took Gillian's plush raccoon to school and lost him. She'd made the first move the time Nora wore her new angora sweater and put a hole in it. And the time Nora refused to meet KC—for two months—because he did occasional contract work for PG&E. . . .

Gillian's fingernails scored her palms. *Nora's not stubborn like Dad. She's ten times* more *stubborn than Dad.*

Nora shoved past her, box in arms. Gillian ground her

teeth and followed her to the door. "Nora," she said.

Nora set the box by the open door. "I have nothing to say to you."

"Nothing to say to me," Gillian said, shoving her fists in her pockets. "God, Nora, I hope you're over this by Thursday—"

Nora turned on her with a look that could have frozen mercury. "I'm busy Thursday."

Gillian stared at her. "Nora, Thursday is Thanksgiving. We're family—"

"I have no living family," Nora said. She spun on the ball of her foot and marched to the far end of the trailer.

Gillian reached for the door frame to steady herself. Her chest constricted; with great effort, she forced it to loosen and allow her lungs to fill again. She walked down the steps, gripping the cold railing.

"Hi, Gillian!" Debbie said. She grinned and held up two steaming cups. "If I'd known you were coming, I'd have gotten you one, too."

Gillian forced a smile. "Just dropped by after school. The trailer looks great."

Debbie sipped from one of the cups. "How're the kids?"

Gillian thought a minute, sorting through her students' faces. After the aftershock this morning Lucinda had tugged at her braids and whispered, "Her thayth Aunt Eth won't come yethterday 'cause her'th 'fraid of quaketh. We're gonna have turkey anyway. . . ."

"They're doing okay," Gillian said. "It's still rough. It doesn't look like we'll have that many this week. A lot of people left town early for the holiday."

"Nora and I are joining Rich for Thanksgiving," Debbie said. She swirled her cup. "Nora's making candied yams."

Gillian's smile froze.

Debbie sipped from the second cup. "There it is!" she said, relieved. She looked up with a smile. "The city council might put up tents."

"Tents?" Gillian said.

"Big ones, like circus tents." Debbie frowned. "I think that's what Rich said. Mmm, you smell good."

"Thanks. My new house—" Gillian coughed, trying to clear the guilt lodged in her throat. "Canice gave me a new perfume oil."

Debbie nodded. "Sort of like the wind."

Tents, the wind . . . it must make sense on some level. Gillian murmured, "Hmmm," and glanced across the parking lot at the Action Trailer Café. A handful of customers hunched over the tables clustered around the silver trailer. Beyond the Action a Cyclone fence shielded the devastated downtown.

"The city's supposed to decide next week what comes down and what stays up," Debbie said. "I mean, what comes down that hasn't already come down."

"They should let the property owners start rebuilding," Nora said, brushing past Gillian and reaching for a cup. She raised it to her lips and glared at Gillian through the steam. "If you'll excuse us, we have work to do."

"Don't let me stop you," Gillian said. She smiled at Debbie. "Nice talking to you."

Gillian walked away. Stumbling on a ridge of buckled asphalt, she caught herself and slowed her pace. Then she stopped. The Cyclone fence loomed ahead of her, wrapped around Rio Santo's downtown like gauze.

Her shoulders bowed forward. She rolled them to break the tension. Weird gaps marred the lines of buildings, like a comb with missing teeth . . . or a war zone battered by bombs. An eerie, helpless feeling prickled her skin. What had Jenna Pelligrini said on the playground at lunch today? Something about facing the pain before she could heal . . .

Surrounded by her own darting, shouting first graders, Jenna had shaken her head. "I know you were down there right after the earthquake—Brandon, what did we talk about? Leave Leti's hair alone. Gillian, you need to go down there, *see* it. You need to *know* how bad it is so you can let go of all your expectations."

Gillian sighed. "I don't have any expectations—"

"We all do," Jenna said quietly. "Expectations of the

past. Only the past isn't there and will never be there
again—Ian, don't hit him. I know he bumped into you,
but that doesn't mean you can hit him. Gillian, your head
knows, but your heart doesn't, not till you've seen it. You
need to face the pain now so you can accept the future,
because it won't be the one you took for granted. . . ."

Gillian scraped her toe along the broken asphalt and
glanced at the Cyclone fence. Maybe Jenna was right,
maybe she did expect the world to fall back into place like
the pieces of a child's puzzle; everything would fit and the
picture would be the same. Gillian crossed the fractured
parking lot to the barrier. Grasping the wide mesh, she
stared at the shattered maze.

Beyond the fence lay a pedestrian alley flanked by two
chipped, stucco buildings. Yellow tape stretched across the
doors of the building on the right; the door to the left stood
ajar. Although the fallen plaster and broken planks had
been removed, a sludge of dust choked the alley, undis-
turbed by human feet. At the end of the passageway, where
Nora's shop used to be, there was nothing.

Nothing, until the rounded, carousel window of the new
bookstore, two blocks away.

They were just buildings. Not people, but things. Not
even home—

An ache spread in Gillian's chest. "But it could have
been home," she whispered. She sniffed. *Might as well
leave now and avoid the pain of rebuilding. Why wait till
summer? Rio Santo isn't home. . . .*

So why was this hitting her so hard? These were broken
things. She traced a chain with the tip of a finger and began
to walk along the fence.

But it wasn't about the loss of things. It was about the
loss of place. A living place with skin of brick, wood, and
plaster, its blood the flow of human life. She'd been part
of that flow, part of the pulse of the city, wandering up
and down the main street, sunning herself in cafés, standing under gum trees, Japanese maples, and ginkgoes while
street musicians played guitars, harps, saxophones—even
glasses of water. All around her the blood of the city bub-

bled and churned with change: the leaves turned and fell, shrubs flowered, hemlines and hair lengths lowered or crept upward. Music drifted from folk to rock to heartbroken jazz to bluegrass. Shops opened, closed, changed names. But the buildings, the *place,* stayed the same— solid and dependable and constant in a way people couldn't be.

Flames licked the edges of her thoughts. Her breath wedged in her chest. Oh, God, Gillian thought. Oh, God. There were no constants, were there? Nothing to depend on—not cities, not homes. Not even families . . .

Her breath seeped out in a murmur. She walked on.

She passed the back of the Whitman building and stopped. Her fingers locked around the rough wire links. Beside the battered blue hulk of the Whitman a gaping hole stretched the length of an entire block. The Palisade was gone.

Jagged teeth of brick and concrete framed the maw of churned earth. Like pictures she'd seen of Belfast. Gillian's fingers tightened. A fire, an earthquake, a bombing . . . violence. She closed her eyes.

Someone stopped just behind her. "It's like visiting a dying friend," a soft male voice said.

Gillian opened her eyes. "Yes," she said, blinking back tears. "It is."

"It's a shock to find the friend so frail, so . . . vulnerable," the stranger continued. "You wonder if she'll ever recover, and if she does, what she'll be like, she's lost so much. The only thing you know for sure is that she'll never be the same. And neither will you, because you'll miss what she's lost."

"You make grief sound so selfish," Gillian said, starting to turn.

"It is. That's why it's so healing."

Gillian tensed. Despite the clarity of the *S*s, the timbre of the voice reminded her of the agate-eyed man. She turned and found herself staring into those forest-green pupils.

She glared at him. "What are you doing here?"

"Looking for you," he said.

Something in his voice . . . Gillian glanced over her shoulder. People crowded the tables outside the Action Trailer Café; a couple strolled along the fence, leaning into each other. If he tried to grab her again, all she had to do was shout. She combed her hair out of her eyes with her fingers. "What do you want?" she said.

Encouraged, he took a step toward her.

She took a step back.

He sighed. "I need your help."

Gillian eyed him warily. "Why? To find Melanie?"

"It might be too late to find her." He looked away. "We can't feel her."

" 'We'?" Gillian said. "What do you mean, 'We can't feel her'? Feel her how?"

The muscles along his jaw knotted. He glanced at his feet, then, almost shyly, at Gillian. "I'd like to explain everything from the beginning—well, there's not really a beginning. I'd like to explain it all from the what rather than the how."

Gillian took another step back. "I don't want to be alone with you. I don't trust you."

He looked around helplessly. Then he brightened. "We could go to the café."

Gillian headed toward the Action.

He fell in step beside her. Gaze fixed on the café's tables and chairs, she avoided looking at him, unnerved by his eyes. She needed something to hold on to, something to make him less strange. "What's your name?" she asked.

"Dagan," he said.

"Dagan," she repeated. The shape of the name seemed odd in her mouth.

She sat at the table farthest from The Happy Wanderer's temporary home, scooting her chair so that her back was to the trailer. Dagan sat across from her. She studied his face. "All right," she said. "Start with the what."

Dagan pursed his lips. "The what. What I am, what Melanie was—"

"Is," Gillian said, tensing.

He looked into her eyes. "What Melanie is," he said. "What's happened. Which do you want to hear first?"

"Tell me what you are."

"Me." He drummed the edge of the table. "I am . . . I'm the earth's hands. I walk the surface, when I can, and do what she can't. I'm part of her."

Gillian touched her tongue to her teeth. "You belong to some weird religious cult."

"No, I—no." He frowned. "I don't know how to—I'm a spirit. I'm not human."

Gillian sat back, crossing her legs. "Right," she said. "You're not human. Now what is Melanie? Is she human?"

"Yes. The earth needs a human to nurture her." He nodded toward the Cyclone fence. "So things like this won't happen."

"Uh-huh. And Melanie was chosen . . . ?"

"She was born to it. Her family's been performing the rites for generations, since the settled people arrived and covered the earth with buildings and pavement."

Gillian uncrossed her legs. The dream woman had said something about rites. "These rites," Gillian said slowly. "Melanie's family's been . . . worshiping in secret for thousands of years—?"

"No, no." Dagan shook his head. "Only since people stopped touching the earth. Before that, it wasn't necessary."

"Necessary . . . ?"

"To keep her from hurting. And lashing out."

Why didn't you send Melanie a warning? the dream woman had asked. *Some small display of anger and discomfort? Why an earthquake?*

Gillian cupped her hands. "If the earth is angry, why destroy Rio Santo? Why not everything?"

"Not Earth the planet. The earth of *this* land. She resides here, the soul of *this* place, of *these* hills, *these* beaches." Dagan sighed. "I don't know how other places survive. Melanie's family has always performed the rites—"

"Until six months ago." Gillian met his eyes. "And you have no one to take her place."

"There's no table service," a clipped tenor voice said.

Gillian looked up at a young man of no more than nineteen carrying a bus tray. His callow features managed to convey a hint of menace. "If you want something, you'll have to go inside."

Dagan stared at the young man, clearly confused. "We don't want anything—"

"Do you have herbal tea?" Gillian said, standing.

"We've got herbal tea, black tea, decaf." The young man swiped at the table with a grimy cloth. He just missed Dagan's hands. "Chai."

Gillian nodded. "I'll be right back."

Dagan started to his feet. "Where are you going?"

"To pay for the table," Gillian said.

The young man smirked and moved on.

Makeshift counters crowded the trailer's interior. Gillian laid a five beside the register. "Pot of peppermint tea, two cups," she told the woman behind the counter.

" 'S a minute," the woman mumbled.

Gillian turned and leaned against the counter. She had a few minutes to sort things out—or get away from him. She peeked at Dagan through the trailer door. His confusing plea for help anchored her dream like a ribbon tied to a balloon. Anchored it, but made little sense of it. Rites, the earth, help, Melanie . . . Gillian bit her lower lip. His words eddied against her common sense: *I'm a spirit. I'm not human.* And at the garage sale: *Use the contractions I taught you. You'll sound more human.* She'd thought he was just being rude to his companion—

We can't feel her. Gillian's stomach knotted. *We.*

I'm part of her. Part, as in only one piece. . . .

" 'S your tea," the woman behind the counter said.

"Thanks." Gillian picked up the plastic tray. Her change rattled between the mugs and the ceramic teapot.

Dagan rose when she reappeared. "Will you help me?"

"I don't know." She set the tray down, then poured

them each a cup of tea. She shoved one toward him and sat down.

He eyed it suspiciously. "What is this?"

"Peppermint." She wrapped her hands around the mug. "I need to know what you want from me."

He leaned toward her, touching her sleeve. "I need the ceramic face or any other clues that might help us find Melanie."

Gillian squeezed the cup. "And that's all you want."

Dagan hesitated. "Maybe."

"Unless you can't find Melanie."

He hesitated again, then nodded.

You should be searching for Melanie, the dream woman had said. But what if it hadn't been a dream, and he'd been the man . . . ?

There was one way to find out. Gillian took a deep breath. "If I'm not—if you use me and I'm not the right one, I won't be able to stop the earth's pain, will I? She might kill me."

He withdrew his hand and looked away. "And she might not."

Gillian stared at his averted face. *Play along, Gilly. Trip him up. Make him admit he was in your house.* "Because I'm a prayer, right?" she said.

Dagan looked at her, gaze steady. "If you're not the right one, she'll reject you. She'll open a fissure beneath you and swallow you whole. The tremor that follows will grind you between the rocks like a seed between mortar and pestle."

Gillian's heart pounded. "And Rio Santo?"

"Will fall." His eyes narrowed. "Melanie talked to you, didn't she? She told you about us—"

"Melanie didn't tell me anything." Gillian circled the rim of her mug with her finger. "What will happen if no one performs the rites?"

"She's already sent two small warnings. The earthquakes—"

Gillian gaped at him in disbelief. "Small? A seven is hardly small—"

"Small." Dagan lowered his voice. "Imagine one that shakes even your little house from its foundation. Imagine one that flattens every structure from the mountains to the sea and creates damage like this"—he gestured toward the Cyclone fence—"thousands of acres beyond that. And not just buildings and structures. Trees will splinter, roads will buckle, the ground, paved and unpaved, will split open. The existing hills will crumble—"

"New ones will rise," Gillian murmured.

A gentle sorrow ached in Dagan's voice. "Gillian, what do you value above all else? Besides your life?"

"People. Children."

"And how many people died in the last two earthquakes?"

"Twelve."

"Twelve." He shook his head. "That's nothing. If no one comes to her . . . ."

Gillian gazed sightlessly into her tea. Her mind blurred with a collage of faces: Beth Ellen, Lucinda—all of her students—Nora, KC, Hiram, Mrs. Timako, even Debbie. They smiled and cried and pouted and laughed, then suddenly froze. Blood seeped from the corners of their slack mouths, red lines reaching to their jaws. Lifeless and hollow-eyed, they looked like ventriloquists' dummies. . . .

Gillian looked up. "How soon does the rite have to be performed?"

"As soon as possible," Dagan said. "The pain is spreading. The *madness* is spreading. Soon it will infect all of us."

Gillian ran her tongue over her dry lips. "You keep saying 'us.' "

"People have arbitrarily broken the earth into bits and pieces," Dagan said. "A park here, a house and garden there. It divides her. It fragments her spirit."

"You were under a house."

"And will be again," he said gently, "if they rebuild."

"The earthquake freed you." Gillian pushed her mug away. "If two 'pieces' side by side become free . . . ?"

"What was separate becomes one."

"And becomes stronger."

Dagan nodded.

Gillian placed her hands on the table. "If Rio Santo falls and the whole becomes one?"

"We'd become one spirit," Dagan said, "driven by pain. Gillian, will you help us?"

"I—" She scooted away from him. "I don't know."

TEN

"AND THEN, TREVOR?" GILLIAN SAID, PROMPTING THE redheaded first grader. She tapped the storyboard lightly. The tap drew Rafael and Lucinda's wandering gazes from the shelves lining Gillian's office back to the task at hand. All three needed to learn to distinguish between past, present, and future—and to communicate clearly with others. The storyboard, with its visual images, seemed the easiest way. "What happens next?" Gillian said.

Trevor squinched his nose in concentration. "The girl goed to the store to buy cranberries—"

The windows rattled, shimmying slightly, then the whole room swayed with the aftershock. Books slapped into each other on the shelves, chairs chattered against the floor.

Lucinda's eyes widened. Clutching her stuffed rabbit, she slid from her chair and backed under the table. Trevor and Rafael scrambled after her. Gillian remained in her seat, her knuckles white as she gripped the quivering table. Was this it? Was this the killer earthquake Dagan had promised?

The world stopped rocking.

The boys' faces shifted from pale fear to rosy swagger. Trevor bobbled the kindergartner's braids with a brush of his hand. "You okay, Lucinda?" he asked.

Lucinda murmured, inching farther under the table. The first graders shoved their chairs out of the way and climbed out of hiding. Rafael held out his hand to Lucinda. She drew back, curling around her bunny. Rafael shook his head. "Kids!" he said.

Gillian got down on her knees. "That was scary, wasn't it?" she said. She offered Lucinda her hand.

Lucinda took it, using Gillian's arm to reel herself into an embrace. "Her don't like it," Lucinda said, snuggling the bunny between them. "Her'th 'fraid."

Gillian hugged Lucinda, smoothing the frizz of stray hair along the girl's neck. "It's okay, Bunny," Gillian said. "The aftershock is over."

"It'th okay, Bunny," Lucinda said, rubbing the stuffed animal's neck. "It'th over."

Over for now, Gillian thought. And if what Dagan said was true? *Forget him, Gilly. He's crazy. Convincing when you're with him—like Manson or Rasputin.* But after leaving him yesterday and getting away from those eyes, her sanity had returned. Or maybe just her skepticism.

She helped Lucinda out from under the table. The boys took their seats without being asked. Trevor pulled at a hangnail with his teeth, a nervous smirk on his face. Rafael jumped at the sudden click of Trevor's teeth. Lucinda circled the room.

"Lucinda, would you like to join us?" Gillian asked.

Lucinda crawled onto her chair and sat with her feet tucked under her. She crooned to the stuffed rabbit. "It'th okay. It'th okay."

Gillian picked up the fallen storyboard. She hesitated. Maybe she should just get out the blocks. How could she expect these children to repeat a story when their world was rattling apart around them?

Not just buildings and structures, Dagan had said. *Trees will splinter, roads will buckle, the ground, paved and unpaved, will split open. The existing hills will crumble. . . .*

People, children—these children—will die. . . .

Gillian set her hands in her lap so that Lucinda, Trevor, and Rafael wouldn't see them shake. She cleared her throat. "The girl went to the store to buy cranberries. What happened next, Trevor?"

THE STAFF ROOM WAS NEARLY EMPTY AT LUNCH. NO ONE wanted to eat indoors, where boxes, copy machines, microwaves, and dishes might fall on them. Gillian went to the table and sat between Jenna Pelligrini and Lupe Valdez, the bilingual third-grade teacher. Setting her lunch on the table, Gillian unwrapped her sandwich.

"Did you go downtown?" Jenna asked Gillian.

Gillian lowered her sandwich, untasted. She nodded. Jenna closed her eyes.

Lupe stirred her instant soup. "Hear about Paul Kestrel? School board asked him to take a leave of absence. Having those shutters closed all the time freaked out the kids. One of the parents threatened to sue."

Jenna opened her eyes. "Are you sure? I heard he left early for Thanksgiving. Going to Albuquerque, or something."

Lydia, the school secretary, sat down next to Jenna. "Nope," she said. "Leave of absence."

"I think we should all leave," Lupe said. "Everyone, just pick up and get out of this town before something worse happens."

ONE FORTY-FIVE—GILLIAN'S LAST SESSION OF THE DAY. She ushered Tess and David into the room, then stepped out into the hall. No Amanda—yet. No use looking for Rosa and Jason. They'd been absent since the second earthquake. Gillian walked back into the room. The two second graders huddled together beside her desk.

Gillian smiled at Tess. "What a pretty sweater—"

The windows rattled, the shutters clacking together. Gillian looked around wildly. The shelves, the chairs, the floor, everything else was still—

Tess and David dived under the table before Gillian could stop them. David's wheezing harmonized with Tess's mumbled prayers.

"It's all right," Gillian said, crouching beside a chair. "It was just someone at the window."

Amanda crept into the room. Tears beaded her eyes. "I'm sowwy. It was just me. I didn't mean it. I didn't."

Gillian sat on the floor. Tess crawled from under the table and snuggled against her. Amanda hugged herself in the middle of the room, rushing to Gillian's other side as soon as Gillian gestured for her to come. David clawed at his pockets, his breath growing more labored. "Can I go . . . to the nurse?" he said, squeezing the words out between breaths. "I need . . . my inhaler."

Gillian nodded.

Amanda whimpered.

Blocks, Gillian thought. *We're going to play with blocks. At least until things calm down.*

But according to Dagan, there was only one way to calm things down.

GILLIAN SWITCHED OFF THE IGNITION AND SAT FOR A MINute, staring at her garage door. A crack crept down the trim like a tiny lightning bolt. She popped open the car door and got out.

If only KC was home . . . she walked over to the rosemary hedge. Hard to tell if he was or not. Probably not. It was only three-thirty. With all the damaged houses and devastated buildings, KC had been in demand.

Gillian stroked the rosemary's oily leaves and blue flowers, releasing the sharp, pungent scent. She'd gone straight to his house yesterday, as soon as she got back from the meeting with Dagan. She'd walked in, badly shaken—no, terrified. Trembling like an uncontrolled vibrato. And she'd tried to tell him about Dagan, but didn't know how. What was she supposed to say? "I met this guy downtown who says he's a spirit. He says the earthquakes are all Melanie's fault and if I don't worship the earth we're all going to die. Oh, and I think he's the guy who broke into my house and listened to my answering machine"?

Instead she'd told KC about Nora and Thanksgiving, assuring herself that she was working up to Dagan. But as she talked, the immediate terror stripped away. Dagan seemed like another one of those lost souls wandering around downtown, talking to imaginary friends, cursing the universe, finding conspiracies and extraterrestrials under every rock. A raver, as Nora would say. A convincing one.

A shiver bowed Gillian's shoulder blades. And she'd agreed to meet him Wednesday. Tomorrow. She shook her head and walked toward her house. Forget Dagan—*she* was the crazy one.

Gillian took the steps two at a time, then tried the knob. The door swung open. Good. Canice was home. She needed to tell Canice that KC had invited them to join him for Thanksgiving. . . .

Gillian shrugged out of her coat and hung it in the closet. She was not looking forward to Thanksgiving. She'd never had one without Nora. She stood for a minute, holding open the closet door. That first Thanksgiving, without Mom and Dad, had been so awful. It had rained the whole weekend—at least, that's how she remembered it. As if everything had been glimpsed through rain-blurred windows.

She'd mentioned it to Nora once. Nora had shaken her head. "It didn't rain, Gilly," she'd said. "We spent the whole day crying. Crying and—remember the gravy? It was so salty. I just kept crying into it, into everything. Even the cranberry sauce was salty."

Tears and salt. Gillian shut the closet door.

"Canice?" she called, stepping into the living room. "Are you home?"

Voices murmured in the kitchen. "It's all right," Canice assured someone. "In here!"

Gillian halted in the kitchen doorway. Canice rose from the table and smiled. "Come on in," she said. "I was just consulting with one of my clients. Dera, this is my housemate, Gillian."

Gillian nodded to the frail woman seated at the table. The woman clutched a huge plastic tumbler in her bony hands. "Hi," Gillian said. "Nice to meet you. I didn't mean to disturb—"

"No, no, please," Dera said. She tossed her long, red hair, so that it raged, split and brittle, in a tangle down her back. A smile creased her sunken cheeks. "We're done. Don't let me chase you from your own kitchen. I need to get going—"

"Don't let *me* chase *you* out of my kitchen," Gillian said. "I'm going to change into some sweats—"

"No, no." Dera glanced sideways at Canice, releasing the tumbler. "It's time I got back. Thank you, Canice."

As Dera rose Canice laid a hand on her shoulder and gently eased her back into the chair. "You haven't finished your water," she said.

The woman's eyes glittered feverishly. "I'd hate to waste water during a drought." She grasped the tumbler in both hands, then drained it in one long, slow gulp.

Canice removed her hand from Dera's shoulder. "Go in peace," she said.

Dera stood. Even stooped, she towered over Canice. "You'll talk to them?"

Canice nodded.

"A little fog, anything." Dera shuddered with a sigh. "Well. I thank you again."

Canice took Dera's elbow and guided her toward the living room. "I'll see you to the door."

Gillian backed out of their way. Dera's arm brushed hers, Dera's rough skin scraping Gillian's. The scent of parched, dusty loam clung to the woman like old sweat. Gillian dry-swallowed, suddenly thirsty.

She waited till Canice and Dera left, then yanked open the refrigerator. She reached for the water jug. In the back of the refrigerator stood the baking soda, the margarine tub just visible behind it. The margarine tub with the medallion, the one that might lead Dagan to Melanie . . .

Gillian squeezed her temples, trying to relieve the guilt throbbing through her head. If she gave it to him, he might find Melanie. Melanie already knew the rites. According to Dagan, she'd been performing them for years. But if

Melanie refused, the vengeful spirits, like Petra, would kill her.

With Melanie's life at stake, how could Gillian give Dagan the ceramic face?

Because the next earthquake will kill everyone.

The sacrifice of the one for the many.

Gillian carried the water jug to the table and sat down. The refrigerator door clapped shut.

Canice returned and dropped into the nearest chair. "You going to drink that straight from the bottle or are you going to get a glass?"

Gillian blinked. "What? Oh. A glass." She went to the sink and got a tumbler from the strainer. She picked up a second one. "You want one?"

Canice rumpled the front of her hair. "Sure. You okay? You seem a little spacey."

"Yeah, I bet." Gillian poured two glasses of water. "I've had a lot on my mind."

Canice took one of the glasses. "Want to talk about it?"

Gillian rubbed the side of her nose. She did—and she didn't. Maybe if she started with Nora. . . . "KC invited us for Thanksgiving," she began.

"Yeah, that's what you said last night." Head cocked to one side, Canice studied Gillian carefully. "That's not what's on your mind."

"I met—" Gillian swirled her water, then looked up. "If I'm out of line, say so. But—that woman's not planning to have a baby, is she?"

A surprised laugh escaped Canice. "*Dera?* No way. I'm trying to help her get well. It may be more than I can do. She's been . . . sick for a long time."

Gillian sipped her water. "Is she anorexic?"

"No. Something simpler and more complicated." Canice raised her eyebrows. "This isn't what's on your mind. What's going on?"

Gillian rolled the tumbler between her hands. "I . . . met this man."

Canice whistled. "KC will be disappointed."

"Not that kind of man."

"Oh?"

Gillian braced herself. "He says he's a spirit. He ... wants me to help him stop the next earthquake."

"He what?"

"He thinks I have something he needs, something that used to belong to Melanie. He's hoping it will help him find her, but if it doesn't, he's hoping I'll help him perform these rites."

Canice hissed between her teeth. "And you believed him?"

Gillian shrugged helplessly. "At the time. He was so convincing. Afterward ... I don't know. I mean, nothing he said made any sense, but Canice, you should see him. He's got these eyes—they're just not human."

A fleeting smile touched Canice's face and was gone. Her frown deepened. "You didn't agree to help him?"

Gillian scooted away. "No. But I told him I'd meet him tomorrow."

Canice stared at her. "Meet him? Gillian, the guy's certifiable. Stay away from him."

"And if he shows up here?" Gillian said.

"This creep knows where you live?"

"He was at the garage sale. When I sold Melanie's things."

"If he shows up, we call the cops." Canice sniffed. "You're not wearing the oil I gave you."

Gillian frowned, confused. She set the tumbler on the table. "I was running late this morning."

"You've got to wear it," Canice said. "I can't protect you if you—"

Distant thunder swallowed her words. The cardboard tucked into the lower pane of the window breathed in and out rapidly, the glasses stuttered on the table. Gillian shoved Canice toward the living room door as the aftershock struck. A swell caught Gillian, pitching her into an unsteady Canice. As they fell to the floor in a tangled heap, one of the cupboards flew open, spewing its contents amid a crash of glass, plastic, and cardboard. Gillian inhaled a lungful of confused scents: mint, eucalyptus, chamomile, black tea, coffee, honey. Crawling out from under Canice, Gillian crept to the door frame. She curled into a ball, covering her head with her arms, and waited for the earth's convulsions to end.

The top panes of the kitchen window exploded in a shower of glass.

ELEVEN

THE WORLD QUIETED.

Gillian hoisted herself to her feet, hands inching along the door frame. A huge crack bisected the wall between the kitchen and the garage, its lines blurred by tufts of plaster. Tinier cracks trickled like freshets or springs from the corners and the ceiling.

Canice rose to her hands and knees. "You impatient fool," she murmured. "You impatient, stupid fool."

"Who are you—?" Gillian choked, her lungs clouded with the thick, oily stench of gas. She swooped and grabbed Canice by the upper arm, dragging her to her feet. "There's a gas leak. Let's get out of here."

They stumbled through the living room, dodging avalanches of books and boxes. One of the bookshelves had fallen again. Gillian tugged Canice to the entry. Canice's denim jacket sprawled across the carpet, its arms reaching toward the front door.

The door stood open, the warped frame no longer able to contain it. Gillian hurried outside and down the steps, Canice close behind. People spilled from the other houses, collecting like a puddle in the street. Hiram fought against the current, metal rod in hand.

"Hiram, hurry!" Gillian shouted. "We've got a leak!"

Hiram nodded. He walked to the gas main between her

house and KC's. Gillian and Canice joined the crowd drifting toward Linnet Park.

"Nick, round up the children and take them to the barbecue, will you, dear?" Mrs. Timako said.

Nick Trestle clasped the collar of his youngest boy.
"You got it."

"At least a six," someone said.

Someone else snorted. "Six-point-*five*."

Jake Rubio waved his arms. "Hey! Who owns the Buick
Skylark? We gotta get that thing off the fire hydrant."

"Has anyone seen the Singhs?" Lily Gerber said.
"Maybe someone should check on them."

"They left Monday," Mrs. Timako said. "Has anyone
seen my Frankie?"

"The Wernickes and the Fischers took off yesterday,"
Jake said. "Hey, Nick! How 'bout giving me a hand with
the Buick?"

"Hiram, which mains still need to be turned off?" Lily
asked.

"Start with Rubio's and work your way toward Orange
Street," Hiram said.

Gillian turned to Canice. "Looks like we'll be sleeping
in the park again—" Her stomach curdled into a ball. Canice wasn't there. "Canice?"

A small hand slipped into Gillian's. Beth Ellen's eyes
burned with a fear too bright to echo her smile. "It wuh-
works," she said, holding out her hand. The tiger's eye
rested like a stigmata on her right palm. "Most of the
time."

Gillian slipped an arm around the girl's shoulders. Beth
Ellen nuzzled her way into a hug. Gillian stroked the long,
blond hair, rocking the child gently. "It's okay," Gillian
murmured. "It's okay to be scared."

Beth Ellen trembled and locked her arms around Gillian's waist. "Are they ever going to stuh-stuh-stop?" she
said.

Dagan's intense agate eyes glittered in Gillian's mind.
"They'll stop," she said, leaning over to kiss the crown
of Beth Ellen's head. "I promise. Where's your mom?"

"At wuh-work. She wuh-works till five."

Not today, she's not, Gillian thought. She slid gently from Beth Ellen's Velcro grip, taking the girl's hand. "Well, you just stay with me, okay? Let's see if we can help Mrs. Timako."

Canice walked up, carrying blankets and a jug of water. "Looks like we'll be sleeping out here tonight."

Beth Ellen's hand throttled Gillian's. Gillian forced herself not to wince. She looked down into the girl's pale face. "Hey, what's wrong?" she said, smoothing a lock of hair from Beth Ellen's eyes. "We've done this before."

Beth Ellen inched closer. "Can I sleep with you?"

"You sure can," Gillian said, pulling the child into another embrace. Her heart ached. If she could somehow quench the fear in Beth Ellen's eyes . . . and Lucinda's, and Trevor's, and—

If what Dagan had said was true, she could. Gillian hugged Beth Ellen tighter.

Jake Rubio rushed past them. "Whoa, whoa, whoa, Mrs. Timako! Let me get that. Damn, where'd you get all this stuff?"

"Costco," Mrs. Timako said, relinquishing a flat of canned goods. "There's more in the garage. Hiram and I bought as many cases as his van would hold. I wish we'd had room for more."

Jake grunted and lugged the flat to the barbecue area. Mrs. Timako patted her sweat-beaded forehead. She turned to Canice. "My, I hadn't realized how heavy—oh, wonderful! You've brought water!!" She then leaned over to Beth Ellen. "Have you seen my Frankie?"

Beth Ellen shook her head.

Jake hunched his shoulders as he walked past. "We're sure gonna miss Melanie tonight."

"Who's Frankie?" Canice whispered.

Gillian leaned over Beth Ellen. "Mrs. Timako's Chihuahua. Beth Ellen, why don't we go to your house and get some blankets, okay?"

"Beth Ellen?" a frantic voice called. "Has anyone seen Beth Ellen?"

"Mom!" Beth Ellen launched herself from Gillian's side. She threw herself into her mother's arms. Her taut body shook with sobs, her clenched right fist startlingly white against her mother's blue-black coat.

Gillian flexed her own hands. She imagined Lucinda, clutching her stuffed rabbit, chewing its ear, her eyes deep and dark and bottomless with fear. Trevor and Rafael, Tess and David crept deeper under the table—

Gillian marched toward the house. "I can't take this anymore. This has got to stop."

Canice started after her. "Gillian—"

Jake caught Canice's elbow. "Uh, I don't know you or anything, but you think you could help me? You wouldn't believe how much shit Mrs. Timako's got in her garage."

Gillian darted across the street, shedding Canice like a scratchy sweater. She ran up the front steps, gulping a lungful of air before plunging through the front door. She hurried through the living room to the kitchen.

A whiff of gas remained. She coughed and cleared her throat. Coffee beans cobbled the floor, mired in loose tea and honey. Glass, tea bags, and small boxes stuck out here and there like clumps of crabgrass. Gillian picked her way carefully toward the refrigerator, wondering if she should get her rubber boots. She shook her head. There wasn't time for that. If she was going to find Dagan today, she had to get going now. She yanked open the refrigerator.

The interior remained hidden in shadow. The electricity was out again. Of course. Gillian reached inside, feeling along the top shelf. There—baking soda . . . margarine tub. She grabbed the plastic container and pulled it out. Peeling back the lid, she peeked inside. The foil-wrapped medallion nested in the bottom of the tub.

Gillian touched the foil. Now all she had to do was get the medallion to Dagan so he could find Melanie—a breath hardened in her chest. But Melanie didn't want to be found. Why? Fear of Dagan and the other earth spirits? What could they do to her that would be worse than the destruction of Rio Santo?

Gillian bit her lip. Was it right to help Dagan drag Melanie back to Rio Santo against her will?

Beth Ellen's face filled Gillian's mind, eyes huge and round above fear-hollowed cheeks. Gillian's arms still tingled with the touch of the child's shivering body. Whispers flowed through Gillian's mind—Lucinda, Trevor, Rafael, Tess, Amanda, David—a gathering stream of voices seeking reassurance and safety. . . .

Was it right to stand by and do nothing while people died, knowing she might be able to stop it?

Gillian snapped the container's lid in place. The rites had to be performed. Now.

Her lungs burned. Still too much gas to be safe. She tore the cardboard from the bottom of the window, then hurried out of the kitchen.

Staggering outside, she inhaled deeply. The air tasted sweet. Now she had to find Dagan.

Gillian sucked in another breath. What had he said, about being trapped? The building above him had fallen, the foundation cracking open to release him. The Palisade's gaping maw flashed across her thoughts. No, nothing downtown. The buildings there hadn't fallen till days after the original earthquake; he had come looking for Melanie the morning after the tremor.

A jolt swelled and ebbed. Gillian darted down the steps, taking them three at a time. The house could still blow—

A house had exploded the night of the first earthquake. That was Dagan's land, it had to be. But *where* was it, who would know?

Hiram walked up, his bow tie askew. "The gas is off. That should take care of it."

Gillian nodded absently, then touched his arm. "Hiram, you remember the house that blew up, the night of the first earthquake?"

Hiram shook his head. "Wasn't that a show? Over on Frigate Street. Poor people lost everything. Nearly lost the house next door."

"Frigate Street," Gillian repeated, backing toward the garage. "Thanks, Hiram."

Gillian yanked open the garage door, then swung to face the park. She searched the milling crowd, finally spotting Beth Ellen. The child's white fist still shone like a star against the folds of her mother's midnight coat. Gillian grabbed her bicycle and wheeled it onto the drive.

GILLIAN LEANED OVER THE HANDLEBARS, STARING AT THE vacant lot. Someone—the owners?—had already cleaned up, reducing the concrete foundation to rubble and raking the skeletal, charred plants into little heaps to the rear of the property. Blackened soil mixed with freshly turned earth corrugated the two-acre plot.

"How did you find me?" a soft voice said.

Gillian looked up. Dagan stood beside her. Weariness hardened the lines of his face. "How—" he began again.

Gillian handed him the margarine tub.

He glanced at it, then met her eyes. He pried open the plastic container. The foil-wrapped medallion caught the last rays of afternoon sun, reflecting wrinkles and furrows onto Dagan's face. He handed it back to her.

Gillian took the margarine tub reluctantly. "You—you found Melanie?"

"One of the other earth spirits found her. Petra." His voice flattened like a failed EKG. "Melanie's dead, Gillian."

Gillian's breath escaped in a rush. No tears, no racking sobs—just an enormous weight squeezing down on her chest, compacting every hope and fear into one diamond-hard, jagged ache. "When?" she said. "How?"

"This morning. Crushed."

Gillian stared into the medallion's marbled eyes. "What do I need to do?" she said.

TWELVE

NIGHT HUGGED THE EARTH. ONLY THE STARS AND A CLUS-
ter of hurricane lamps near the barbecue area slit the darkness. Gillian pushed her bicycle past KC's house, her
bruised hip forcing her to swing her leg in a stiff circle.
Gillian stopped to listen: voices drifted from Linnet Park,
some high and forced, others low and hushed. No crickets
sang to the night—when had they stopped, how many days
ago? Had autumn lulled them to their usual silence or had
the aftershocks killed them? *Like they're killing us,* Gillian
thought. Leaning into the handlebars, she guided the bicycle down her driveway and into the open garage.

Footsteps plodded toward her. Gillian turned, forcing
her shoulders to relax.

"Where have you been?" KC said. "Canice and I have
been worried sick about you."

A twinge of jealousy tempered Gillian's annoyance. She
squelched it. He was free to see anyone he liked. "Filling
in for my parents?" she said.

"No, for Nora. What happened? Why are you limp-
ing?"

Gillian relaxed a little. She leaned against KC, hungry
for the warmth of him. His hand settled on her shoulder.
"I got thrown from my bike by one of the aftershocks,"
she said. "I hit a car."

KC gaped at her. "You *what*?"

"You should have seen the driver's face—"

"Where have you been?" Canice said, grasping Gillian's shoulder.

Gillian pulled away from both Canice and KC. So much for comfort. "I was worried about Nora—"

"Why didn't you tell me?" Canice said. "I'd have gone with you—"

"Gee, Mom, I didn't think about it." Gillian brushed past Canice. She strode toward the park, trembling with the fierceness of her anger. Why were they treating her like this, like she was a child? Especially Canice. She hardly knew her—so where did Canice get off playing mother hen?

Gillian snorted. *And why am I so pissed about the whole thing?*

KC stumped after her. "Gillian—"

"Gillian, come on." Canice fell in step beside her. "We have no idea what's going on out there. Mrs. Timako can't get anything on the radio. If what's happened here reflects what's out there—" Canice shuddered. "Hiram's chimney smashed his car."

"The Fischers' house jumped six inches off its foundation," KC said.

Gillian stopped and squeezed her temples. Six inches—six inches was nothing. That house on Diego, the gray Colonial, had skidded until it met a barrier of pines more than a foot away. The porch had accordioned against the trunks, stripping the bark to release the sap's sharp, snowy odor. . . .

Gillian closed her eyes. Tomorrow at noon she would meet Dagan and they would put an end to all this. Tomorrow, after they performed the rites, the earth would rest and Rio Santo could rebuild and heal.

Would she survive to see it?

"Gillian," Canice said.

Gillian blinked. "Six inches is nothing."

Canice and KC exchanged looks. Gillian ground her teeth and stalked off. Goddamn, patronizing—

"Are you okay?" Canice said.

"I'm fine!" Gillian shouted. "I'm not a child, okay? I'm fine!"

Her leg twisted and she staggered. KC caught her arm.

Gillian shook him off. "Why don't you two go mother each other? If I need a mom, I'll go find Nora."

"Gillian—" KC began.

Canice caught his eye and shook her head. The two of them faded back.

Gillian followed the glow of the hurricane lamps to the picnic tables. A whiff of kerosene tinged the air. Plastic ice chests and metal coolers crouched under benches. Two empty cardboard flats leaned against the barbecue pits. Mrs. Timako sat alone at one table, fiddling with the knobs on her radio. Static crunched and hissed. Gillian sat down across from her.

Mrs. Timako looked up. "There you are. I saved you a can of refried beans."

Gillian smiled. "Thanks."

Mrs. Timako pushed herself to her feet and went to the nearest barbecue. With a pair of tongs, she fished an open can from the white coals. Placing the can, a towel, and a plastic fork in front of Gillian, she said, "Be careful, dear. The can is hot."

"Thanks," Gillian said, wrapping the cloth around the can. She spied KC and Canice a table away, just out of earshot. "What's been happening here?"

"Well, there's not a windowpane for blocks." Mrs. Timako braced her hands on the lip of the table and sat down. "Hiram's afraid of looters. He's got that shed out back, you know—windowless, sturdy. He and Jake have been collecting everyone's valuables. CD players, VCRs, things like that. Canice and KC moved your things in there. She's very nice. And she and KC seem to get along well."

"They do, don't they?" Gillian whipped the beans with the fork. Nora and KC got along okay but not well. Okay was better. She missed KC more when he got involved with someone she knew. That time he'd gone out with

Marci Gomez . . . okay was definitely better. He and Melanie had gotten along okay—Gillian curled around the grief taking root inside her.

Mrs. Timako covered Gillian's hand with her own. "If you keep stirring those, dear, I'll have to get you a spoon."

Jake Rubio flopped down beside Gillian. Sour sweat radiated from him. Reaching over his shoulder, he tried to massage his neck. "Damn, I wish Melanie was here."

Gillian dropped the fork. The handle melted, folding over the side of the can. She tucked her arms to her sides to keep from shaking.

Jake rubbed his bearded chin. "Said she'd marry me if I disconnected my truck alarm. I'm gonna hold her to it."

Mrs. Timako drew closer to Gillian. "You heard something, didn't you, honey?" she said softly.

Gillian nodded, cleared her throat, nodded again. Sorrow spread through her like a creeper growing out of control. She stiffened around it, trying to contain it. "Melanie—" she began. Her voice escaped in a tear-strangled squeak. She willed her throat to relax. "Melanie's dead."

Saying the words made it true. She buried her face in her hands, the hot tears burning between her fingers. Someone knelt behind her, curling around her. The scent of lavender surrounded her. She leaned into KC's arms.

"WE'RE NEAR THE PICNIC TABLES," KC SAID, GUIDING Gillian across the park. His arm circled her shoulders.

His touch held her together. Gillian's body felt as fragile as a dried tomatilla husk—little more than a lace of brittle veins cupping nothing. Aching with spent tears, her eyes refused to focus. Gillian gazed at the blanket-quilted lawn.

Someone crunched toward them between the sleepers. "Are you all right?" Canice asked.

Gillian looked up, then averted her stinging eyes. "I think so. We've been sitting in KC's car. I had to get away from the destruction for a while."

Canice murmured. The three of them wound their way through the maze of bodies. "Here we are," Canice said, stopping beside three mounds of blankets sandwiched between other sleepers.

"Frankie!" Mrs. Timako called.

Gillian looked sideways across the park. Mrs. Timako stood on the far curb, peering down the street.

Gillian's heart ached. "Poor Mrs. Timako."

"He found his way home after the last big aftershock," KC said.

"Yeah, but he was only gone an hour." Gillian slipped from under KC's arm and stepped toward the lone woman pacing the sidewalk.

"Gillian?" a small voice said.

Gillian turned. Beth Ellen looked up at her from under the lip of a down sleeping bag scooted close to Gillian's worn blue comforter. Gillian squatted beside the girl. "Hey," she said. "That looks like a warm bag."

"I waited for you," Beth Ellen said, rising on her elbows. "I wuh-wanted to say good night."

"Frankie!" Mrs. Timako called.

Gillian smiled at Beth Ellen. "I'm glad you did. I need a good-night."

Beth Ellen pressed her lips together. "You—you said I could suh-sleep next to you. You promised."

Gillian reached for Beth Ellen. Beth Ellen clung to her. "I was hoping *you* wouldn't forget," Gillian said, rubbing her cheek against the blond head. "Think you can get some sleep?"

Beth Ellen drew back and nodded. "Uh-huh. 'Cause you're here. You're luh-like the tiger's eye."

Gillian raised her eyebrows. "Am I?"

Beth Ellen grinned, a twinkle in her eye. "You're blue and shiny."

Gillian laughed.

"Beth Ellen," Ms. Jansen mumbled from the depths of a second down bag. "Leave Ms. Wheatley alone. Get some sleep."

"Sorry, Mom." Beth Ellen snuggled into her bag. " 'Night, Gillian."

" 'Night, Beth Ellen."

Across the park, Mrs. Timako and Lily Gerber harmonized. "Frankie!"

Hiram called out, "Frankie! Come on, boy!"

Gillian slid under the covers. She glanced at Canice and KC. Canice had already curled up under a mountain of blankets; KC sat between them, watching Gillian. "You okay?" he said.

"I'm fine," Gillian said.

AN AFTERSHOCK PRODDED GILLIAN AWAKE, THEN groaned to a standstill. Gillian stared up at the stars, listening to the pounding of her heart fade. She yawned and rolled over. The crying had exhausted her, freeing her from her spring-wound tension. The keys to that tension were still there—Melanie's death, the fight with Nora, the devastation, Dagan and his rites—but she wasn't about to let them wind her to the breaking point again.

She dozed. Mom cocked her head to one side and said, "Listen to all those vampires, Gilly! Must be at least a hundred people camped out there."

"About half that, Mom," Gillian mumbled. "Maybe more."

"Gillian?" Mom said tentatively, shaking Gillian by the shoulder. "Gillian, I have to go to the bathroom."

Gillian shook herself and sat up. "You what?"

"I got to go real bad."

Gillian blinked. Beth Ellen sat beside her, thighs squeezed together. "I been tuh-tuh-tuh—I've been huh-holding it, but I don't think I can hold it anymore," Beth Ellen said.

Gillian folded back her blankets. Cold sluiced over her, waking her bladder. "I need to pee, too," she whispered, offering her hand to Beth Ellen. "Let's go."

They picked their way between makeshift beds and sleeping bags, stepping over two sprawled sleepers who blocked their path. The fertile stench of human waste greeted them within five feet of the maples.

Beth Ellen stepped back. "I don't have to go anymore."

"It's worse to hold it in," Gillian said. She tugged Beth

Ellen's hand. "Take a deep breath and hold that instead."

They gulped air, then walked between the maples to the trenches Jake and his housemates had dug earlier. They unzipped quickly, then shimmied their pants to their ankles. Gillian braced against the cold. She forced herself to pee.

Beth Ellen peed and fled.

"Their roots were shallow," a dry, cracked voice said. "All of our roots are shallow. When the big aftershock hit . . . ."

Gillian pulled up her pants. Dera? Here?

"You can't go to her," someone replied. Canice? "The salt air will kill you. Let me go—"

"When, Canice? We lost nine yesterday. How many more must die?"

"Today, Dera. I promise."

Someone rustled behind Gillian. Beth Ellen snatched at Gillian's sleeve. Gillian followed her away from the maples.

Beth Ellen exhaled noisily. "Phew! How can you stand the smell?"

"There are worse things," Gillian said. Death, for one. Who was Dera talking about? Nine people. . . . "Come on. Let's go wash our hands at the picnic tables."

"SLEEP TIGHT," GILLIAN SAID. SHE TUCKED THE DOWN bag under Beth Ellen's chin. "I'll see you in the morning."

"There won't be any school tomorrow," Beth Ellen said.

"No, there won't."

Beth Ellen wriggled closer. "That's the scary part. Having nothing to do except wuh-wait for another earthquake."

Gillian nodded. "I have some games and things. Maybe some of the other kids would like to play."

Beth Ellen's voice brightened. "Do you have Monopoly? That's my favorite."

"I sure do." Gillian smiled. "Try to get some sleep, okay?"

Beth Ellen nodded and closed her eyes. She rolled over to face her mother.

Gillian sat up a little and peeked over KC. Canice sighed in her sleep, stretching into a new position. Gillian frowned. That voice by the maples . . . it had sounded like Canice, but . . . how had Canice managed to get back before them *and* fall asleep? Gillian lay down and burrowed under her covers.

She closed her eyes, waiting for her mind to settle. Instead it raged like a whirlwind, tumbling her thoughts. Nine people dead—and those were just the ones Dera knew. *If* that had been Dera speaking and not some waking dream. Nine people. How had they died and where?

What if Nora—? Gillian squirmed farther under the covers. Nora was fine, she had to be. Better not to think about her till morning. In the morning Gillian would get up, get out the games, and set up an area for the kids. She'd set up Monopoly first, since that was Beth Ellen's favorite. It was Nora's favorite, too. Nora bought every square her money allowed, weighting them with motels and houses. "Pay up or die," she'd say whenever someone landed on one of her squares. Gillian smiled. *Pay up or die.* As far as Nora was concerned, Monopoly was *the* game about taking over the world, not Risk. Maybe tomorrow evening, after the rites, Gillian could invite Nora over to play Monopoly—

Nora's voice tore through her like cracks across ice: *I have no living family.* "You do," Gillian whispered, "but for how long?"

Dagan promised her she'd be safe. He'd guide her, step-by-step, through the rites. Protect her. But the other spirits would be there, including Petra. Gillian shifted. Petra found Melanie. Gillian had been afraid to ask—had Petra found her dead or alive?

GILLIAN GROANED AND PUSHED THE BLANKET AWAY FROM her face. Sunlight pierced her eyes. She winced, tug-

ging the covers back over her head. She'd thought she'd
never get back to sleep last night, but obviously she had.

She hummed low in her throat, then listened to the bus-
tling park. Metal scraped metal over by the barbecue area.
A tea kettle whistled, people chattered and grunted. She
peeked at the sun. Still fairly early. Probably around seven-
thirty or eight.

Shoes snicked through the dust near Gillian's head. "Be
sure they remove even the tiniest bit of glass," Mrs. Timako said. "I hope we bought enough of that plastic sheet-
ing."

"If we didn't, we'll just have to cover some of the windows with cardboard," Hiram said.

Gillian waited till Mrs. Timako and Hiram walked away,
then struggled into a sitting position. She rubbed her eyes.

"Morning, sleepyhead," KC said, squatting beside her.
He handed her a cup of hot chocolate. "How about a jump
start?"

"Thanks." She took a sip. Heaven. "Sounds like the
troops are mobilized."

KC laughed. "Hiram's organized a food-and-water
drive. Lorna and Canice are setting up an infirmary, Jake
and I will be checking out chimneys—"

"Lorna?"

KC pointed to a two-story gray house bordering the
park. "Lorna Chang. Five units from her RN. How about
some breakfast? They've got a mean barbecued Spam over
there."

Gillian wrinkled her nose. "I'd rather have fruit cocktail."

"I don't know if there is any—"

"Gillian!" Beth Ellen raced to Gillian's side. Her friend
Bibbie stopped a foot away, tugging the end of her black
ponytail. Beth Ellen grabbed Bibbie's elbow and pulled
her forward.

KC stepped aside. He winked at Gillian, then wandered
over to the barbecue.

"Gillian," Beth Ellen said, "me and Bibbie wondered
if you had any Barbies. We want to play Barbies."

Gillian rose slowly to her feet. Her joints ached. "I thought you wanted to play Monopoly?"

Beth Ellen's eyes lit up. "Yeah!"

Bibbie looked less than enthusiastic.

Gillian suppressed a smile. "I'll go get some games. Tell KC I'll be right back, okay?"

Beth Ellen glanced at KC, then motioned for Gillian to lean over. "Are you guys in love?" she whispered.

Gillian gaped at Beth Ellen. "What?"

"You and KC," Beth Ellen said. "Is he your boyfriend?"

Gillian shook her head. "No. We're just friends."

Beth Ellen and Bibbie looked at each other and giggled. "That's what Mom said and then Tim started spending the night," Beth Ellen said.

Gillian ran her tongue along the inside of her cheek. A whole different world from the one she grew up in. "I'll be back in a few minutes."

A rustling sound greeted Gillian when she stepped into the entry. Rats or cascading plaster? A puff of white dust huffed from the living room. Plaster. She crept into the hallway. Cracks threaded the walls; it was like walking into a spiderweb. A flap of Sheetrock yawned above her bedroom door. Gillian darted under it and into her room.

The drawerless dresser had belly-flopped across her bed, splintering the headboard. Boxes and drawers skimmed across the floor. Gillian slid open the closet. Shoved to the back, the case of fruit cocktail peeked from under her dresses and slacks. She stockpiled four cans, then dragged the case out into the bedroom. If things got bad, she'd give up her private stash, but until then. . . .

A small vial rolled ahead of the cardboard case. Gillian picked it up. Canice's oil. She opened it and daubed some on—why not?—then set it aside. The wood tones mingled with the floral as her pulse warmed the oil. Gillian felt along the bottom of the closet for the games. Monopoly, Polar Dare, chess, Candyland, Blockhead—that should be enough for now.

She piled the games on top of the case, then squatted

and tried to pick it up. She grunted. She'd come back for the cocktail.

Gillian tottered out the front door and down the steps. Her bruised hip twisted under her once, but she caught herself, straightened, then carried the games to the barbecue area. As she set them on a table Beth Ellen and Bibbie crowded her.

"No Barbies," Bibbie said, weaving her ponytail through her fingers. "She got penguins."

"Penguins?" Beth Ellen said. "Where?"

Bibbie pointed to Polar Dare, then sighed. "Can't dress penguins."

Gillian set Monopoly in front of Beth Ellen. "Here you—" She stared at the lid.

Nora's handwriting flowed across one corner: *Merry Christmas, Gilly. Pay up or die!*

"I get to be blue," Beth Ellen said.

Nick Trestle backed into the table. KC planted himself beside him. Nick pointed to his house. "Look at it. It's still standing! There's no reason I can't start a fire—"

"Standing doesn't mean anything," KC said, folding his arms across his chest. "If there are any cracks or if the chimney's shifted at all, the whole place could burn down. You'd lose everything."

Gillian stepped back. Just as she'd lost everything. Mom, Dad, home—gone in a crackle and a flash. Everything but Nora.

An emptiness filled her, an emptiness lined with the cold, fine ash of loss. She swallowed, trying to moisten the grittiness in her mouth. Glancing up at the sun, she limped toward her house. She had to meet Dagan at noon—time enough to go to Nora and heal the rift between them. If she survived, they'd be family again that much sooner. And if she didn't . . . Nora didn't need the guilt of proclaiming her dead.

Gillian stopped midstep. Dead. She swung around. Beth Ellen and Bibbie had already set up the Monopoly game. Three other children swarmed over the table, shaking open boxes, spilling plastic penguins and chess pieces. If Gillian

didn't try to appease the earth, any one of those children—
any one of these people—would die. Including Nora.

Gillian jogged to the garage. Whether Nora talked to her
or not, at least she could say good-bye.

It was more than she'd been able to say to Mom and
Dad.

THIRTEEN

GILLIAN WHEELED HER BICYCLE INTO THE DRIVEWAY, staring up at Nora's Queen Anne Victorian. The tall, rounded house rested on a patch of scraped dirt and splintered wood inches from what little foundation it had. A gap had opened between the front porch and the rounded turret window. The coral welcome mat dangled like a tongue from the porch.

Gillian scraped her teeth across her lower lip. "First the shop, now the house," she murmured. "Oh, Nora . . . ."

She wheeled the bicycle a little closer, then stopped and squatted beside the house's right front corner. Something had peeled away the brittle wood, fanning and splintering the planks like an exposed and broken rib cage.

"Debbie hit it last night," Nora said from behind her. "What are you doing here?"

Gillian stood, heart pounding. "How'd she do it? Is she all right?"

"She lost control of the truck." Nora placed her hands on her hips. "What do you want?"

Gillian rubbed her damp palms together. "I wanted to be sure you were all right."

"I'm fine." Nora spun on the ball of her foot and walked away.

Gillian followed her. "Nora, can't we talk this out?"

Nora turned on her, nostrils flared. "I don't think so. All I asked was one little favor, Gillian. Just one little favor."

Gillian squeezed the bridge of her nose. If she could figure out what they were really arguing about, she might be able to break through this barrier. "I know you're angry," she said. "I'm not sure why—"

Nora bristled. "Don't use that reflective listening crap on me. Save it for your kids."

"Hi, Gillian," Debbie said, shutting the backyard gate. "Think it'll rain?"

Gillian blinked, then glanced at the sky. Blue, with an abundance of black, oily smoke. "No, I don't think so. . . ."

She turned to Nora. Nora glared at her, lower lip curled under in a thin sneer. Gillian took a step back. She knew that look. What would Nora open up with? *You're too selfish to know how to give. All you do is take.* Or: *Love escapes you, doesn't it? You don't even know what it is. Every time someone tries to get close to you, you fence them out. Me, KC, even your precious Melanie . . .*

Gillian pressed her palms together. Not this time. Not if it might be the last time. "Nora—"

"Would you like some coffee?" Debbie asked brightly. "We've got the Coleman set up in the gazebo."

Gillian forced a smile. "No, thanks. Nora, if we don't see each other again—"

Nora sniffed. "I wish."

Not like this. Gillian didn't want the last of her existence to be like this. "Be careful what you wish for," Gillian said quietly. "Whatever happens, I want you to know I love you. Good-bye, Nora." She nodded to Debbie. "Bye."

Nora's anger hardened into an expressionless stare. She turned and walked briskly toward the back gate. "Is the coffee ready?" she asked Debbie.

Gillian waited several minutes after the gate creaked shut behind them. Paint flaked along the boards, a nail had worked loose near the latch. Gillian mounted her bicycle and rode away.

ONLY ONE CAR PASSED GILLIAN ON HER WAY DOWN-town.

She swerved out of its way, then glided between a top-pled mailbox and a heap of chipped bricks. People wandered the streets, crept cautiously across yards, poked ineffectually at both ruined and untouched houses. One man sawed the frayed boards binding his porch to his house while a woman dragged the planks free and dropped them in a pile on the sidewalk. A few doors down, another woman sat on the curb holding a hammer.

Gillian pedaled faster.

Nearer downtown, red tape and tags hung from the most battered houses. Yellow tape stretched across others. Chimneys flowed across arid lawns, planks crisscrossed like pickup sticks. Houses listed to one side or knelt as if in homage to the street. A few had burned, leaving charred cavities that crept toward neighboring homes.

An aftershock rumbled and shimmied. Gillian planted a foot on the curb to steady herself. She lurched and swayed, gripping the handlebars until her fingers ached. As soon as the ground quieted, she dismounted. Knees shaking, she leaned on the bicycle for support.

Steering the bicycle between clods of concrete, Gillian made her way to the Cyclone fence surrounding the downtown. Most of the buildings looked as if they'd weathered the last big aftershock fairly well. A few braces had snapped and fallen, causing the dependent buildings to sag a little more.

Gillian groaned. The Action Café had dissolved into a stew of wood, brick, and plaster. Its thick wooden sign rested like a rumpled napkin beside it. Poor Rich. Gillian steeled herself and walked on.

She stopped in front of the old Seraphim Theater. She'd avoided it on her last visit, afraid of what she'd find. Her shoulders tensed as she gazed at the stately old theater.

Its sculpted columns and wide, expansive steps were

largely intact. The slender, Art Nouveau angels shouldered the lintel of darting seraphim, the angels' faces somehow wistful and stern at once. Two angels waited near the buckled sidewalk, one on each side of the steps, their wings slightly unfurled and rising above their shoulders to sweep to the ground below. Yellow tape belted their waists and stretched across the steps. One of the two guardians had lost her nose, but that had nothing to do with earthquakes. Someone had chiseled it off as a trophy years ago. Every year some minor politician championed her restoration, and every year the money was spent on better acoustics, new plumbing, or structural improvements.

Like the recently added left wing, the one now folded in on itself like a fan. The wing slid away from the main building as if the earth was determined to pull the original theater down with it. . . .

She left her bicycle and pulled herself along the fence. A large crack stretched across the face of the theater. Gillian murmured low in her throat.

Such a beautiful old building. KC brought her here the first time, for Doc Watson's farewell tour. She'd been reluctant to leave the angels and go inside, she'd been so enchanted by their willowy figures and dreaming faces. After the concert KC insisted they examine each angel. They caressed the feathered wings, fingered the folds of each robe, traced the slope of a cheek. KC kissed her behind the disfigured angel. His lips were softer than she'd imagined, warm and sweet. . . .

Someone tapped her elbow. "You're early," Dagan said.

DAGAN WHEELED GILLIAN'S BICYCLE ALONG THE FENCE. He glanced at the Seraphim. "What does the yellow ribbon mean?"

"Caution," she said. "The building's damaged. Only people with the proper authority are allowed inside."

Dagan made a clicking sound. "Are they going to tear it down?"

Gillian hunched her shoulders. "They might. Red is definite, yellow is maybe."

Dagan exhaled through his teeth. "Come on," he said.

He veered away from the Cyclone fence. They took to the street, hurrying past the downtown's outer offices and shops. Although none of the buildings had fallen, yellow tape bisected their faces. Dagan glanced back at the Seraphim again.

Gillian studied him. "Why are you so worried about the Seraphim? Wouldn't the earth be happier if all the buildings fell?"

"Not that one."

"What's so special about the Seraphim?"

"It's well placed."

"What do you mean, 'well placed'?" A knot formed between Gillian's shoulder blades. "Dagan, what's under there? Isn't it just another piece of the spirit? Couldn't it become part of you if the rest of the buildings and pavement were stripped away?"

He paled. "It's possible. Let's go."

Gillian slowed. "What's different about that piece of land? What's under there?"

"We need to hurry—"

Gillian stopped. "Tell me, Dagan."

Dagan kicked at a stone. "How much do you know about Rio Santo? About its history?"

"A little," she said. "*Rio santo* means 'sacred river.' Two monks wandered away from an expedition exploring the California coast and saw a vision of the Virgin Mary standing on the banks of the river—"

Dagan shook his head. "They didn't just see her, they talked to her. They talked to the spirit of the place—"

"Of *that* place? But none of this had been divided then."

Dagan began walking again. Gillian fell in step beside him. "People aren't the only ones who make divisions," he said. "There are a few . . . natural divisions. The land under the Seraphim—that's one of them. Sacred places, people call them. Holy ground. Great power dwells there.

People can feel it when they walk on it or near it.''

"And this power talked to the monks?''

"As a sacred person the settling people understood. Until then, the spirit appeared as one the wandering people understood.''

Gillian frowned. "Dagan, those monks saw the Virgin Mary by the river. The river doesn't run through downtown.''

"The river was diverted over a century ago, to the edge of the floodplain.'' Dagan stared at her. "Didn't you know that? That's why the ground is so unstable. It's clay. It ripples.''

A chill pricked Gillian's scalp. That's why the banks of the river were so heavily fortified with concrete and stone, to keep the river from reverting if a heavy storm caused it to swell. She'd always assumed the levy was one of those Army Corps of Engineer jobs—

The *edge* of the floodplain? That was at least a mile from downtown. . . .

Gillian started at the sound of two people shouting to each other. She looked around quickly—she and Dagan had drifted into a residential neighborhood. People swarmed over houses and yards, stacking bricks and scrap wood, removing shattered windows. A woman wearing a red bandanna jogged alongside them. "Any news?'' she said. "Any word on the National Guard?''

"Not that I've heard,'' Gillian said. "We haven't been able to get anything on the radio.''

The woman grunted and dropped back. "Yep. Same ol', same ol'. Thanks!''

Gillian nodded, then turned to Dagan. "The spirit under the Seraphim—is it powerful?''

"Very powerful—and angry.'' Dagan walked faster. "People have always worshiped that bit of ground. The wandering people stopped to make offerings, sing a little, ask favors of the land. Then the settling people came, and despite the warnings, they built there, trapping the spirit.''

"What warnings? Earthquakes?''

"Collapsed buildings, fires. None of the early buildings

had foundations. The spirit shook them off like a duck shakes off water. Then the settling people's skills grew and developed. When the Seraphim was built, a thick foundation was laid.''

"And the spirit was trapped," Gillian said. "How do you know it's angry? You were trapped under a house—you're not angry."

"After all those years of worship and care, to be so badly abused . . . ." Dagan shook his head. "I'm part of the earth. I can feel her many parts. That spirit is angry. Very angry."

"The earthquakes . . . did that spirit cause them?"

"No," Dagan said, lifting the bicycle over a crumpled fender. "I told you. The earth needs peace."

" 'Peace,' " Gillian muttered. Her temples pounded. "What do you mean, 'peace'?"

Dagan shrugged. "Peace. You know—tranquillity, calm, composure."

Gillian stared at him. "And *I'm* supposed to give this to the earth?"

"Yes."

"Right. And how am I supposed to do that?"

"You'll know," Dagan said.

"Dagan—"

"You'll *know.*"

Gillian gritted her teeth. They continued in silence. After several blocks Dagan nudged Gillian to the right, through the wrought-iron gates of Avenida de Mantequilla. Gillian murmured, taking in the sampler of large, expensive homes. Unlike the downtown neighborhoods genteel with row houses and Victorians or the newer tracts crowded with ranch houses, Avenida de Mantequilla boasted Tudors, Georgians, Colonials, a Frank Lloyd Wright rip-off, haciendas . . . and lawns—broad, parklike slopes of singed grass bordered by shrubs and trees.

But even wealth had proved no protection against the devastation. Columns had cracked and fallen, balconies drooped like ragged mustaches. Three alabaster nymphs toppled across green stepping-stones, a shallow bowl wrenched from their hands. One driveway ran red with shattered roof tiles, another with white paint. Down the street and to the left, a Tudor crosshatched with roses folded in on itself. Bright red tape stretched across its door.

Gillian pursed her lips. Something about the neighborhood unnerved her. Not the damage. God knew she'd seen enough of that the last three weeks. She frowned in concentration, trying to pinpoint just what bothered her—

The silence and the lack of people. No one clambered across the roofs to check chimneys or wrenched broken glass from window sashes. No one sat outside or sought the solace of neighbors. The silence of Avenida de Mantequilla ached with desertion. These people left, forsaking Rio Santo. Gillian hugged herself. As she had wanted to, days ago.

KC, Beth Ellen, Lucinda, even Nora—the faces of Rio Santo clamored in her mind, begging her not to abandon them to the spirits. . . .

She glanced at the condemned Tudor as she and Dagan passed. A drainage ditch bordered the lawn. A plaster Virgin Mary stood beside the crumbling bank, her robes painted a vibrant blue.

Goose bumps rose along Gillian's spine.

Very angry, Dagan had said of the Seraphim spirit. Judging by the destruction of this house, it wasn't just that spirit, but the entire earth.

Gillian looked away. Avenida de Mantequilla curved past five or six more houses then narrowed to a footpath as it passed under a vine-wreathed arbor.

Gillian faltered a step, then hurried to catch up to Dagan. "We're headed for Briar Hollow."

He nodded.

"The site is in the park?"

"Yes."

"That's a public park—" An incredulous laugh escaped her. "I have to perform the rites in public?"

Dagan blinked at her, puzzled. His eyes widened slowly with understanding. "No, no. You'll see. Trust me, Gillian."

She sighed. "Do I have a choice?"

The arbor loomed ahead. Vines clung to its trellised arch and rambled along the Cyclone fence on either side. The runners drooped, their few remaining leaves less an autumn carmine than a drought-withered brown. Gillian frowned, trying to remember: the west arbor . . . blackberry? She'd never been to this entrance before. She'd always been a little intimidated by the affluence of the neighborhood. The other two arbors, the south and the east, were flanked by narrow parking lots and signs, making them a bit more welcoming. Raspberry climbed the south arbor. Wild roses adorned the east.

Gillian stopped and peered through the arbor. Even driven back by drought, brambles raged along the sides of the trail. Drought had thinned the leaves, but not the thorns. If only she had her rubber boots. . . .

Gillian scratched her leg. "Do we have to wade through the brambles to get to this site?"

"There's a trail." Dagan steered her bicycle through the arbor. "It's not hard to follow. If you know what to look for."

He leaned the bicycle against the fence, then hid it beneath a thick mass of blackberry. Thorns shredded his arms as he pulled them out of the briars. His skin crumbled like dry soil, his flesh pitted where the soft clods had worked free. He rubbed his arms with his hands. The rust-colored skin stretched perfect and smooth again. "Are you ready?" he said, holding out his hand.

Gillian hesitated. *I'm in over my head*, she thought. *How can I hope to succeed?* She reached for his hand. *Faith, Gilly. Have faith in yourself. Dagan does or he wouldn't have come to you—not for something this important.*

His damp fingers closed around her palm. He led her into Briar Hollow.

Banks of dripping vines cramped the trail. Gillian stayed in the middle of the dusty path, crowding Dagan. She wondered what kind of vines these were. They looked like blackberry, but without berries or flowers, it was hard to tell. Brambles of every description crept and tangled throughout the park, wrapping themselves around the trunks of the bay laurel, elm, and oak trees hearty enough to brave the thorny vines. Although blackberry and wild roses claimed much of the park, the raspberry and ollalie berry held their own. Gillian had read somewhere that one of the docents had even planted marionberry and boysenberry, protecting the small patches with strips of ragged lawn. "I want a collection of brambles," Gorse Blanchard, the founder of the park, had said. The brambles had flourished.

Until the drought.

Curled, wilted runners tangled along the sides of the path, coated with dust. In wetter times, in the late spring, white and baby-pink blossoms rode waves of dark leaves, followed by black and red berries in the late summer. But in the last two years both flowers and berries had grown fewer and fewer.

Even so, Briar Hollow retained its rampant strangeness. "What a weird idea for a park," KC had said the first time she brought him here. "It's like a fairy tale run amok."

"What, like a nightmare?" she'd said. "KC, this place is . . . romantic. Not in the love-and-lust sense—in the old-fashioned, poetic sense. Nature being true to nature. Beauty reverting to the wild."

"It's wild, all right," he'd said. But he'd insisted they come back, many times, especially those times when the affection between them blurred. . . .

She shut KC out.

She tramped behind Dagan, wondering at the eeriness binding her heart like the vines. KC was right—a fairy tale run amok. Like Sleeping Beauty—only Gillian hoped to lull the princess to sleep, not wake her.

Rounding a curve overflowing with vines, she and Dagan stepped onto the park's main trail. Trees sprouted from the brambles, their bare branches chattering in the wind. Gillian's gaze darted from tree to tree, resting at last on the stone bench. She shook her head. This was impossible. The trees, the ground, the bench—none of these things had suffered in the earthquakes. She expected some devastation—fallen trees or fans of churned dirt—but the tremors hadn't touched Briar Hollow.

Hadn't touched it, while less than a half mile away, the Tudor with its Virgin Mary had been destroyed. . . .

Gillian's shoulders rose. If the earth could selectively spare and destroy, what else could it do?

Gillian forced her shoulders back. *Don't think about it; act.*

She coughed. "You—you mentioned the settled people," she said. "You mean white people, like me?"

"You're all settling people now," he said. "There are a few wandering people left, but not many. Even those who don't build houses or stay in one place use roads."

"Roads? But people use roads to wander—"

"Roads are permanent. Fixed. They trap the earth the same as any other structure." He nodded toward the hint of a trail leading off to the left. "This way."

Gillian balked. Brambles choked the path.

Dagan waded ahead. Gillian followed. Thorns flailed at her ankles and calves, biting through her jeans. Sharp stings rose in welts above her thick wool socks. After fifteen feet the path swerved to the left again. Brambles loomed a foot over her head on either side.

"It's not much farther," Dagan said.

Gillian eyed the towering brambles. "Okay."

Eight more feet and the tunnel of thorns emptied into a brittle, gold meadow shaded by a small butte.

Gillian stared. "I've never seen this before."

"The trail isn't very welcoming," Dagan said, leading her across the meadow. "Even those who notice it rarely try it."

They crossed the yellow grass to the foot of the butte, then skirted its rocky base until they came to a rift in the stone. Dagan stepped inside, gesturing for her to follow. She took a step forward, then stopped. Looking up into the sky, she marveled at how blue it was. *Like the Virgin Mary's robes.*

Gillian raised a trembling hand to shade her eyes. The

sweet, grassy scent of Canice's oil surrounded her, warmed by her racing pulse.

"Gillian," Dagan said gently.

She stepped into the rift.

FOURTEEN

GILLIAN STEPPED OUT ONTO THE WORN, DIRT FLOOR OF A circular "courtyard" enclosed by cliffs. She exclaimed, a short catch of breath, as wonder overpowered her fear. The walls rose a good twenty feet, weathered and straight, the manzanita-red stone topped with a fringe of grass and gray twigs. Not one root or vine, not even a rash of lichen marred the cliffs. Except for the green tufts above her, the enclosure was nothing but dirt and stone. Earth. Gillian shielded her eyes and looked up. That same virgin-blue sky stretched like the vault of a cathedral overhead.

Gillian lowered her gaze. About thirty feet across, the courtyard held nothing but a trunk-sized granite slab—an altar?—that squatted in front of an arbor of white stone. A spray of roses climbed the arbor, two or three trailing down the sides of the arch. Carved from a variety of quartz-laced rock and dull stone, each rose was wildly different. Some only resembled flowers, others unfolded in carefully chiseled petals. One looked as if its creator had chipped slivers of jasper then glued them together in a lopsided cabbage rose. One blossom, delicate and well crafted, sparkled with veins of rose quartz.

Below the arbor, the altar was little more than a crude block. Gillian glanced at Dagan, then walked to the granite slab and knelt. She stared at it a second, not sure what she expected to find, then shivered with relief. No stains—no *blood* stains.

She hesitated, then ran her hand along the worn top. Its surface reflected a little, unevenly polished as if by frequent use. Gillian's hands traveled the face of the block, along the right front corner. Chisel marks and shallow carving curved and receded under her fingers. She scooted closer, bending to examine a graceful knotwork border.

Dagan knelt beside her. "Everyone adds something to the arch or to this," he said. He took her hand and placed it on the side of the stone. "Feel that? That was Melanie's gift."

He dragged her fingers across two spidery outlines. Gillian frowned. "What is it?"

Dagan smiled and released her hand. "See for yourself."

Gillian leaned across him. Chipped shallowly into the stone were two hands, fingers spread, poised to massage any stress and tension from the stone. Gillian smiled. How like Melanie—

Melanie's dead, Gillian. . . .

Gillian pulled her hand away as if the granite had turned to dry ice.

"Gillian?" Dagan said, alarmed. He pressed against her.

Gillian pushed him away, sneezing at the cloying, musty smell of him. Sniffing, she inched away from the granite slab, looking around. Not a stroke of graffiti, not a scrap of litter . . . aside from the arbor and the altar, there were no signs of human trespass. If she died here, if Dagan or the earth killed her, would anyone find her?

Would anyone know?

"No one—" Gillian fought to steady her voice. "No one knows about this place, do they? I can't believe hikers haven't seen it from above and come looking for it."

Dagan pointed to the grass and bare twigs above. "The bluff is rife with poison oak. She drives back anyone brave enough to wade through it with an earthquake. No one has been here that doesn't belong."

Gillian's lower lip trembled. *She's not right for you. If you use her, you might kill her. . . .*

"If someone . . . came here that didn't belong," Gillian said slowly, "what would happen? What would the earth do?"

She's not what you're looking for. . . .

A slight frown dimpled Dagan's brow. Then his eyes widened. He cupped her chin in his hand. "You're afraid."

Gillian shrank from his touch. "What if I'm not what you're looking for? What if this doesn't work?"

A glossy hardness sheened Dagan's eyes. "It'll work. Every person who touches the earth gives to her—"

"Then why me, why not anyone?"

"Because right now she needs someone special, someone who offers more than a normal person. Someone . . . aware." Dagan reached for her, grasping her wrists. "Gillian, I need you. *She* needs you. If you don't do this, Rio Santo will be destroyed."

Gillian closed her eyes. Voices clamored through her mind: *She is language,* whispered the first. *Then she is also prayer,* replied the second. *Let me use her once.*

Gillian shuddered. All right—once and only once she would be a prayer pleading for the lives of Rio Santo. Gillian opened her eyes. "Show me what I need to do," she said.

He tilted his head slightly; his eyes glinted in the slanting rays of the sun. Calm seeped into her fear, furrowing it like a wave dissolving a sand castle. She backed into the altar. The calm felt wrong, like the quiet before an earthquake.

Gillian looked away. "Show me what to do," she said.

"Close your eyes," Dagan said. "Close your eyes and feel this place. Feel the earth's pulse beneath your feet."

Gillian closed her eyes. A hum tingled beneath her. She reached down and fumbled with her shoes and socks, tugging them from her feet. The hum tickled the soles of her feet.

"Hear her as she calls to you," Dagan said.

Gillian held her breath. A gentle crumbling whispered through the courtyard, the sound of ground settling. A rock tumbled down the nearest cliff face, pinging against the wall twice before striking the floor.

Gillian bit back a nervous laugh. *Don't fall apart on me now,* she wanted to say—anything to break the tension. She sobered, exhaled, then filled her lungs with the rich, loamy scent of freshly turned earth.

Dagan took her hands, barely touching her fingertips, and turned her so that she faced the arbor. His hands fell away. "Open your eyes and see her," he said.

Gillian opened her eyes. The cliff towered over her, its face streaked with sienna, umber, and deep walnut. Burnished by the late-morning sun, the layers of stone shimmered with a pulse of radiant heat. Gillian's heart caught. A spectrum of earth and time, too beautiful for words—

"Know Her," Dagan said.

The hum resonated against the soles of Gillian's feet until it vibrated along her very core, filling her with the Earth's life and hope and promise. And Her pain.

Dagan's voice caressed Gillian. "I'll lead you through the rites this first time—"

"This first time!" Gillian swung to face him. "You asked me to do this once, *once,* to help you buy time while you searched for someone else—"

Someone right for the Earth.

Dagan's pupils swelled, then receded to pinpoints of green. "Yes, I said that."

Gillian's shoulder blades strained to touch. "But if you can't find someone else—"

"I'll ask you to come again," he said.

"Unless I'm not right," Gillian said. "Unless I die."

Dagan's jaw hardened. "You won't die. I won't let you. You *are* right for this. You are language and language can be used—"

"For prayer." Gillian twisted her hands together. "What does it mean, I am language? What is this prayer you want so badly? Or is it really a promise you want— *my* promise to return?" A chill spilled through her, quenching the hum of the Earth. "What have I promised by being here at all—to bind myself to this place?"

Dagan took her hands. Desperation strained his voice. "Being here won't bind you. Only a rose will bind you."

A rose? Gillian glanced at the arbor, then back at Dagan.

Dagan released her hands. "The roses are promises. To return. To give to Her. Every month for the rest of one's life."

Gillian sought his gaze. "I'm only bound if I bring a rose."

"Well . . . ." Dagan looked away. "And until we find someone else."

The chill inside Gillian turned glacial. She'd be bound to more than the Earth. She'd be bound to Rio Santo. Even if she moved away, found a home, a real home, she'd be tethered to Rio Santo by a short leash. If she wanted more than a small city school district, if she met someone and wanted to follow him to Montana or Georgia—or Maine. . . .

Her heart thudded wildly against the icy fear crystalizing inside her. And if Rio Santo never recovered from these earthquakes and people deserted the city . . . ? The cold spread to Gillian's fingers. She fisted her hands.

If Rio Santo never recovered, the young people would flee first, looking for more, for *life*. Then the older people would follow or slowly die. Gillian imagined Rio Santo's shored and broken downtown layered with neglect and grit, its fractured houses crumbling under the weight of disrepair. Rio Santo faded, became a fragile ghost of itself.

And there, amid the ruins, Gillian imagined herself with her clothes in tatters, her hair felted into cords and sheets, crazed with loneliness. A visitor in Rio Santo, always, but bound to it.

Bound to Rio Santo . . . suddenly Gillian heard the resignation underlying the contented sense of place in Melanie's voice. She heard the hunger behind Melanie's gift for opening people up, encouraging them to talk about places they'd been—Australia, Europe, Latin America, San Francisco, Arizona—a hunger fed only by a passing whiff, like a penniless person tasting fresh bread by scent.

Gillian had always envied Melanie's sense of home. To find out it was only a trap. . . .

Gillian opened her cramped hands. "But you will," she said. "You will find someone else. And right now this isn't dangerous . . . ?"

Dagan faced her. "Less dangerous than leaving Her angry."

A third earthquake . . . a trail of bodies and fires flowing like lava through the rubble . . . Beth Ellen and Lucinda, KC, Nora, and Canice gazing sightlessly at the sky as children's blocks buried them in a confused heap of red, yellow, green, and blue. . . .

Gillian forced the images away, banished her own needs and fears. She'd promised Beth Ellen there would be no more earthquakes; she couldn't back out without trying. Gillian spread her toes, clutching at the soil, reaching for the hum of the Earth until it filled her again. "Show me," she said.

Dagan studied her for a few seconds, then reached behind the altar and retrieved a plastic vegetable bag filled with the things he'd bought at the garage sale: Melanie's coins, the ceramic face, the velvet pouch, and the mortar and pestle. He removed each carefully from the bag and placed them on the stone. He reached behind the altar again, then straightened, holding the four candlesticks. He set one at each corner. Then he crouched one last time and set the mortar and pestle at the center of the stone.

"You have to arrange them," he said.

Gillian gazed at the handful of coins and other objects. She picked up the velvet pouch, squeezing it in her hand. Something hard had been tucked inside. She peeked. The Zuni badger. "How do I arrange them?" she said.

Dagan nudged a coin toward her with his finger. "Feel the shape of them. You'll know."

Gillian frowned. Feel the shape . . . she left the candlestick holders at the four corners, then made a circle with the coins. She set the mortar and pestle in the center of the circle. Opening the pouch, she poured the badger into her palm, then placed the fetish beside the mortar and pestle.

Dagan's brow puckered as he examined her placement. He wet his lips. "Is this how you want them?" he said.

Gillian looked over the objects on the altar. She reached for the mortar and pestle, hesitated, then pulled her hand back. The mortar and pestle didn't seem to fit, not just the design she'd set up, but the whole *feel* of the thing. And something seemed to be missing. . . .

"Where are the candles?" Gillian asked.

Dagan shrugged. "Melanie never used candles."

Gillian flexed and unflexed her hands, then studied the altar again. The mortar and pestle still felt wrong, but who was she to question the sacred objects? Dagan and the other spirit, Petra, had taken such pains to collect them. "There's something missing," Gillian said.

"Missing? Oh!" Dagan fished in his shirt pocket and pulled out the ceramic face. He handed it to her.

Gillian weighed the medallion in her hand. She set it beside the candlestick holder in the far right corner like a sun in a child's drawing. She traced its lips with her finger. That felt a little more right, but not completely. *Trust him, Gilly,* she warned herself. *He knows what he's doing. He needs this to work more than you do.*

Dagan nodded. "Now you have to find something to offer Her. Something you can grind."

Gillian looked around the bare courtyard. What could she possibly grind? One of the other objects—the badger, a coin, the medallion? No. She squinted along the cliff face to the bright sky. A rock, maybe a fallen leaf . . . a sliver of the cliff itself? But there were no rocks or leaves, and she had nothing to scrape even a flake of stone from the walls. She twisted her mouth to one side until her gaze fell on a single stone petal curled at the base of the arbor like a wisp of sawdust. She walked over and picked it up. Dried glue crusted one edge. She set the petal in the mortar.

"Now what do I do?" she asked.

Dagan backed away from the altar. "Send Her your thoughts. And when the time is right, offer Her your gift of peace. Don't let anything distract you. You must give Her your full attention.''

Gillian's throat tightened. It was all so nebulous. She glanced over her shoulder. Dagan stood five feet away, watching her. A sense of isolation draped her like a cloak. ''What do I say?'' she said. ''How will I know when to make the offering?''

''It comes from the heart,'' Dagan said. ''It must always come from the heart.''

Gillian faced the altar. From the heart . . . and hers was sinking beneath the weight of doubt and fear. Gillian focused on the Earth's pulse, matching it with her own.

Send Her your thoughts. Prayer.

Gillian opened her heart. ''Please have mercy on us,'' she whispered. ''I know You are in pain and that we—uh, humans—have somehow caused that pain. Please forgive us and accept this gift of peace. . . .''

The vibration quickened inside Gillian. She fought her own rising panic, scouring her mind for the words to calm the Earth. ''You've suffered greatly, I realize. You've struck out like a wounded animal—'' Gillian bit her lip. *Great. Insult the Earth.* ''You've struck out and reached for the comfort You deserve—'' *Patronize Her, really piss Her off.* ''Forgive us. We had no idea we'd hurt You so badly. We never meant to. Please teach us—teach *me*—to give to You and—''

The resonance shuddered through her. The wildness of it, the pain, raged inside her, threatening to shake her apart, erode her . . . like an earthquake. A seed of calm planted itself in Gillian's heart. She eased into the madness. ''I understand,'' she said softly.

Her words escaped through skull-rattled teeth. ''I can't promise You this will never happen again. We've built barriers between You and us—roads, buildings, parking lots, shoes—and we don't touch You as we used to. We don't become part of You. People are many, but people who seek the warmth of Your soil beneath their bare feet are becoming fewer. People who sit with You and absorb You and give back to You . . .''

The uncontrolled spasming slowed to a tremble. Gillian caught her breath. "I can't promise You any more than You can promise us. I can only offer You myself and the peace I wish for You. Please accept these wishes and this prayer. Please restore the calm."

Gillian's body stilled to that first low hum. She swayed a little, weakened by the quivering and shaking, then dropped to her knees before the altar. Propping her elbows on the granite block, she rested her head in her hands. What now? She lifted her head and her gaze fell on the mortar and pestle. She straightened, forcing her shoulders back. She picked up the pestle. It weighed heavily in her hand.

She thrust the pestle into the bowl of the mortar and began to grind the stone petal.

"Stop her!" someone said. "She must not do that! She is destroying an earlier offering!"

"Leave her alone," Dagan warned. "It is her offering now."

Gillian faltered, glancing over her shoulder at Dagan. He nodded for her to continue. "Go on," he said.

Gillian leaned into the pestle. She focused on crushing the sliver of stone. "This is for You," she told the Earth.

Someone growled behind her. Gillian glanced quickly over her shoulder. The white-haired woman from the garage sale, Petra, snarled at her, teeth bared. Gillian stared into the mortar, trying to concentrate on her gift to the Earth, but Melanie's face haunted her. Like a flash of lightning, the image of Melanie strangled by the hate-filled Petra flared through her mind, then disappeared. Gillian slowed her grinding and looked over her shoulder again.

A figure stood beside Petra, clutching his head and moaning. Another crouched beside him, her eyes rolled up into her head. Six more surged from the shadows. Gillian turned back to the altar and attacked the stone petal.

Gillian murmured to herself, concentrating on the offering. A brown silt lined the bottom of the mortar.

A sultry male voice said, "She is not the one, Dagan."

"No, she is not," Petra said. "Yet she dares to destroy

the gift of one who was. She must be stopped!"

Gillian's shoulders rose. Ignore the spirits, that's what she had to do, and give herself wholly to the Earth. "Please," she prayed, not sure whether to direct her plea to God or the Earth. "Please, send them away."

"She falters," Petra said. "I warned you, Dagan. She is not right—"

"I offer You peace," Gillian said, her voice rising shrilly. "I offer You peace and ask You to restore peace to us—"

The hum tingling through Gillian's body deepened to a low rumble. A rock tumbled from the edge of the cliff and then another. The mortar wobbled out of Gillian's hand. It wasn't just her this time. Gillian dropped the pestle and pushed herself to her feet.

Gillian bent her knees to absorb the aftershock. "Have mercy on us—"

"Kill her!" Petra screamed.

A fierce jolt flung Gillian to the ground. The ground bucked and shimmied, accompanied by Petra's howls. Gillian grasped the edge of the altar and pulled herself to her knees. The candlestick holders toppled and rolled, scattering coins, fetish, and pestle. The mortar tipped, spilling brown dust. It bounced from the altar, striking the ground with a thump.

The ceramic face remained still.

Gillian clawed at the altar, dragging herself toward the medallion, but every time she gained an inch, a deep shudder knocked her back. She clung to the stone, then crept forward again. The tremor calmed a little, idling like some monstrous engine.

A loud crack echoed through the courtyard.

"Gillian!" Dagan shouted.

Petra laughed. "Leave her!"

Gillian glanced back. Three strangers held Dagan. He struggled against them, yearning toward her. Petra wound her arms around him like a harness. Dagan whipped his head side to side, smashing the face of one of his captors. The man's features crumbled like sandstone. "Gillian!"

Dagan yelled. "The altar! Get on the altar!"

"I'm trying," she muttered through gritted teeth. She grasped the far side of the granite block, dragging herself partway onto the stone. The ground lurched from under her. Her hip smacked the altar. She grimaced, clinging to the rough stone.

Another crack echoed through the courtyard.

"Gillian!" Dagan screamed.

She turned. A rift had opened between Petra's feet. As if on cue, the six spirits circling Dagan and his captors stamped the ground with their feet, fracturing the earth, then stamped again. Seven fissures raced toward Gillian with a deafening growl.

Gillian gasped and pressed her fingers into the stone, clawing and wriggling, struggling to embrace the altar and pull herself onto it. Her fingers, scraped raw, striped the stone with streaks of blood.

The ground crumbled away beneath her. Legs dangling, she hugged the stone. Her jaw cracked as she ground her teeth tighter. "I tried, damn it," she said. "*I tried!*"

Her shoulders burned. Electricity sizzled through her body as the nerves and sockets in her arms popped. She cried out, closing her eyes.

A rush of wind ruffled her sweat-damp hair. Cool wind, not the hot breath of the earth she'd expected. She moaned. Her fingers ached. . . .

Hands caught her wrists and pulled her upward. A fiery pain seared through her arms as her sockets wrenched still farther. Then arms wound around her, folding her into an embrace. Her feet scraped something solid—the altar. Gillian opened her eyes and looked up into Canice's fierce and storm-dark face.

FIFTEEN

CANICE FOLDED HERSELF AROUND GILLIAN LIKE AN AN-
gel. She seemed taller, much taller than Gillian remembered—and very, very strong.

Canice hissed. "What did you think you were doing? I
told you—she's not right for you."

Gillian tensed.

Jerking free of Petra's grip, Dagan swaggered toward
Canice. He stopped, straddling a fissure. "She might be,"
he said. "She *could* be, if the rest of you would only trust
her."

He turned and glared at the spirits huddled behind him,
then faced Canice again. Defiance simmered in his eyes.

"It's not a matter of trust, Dagan," Canice said. "It's
a matter of heart. Her heart speaks to the Four, not just
the Earth. She'll never be able to focus the way you need
her to."

"You're wrong," he said. His voice softened with en-
treaty. "Gillian, please. Try again. For the sake of Rio
Santo—"

"No!" Canice pulled Gillian closer, nearly crushing her.
"Gillian, for the sake of Rio Santo, you mustn't try
again."

"I agree with Canice," Petra said. "She is not right.
Bring her here again, Dagan, and I will kill her."

Gillian squirmed, struggling to break free. "Save your threats. I'm leaving."

Canice released Gillian. Gillian stalked toward the rift, her legs trembling under her. She lifted her chin. *Courage, Gilly. Make them believe you aren't afraid.* She turned before entering the cleft.

Canice glared at the spirits. Her gaze lingered on Petra. "If any harm comes to her, I know who to look for."

Dagan shifted uncomfortably. Petra sneered. The other spirits dissolved, leaving Dagan and Petra to face Canice.

The white-haired spirit growled low in her throat. "You do not scare me, Wind Spinner. What could you possibly do that *they* have not?"

Gillian frowned. Wind Spinner . . . wind. Some memory, some lost remark. . . .

Canice smiled, sweet and cruel. "I can sweep the topsoil from your pathetic little plot. Just keep wearing you down until you're nothing but useless rocks and clay. No human would bother to cross your miserable little parcel then, would they? You'd be without the comfort of their touch. . . ."

Despite her brash pose, Petra flinched. She spat, then crumbled to a fine dust.

Only Dagan stood his ground. He yearned toward Gillian. "Gillian—"

Canice hissed. "Leave her alone. I don't want you anywhere near her."

"But the Earth is one of the Four—"

"And the Earth can send one of the others," Canice said. "Anyone but you or Petra."

Dagan's shoulders slumped. "The others are insane—"

"I don't want you near her," Canice said. "I don't trust you."

Dagan opened his mouth to speak, closed it, then opened it again. He gazed at Gillian, pleading—for forgiveness? Help?

"Don't," Canice said in a low, even voice. "And Dagan, tell Her to stop the aftershocks. It isn't just Her lack of contact with humans that's hurting Her. Part of Her pain comes from the silence of the Four. It's been far too long since She and the other Three have spoken. Fresh Water refuses to talk—don't tell me She hasn't noticed the drought. And Ocean sends little to no fog. Tell Earth to be patient.''

"I'll tell Her," Dagan said. He closed his eyes and melted into the soil.

Canice watched him disappear, then walked across the courtyard to join Gillian. Grabbing Gillian by the elbow, Canice herded her into the rift. "Come on," Canice said. "Let's get out of here."

NEITHER GILLIAN NOR CANICE SPOKE AS THEY WADED through the brambles to the main trail. Images tumbled through Gillian's mind: the spirits dissolving, Dagan's pleading eyes, Petra's twisted, angry mouth, Canice towering over the quailing spirits. Words shrilled through her thoughts like a storm through the eaves: the Four, trust, heart, silence, Wind Spinner. Wind. Gillian resisted her mind's conclusion. Canice couldn't be a wind spirit. That was impossible—and the idea of earth spirits was impossible enough. But if she was a wind spirit . . . the Four. Dagan had said he was one of the Four. Earth, Wind, Fresh Water, and Ocean? Gillian shuddered involuntarily. God, who—*what* would she have to meet next?

Gillian stopped. *Sort of like the wind,* Debbie had said. Gillian had thought she meant the perfume.

Gillian grasped Canice's sleeve. Canice stopped and looked at her, a guarded expression on her face. "What does your name mean?" Gillian demanded.

Canice blinked, staring at her in surprise. Then she laughed. "My *name*? After everything that happened back there, you want to know what my *name* means?"

Gillian's cheeks flushed. She nodded.

"Daughter of the Wind," Canice said. "It's Greek. You've been spelling it wrong, by the way. It's C-A-N-A-C-E. I didn't correct you because I was afraid you'd look it up."

Gillian's face grew hotter. "And you didn't want me to figure it out."

Canace pressed her lips together. "Not until I was sure about you. Not until I was ready to explain everything. You'd already met Dagan and I didn't know if you'd, you know, connect . . ." She shrugged helplessly.

Gillian fought to calm her racing heart. "Are you ready to explain everything now?"

Canace took a deep breath. She held it, then hissed. She pointed toward the west arbor. "Let's get out of Briar Hollow first. I have a promise to keep and I think you'd better come with me. I don't trust Dagan."

"A promise," Gillian said. "To Dera."

Canace nodded.

GILLIAN PUSHED HER BICYCLE PAST THE DESERTED HOMES of Avenida de Mantequilla. She averted her eyes from the plaster Virgin and the crippled Tudor. Canace walked beside her, chasing a rock down the street. She kicked it, it clattered ahead, rolled to a stop, she kicked it again.

Gillian cleared her throat. "We're out of Briar Hollow."

"We are." Canace kicked the rock and sent it tumbling a good fifteen feet. "What did Dagan tell you? About what you were supposed to be doing back there?"

"Not enough, apparently," Gillian said. "I'd like to hear your explanation."

"Mine." Canace ran a hand through her hair. "Okay . . ."

The silence stretched, expanding across a minute. Canace kicked the rock. Gillian started to clear her throat again. "Well . . ." Canace said.

"Yes?"

Canace glanced at Gillian sideways. "I'm not sure this will be any better. The Earth needs people. We all do— but the Earth . . . ." She screwed her mouth to one side. "It's like a mother breast-feeding her baby. The baby draws milk, comfort, and love from the mother and the mother is relieved of the heaviness of her breasts. *And* she is spiritually and emotionally nourished by the love and need of her child.''

"A circle,'' Gillian said.

"Hmm? Yes—exactly.'' Canace kicked the rock. "But the circle gets broken. People still touch the Earth, but a lot of them only nourish her with fertilizers and compost. Sure, they massage and turn the soil with their tractors and machines—even with their hands—but for most of them, She's just something that needs tending, not loving. They forget She has a soul. A heart.''

Gillian rolled the tension from her shoulders. "What She needs is someone to complete the circle.''

"Right. Someone born to Her, *of* Her, in a spiritual sense. You weren't.''

But Melanie was.

Was.

Gillian's knuckles turned white as she clenched the handlebars. Tears burned along her lower lashes.

Canace, taking another swing at the rock, didn't notice. "When She's undernourished, She does what people do. She gets unbalanced. She goes crazy, gets angry, withdrawn, disconnected—desperate.''

Angry like Petra, desperate like Dagan. Gillian wriggled with a shiver. "You said the Earth needs people, 'We all do.' This 'we'—is that the Four? You told Dagan I speak for the Four. Do They need me?''

"Yes, we do.''

"But the Earth almost killed me. She's one of the Four.''

"She is. She rejected you because your attention isn't focused on just the Earth, that's not who you are. Your attention encompasses the Four.''

Gillian frowned. "And the Four need me to complete Their circle. . . .''

"Not—'' Canace hesitated. "Not to complete a circle, no. You're . . .''

"Language,'' Gillian said.

Canace smiled. "Yes.'' She stopped at the end of Avenida de Mantequilla. She pointed right, toward the sea. "This way."

Gillian followed. "Explain it to me. I want to be sure I understand all this. The Four are Earth, Wind, Ocean, and Fresh Water."

"Yes."

"What about Fire?"

Canace snorted. "Earth and Wind make fire."

Gillian tilted her chin. "Why do you need me?"

"You're our tongue, our language," Canace said. "Without a common language we don't communicate— very well. It's like people who speak different languages trying to discuss world peace. We catch a little of what the hand waving is all about, but the nuances aren't there." Canace wrinkled her nose. "And we don't get along very well. You heard Dagan and me. That's about as good as it gets."

"So I'm the referee," Gillian said.

"No." Canace touched Gillian's arm. Her fingers caressed Gillian's skin like a tropical breeze. "You're the language we use to communicate. You draw us together, ease our frustrations and sorrows by allowing us to understand each other. This way."

They turned down another street, this one flanked by the levee. Gillian stared at the cement slope cupping the parched river, not really seeing it, too confused and too unsettled to allow herself the distraction of her surroundings. The language that drew the Four together—and what if *she* didn't understand? What if she misspoke or added her own misguided interpretation?

Why did They need *her*?

What was she supposed to prevent now?

"Canace," Gillian said slowly, "Melanie was raised to all this. I don't know anything about the Four. How am I supposed to help you communicate?"

"Treat us like your students," Canace said. "Teach us to speak clearly. Help us to understand each other."

"Why *me*, Canace? How can you be sure I'm right this time?"

Canace squeezed Gillian's arm. "I felt you, through Melanie. We're all connected. The Earth sensed you a year ago and asked the Wind to watch you. I've been observing you, making sure you were . . . expressive enough. You've grown stronger and stronger in that time—not strong enough, but when Melanie fled . . . well, the Earth went mad and I thought it might be wise to protect you."

"Protect me?" Gillian said. "Why isn't the Wind trying to rush me into this like the rest of Them? She must be just as hurt and crazy as the Others."

"The Wind has more contact with humans than the other Three. She has more contact with *you*. Every breath you take, you hold a piece of the Wind. That contact makes Her more understanding and more patient."

Gillian tongued her front teeth. "Then Her pain doesn't come from a lack of people, but from not communicating with the Others."

"Exactly!" Canace sniffed. "Although She's not too thrilled with the pollutants humans insist on spewing—oh my God!"

Canace sprinted to where Dera sprawled across the sidewalk, hands cupped to the cloudless sky, sienna hair trickling across her narrow, sunken face.

SIXTEEN

CANACE SAT ON THE SIDEWALK, CRADLING THE UNCON-
scious Dera in her arms. Gillian set her bicycle down and
sank to her knees beside them. Canace's fingers crept
along Dera's throat until they found a pulse. With a shallow laugh, Canace hugged the still form to her chest. "Still
alive," she murmured.

Canace brushed the matted hair from Dera's face. Gillian gasped.

Dera's face, wasted and drawn the day before, was now
little more than a skull, the eye sockets and chin sharp
ridges under a thin sheet of skin. Her chapped lips
stretched across the cobbles of her teeth. Canace stroked
the prominent jawbone. Flakes of skin puffed beneath her
fingers.

"What—what's happened to her?" Gillian said. "Yesterday . . . she didn't look fine, but she didn't look dead.
Canace—"

"She shouldn't be here," Canace said. She stroked the
taut brow. "It's killing her, being this close to the sea.
Help me wake her. You'll have to take her back. I'll take
you to the Ocean tomorrow—"

"Take me today," Dera whispered. Her eyes fluttered
open. "Today. You promised."

Canace sagged. "I never promised to take you to the

sea. I promised to talk to the Ocean for you. Dera, I'm
sending you home with Gillian—''

"It's too late, Canace." Dera struggled to sit up. She
dropped back panting. "Two more fell this morning. I
can't stand by and watch anymore."

We lost nine yesterday. Gillian rubbed the chill bumps
from her arms. Eleven people . . . or were they people?

Dera's body bowed with a sharp intake of breath.

"Tell me what to do," Gillian said. Taking Dera's hand,
she met Canace's gaze. "Where is home? Where do I take
her?"

Canace slapped Gillian's hand away. "Don't touch her.
You need to guide her back to the forest—without touching her. We've got to get her away from the sea air."

Gillian inhaled, drawing the breath across her tongue.
No salt roused her taste buds. "We're almost a mile
away—"

"She's too close," Canace said. With a grunt, she rose,
lifting Dera to her feet. "And she needs water. See if you
can find some."

The levee rose like the rim of a bowl to one side—a
bowl of fine, arid dust. Gillian stood, looking at the nearest
house. A ranch-style home, its porch and trim had been
pulled away like strips of perforated paper. The walk
folded in huge, crumbling pleats. A red tag hung on the
door. The three nearest houses wore red or yellow tags.

"Gillian, anything," Canace said. "Toilet water, pond
water, anything but seawater."

Gillian recoiled. "She's already sick—"

"She's already dying." Canace draped Dera's arm over
her shoulder. Dera listed to one side. "Never mind. Let's
just get her out of here. The salt is killing her."

"It's too late, Canace," Dera said. She winced and
pulled away from Canace, bracing her trembling legs. She
straightened, her head held high. "I am dying. But the
others don't have to. When the Ocean sees me, She'll understand. She'll feel our pain and She'll send fog."

Canace's eyes flashed. She reached for Dera. "This is
suicide. I can't let you—"

Dera turned to her, eyes narrowed with intent. Her posture, her expression declared her immobile—*if* she wanted to be.

Canace sighed. "All right," she said. "But let us help you. It's going to get—"

"Worse," Dera said. "I know. I don't need your support yet. And no water. I don't want to prolong this."

Canace nodded. She gestured to Gillian to stand by her side, the side away from Dera. Gillian righted her bicycle and wheeled it across the ridged sidewalk. The three of them walked toward the sea.

Gillian peeked around Canace, her mind shuffling possibilities: Dera must be some kind of spirit. She wasn't Earth, Wind, or Ocean. A Fresh Water spirit? No, or she wouldn't be so parched.

Gillian glanced at Dera again. Tall, proud, the woman was withering away before their eyes. Her skin had shriveled to her bones; her lashes blinked over eyes dull as dust. Her hair hung in deep sienna scraps . . . like redwood bark.

Gillian stopped. *All of our roots are shallow. . . .*

Two more fell this morning. . . .

Dera . . . *madera.* Spanish for wood.

Gillian hurried to catch up. She plucked at Canace's sleeve. "She's . . . a tree?" Gillian whispered.

Canace shook her head. "A dryad. Her life and her sisters' lives are tied to their trees. And right now the redwoods are dying—"

Dera stumbled, pitching forward. Canace caught her by the elbow, steadied her, then wound an arm around the dryad's waist. Dera dangled there for a few seconds, then slowly staggered into an upright position. Strain creased her face. Gillian switched her bicycle to the other hand and hurried to Dera's side, ready to wedge her shoulder under Dera's arm.

"Gillian, no!" Canace shouted. "I told you not to touch her!"

Startled, Gillian pulled back. "But—"

"Have you ever really looked beneath a redwood tree?" Canace said. "Not much grows there, for some very good reasons. For one thing, redwoods leach all the water from the soil, every drop they can. She's dehydrated, Gillian. Do you think she'll be able to stop herself from leaching water from you?"

Gillian stared at Canace, then looked up at Dera. The dryad smiled sadly. "Listen to her," Dera said. "My thirst is too great. I wouldn't even know I was taking from you."

Gillian took another step back. "Thanks for warning me."

Dera nodded. They walked on, through broken, shattered neighborhoods, following the captured river to the sea.

THE BICYCLE'S PEDAL WHACKED GILLIAN'S THIGH, ENcouraging a dull throb. Gillian spun the pedals, positioning the offending one lower, but it crept up again as she followed Dera and Canace past the corner of Sand and Beach. Planks and churned concrete narrowed the sidewalk. A smashed Tonka dump truck twisted from under a block of cement as if someone had tried to pry the toy free.

Gillian shook her head and looked around. The streets had become increasingly more deserted for the past four or five blocks, the houses and shops more broken. "People's afraid of tidal waves," that man on the last block had said when Gillian called out to him. He'd been sitting on his porch, whistling and looking up into the sky. The house had wrenched away, leaving the porch in the middle of the front lawn like a raft on a winter shore. "Folks come creeping back," the man had said, "when the shocks get littler. Then a big one hits, and *pow!* All them people go scrambling for higher ground."

Gillian shivered. Tidal waves. She licked her lips, her tongue burning with brine. The air tasted of salt and rotting kelp.

Strangled gasps sawed the quiet. Gillian looked at Dera. The dryad sucked at the air, her shoulders quivering with the effort, then wheezed out a tiny sigh. Each breath sounded like it skimmed her lungs. Gillian's shoulder hunched. The closer Dera got to the sea, the shallower her breathing and the more plodding her step. If the dryad made it within sight of the ocean, it would be a miracle.

Canace shouldered a little more of the dryad's weight. "Dera, you don't have to go all the way to the beach. This is close enough. She'll know how important it is to you."

"I've come this far," Dera said. Her voice scraped across Gillian's ears. "I will see Her. She must send fog."

Gillian guided her bicycle to the street, then jogged up alongside Canace. "Isn't there anything I can do?" Gillian said.

Canace hissed between her teeth. "No. The salt is drawing the moisture from her pores. There isn't enough water to stop that. How much farther is it to the beach?"

Gillian studied the intersection. Marduga Avenue ... Laundromat, mom-and-pop market, T-shirt store, the weather-beaten Driftwood apartments. At the next intersection, Playa Street ran perpendicular to Beach. . . .

Gillian pointed. "Right there, then a quick left on Beach."

Canace nodded. She turned to Dera. "We're almost there."

The dryad shuddered with another breath, then smiled. "Good."

CANACE AND DERA HALTED BEFORE THE ROUGH GRAY stone of the seawall. A ragged palm tree swayed above them, one of eight that lined the beach. Behind them, across the street, a chain of whitewashed villas slumped, their Mediterranean splendor faded even before the earthquake toppled them from their foundations. "This is close enough," Canace said.

Gillian joined them, leaning her bicycle against the wall. Cupping a hand over her eyes, she squinted at the brightness of sea and sand. Salt clung to the breeze and coated her upper lip. Blue-green waves slammed and clawed the beach, each concussion punctuated by the hiss of yellowed foam. A man and woman combed the beach, five children between the ages of four and eleven trailing after them like sandpipers. Wandering in the opposite direction, a man in gray coveralls and a panama hat swept the beach with a metal detector, dodging the kelp and driftwood flung like streamers across the sand.

Some of the driftwood was yellow and white, blue and pink. One piece, a porch railing, stretched like train tracks across a ramp of seaweed. Gillian's breath whistled between her teeth.

Dera gasped and hacked, the cough scraping through her lungs. Her body spasmed as she sucked at the air, but her lungs seemed to expel it without filling. She leaned against the seawall and stared at the waves, her eyes yellowed and lusterless. Her hands slipped. Canace caught her, then propped her against the rough stone.

"Wait here," Canace said. "The Ocean will come this far."

"No," Dera wheezed. "I must . . . prove to Her . . . how serious I am."

Canace's voice broke. "Dera, She knows. She *knows.*"

Gillian touched Canace's arm. "Canace, if She knows, why hasn't She sent them fog?"

The crash of the waves drowned the dryad's airless laugh.

Canace looked away. "If the Ocean sent the redwoods relief, She'd also have to send the Earth and the humans relief. Her pain is too great. She's lashing out, just like the Earth."

"But that's not—" Gillian began.

"Fair?" Canace finished. "No. That's why the Four need to talk. That's why They need a common language."

Gillian's shoulders hunched. *A common language. Me.*

Gillian faced the land, afraid to ask more right now. She gazed at the house across the T-intersection from the Mediterranean villas. An older house, it poured into the street, a spring of crumbled cement and brick. A twisted chair floated on top of the rubble.

"Dera!" Canace shouted.

Gillian swung back to the beach.

"You're too weak," Canace said, easing Dera down

from the top of the wall. "There's a stairway further down—"

"Too far," Dera whispered. She struggled to remount the wall.

Canace hesitated, then boosted the frail dryad onto the stones. Dera slumped forward, panting shallowly, then smiled. "She comes," she said.

Gillian walked over beside Dera and pressed against the seawall. A wave rushed toward the shore, rising in a curl of green and white. As the wave began to fold in on itself, a blue-green figure stepped from the curl. The wave crashed in a swirl of foam. The figure walked toward shore, its shimmering body turning from sea green to palest peach. A sheath of tattered lavender cloth clung to rounded breasts and hips, dripped between short, powerful legs. Long black hair twisted down the woman's back like wet rope. Every hair, every pore on her body glistened as if fog-kissed.

Dera laughed until she choked. "Oh, Canace," she whispered. "She comes."

The woman walked toward them, her gaze fixed on Dera. The dryad scooted closer to the edge of the wall only to lose her balance. She flailed toward the sand. Gillian caught her arm, jerking her back onto the wall. Canace cried out, winding her arms around Dera's waist. She anchored Dera to her perch.

Gillian let go. Chapped and dry, her palms ached. She rubbed them against her thighs, releasing a flurry of dried skin. Thirst burned through her.

Canace hissed. "Gillian, I warned you—"

"I'm not going to watch her fall," Gillian said. A bitter tang coated her mouth like the aftertaste of strong black tea.

Canace pressed her lips together.

"Thank you," Dera said, then doubled over in a fit of coughing.

The vibrant scent of the sea grew stronger, the scent of salt water, kelp, and baked sand. The Ocean spirit stopped in front of the dryad, her skin still sparkling as if faceted with dew.

Gillian swallowed involuntarily. Her parched throat ached. She sucked at her lower lip as the spirit placed her damp palms together and touched the tips of her fingers to her chin. "Dera," the Ocean spirit said, "has it come to this?"

Dera's breath rasped. "We're dying, Marea. The drought . . . too long. So little rain, no fog . . . please. Send fog. We can't . . . survive much more. But with a . . . little fog . . . ."

The glistening woman's gray-green eyes swam with tears. Her voice, liquid and full, reminded Gillian of a comment her high-school choral teacher once made: it was a voice that flowed too freely, a voice too in love with the song. "Oh, Dera," the Ocean spirit said. "If I could help you. I've tried to send the fog, but it evaporates before it crosses the sand. The Earth and the Fresh Water are too angry. And the Wind"—she glanced at Canace—"is a fickle ally."

Canace said nothing, only gazed out to sea.

Dera shuddered, clutching at herself. Dust rose under her hands. "At least . . . the Wind sends . . . cool breezes."

The Ocean spirit sighed. "I've tried, but I cannot persuade the Fresh Water to help me help you."

"We die," Dera said, "because the Four . . . will not work as one."

Canace massaged the dryad's hunched shoulders. "Everyone suffers because the Four refuse to communicate," she said softly.

Dera shook her head. "The two-legged . . . don't suffer. They bring water . . . from other places. They . . . shelter themselves . . . from the heat . . . and strong winds. They retreat before . . . the sea becomes turbulent and vengeful. They *resist*. We cannot. We—"

A racking cough cut Dera short. After it passed, she sagged forward. Her breath scraped like claws on slate.

"Even the two-legged can't escape the Earth's madness," Canace said.

Gillian shrank around the echo of Melanie's voice: *What have I done?*

What could Gillian do now?

An ironic smile curved Dera's mouth. "We cannot escape . . . the Earth either. If we survive . . . we must have water. Enough to soak the ground. To plunge our roots . . . deeper. Nourish *and* anchor ourselves."

"Even if I could send fog," the Ocean spirit said, "it would never go deep enough."

A moan escaped the dryad. She slumped against Canace's chest. Canace held her, looking over her bowed head at the Ocean spirit. "Send them a little, Marea. I'll help you—"

"And the Others?" The Ocean spirit laughed bitterly. "Without Their help, it will all be for naught. We need to communicate, as you said. Have you found a tongue yet that we can share?"

Canace smiled. "I have."

Marea drew back in surprise, then leaned forward. "Truly?"

Canace nodded, then tipped her head toward Gillian.

Marea looked at Gillian for the first time. Suspicion narrowed her eyes. "It's hard to tell by looking at her. How do you know that we can use this language to understand each other?"

Gillian's cheeks smarted as if slapped.

Use.

Canace's smile broadened. "This is the longest uncontested conversation you and I have had since Jamison died."

Realization flickered in Marea's eyes. A smile followed. "Yes," she said. "So it is. Do the others know? Have they tried to use it?"

Canace glared at her. "It, Marea? *It?* When will you get it through that coral-encrusted brain of yours that language, all language, is a living thing? *It* is a woman and her name is Gillian. She's met everyone but Fresh Water."

Marea shrugged. "I'll reserve judgment, then." She tossed her dark, wet hair and looked up into Dera's face.

Sorrow pleated her brow. "Why, Dera?" she whispered. "I am death to you. Why did you come here?"

Dera inhaled with a creak. "You are death . . . and you are . . . life. Send fog. For the others. It's too late . . . for me. I am tired . . . of dying slow."

A murmur scraped in Gillian's dry throat. "You've got to help her, Marea."

Marea smoothed her own brow with the tips of her fingers. "Is it still too slow, Dera?" she asked.

A dry sob escaped the dryad. "Yes."

Marea took a deep breath, braced herself, then reached for Dera. Canace hesitated, her gaze searching Marea's face, then released the dryad.

Marea pulled Dera into her arms, crooning softly to the bowed head. Dera jerked, uttering a strangled cry, then wilted in Marea's arms. Marea pressed her face into the dryad's hair.

Several minutes passed. The crash of the waves seemed muted. A breeze lifted Dera's auburn hair, tangling and untangling it. Then Marea laid the body on the sand. "Peace follow you, little one," she said. "Return in your time."

Humming softly, the Ocean spirit ran her hands the length of the dryad's body. She passed her hands over the corpse a second time. The desiccated form became the tip of a redwood, fringed with scorched, brown fronds and shriveled cones.

Gillian looked up at a shout down the beach. The man and woman were stoking a driftwood bonfire. A boy of seven stood a few feet from Marea and the fallen redwood, his hungry gaze flicking from one to the other. Gillian's heart constricted.

Gillian jumped from the wall and knelt beside the redwood. A piece of Dera had to remain, had to be given back to the world. Gillian snapped a handful of fronds and several cones free. She cradled the last of Dera in her hands.

The boy turned and raced back to the bonfire.

"What will you do with these twigs and cones?" Marea said.

Gillian stepped back. "Remember her," she said. "And when the drought is over, return her to the forest."

Marea raised her eyebrows, gazing thoughtfully at Gillian. "A compassionate tongue, Canace," Marea said. "But will we learn to use it—"

"Marea," Canace warned.

The Ocean spirit shrugged. "Will we learn to *understand* her in time?" She challenged Canace with a look. "Will we master her?"

Master her. Gillian bridled, but for once Canace seemed unfazed. Gillian squelched her own annoyance and looked to Canace for guidance.

Canace frowned. "In time? What have I missed, Marea?"

"Can't you feel it?" Marea shook her head. "How long have you walked like them? Fresh Water grows angrier by the day and you can see the Earth's madness. With both thwarting the Ocean's every move, the Ocean is fast losing patience." She sniffed. "We have no reason to trust *Wind* either. Of course, I cannot speak for Fresh Water or Earth. This is all—what do the two-legged say?—interpretation."

Uneasiness invaded Gillian like a column of ants. "What are you getting at?" she tried to say, but her voice came out in a croak.

"Talk to Her, ask Her for patience," Canace said. "Tell the Ocean—" Her gaze fell on Gillian. "Tell Her I need a week to work with the language so that she understands and can gather the objects she needs to teach us to communicate. I've talked to the Earth—"

"And Fresh Water?" Marea said.

Canace snorted. "Fresh Water is already taking Her anger out on them. Look at this drought. She's killing them slowly. They could barely bring in enough water before the earthquake. Now . . ."

Gillian touched her throat. Her thirst still raged unchecked. What she wouldn't give for a glass of water. . . .

"I speak only for the Ocean," Marea said. She smiled

at Gillian, a sudden and surprisingly warm smile. "You must be language. The longer I stay with you, the less desire I have to guess, the greater to be understood."

"That's a step," Canace muttered.

"I'll talk to the Ocean," Marea said. "I don't know that She'll be willing to wait a week. . . ."

Marea shrugged again, then took Gillian's hands. "Gather your objects, whatever you need to help us communicate with each other. If you need me, come to me. I must go."

The Ocean spirit squeezed Gillian's hands once, then dropped them. She walked back toward the waves, sunlight glittering on her water-beaded skin. At the foam's edge she turned. "Canace, keep the Wind steady," she called.

Canace waved.

Marea waded through the swirling foam. A wave rose like a door before her. She stepped through it and disappeared.

Gillian caught her lower lip between her teeth. Everything was getting stranger and stranger—

Canace brushed Gillian's shoulder. Gillian shrank from the Wind spirit. "Don't," Gillian said. "I'm sorry—I just—I need time to think about all this. Canace, what did I agree to? What did *you* agree to for me?"

Canace sighed, her face pale and tired. "You're right. You do need time to think. You've taken in too much too fast. Come on, let's go home. I'll explain the rest tomorrow."

Relief dampened Gillian's curiosity. It was too much, much too much. She accepted Canace's outstretched hand and let the Wind spirit pull her up onto the seawall. They hopped down. Gillian grasped her bicycle by the handlebars and wheeled it away from the wall.

"Gillian," Canace said.

Gillian looked up.

"You haven't agreed to anything," Canace said. "The decision is still yours."

SEVENTEEN

GILLIAN SET THE TUMBLER ON THE PICNIC TABLE, THEN rested her head in her hands. She squeezed her temples, trying to dull the headache. The radio announcer's voice bored through her thoughts like a drill: "... no aftershocks since twelve thirty-eight this morning—"

Mrs. Timako turned down the radio. "More water, dear?"

Gillian nodded. "Please."

Mrs. Timako filled the tumbler from an old plastic milk jug. Gillian fumbled greedily for the glass. Grasping it in both hands, she drained it in three swallows. The tannic-acid bitterness still soured her mouth.

A hand closed on her shoulder. Gillian looked up. Canace bent over her. "Sip the next one," Canace said. "Slowly. Gulping it won't make the headache go away any faster."

"I can't drink another one," Gillian protested. "We need to conserve water—"

"One more, coming up," Mrs. Timako said, refilling the tumbler. "Don't worry, dear. The National Guard is coming tomorrow with a whole convoy of tankers. KC and Jake are going to ask that one be placed here at the park."

Gillian sipped. Thirst still burned along the back of her throat. She chugged the water. How had Dera managed to wring so much moisture from her in such a short time?

The wind rattled the branches of the maples like rusty sabers. Gillian lowered the tumbler slowly. No wind would touch Dera again. *If it eased your suffering, Dera, welcome to it. Peace be with you.*

Lorna Chang jogged toward them. "Canace! D'you hear? National Guard's bringing in a bunch of water tankers. I'd love to inventory the herbs with you, darlin', maybe measure out a few for infusions and what not."

"Sounds good," Canace said. She patted Gillian's shoulder. "Mrs. Timako, pour her another one. And keep pouring them until she sips one or has to pee."

Gillian swung her legs over the picnic bench and snatched at Canace's shirt. "Wait a minute! We need to talk—"

"Later," Canace said, gently loosening Gillian's fingers.

Gillian lowered her hands to her lap, watching Canace and Lorna stalk across the white lawn. Gillian leaned back against the picnic table, suddenly tired. Her limbs hung like lead bell clappers, heavy and loose. Mrs. Timako handed her the refilled tumbler. Gillian murmured thanks and sipped the water.

Mrs. Timako shook her head. "You certainly worked up a thirst. What on earth have you been up to?"

Gillian took another sip, holding the cool water in her mouth and letting it trickle down the back of her throat. What *had* she been up to? She'd tried to pacify the Earth, been rescued by the Wind, walked a dryad to the beach, and watched her die. She'd met the Ocean and been hailed as the new language. She had seven days to gather her objects so that she could teach the Four to speak. . . .

"I'm not sure," Gillian said. She swirled the water. "A lot of running around, I guess. When did the radio come back on?"

"Two, three hours ago." Mrs. Timako sat down beside her, cradling the jug in her lap. "Aside from the National Guard, there's not a lot to tell. The north and east roads are still closed. The south is only open to emergency vehicles." Mrs. Timako raised the jug. "More?"

Gillian hesitated. Her head still throbbed, but her throat no longer stung with that horrible dryness. "No, I'm fine. Any word on Frankie?"

Mrs. Timako sagged, the jug dangling from her hands. "No," she said, her voice a colorless whisper. "Hiram and I went door-to-door . . . he couldn't have gone too far. His legs . . . he's such a small dog. He must be so frightened."

Gillian touched Mrs. Timako's knee. "Maybe—maybe someone took him in. When things get a little more normal . . . ."

Mrs. Timako covered Gillian's hand with her own. "It'll be years before things are normal again. But thank you." She sighed. "No. I'm afraid I need to face the possibility that Frankie might not be coming home."

"It's only been two days—"

"Two days." Mrs. Timako sighed. Her gaze turned inward. "The longer he's gone, the less likely . . . no, I have to prepare for the worst. I—" She looked up and smiled. "Well! And what's on tonight's menu?"

Hiram plodded toward them, lugging a cardboard box crowded with family-sized cans. The cans thunked together as he hoisted them onto the picnic table. Sweat stained the edges of his bow tie. "The twins here are pushing for chili," he said.

Beth Ellen and Bibbie swarmed past him. "You're back!" Beth Ellen said, running up to Gillian. She handed Gillian a stick fashionably dressed in denim and Spandex, a foil knob stuck on one end. "Like my Barbie? I made her head myself. Bibbie's is better. Her mom had a Styrofoam ball."

Bibbie thrust her Barbie in Gillian's face. The stick's Styrofoam head sported twig hair and seed eyes.

Gillian leaned back to uncross her eyes and examine Bibbie's doll. A smaller stick had been fastened like a T-bar to create arms. "They're lovely. How'd you get the arms to stay?"

Beth Ellen beamed at Hiram. "Hiram did it. He made their bodies and we made their heads."

"Yeah." Bibbie lowered her Barbie and stepped back. She nudged Beth Ellen. "Ask," she whispered.

"I will, I will," Beth Ellen whispered back. "You gotta do small talk first." She twisted her mouth to one side and looked up at Gillian. "We overheard KC talking and he said you don't have any family . . . well, you do, but your sister's acting like a—"

Bibbie elbowed her. "Don't say that word."

"I wasn't going to," Beth Ellen said through gritted teeth. "He said she's being a—a weenie, so you don't have anybody—"

"Have Thanksgiving with us," Bibbie said.

Beth Ellen gave Bibbie a dirty look, then turned to Gillian. "We want to be your family."

Gillian brushed at her cheek. She'd faced all the trauma without breaking down and now someone was nice to her. "I'd love to. Whose house—where is it going to be?"

Mrs. Timako squeezed her knee. "Right here, dear. Several people bought turkeys before the last big quake. Hiram's going to barbecue them."

"Lily's going to make stuffing out of bread crumbs and cereal," Hiram said.

"I've got some fruit cocktail," Gillian said.

"Wonderful! Oh, and KC said you love candied yams," Mrs. Timako said. "Gloria Hidalgo—the woman in the red house on the corner? Used to be married to a policeman? She has a whole bag of yams."

"We're going to have canned pumpkin, too," Beth Ellen said.

"Pretend pie." Bibbie puckered her lips and nodded gravely. "We got lots to be thankful for."

Gillian caught Bibbie's hand and held it. "We do, Bibbie. We really do."

"There you are!" KC shouted, swooping down on her from behind. His arms circled her, pulling her into a bear hug. Beth Ellen and Bibbie giggled. He hugged Gillian tighter, then let go. "I've been looking everywhere for you."

The sharp clean scent of KC's lavender soap clung to Gillian. She inhaled slowly, savoring it. "I went to Nora's."

"This morning," KC said. His fingers strayed along her shoulder. "I went by there after Jake and I checked chimneys. She was pretty cold."

Gillian winked at the girls. "A real weenie, huh?"

KC made a face. "Beyond weenie."

GILLIAN SET A STACK OF DIRTY DISHES AND SILVERWARE in front of Canace. Canace slid them into the shallow washtub, then swiped at her forehead with the back of her hand. A spray of bubbles blossomed over one eye. "Thanks," she said. "Silverware goes to Jake. Lily, ready for a rinse?"

Lily gathered up a load of dishes and carried them over to another table.

Gillian removed the silverware from the top plate. "When can we talk?"

"About?"

"Today. The Four. All of it."

Canace peered at Gillian through the dim lamplight. "You need to think about what you already know. Become comfortable with it. I'll look for you later."

Gillian set her teeth. "Canace, how can I be comfortable with what I already know when I haven't got a clue how all the pieces fit together?"

"No, you don't know how they fit," Canace said. "But you also haven't fully accepted them, either. Go on. Mull them over. Let them become part of you, then we'll talk. Until then . . . ." She raised her eyebrows.

Gillian scowled. "Thanks, Canace."

A smile quirked Canace's face. "No problem."

Gillian shoved her hands in her pockets and wandered away. Mull it over, accept it. Accept that she'd met spirits and been told that they needed her to help them communicate. Become comfortable with the idea that *she* was the only way they were going to communicate. Accept and become comfortable with the idea that *she* had somehow become responsible not only for the Four but for all of Rio Santo.

At what cost? She snorted. Wasn't the responsibility enough?

"Gillian," KC said, falling in step beside her.

Gillian looked up. KC's eyebrows met in a concerned frown. His cheeks hollowed a little beneath the reddish beard.

Gillian stopped walking. "Have you lost weight?"

KC's eyebrows parted slightly. "A little. I've been stressed lately."

Gillian gave in to a smile. "Stressed? No kidding?"

KC looked around furtively. "Don't tell anyone."

"What, this little earthquake?" she teased. "So all roads to Rio Santo are blocked and the downtown's destroyed. So the ground refused to stay still for several weeks. That's something to be stressed about?"

KC struck his forehead with his palm. "God, what a wimp I've been!"

Gillian slipped an arm around his waist. "I mean, if you're going to let something as trivial as an earthquake get to you—"

He side-hugged her. "You're right. Thanks. I guess what I really needed was perspective."

"Glad to oblige." Gillian waited a beat. "So what's *really* bothering you?"

KC opened his mouth, then caught her eye. They both laughed. Gillian snuggled against the reassuring solidity of him.

Their laughter calmed. KC's hand strayed to her hair. Stroking it gently, he fingered a lock. "Actually there is something else."

"Go on." She pretended to be serious.

Realizing too late that he was.

He tilted her chin so that she looked up into his face. His eyebrows met again. "I've been worried about my best friend," he said, attempting a lightness of tone. "She's been a little distant lately and I'm worried about her. I miss her.''

My best friend. Gillian tongued her front teeth. He'd never called her that before.

"We usually talk about everything, even the most painful things, so I'm a little confused,'' he said. "She's talked to me about the earthquake and her fears for her students and about her sister the weenie. But I get the feeling there's more to it.''

There is, Gillian wanted to say, but the words caught in her throat.

KC searched her eyes. "Her friend Melanie died and she hasn't talked about that at all. That's not like her. I'm not sure, but I think Melanie's only part of the moat she's built around herself. A small part.''

They gazed at each other in silence. Gillian's heart pounded. What a relief it would be to talk about it all, just lay everything out in front of him and get a good look at it, like she had with so many other things. Silly things, looking back on them. No, not silly, just nothing as portentous as this.

But if she told him about the spirits and the Four, he'd think she was crazy. And worry about her even more.

And if he believed her—

Gillian's heart skipped a beat. If he believed her, he might well be in danger. Who knew what the spirits might demand if they knew he believed? Dagan might try to persuade him to worship the Earth . . . Gillian cringed. Persuade him to sacrifice himself, more like. KC was not what the Earth needed, she sensed that much. Fissures opened in her mind, sucking KC into darkness.

And the other spirits . . . she didn't even know what they wanted from her—

"Gilly,'' KC said, his palm cradling her cheek. "This morning, I got this feeling I couldn't shake, this feeling that your life was in danger. That you were about to die. I started asking everyone if they'd seen you. When I asked Canace, she took a deep breath and stood still for a minute, as if she was listening to something far away, then her face went white. She didn't even answer me, just took off running.''

Gillian cupped his hand with hers. "When—when was this?''

"Around twelve, I think," he said. "I took off in my truck looking for you. I was going to follow Canace, but she disappeared. The only place I could think to look was Nora's. Then that last aftershock hit and I thought I was going to go insane. The anxiety just ripped me apart. Then I just stopped being afraid.''

A gurgle escaped Gillian's throat.

KC eyed her suspiciously. "You *were* in danger during that aftershock, weren't you? Where were you, Gilly? What was—no, what *is* going on?"

Gillian shook her head. *I don't want you involved in this. I don't want you hurt. . . .*

"It's not over, is it, Gilly?" he said.

"No," she whispered. "Don't ask me any more—"

"Damn it, Gillian! You've never held anything back. You've always been completely straight with me, even when you decided you didn't want—" KC flinched and looked away. "Even then. That's one of the things I've always loved about you, that honesty . . . that—that openness. I want to help, Gilly. Don't shut me out."

An image flickered through Gillian's mind: her parents' house, the flames climbing toward the open window where Mom and Dad waved down at her, Nora, and KC standing beside them.

Death will always be a burning house, she thought.

"Please, Gilly," KC said.

"I can't tell you anything. It's too dangerous."

"Let me decide that."

"No, *I'm* deciding that. You want to help me and I want to protect you." Gillian shivered, suddenly cold. She looked up, studying KC's face. What she wanted—but even the asking would change everything between them forever.

But everything had already changed. Everything.

Gillian wet her lips. "You want to help me?"

"You know I do."

"Will you—will you stay with me tonight and hold me?" she said. "Just hold me. I can't tell you anything. You'll have to accept that. But I'd like you to be there."

KC blinked, surprised, then nodded. He bent as if to kiss her, then drew back. "I'd like to be there," he said.

EIGHTEEN

"GILLIAN," KC WHISPERED.

Gillian squinted at him. Already fully dressed, he knelt beside the bed in the predawn gloom. Gillian tugged the comforter to her throat, covering her nightgown. "Where are you going?" she said. Her mouth tasted sour. "It's not even morning yet."

KC brushed her cheek with his finger. "It's after six. Jake and I are heading downtown at six-thirty. We want to be there when the National Guard arrives."

"Hmmm." Gillian leaned into his hand. "You'll be back in time for Thanksgiving?"

"Wouldn't miss it."

"Are you part of my family?" she teased.

A fleeting sadness crossed KC's face. "I'd like to be. Gilly, last night, after you stopped talking in your sleep—"

Gillian flushed. "I didn't. KC, I'm sorry. What did I say?"

KC shrugged. "Something about, 'He doesn't think of me that way.' "

Gillian slid a little farther under the covers. Talking to Mom about KC again. Gillian cursed herself silently. She usually woke to the sound of her own voice; why hadn't she last night?

As if reading her mind, KC said, "I thought you were awake at first, so I answered you. It was an interesting conversation."

Gillian wrinkled her nose. "Did it make sense?"

"Enough. It got me thinking—"

"KC, it didn't mean—"

He put a finger to her lips. "Hey. Let me finish. It got me thinking. You mean a lot to me, Gilly, more than you know."

"But," she prompted.

"But things need to change. It's too painful. For both of us."

"This isn't a good time—"

He withdrew his hand and turned away. "It's never a good time."

Panic spread through Gillian like red wine across a tablecloth. Not KC, she couldn't lose KC, too. She started to reach for him, then drew back. *Don't reel him in out of fear of being alone, Gilly,* she scolded herself. *If you reach out to him now, it has to be because you want* him, *not just someone.*

And if it doesn't work out? her fear challenged. *If you lose his friendship?*

KC turned back to her. His eyes held the sadness this time. *If we don't try,* she thought, *he'll be gone anyway.*

A friend, but no longer a close friend.

"You're right," Gillian said. "There is no good time. After dinner—can we talk then?"

Hope muted the sadness. He smiled. "We'll make it a good time." He glanced at his watch. "I better go. Jake's probably waiting for me."

Gillian touched his arm. "Good luck."

He bent forward, hesitated, then kissed her lips. It was more a brush than a kiss, but as sweet and soft as it was quick. He rose and hurried out.

GILLIAN POURED THE EIGHTH CAN OF FRUIT COCKTAIL into Lily Gerber's punch bowl. She sucked at her lower lip, trying to ignore the lump in her throat. The slick, shiny fruit reminded her too much of Nora. What was Nora doing now? Was she boiling potatoes over her camp stove? Nora loved mashed potatoes—

Gillian turned to Beth Ellen and Bibbie. "How many cherries?"

"Four—no, five," Beth Ellen said.

Bibbie nodded. "Five."

"Bibbie got it on the nose," Gillian said, reaching for another can. She held it up to the girls. "How many in *this* one?"

Bibbie's mom, Ms. Leeds, walked up behind Bibbie and tugged her hair. "These girls in the way?"

Gillian picked up the can opener. "No. We're practicing ESP. So far they've got equal ability."

Ms. Leeds smiled. She wrapped her arms around Bibbie's shoulders and folded her into a hug. "Got some beaters over there need tongues."

Wriggling free, Bibbie looked up at her mother. "Brownie beaters?"

Ms. Leeds nodded. The girls darted to the farthest table with a whoop. Ms. Leeds grinned, then called out, "Got to share with the brother!"

Beth Ellen raced back and tapped Gillian's elbow. "Six. This can's got six," she said before bounding away again.

Gillian shook her head. The can-opener blade bit down on the can with a hiss.

Looking out over Linnet Park, Gillian spotted Canace and Lorna over by the sand volleyball courts. Lorna stood with her hands on her hips, Canace with her arms folded over her chest. Both listened intently to Lily Gerber, whose hands fluttered and fell as she spoke. Lily pointed to the Trestles'. Lorna shook her head. Canace's frown deepened.

Gillian cranked the can opener. This morning's talk with Canace had been good, if a little frightening. . . .

Canace had waited till KC left, then knocked on Gillian's bedroom door and poked her head in. "You awake?" she'd asked.

"Yes," Gillian said, sitting up.

Canace stepped inside. "It's going to be a busy day today. Are you ready to talk now?"

"I've *been* ready. I've only got six days to do I don't know what. I can't find the objects if I don't know how I'm supposed to use them."

Canace crossed over and sat on the bed. She took Gillian's hand. "Tell me what you know."

Gillian took a deep breath. "You're a Wind spirit. The Wind is one of the Four. The other three are the Earth, the Ocean, and Fresh Water. None of you get along very well on your own—you act like you hate each other. You need a language—me—so that you can communicate. Apparently you haven't had one in a while and everyone's on edge. The Earth has gone completely insane, but that has more to do with imbalance than a lack of communication. Maybe the rest of you are off balance, too, and that's the real reason you can't get along. I don't know."

Gillian looked deeper into Canace's eyes. "I'm supposed to help the Four communicate, using objects of some kind. What, I don't know. I use storyboards and games with my students, but I don't think those things will help you. I also don't think someone helping you pronounce your *S*s and *R*s is what you're looking for either." She hesitated. "I also get the feeling that if I don't help the Four, something terrible is going to happen."

"Rio Santo will be destroyed," Canace said quietly.

Gillian pulled the comforter to her shoulders. "Why, Canace? The anger and frustration seems to be between the Four—well, except for the Earth. Why take it out on Rio Santo?"

Canace smoothed the comforter across Gillian's knees with her free hand. "Rio Santo is a special place. It's always been a special place—"

"Holy ground," Gillian said.

Canace nodded. "Yes, if that's what you want to call it. It's a place where the Four come together. We can meet here as equals—no one is stronger than anyone else. You said we act like we hate each other. We don't. But we don't trust each other because we don't understand each other. When that distrust and frustration becomes too great, we lash out at each other, like neglected children, hoping for any response, any sign that we've been heard. That's where you come in. You help us respond and hear each other so that we don't have to lash out. You're the words and tones and gestures we use to open up to each other.''

Gillian sank farther beneath the comforter. The hand caught in Canace's grew cold. ''You'd destroy holy ground—you'd destroy *us*—just to be heard?''

''*I* wouldn't,'' Canace said. ''But *we* would. Gillian, imagine a family that hasn't really talked or expressed its sorrow, joy, fear, disappointment, and anger for years. Imagine all of that emotion seething inside of each family member. It's poison, Gillian. It kills each person little bit by little bit, but everyone reacts to the poison in different ways. Some people explode, others withdraw. Others strike out in subtle ways—innocent by all appearances, but deadly.''

''Why destroy the house you live in?'' Gillian said. ''Why not turn on each other?''

Canace squeezed Gillian's hand. ''Because we can't destroy each other.''

Gillian shrank against the headboard. Her throat ached, not with the thirst she'd suffered after touching Dera, but with a dry fear. She forced herself to swallow. ''Canace—''

''Don't try to understand us,'' Canace said. ''Don't try to bring us into focus using a human lens. We're not human. We've learned from you, but we are not you. It's not your job to understand us but to help us understand each other.''

Gillian slid her hand from Canace's. ''What do I have to do?''

''You'll do it?'' Canace said. ''You'll help us?''

''I have no choice.''

''You have a choice. Say no, and I'll be sure none of them touches you. I'll get you away, to someplace safe.''

Gillian closed her eyes and drowned in that same sea of faces Dagan cast her into: KC, Nora, Beth Ellen, Lucinda,

Mrs. Timako, Jenna, all of Rio Santo—sucking and choking on dust and smoke. Dying.

"I'll do it," Gillian said, opening her eyes. "Tell me about the objects first."

Canace's smile barely contained her excitement. "It might help to think of the objects as symbols . . . physical metaphors for each of us."

"For things that remind me of the Earth, the Wind, the Ocean, and Fresh Water," Gillian said.

Canace nodded. "They can be anything. Jamison had a rusty beer can—a real pre-aluminum one—that reminded him of the Ocean."

"Okay." Gillian's throat tightened. "And how will you 'use' me?"

"Each of the Four will enter you—"

"Like a possession?"

Canace shook her head. "You won't be taken over. You're more than a voice. You're a language. Language is alive, it shapes the speaker's thoughts and understanding."

Gillian stared deep into Canace's eyes. "Is it dangerous?"

Canace hesitated, but did not look away. "It can be dangerous. There are those who abuse language. . . ."

Gillian stared at the can of fruit cocktail in her hand. Thinking back on the conversation, the same thoughts filled Gillian's mind: *Who might abuse me? Not Canace. But which of the others? Dagan? Marea? Fresh Water?*

With a jerk of the wrist, Gillian plopped the fruit cocktail into the bowl. Six cherries garnished the dollop of processed fruits. *God protect you, Beth Ellen,* Gillian prayed.

"They're here!" someone shouted.

Gillian looked up. KC pulled his truck over to the curb along the far edge of the park, a large, bulbous truck easing in behind him. The water tanker had arrived.

GILLIAN STOPPED IN FRONT OF THE LAST HOUSE ON TINKER Loop, a blue two-story Colonial, and squinted up at the sun. Not quite noon. Hiram had warned all the "messengers" to be back by one. "The turkeys will be done by then," he'd said. "No one should be forced to eat cold turkey on Thanksgiving. If you miss a few houses, you can always go back."

Mrs. Timako had pulled Gillian aside. "He's worried there won't be more than a taste of turkey for everyone. Here's your pad of paper, dear. Good luck."

Gillian looked down at the pad. After three blocks only four or five sheets of paper remained. She'd tucked a lot of notes into the cracks between door and doorjamb to let people know about the water tanker and the crates of food. A good two thirds of the residents had either fled Rio Santo or gone ahead with Thanksgiving plans—elsewhere.

She studied the blue house. Home or not home? Plywood and weathered planks shuttered the lower windows, from the inside. Sheets stretched across the paneless top-story windows, wavering in and out as if the house was trying to breathe. The chimney had disappeared without a trace. Someone had been here, but was he or she still here? Gillian walked up the fractured cement path and knocked at the door.

She waited. Turning toward the picture window, now a mosaic of boards and bent nails, she recoiled. A redwood burl plaque hung beside the door frame, the name "Kretski" branded into the rich sienna grain. Gillian's stomach soured. "Please don't let anyone do that to Dera," she whispered.

After another ham-fisted knock, Gillian slipped the pen out of her back pocket. Leaning against the door, she jotted a quick note.

Low voices murmured from the other side of the door. "See if she's gone," someone urged.

Gillian lowered her pen. "Mr. and Ms. Kretski?" she called. "Hello?"

The whispers started up again, almost rose to conversational levels, then stopped abruptly. Cautious footsteps shuffled to the door.

"Mr. and Ms. Kretski?" Gillian said.

The door opened a crack. A grim, black-haired, bearded face peered out. "You with the Red Cross?" he asked.

"I'm a neighbor—"

The door slammed shut.

Gillian gaped at the door. "Mr. Kretski! Please, it's about the water—"

"It's ours!" shouted a woman's voice, angry and shrill. "We need it all! We don't have anything to share—"

"We don't *have* anything," the man growled. "Now get off our property. We have a right to survive."

"That's why I'm here," Gillian said. "To help you survive. We've got a water tanker at Linnet Park—"

The door opened a sliver. "Water tanker?" Mr. Kretski said. "You sure you aren't with the Red Cross?"

"I live across from the park," Gillian said, pointing. "The National Guard brought in a bunch of tankers. There's one in the park. If you have a jug or something—"

"You bet we do," the man said, opening the door wider. "Dorcas, hand me that bucket. You stay here and guard the house while I get us some water."

Dorcas padded to the entry, bucket in one hand, hunting rifle in the other. "Go for it, hon. I've got us covered."

Dorcas shifted a little, allowing Gillian a clear view of the living room. Four kerosene lamps flickered in the gloom, illuminating two four-burner camp stoves set side by side on the coffee table. Extra fuel tanks flanked the floor-to-ceiling bookshelves along the far wall, as well as a drum labeled KEROSENE and a kerosene heater. Well prepared, Gillian thought, then blinked in amazement. Those weren't bookshelves; they were cases of ravioli, creamed corn, spinach, Vienna franks—

"My God," Gillian said.

"She's seen it, Reg," Dorcas said. "She's seen our supplies. That's it. Now they're all gonna come over here and plunder us. We've got to stop her from going back."

Reg squinted at Gillian. "Mighty clever trick, missy. Making us reveal our stash. There isn't any water, is there? Well, you tell whoever sent you, we're not giving any of it up, not one can. Not without a fight. We got guns here, plenty of 'em, and ammo, too, so you just tell everyone to stay away from the Kretskis.''

Gillian nodded, stepping back, then shook herself. She caught the door before Reg could shut it. ''No, wait,'' she said. ''I didn't know. There *is* a water tanker at the park and you're welcome to . . . .''

The words died on her lips. Nailed to the entry wall behind Dorcas Kretski was Frankie's tiny black and white pelt, his head still intact.

NINETEEN

A STORM OF QUESTIONS DRUMMED ACROSS GILLIAN'S mind as she walked the three blocks back to Linnet Park. Why had the Kretskis killed Frankie? Not for food—there wasn't enough flesh on a Chihuahua to feed a cat, let alone two people. Why, then? Fear? Were they afraid he had rabies or some other disease? Or had they simply been practicing in case they needed to skin something bigger? Some larger animal—

Flickers of vomit seared the back of Gillian's throat. The Kretskis wouldn't skin and eat a person. They were just two paranoids practicing their survival skills . . . weren't they? Gillian flinched, remembering the hatred on Dorcas Kretski's face as she raised the rifle: *We've got to stop her from going back.* And the determination in Reg Kretski's voice: *We've got a right to survive.*

Gillian walked faster. Just around the corner, half a block, and she'd be among friends, among people working together to survive, people helping each other. Her steps rang along the fractured sidewalk. How far would the Kretskis go to ensure their survival? Would they turn on their neighbors next? No, no—they'd have practiced on *her* if they were willing to do that. But if they got desperate enough? Gillian thought of Frankie's glossy black-and-white pelt stretched like a map across the wall. A map of hell.

Gillian stopped suddenly.

How was she going to tell Mrs. Timako?

JAKE RUBIO JOGGED TO MEET GILLIAN AS SHE CROSSED the park. "You went all the way to Tinker Loop, right?" he said. "D'you get everybody?"

"In person or by note," she said, scanning the park. Mrs. Timako talked with KC over by the tables.

Jake thumped Gillian on the back. "Way to go! Hey, KC! 'Nother three!"

Gillian smiled weakly and doubled back toward her house. Head lowered, she aimed for her front door. She couldn't face Mrs. Timako now.

Footsteps slapped toward her. KC caught up to her, slipping his arm around her waist. "How'd it—Gilly, what's wrong?"

Gillian sucked in her cheeks. "I found Frankie."

KC searched her eyes, then steered her gently toward the park. "Mrs. Timako needs to know."

Gillian planted her feet. "I *know* she needs to know. In my own time, all right?"

KC withdrew his arm from her waist. "Where's the body? Is it trapped?"

"It's tacked to a wall." Gillian hugged herself. "The skin. Somebody skinned him."

"Shit." KC paled. "She still needs to know."

Gillian nodded. "But how much?"

"Let her decide," KC said.

They strode across the park in silence. Gillian stopped at the first picnic table, resting her hand on the dinosaur tablecloth. A confusion of scents rose from bowls and steaming serving dishes. Garnet yams, barbecued in their skins, had been burst open to reveal their sunshine-orange centers, each crowned with a walnut. Mounds of mashed potatoes, a slightly wilted salad, several can-shaped cranberry sauces, the punch bowl of fruit cocktail—someone had even attempted a Jell-O salad. Not quite set, the red gelatin oozed over Mandarin orange slices. A stack of chipped platters waited for turkeys.

"Looks good, doesn't it?" KC said.

Gillian inhaled deeply. And somewhere—somehow—someone was cooking brownies and pumpkin. Gillian looked up.

Mrs. Timako stood beside Hiram at one of the barbecues, peering over his shoulder. He pulled open a huge ball of foil to reveal a turkey. "Just about," Hiram said.

Gillian joined them. "Mrs. Timako?"

"Five minutes ought to do it." Mrs. Timako turned to Gillian. "Yes, dear? Gillian, is something wrong?"

"Mrs. Timako," Gillian said slowly, "I found Frankie."

Mrs. Timako's gaze locked Gillian's. "He's dead."

Gillian nodded.

Mrs. Timako took Gillian's elbow and squeezed it. "Thank you. Now I can let go of him." She released Gillian and turned back to Hiram. "Hiram, just a little piece of skin—thank you."

Gillian's stomach lurched. *Skin.*

"Gillian, could you get that stack of platters?" Mrs. Timako said, pointing. "There's a dear."

Gillian brushed past KC as she returned to the dinosaur table. He handed her the platters. "After all that searching . . ." she murmured, then sighed. *After all that searching, maybe the relief of knowing is a kind of peace.*

Gillian set the platters beside Mrs. Timako.

Mrs. Timako smiled. "Thank you, dear." She picked up a platter and turned her back on Gillian. "Did he suffer?"

Gillian ran her tongue along her teeth. Was it really a lie if Gillian didn't know? "No," she said. "No."

A HUSH SOFTER THAN CANDLELIGHT ENVELOPED THE PICnic tables. Gillian helped herself to another spoonful of fruit cocktail. Seated beside her, Bibbie tugged at Gillian's sleeve. "More potatoes?" she said hopefully.

Gillian smiled and reached for the cracked blue bowl.

"There's only a little left," she said, scooping them onto Bibbie's plate.

Bibbie's six-year-old brother dropped his fork onto his cranberry-smeared plate. "No fair," he whined. "Me, too."

Ms. Leeds looked up from cutting a slice of turkey into bits for the tiny girl leaning against her. "Bibbie, share."

"Yes, Mom." Bibbie scraped a third of the potatoes onto her brother's plate. She twisted her mouth to one side and pointed at her three-year-old sister. "Baby, too?"

"No, Peanut," Mr. Leeds said. "You eat them."

Beth Ellen tugged at Gillian's other sleeve. "Are there any yams left?"

KC handed Gillian the bowl with a wink.

"One left," Gillian said. "I'll split it with you."

Beth Ellen's eyes lit up. "Can I have the walnut?"

"Beth Ellen!" Ms. Jansen said. "When did you start eating walnuts?"

Beth Ellen shrugged and looked up at Gillian.

"It's yours," Gillian said. She cut the yam in half and placed the piece with the walnut on Beth Ellen's plate. Hiram and Canace's sudden laughter broke from the next table. Gillian glanced over at them. Mrs. Timako leaned forward as if telling them a story or a joke.

A twinge of loss caught Gillian off guard. Nora leaned forward like that when she told stories—

Gillian lifted her chin. And Nora was still alive. All of these people, these wonderful people, were still alive. Considering all that had happened in the last three weeks, that was miracle enough. The only real casualty she'd had to face was the death of a small dog.

And Melanie.

Melanie. Gillian hesitated, then took a bite of yam. She savored the sweet, buttery flavor. Focus on the good, on the possible. She'd patch things up with Nora. It would just take a little time. And she'd work with the Four to calm Them and ensure that these people, that all the people of Rio Santo, were safe—

Until the Earth's pain caused Her to lash out again, enraged and desolate over Melanie's desertion.

Gillian swallowed. Perhaps helping the Earth communicate with the other Three would placate the Earth until Dagan had a chance to find Melanie's replacement. Perhaps by being the language, Gillian could buy Dagan and Rio Santo that chance.

A chance. That, at least, was something to be thankful for.

TWENTY

GILLIAN AND KC SAT ON HER TOP STEP WATCHING THE
evening fold over the park like the closing of a bird's wing.
The coming night allowed only a glimpse of the people
still drifting from picnic table to picnic table, gathering the
last piece of flatware, the last dish, the last saltshaker. A
few sleeping bags and blankets still patched the lawn, but
most people had retreated to the illusory safety of their
houses. Even Mrs. Timako and her radio had slipped away
in the first rays of sunset, accompanied by Lily, Hiram and
a bottle of Hiram's best wine.

"Do you think they're having a wake?" Gillian said.

KC rested his hand on her knee. "Who?"

"Mrs. Timako, Hiram and Lily. For Frankie."

"Probably."

Gillian tucked her hands between her thighs. She and
Nora had wanted a wake or a memorial for her parents,
but Pastor Drysdale, her parents' minister, insisted on a
funeral. "Your father talked to me at length about the kind
of service he wanted," Pastor Drysdale said. "It is best to
honor the dead's wishes."

Nora had seethed about it. "Right," she said. "Like
Dad always talked about death. That old fraud! The funeral
isn't for the dead, it's for the living."

"But maybe Dad did talk to him about it," Gillian said.

"Maybe we should just let Drysdale have his funeral. And we'll have a memorial."

But the funeral had been hard enough. She and Nora stood, still as towers, in the brightly lit foyer, amid fountains of carnations and sprays of roses. Gillian wore a purple scarf—purple was Mom's favorite color—and Nora wore a turquoise one for Dad. Together they clasped the hands of people they hadn't seen in years and would never see again. They clasped the hands of strangers and the hands of relatives known largely through Christmas newsletters and formal announcements. Friends and close family delivered kisses. It was all too much, too overwhelming, to think of planning a second good-bye.

The memorial consisted of Nora and Gillian and a pitcher of strawberry margaritas, trading stories from and about Mom and Dad over a basket of chips and salsa. . . .

And if I don't make it, Gillian thought, *does anyone know what I want?*

She butted KC with her shoulder. "I don't want a funeral. I want a memorial."

KC started. "Okay."

Silence settled over them again. Gillian tried to slow the rhythmic hammering of her heart. She could die helping the Four. If she wasn't the right person, They might well destroy her, as the Earth would have done if Canace hadn't rescued her. Canace believed Gillian was the right person and if Canace believed—but that wasn't enough, Gillian knew. *She* had to believe. She hadn't with the Earth. Did she believe now?

Yes, I believe—

"So what do you think?" KC said.

Gillian blinked. "About . . . ?"

"You're miles away, aren't you?" KC said, a hint of disappointment in his voice.

About us. . . .

"Sorry, there's just so much going on." She slipped a hand from between her thighs and took his. "I've been thinking. And I'm afraid—"

"We've both been afraid, for years."

"I know. But right now, with Melanie . . . gone and Nora refusing to talk to me . . . ." Gillian kicked the lower step with her heel. "I wouldn't know if I was getting together with you because I wanted you or because I was afraid of being alone—that didn't come out right. I do want you. I guess I always have. But I want us to get together out of desire, not out of need."

KC sighed. "There's always going to be something, isn't there? Some hurdle. Gillian, there is no good time. I've been waiting for years, but it never comes. Sure, I've gotten involved with other women, but I always find myself missing you."

Gillian shifted. "I know. I miss you, too."

"Don't pull away from me," KC said gently. "It's not going to get better. Eventually it'll dismantle our friendship—it's *already* dismantling our friendship. I just think we should try, Gilly. We've never really tried."

Gillian bowed her head. After her parents died. . . . "You're right," she said. "I don't—there's so much going on right now. I don't know how to start."

Or when, she thought. Would it be harder for him to lose her if they'd started something before she went to the Four? Or if nothing ever happened between them?

This was ridiculous. She'd be fine. She'd go to the Four and They would use her and she would be fine. She was language—

Canace's words whistled through her mind: *There are those who abuse language. . . .*

"I don't know when to start," she said, looking up. "KC, give me a few days, to clear up a few things. I can't tell you about them now, but when they're over, I'll tell you everything. I promise. Just a few days."

A guarded look crossed KC's face. He forced a smile. "Sure. I'll hold you to that promise."

Gillian leaned against him. "You better."

He put his arms around her. "Gilly, you can talk to me about anything, you know that."

"Not this," she said. "Not yet."

KC hugged her tight. "Okay. I'll stop pushing. Do

you—would you like me to hold you tonight?''

"No. Not tonight." Gillian pulled away and rose to her feet. "I'll see you tomorrow morning."

KC stood. "Not too early. Jake and I are going to finish digging latrines."

Gillian shook her head. "In people's backyards?"

KC winked. "I dug yours first."

Gillian feigned coyness. "Part of the courting ritual?"

KC bowed. "Of course."

He kissed her good night—shy, gentle, his lips warming hers before pulling away. "See you in the morning," he said.

"First thing," she said.

GILLIAN SQUINTED AT THE SOFT GRAY LIGHT THAT CREPT through the plastic-covered bedroom window. Must be at least eight. She'd gotten up just before dawn to use the "latrine"—KC had dug the ditch behind the three liquid amber trees—then crawled back into bed. Not to sleep—she'd hardly slept all night—but to stare into the darkness and worry. Not that *that* did any good. The spirits would do as they wished. And in five days—

Five days. And she still hadn't found any metaphors.

"Well, if Canace isn't worried," Gillian muttered. She picked up the scarf in her lap and tied the purple and turquoise cloth firmly over her head in gypsy fashion. Her hair clung to her neck in greasy spirals. What she wouldn't give for a shower. Sponge baths were fine, but there was no way to wash her hair. Reaching for Canace's oil, she daubed the scarf and a few stray locks to cover the grimy fur smell.

"Wait a minute," she said aloud. The oil—this must be how Canace found her at Briar Hollow. . . .

Gillian shrugged and added another dab to the hollow of her throat.

She got to her feet and padded down the hall. The front door still hung at an angle. Light oozed into the entry. Gillian nudged the door open, then stood in the doorway a minute, rocking her neck side to side to loosen the kinks.

"Gillian," someone said behind her.

She turned. Dagan stepped out of the darkened living room. Rumpled and worn, he slunk toward her. "Gillian, when are you coming?" he said. "To meet with the Four?"

Pain muted the light in his eyes, muddying the clear agate with a touch of wildness. His chin quivered slightly.

Pity welled up in Gillian, diluting her initial anger. Fear overlaid both. She backed into the doorjamb. "Five days," she said. "As soon as I find the objects I need."

He moaned. "Sooner, please," he whispered. "She grows more insane every day. I can't—I'm having trouble resisting Her madness."

"As soon as I find them, Dagan," Gillian said. "I promise."

He hung his head, then, with a low growl, rushed her and grasped her arms. The moist, warm scent of turned earth filled her lungs, spiced with fresh clover and mint. His fingers dug into her flesh.

Gillian tried to wrench free. "Let me go—"

Then she met his gaze.

"Come back to Briar Hollow with me," he said. "Promise Her it will be soon. Promise us. Ease Her pain a little. Gillian, She needs you."

Gillian stared at him for a few seconds, then renewed her struggles. "Needs me? She nearly killed me the last time! I'm not going near that place—"

"Please; Jamison went to Her. He soothed Her."

Gillian stopped struggling. "Jamison. The other language."

Dagan nodded.

"Where is Jamison?" she said. "What happened to him?"

"He died seven years ago."

A prickle ran the length of Gillian's spine. "Seven years ago? And there's been no one to take his place?"

"A complete language is hard to find," Dagan said. "Most of us have been very patient."

"Most of . . . ." Gillian stiffened. The drought had started five years ago. . . .

Dagan slid his arms around her, pulling her into an embrace. His breath whispered across her cheek. "Just talk to Her, Gillian. The hope might lessen the pain—"

"Gillian?" KC called. "I'm going downtown and I wondered if you wanted—oh."

Gillian strained against Dagan, but it was like pushing against the base of a cliff. "KC—"

Dagan's arms locked tighter. "Promise me," he whispered through gritted teeth.

"Is he one of the things you have to clear up?" KC said. His tone dripped bitterness.

Gillian wriggled in Dagan's arms, unable to see KC. "Yes—no. Not the way you think."

"I don't know what to think," KC said. His steps retreated.

"KC!"

"Promise me," Dagan said.

Gillian glared at him. "Let go of me—"

"What are you doing here?" Canace demanded.

Dagan released Gillian and backed away quickly. "I asked her to—I need help—"

Canace slid between the Earth spirit and Gillian. Gazing into his eyes, Canace hissed. "Is She in that much pain?"

"Yes," Dagan said. "I can't feel anything else. I can't clear my mind of it."

Canace shook her head. "Why did you come to Gillian? Why didn't you come to me? I can smooth away some of it. What can she do?"

Dagan closed his eyes. Sweat sheened his face.

Canace reached out to him, her fingers brushing his forehead, his cheeks, the nape of his neck, like a breeze blowing over the dunes. Slowly the tension lifted from Dagan's body and face. His eyelids fluttered open. The madness had retreated to a mere twinkle in the depths of those moss-agate eyes.

He smiled at Canace, then turned to Gillian. "I'm

sorry," he said. "I'm so sorry. I never meant to hurt you. I shouldn't have come."

He walked slowly down the steps, then turned. "Good luck, Gillian. If you need help, call on me."

Gillian slumped against the doorjamb.

Canace leaned against the wall beside her. "I can only brush away the topsoil," she said. She shook her head. "He's one of Her most stable spirits. I hate to pressure you, but I think a week might have been wishful thinking."

Gillian rubbed her arms. Dirt flaked from her sleeves. "So do I," she said.

GILLIAN PEDALED ALONG THE NEAR-EMPTY STREETS OF Rio Santo. There were more cars on the road than on Wednesday, when she and Canace walked Dera to the sea, but still not many. The drivers crept along, dodging piles of rubble, the grimness on their faces magnified by their windshields. Gillian slowed whenever a white truck passed, hoping it was KC. Pulling to the curb, she'd touch ground with one foot and peer into the cab. So far, no luck. Jake had said KC was looking for scraps that could be used to repair roofs. Judging by the debris strewn across sidewalk and street, he hadn't needed to go far. He'd been gone over an hour when Gillian took off on her bicycle.

She'd wanted to explain to KC—Gillian squeezed the rubber grips on her handlebars. She'd wanted to explain about Dagan. Which would mean telling KC everything. She'd wandered around the park in search of objects, waiting for KC to return. Bibbie and Beth Ellen trailed after her, chattering and playing. Bibbie had found two Power Rangers—one red, one black—and the girls dressed and redressed the action figures in Barbie clothes. Their voices calmed Gillian until she looked up from sifting the sand in the volleyball court and saw the red Power Ranger dancing on the court's wooden trim, its body all but obscured by a voluminous yellow prom dress and Bibbie's hand. . . .

Gillian shook her head. Trevor and Rafael had used Power Rangers once to scare Lucinda. They'd backed her

into the far corner of the speech room with the action figures after Gillian stepped outside for a minute with the
principal. Gillian had come back inside to find Lucinda
holding her stuffed bunny in front of her like a crucifix,
trying to ward off the taunts of the boys. "Him'th mean,"
Lucinda said, pointing at the green Power Ranger. She
pointed at the red. "And him'th meaner. . . ."

"Oh, Barbie, you look so pretty!" Beth Ellen said, hop-
ping her Power Ranger in time with the words.

"Thanks," Bibbie said.

Gillian watched the two girls in frustrated horror. Beth
Ellen, Bibbie, Lucinda, Trevor, Rafael, Edgardo, Tess—
all of the children, doomed if she couldn't find the right
objects. KC, Nora, Mrs. Timako, Debbie, Hiram—everyone, all the people she cared about, destroyed if she didn't
bring the Four together. Gillian stared at the sand trickling
through her fingers as if they were the waist of some dis-
torted hourglass, then rose to her feet.

She'd gotten on her bicycle, unsure where to go, unsure
where to look. And here she was, cruising the streets of
Rio Santo, looking for metaphors.

Metaphors.

Gillian swerved to avoid a plank with two large nails.
Would she recognize the right objects when she saw them?
What if she became desperate and accepted anything that
vaguely reminded her of one of the Four? Would the metaphor work—or would all Four rise against her as the Earth
had?

She stopped as another white truck rumbled past. Not
KC. Pushing herself into motion, Gillian rolled forward
several feet, scanning the strips of dust and thirsty plants
between the sidewalks and the street. She'd recognize the
metaphors, wouldn't she? Jamison had chosen a rusty beer
can for the Ocean. "Think, Gilly," she muttered. "What
reminds you of the Ocean?"

Making a broad curve, Gillian swung around the corner
and onto Jamarillo Avenue. And stopped, planting both
feet, in front of the third house from the corner.

The top story of the brown stucco house floated in the

choppy, frozen waves of the lower story. Sheetrock and
splintered boards rose like spume around the warped, paneless windows. Chunks of plaster dotted the debris like bubbles. Gillian held her breath. Three boards had been
plunged into the edge of the lawn like pier pilings—or
tombstones. Black ribbons circled each. Black letters
fought the worn grain. SHELLEY. DEREK. TESS.

Tess. Gillian let out her breath in a rush. *Not my Tess,*
she thought. A memory washed through her: Tess snuggled against her, no less frightened on finding out that it
was Amanda who'd rattled the window and not an earthquake. . . .

Trembling, Gillian looked around, trying to get her bearings. If her Tess had lived here—Gillian's shoulders relaxed just a fraction. If her Tess had lived here, she would
have gone to Montoya Elementary, not Lowen.

But if Tess had been visiting this house—

Gillian rode on.

Death still haunted her. Anyone could die in this town
right now and she'd never know it. Gillian swerved to go
back the way she'd come.

Jabbing at the pedals with fast, hard strokes, she rode
to Nora's.

GILLIAN DISMOUNTED AT THE END OF NORA'S DRIVEWAY
and wheeled the bicycle over a ridge of sidewalk. A black
garbage bag perched on the curb, its sides reamed with
holes. Stray dogs, Gillian thought, then wondered what
Hiram had been doing with all the scraps and garbage gen-
erated by the meals in the park. Kept it far from the houses,
no doubt, to stave off an invasion of rats. Just as Nora was
trying to do.

The garbage bag settled, spewing a can from one hole.
The can's label faced her: fruit cocktail.

"Comfort food," Gillian murmured. Maybe Nora was
ready to make peace—

"Hi, Gillian!" Debbie said.

Gillian turned. Debbie padded barefoot down the driveway, dressed in a prairie-length flannel skirt and pullover

sweater. She grinned. "Nora taught me how to bank coals. It sure beats trying to start a fire with kindling."

"Yeah, it does." Gillian frowned. "Aren't your feet cold?"

Debbie wiggled her toes. "A little. But I just had to feel the dirt. I wish it would rain."

Gillian nodded. "Me, too. We could sure use it. Debbie, what do you mean, you had to feel the dirt?"

"Against my skin," Debbie said. With a curtsy, she lowered herself to the barren former lawn. The flannel skirt circled her. "Touching the Earth centers me, makes me feel whole."

Gillian stared at Debbie. Touching the Earth. In the late spring and throughout the summer, Melanie had often gone out into the backyard and lain naked on the dirt beneath the three liquid-amber trees. "Just trying to ground myself," Melanie said—then laughed and laughed at her own pun. Her face radiated peace when she came back inside. Gillian had assumed it was the stillness. . . .

"Centers you," Gillian said. "Gives you a sense of . . . peace?"

Debbie shifted a little. "Mm-hmm. And I get to give something to the Earth."

Gillian stared. *Why hasn't Dagan found you?*

"Nora says I shouldn't do it," Debbie said. "Not right now, when it's so hard to take a bath. She hates it when I climb into bed with my legs dirty. She threatened to make me sleep on the couch last night." She made a face. "I hate sleeping alone."

Debbie might be just what Dagan needed to calm—Gillian blinked. "Alone?"

Debbie sighed. "Yeah. But Nora doesn't really like it either, so she let me stay. She said it was too soon to move in together, but an earthquake's an earthquake, right?" She brightened. "Nora made a pie out of fruit cocktail yesterday. It wasn't easy baking it over the barbecue."

"I'll bet. . . ." Gillian's mind raced. Nora had dated a woman once, six, seven years ago. But since then she'd only gone out with men. . . .

"Is, uh," Gillian said, responding to Debbie's expectant gaze. "Is Nora home?"

"She's out back making soup with the Thanksgiving leftovers." Debbie giggled. "Well, everything but the pie. You should try some. It turned out really good."

"Sounds good," Gillian said. She leaned her bicycle against the house. "Uh, listen. I'm going to go talk to Nora. Keep touching the Earth. She needs you."

Gillian followed the side of the house to the back fence. Nora and Debbie . . . it made sense. Suddenly a lot of things made sense. Lack of long-term relationships with men . . . well, with anybody, really. Nora couldn't even get along with her women friends for very long. But that woman, the one Nora had been involved with—what was her name? Judy? *That* had been something. Brief, fiery, and devastating—Nora had withdrawn completely when Judy broke up with her, refusing to answer the door or the phone for three weeks. She'd used up all of her vacation and sick time at the law firm where she worked, and started taking unpaid days. Out of desperation, Gillian had let herself in with her spare key. Nora nearly burst a vessel. But Gillian's "violation" snapped Nora out of it. She'd had to leave the house to get a new lock. The simple act of leaving the house dissipated the shock of the breakup. She'd gone back to work the next day.

Gillian sniffed. How could she have forgotten that whole episode? Because Nora refused to talk about it. She'd talked about all her other romances—even some that never really got started—but her "lesbian experiment" (as Mom called it) suddenly ceased to exist in the present or the past.

But Nora hadn't even talked about Debbie. . . .

The back gate creaked open and Nora stepped out. She frowned when she spotted Gillian. "What do you want?" she said.

Gillian cocked her head. "Why didn't you tell me?"

"Tell you what?" Nora said, planting her hands on her hips.

"About you and Debbie."

"She's living here, because you—"

"Don't give me that," Gillian said. "Nora, I'm your sister. I'm your *friend*. Why didn't you tell me the truth?"

Nora's cheeks flushed. "I told you the truth. Debbie's living here."

"Because you're interested in her and you were afraid she'd leave town," Gillian said. "That's why you wanted her to stay with me. You weren't ready to make a commitment, but you didn't want to lose her. Why didn't you tell me? I can understand that. What were you afraid of?"

Nora raised her eyebrows. "Afraid? Of you? Why would I be afraid of *you*?"

Gillian's shoulders rose. She fought to keep the frustration and seeds of anger from her voice. "Not of me. Of telling me you're a lesbian."

Nora snorted and pushed past her. "I'm not a lesbian."

Gillian caught Nora's wrist. "Does Debbie know that?"

Nora turned. "I'm not a lesbian," she said coolly. "I'm involved with her now. I've been involved with men, too, remember?"

"And with Judy," Gillian said.

Nora's eyes widened, then grew icy. "And that makes me a lesbian?"

Gillian released Nora's wrist. "I'm sorry, Nora. I didn't mean to—"

"Is that too much for you to handle, Sis?" Nora said. She pretended to pout. "Poor Gilly. Need a label, huh, Sis? Well, why don't you just call me a bisexual, okay?"

"That's not the—I don't care who—I wish—" Gillian massaged her temple. "Nora, why didn't you just tell me? Instead of inventing this tiff about my not doing anything for you—"

"Tell you?" Nora laughed. "*I'm* going to tell Little Ms. Asexual about my love life?"

A cold, icy hurt chilled Gillian. "What is that supposed to mean?"

"Oh, that's right," Nora said. "The last to know. Wake up, Gillian. Poor KC's been practically salivating all over you for years and you never had a clue. Too busy building up a career and doing all your do-gooder stuff for kids. And poor KC's stuck it out because even when you date, it isn't for keeps. Anyone can see that with the kind of guys you go out with.''

A hard knot closed Gillian's throat. She tried to speak, but the knot hardened. Just as well. She'd been about to lash out, *Yeah, well, at least none of them were half-wits.* Why hurt Debbie to get back at Nora?

She tensed. Where was Debbie, anyway? This was not something Debbie needed to hear.

''Poor Sis,'' Nora crooned. ''Looking for a way to make your escape?''

''I'm looking for Debbie,'' Gillian said, turning her back on Nora. ''She doesn't deserve this.''

Nora's voice softened. ''No, she doesn't. And neither do we. God, Gillian, I'm—''

''Save it,'' Gillian said. She stalked down the driveway and picked up her bicycle. Nora's footsteps rustled the debris behind her. Gillian ignored them.

''Gillian, wait,'' Nora said.

''Not now,'' Gillian said. She turned and glared at Nora. ''You don't even know how things stand between KC and—'' She locked her jaw. ''For now, I need you to leave me the hell alone.''

''Gilly—''

''Back off, Nora,'' Gillian growled.

Nora hugged herself and took a step back.

Gillian wheeled her bicycle toward the street. Debbie still sat on the patch of dirt, eyes closed, face lifted to the sun. A blissful smile played across her lips.

Gillian relaxed. *She hasn't heard anything. Good.*

Gillian leaned over the handlebars. ''Debbie?''

Debbie opened her eyes. Her smile faded. ''Are you all right? You're so pale—''

''I'm fine,'' Gillian said. ''Debbie, you . . . really feel a bond with the Earth, don't you?''

Debbie laughed, surprised. ''Of course! Doesn't everyone?''

Gillian shrugged with one shoulder. ''Some more than

others. Listen, I know someone I think would be interested in talking to you. Maybe I could bring him by sometime?"

"Sure." Debbie frowned. "Why me?"

"He . . . shares a lot of the same concerns about the Earth that you do. He sort of takes your ideas a step beyond. I thought you might be interested."

Debbie's smile returned. "Definitely. Thanks, Gillian."

"Don't thank me until you've talked to him," Gillian said.

TWENTY-ONE

WAVES CHASED EACH OTHER TO SHORE, ARCHING THEN slamming the sand with webbed fingers of foam and spray. Perched on the seawall, Gillian swung her legs once, then dropped to the sand below. Her knees bent, absorbing the impact. She straightened and walked toward the crash and blow of the sea.

Scraps and wads of paper scuttled across the sand. *Like my thoughts,* Gillian mused. KC, Nora, the Four . . . Gillian gnashed her teeth. *Concentrate on the Four, Gilly. None of the rest matters if you don't solve that problem.*

Gillian licked the salt from her upper lip. What was it Mom used to say? *Think of each problem as an opportunity. . . .*

Well, this was one opportunity Mom never anticipated. Gillian kicked at a mat of kelp. "Mom, it's my opportunity to save the world," she muttered, bending to pick up a smooth, round stone embedded in the seaweed.

She stood, then froze. The world. When had she started thinking of Rio Santo as the world?

Someone touched her shoulder. "Have you found anything?" Marea said.

Gillian turned. "I'm not sure."

Marea considered this, her head tilted back. Water beaded her skin and hair, weighted the lavender sheath.

"We've been watching you," she said. "You seem pre-occupied."

Gillian ignored the spirit's sarcastic tone. "Who's 'we'? You and the rest of the Four?"

"The Ocean," Marea said matter-of-factly. "I'm just one current. Canace is just a single whisper." She sneered. "Dagan is the underside of a rock."

Gillian turned the stone over in her hand. "I know why Canace is angry with Dagan. Why are you so upset with him?"

"I'm 'upset' with the Earth." Marea glowered. "And Fresh Water. Have you met any of Them yet? Vile, moody spirits. Impatient as humans. Sorry."

"Understandable," Gillian said. She pressed the stone to her palm, then opened her hand. "You know, this rock reminds me of you. Funny, isn't it? It should remind me of Dagan or Petra. But it reminds me of you—it's smooth and it's hard."

Marea took Gillian's hand in hers, refolding Gillian's hand around the rock. "We helped shape this stone. We rounded it, smoothing away its edges and its spines. Why shouldn't it remind you of the Ocean?"

Gillian sucked her lower lip, then nodded.

Marea released Gillian's hand. "This stone came from the Earth originally. Or not so originally, who can tell? From Earth and Fresh Water, from Earth alone. But lately the Ocean made it Hers."

"Everything is connected," Gillian said.

"Everything," Marea said, "is family."

Gillian rolled the stone across her palm. A metaphor of the Ocean's power: smooth as the sea at rest, hard as the waves that shattered the shore. Smooth and hard and honest.

Like the stone she'd given Beth Ellen to calm her stuttering.

"You asked me if I'd found anything," Gillian said. "I have."

Marea smiled.

• • •

SWINGING WIDE, GILLIAN COASTED INTO HER DRIVEWAY, scanning the street for signs of KC. His truck waited next door, parked with its nose to the garage door. Gillian dismounted and propped her bicycle against her house. She adjusted her jacket, squaring her shoulders, then marched along the rosemary hedge. She'd explain, simply and quickly, what Dagan was and why he'd been there this morning, smooth things between her and KC. Clear her mind of that distraction so she could concentrate on finding the right metaphors. "Yeah, like KC's really going to believe Dagan's a spirit," she muttered.

"Better put that bike away," KC called.

Gillian stopped beside the hedge and looked around. Across the street, Lily Gerber chatted with Ms. Jansen and that woman . . . Hidalgo, Gloria Hidalgo, the one who used to be married to a cop. Children raced around Linnet Park in every direction—Beth Ellen and Bibbie kicked up geysers of sand in the volleyball courts—while Mrs. Timako and Hiram puttered around the barbecues.

Gillian scratched the back of her neck under the scarf. "KC?"

"There's been a lot of looting in the neighborhoods downtown," he said. "There won't always be an angel on your roof."

Gillian turned and looked up at her house. KC straddled the roof. He waved a hammer. "Sorry about this morning," he said sheepishly. "It was none of my business."

Gillian folded her arms across her chest. "If *I'm* your business, *it* was your business. I need to talk to you."

"Just a few more patches—"

"I don't have time for a few more patches!" Gillian shouted. "I need to talk to you now!"

KC gazed beyond her. The hairs along Gillian's neck tickled. She glanced over her shoulder. Lily, Ms. Jansen, and the Hidalgo woman stared at her, then ducked their heads.

Gillian looked away, sucking in her cheeks. She just wanted to get this over with so she could clear her mind and find the objects. "KC, I'm coming up," she said.

KC nodded toward the backyard. "Ladder's in the back."

"Lily, keep an eye on my bicycle, will you?" Gillian said, heading toward the back gate.

Lily waved her on. "Go right ahead, honey. I'll watch it."

Gillian grasped the string to release the gate's latch. Footsteps raced toward her. "Gillian!" Dagan called.

Gillian gritted her teeth. Not now, not here. She glanced up but could see only eaves. Which meant KC could hear but not see. She spun on the ball of her foot and marched down the driveway to meet Dagan.

Dagan clasped her arms. "Gillian, the tape—"

Gillian wrenched away. "Don't touch me."

Dagan clasped her arms again.

Gillian glanced at the roof. No KC. She turned on Dagan. "What do—"

She fell silent. His eyes were wild . . . with fear. His pupils swelled and contracted, their marbled coloring more intense and more weird set against the pale terra-cotta of his skin. He calmed a little, soothed by her attention.

Gillian eased from his grip, taking his hands in her own. She kept her voice low and even, as she would with a frightened child. "Dagan, what happened?"

Dagan shifted foot to foot. "Gillian, the yellow. You said yellow is caution—"

The back gate slammed open. KC swept toward them like a cold front driven by storm. He elbowed his way between them, forcing Gillian to let go of Dagan's hands. "Leave her alone," he said.

Dagan stepped back, confused, then riveted his gaze on Gillian. His eyes pleaded.

Gillian touched KC's arm. "It's all right, KC. Something's happened."

KC searched her eyes, his face betraying disbelief, anger, and finally, an uncomfortable truce between hope and distrust. He stepped to the side, flanking her like a stake beside a seedling.

She coaxed Dagan forward with a nod. *He could crush*

us without straining or open the ground beneath our feet,
she thought. *What is he so afraid of?*

"Start again," Gillian said. "You said something about
yellow. Yellow what, Dagan?"

Dagan leaned toward her. "The tape on the buildings.
Yellow means the building is damaged and might have to
be pulled down. . . ."

Gillian's uneasiness swelled. "Rebuilt if possible. Dagan, the house above you was destroyed—"

"Is this man bothering you, Gillian?" Hiram said.

Gillian started and looked beyond Dagan. Hiram, Mrs.
Timako, Lily, Ms. Jansen, Gloria Hidalgo, Jake, and Jake's
housemate, Denny, surrounded Dagan in a half circle. A
wary concern darkened each face. Gillian's heart tripped
once, then raced. Rent by the Earth's madness, Dagan
clung to the merest thread of sanity. Any threat could sever
that thread. . . .

She studied Dagan. He was too absorbed in his own fear
to notice her neighbors' defensive stance.

Gillian forced a smile. "He's not bothering me. He's—
we work together."

"Sure he's not bugging you?" Jake said, swaggering
forward. "I don't like the way he was touching you."

"He's upset," Gillian said.

Dagan grabbed her wrist again. Both KC and Jake bristled. Oblivious, Dagan pulled himself toward her. "Gillian,
the red tape," he said. "Tell me about the red again."

Gillian warned KC and Jake off with a glance. "The
building's been condemned," she said. "It'll have to come
down."

Dagan flung her hand away as if he'd been shocked.
"No," he moaned, "Gillian, if it does, it'll free the spirit."

A shiver spasmed along Gillian's spine. "Which spirit,
Dagan? Which building's been condemned?"

Dagan's shoulders hunched. "The Seraphim."

TWENTY-TWO

GILLIAN'S STOMACH CRAMPED AS IF SHE'D BEEN HIT.

"The Seraphim?" Mrs. Timako said. Her voice wavered. "I was married there, on the steps. . . ."

Hiram slipped an arm around Mrs. Timako's shoulders. "The Seraphim is owned by the city," he said. "It'll be months before those pencil pushers do anything about it. Years."

The knot in Gillian's stomach eased. She glanced at Dagan. His eyes glinted with cautious hope. Still watching him, Gillian said, "Do you really think so?"

"Of course," Lily said. "Besides, the Historical Society won't let the bureaucrats take it without a badger's fight."

Dagan's shoulders slowly relaxed.

"The city may not have a choice," Jake said. "If it's some kind of fire hazard, they'll pull that sucker down fast."

Dagan's shoulders rose again.

Jake's housemate, Denny, shook his head. "Yeah, well, nobody's doing nothing till the power comes back. Not in a disaster."

Jake snorted. "Man, we've been in a disaster since day one and look how fast they took down the Palisade. Six days. Just 'dozed it."

"Man, it's more disaster now than it was then," Denny said.

Gillian touched Dagan's arm, hoping to steady the rise and fall of his hopes. He started, then turned, gaze locked on hers. Jake, Denny, and the others continued to exclaim and chatter, their voices receding into a low, cacophonous background music.

KC bent to Dagan's ear and said in a reassuring voice, "The Palisade was privately owned. Hiram's right. It could take years."

KC's words seemed to soothe Dagan. The Earth spirit inhaled with a hiss. "*If* the Seraphim's not a fire hazard. Gillian, come with me and look at it. Tell me what you think, if it can wait till after you talk with the Four—"

"Dagan," Gillian said through gritted teeth.

He pressed his lips together, nodded almost imperceptibly.

"Let me put my bicycle away," Gillian said. "Then I'll come with you."

KC followed her to the garage. He lifted the door for her while she grabbed her bicycle. "You don't really work with him, do you?" he whispered.

Gillian glanced over her shoulder. Lily stood next to Dagan, patting the crook of his elbow, trying to comfort him. "In a way I do," Gillian said. "It's hard to explain." She leaned her bicycle against the wall and turned to KC. "If you're willing to listen, I'd like to try. When I get back."

"I'm willing," KC said. He touched her cheek. "Do you trust him, Gilly? Enough to go downtown alone with him?"

Gillian's knees locked, bracing against the memory of the chasm racing toward her. "Enough to go downtown with him," she said. "I have to."

KC withdrew his hand with a caress. "Take care."

Gillian took a deep breath. "You, too."

THE SERAPHIM LISTED TO ONE SIDE, BUCKLED AND BRO-ken like jumbled teeth set in a fractured jaw. Toward the front, one of the angels had been driven to its knees by a huge crack. A wide red ribbon fluttered between the pillars, whipping and snapping in the breeze. Gillian touched the Cyclone fence's chill metal strands. The old theater looked worse than the Palisade had. Much worse.

Fingers hooked through the fence links, Dagan stared at the mangled carcass of stone and plaster. "How bad is it?" he said. "Is it a hazard?"

"I don't know," Gillian said. She winced at the stairs along the far corner. The bottom step jagged upward like splintered bone. How could the city not condemn the building? "How much of the foundation has to be destroyed for the spirit to escape?"

"Not much for a little to be freed," Dagan said. "But for the spirit to claim full power, the whole foundation would have to be destroyed."

"Destroyed." Gillian crammed her fists in her pockets. *Great power dwells there,* Dagan had said of the land under the Seraphim. *That spirit is angry—very angry . . . after all those years of worship and care, to be so badly abused. . . .*

"Dagan," Gillian said, "what is it capable of?"

Dagan's voice grazed her mind like sand blowing over a dune. "Anything," he said. "Anything the Earth can do, but within a limited area. Open the ground and swallow people. Shatter roads, topple buildings—"

"Like a duck shakes off water," Gillian murmured.

Dagan's eyes flashed. "Exactly. And, if the spirit wishes, it can destroy neighboring structures and claim the power of the adjoining plots."

Gillian pressed her fists into her thighs. Gaping holes and red-tagged buildings riddled the blocks surrounding the Seraphim. Even the steadier buildings sagged under the weight of the yellow sashes. Radiating from the downtown, rows and rows of houses had crept from their foundations, many of them slumped and crippled. How many deserved a yellow or even a red tag and hadn't yet received it? Gillian shook her head. Few, if any, of the buildings within sight could withstand even a moderate earthquake or aftershock. How could they withstand an enraged spirit?

"Will it—will the spirit be able to move about freely like you?" Gillian asked.

Dagan's whisper escaped between his clenched teeth like steam. "Yes."

Gillian stared at the Seraphim. And what sacred person would the spirit appear as this time? An angry Zeus? No, Dagan said it appeared as someone people understood. Her contemporaries wouldn't understand Zeus. Christ or Buddha, yes, but both were such gentle Gods. Satan? But Satan was profane rather than sacred. . . .

A monster with leathery, pleated wings and fangs rose like an atomic cloud to fill Gillian's mind.

She cleared her throat. "I've got to get to the Four—"

Dagan slapped the fence, jangling the chain. "Gillian, if the city frees the spirit—"

"What if a frustrated member of the Four inadvertently does it first?" Gillian said. "The Seraphim won't be able to withstand another earthquake. What if the Wind sends a tornado? Or if the Wind and Fresh Water decide to join forces and send a hurricane? Hiram and Denny are right. The city's not going to do anything till the initial emergency is over. Look around you, Dagan. There's no electricity, no gas, no water. The Seraphim is not a top priority right now. But the Four *is* a top priority. For us. For *me*."

Dagan locked his jaw so tight it quivered. Finally he relaxed—a little. "Have you found any of the objects you need?" he said.

Gillian exhaled. "One."

Dagan nodded.

Gillian glanced at the Seraphim, starting to turn away when something caught her eye. She pressed against the fence. One of the stone angels' hands lay on the bottom step, a good thirty, forty feet away. The carved fingers curled slightly, beckoning.

Beckoning to Gillian.

Gaze fixed on the broken statuary, Gillian began to climb the fence. She ignored the scrape and bite of the metal links. Her mind clicked with excitement: a hand of stone, of the Earth, motioning through the air—the Wind. Motioning, communicating—as one would with someone who cannot hear. As the Earth couldn't hear, deafened by Her own madness. . . .

Dagan caught her ankle. "What are you doing?"

"The angel's hand," she said, kicking her foot free. "I need it."

"Gillian, you can't. It's been in the spirit's presence—"

"Which can only make it that much more powerful."

"Gillian!" Dagan snatched at her ankle again.

She shook him off.

"Gillian, I can't help you," Dagan said. "If I set foot on its land and the spirit senses me, it might try to use me—"

"I don't need your help—"

"Hey!" someone shouted. "What do you think *you're* doing? Get down from there *now*!"

Gillian turned. Nightstick drawn, a police officer had planted himself ten feet away. Gillian dropped from the fence. Dagan eased in front of her, shielding her.

"Take it easy, guy," the officer said. A ripple of tension rounded his square face. "Step aside so I can see the lady. Both of you, keep your hands where I can see them."

Gillian raised her hands. "Do it, Dagan."

And please don't split the ground beneath his feet. . . .

Dagan growled low in his throat. He moved to the left, his arms spread wide, palms toward the officer.

The officer took a cautious step toward them, tapping the nightstick against his palm. "We've had a lot of looting downtown. Lot of stuff's been disappearing. You aren't into that, now, are you?"

Gillian shook her head. This guy's nerves were strained. What had he had to face during the last few days? Gillian stiffened as the answer hit her: people like the Kretskis. . . .

"No," Gillian managed. "No, we're not."

"I didn't think so." The officer shifted, focusing on Dagan. Dagan glowered at him. "You know," the officer continued, "that fence isn't just there to keep stuff from getting ripped off. It's there to keep disaster tourists from getting into things they shouldn't and getting hurt. That slag heap there—it's a real death trap. So you want to tell me why were you climbing the fence?''

Gillian coughed, trying to attract the officer's attention. ''I wanted—'' A breeze cooled her flushed cheeks. ''I wanted to get a better look?''

Dagan laughed, an ugly barking sound.

The officer raised the nightstick into a ready position. ''Watch it, buddy. I want those hands where I can see them. *Now!*''

Gillian glanced at Dagan. He'd moved a little away from her, head twisting and bobbing as if ducking a mosquito. The breeze lifted his hair in a dandelion fringe. He swatted at the air around his ears. ''The hand,'' he whispered to a point above his head. ''She wants the hand.''

The officer's body tensed. He took another step forward. *Trying to decide if Dagan's a harmless nut. . . .*

Gillian eased farther from Dagan and the officer. Between the nightstick and any sudden fissures—

''I don't want to work with you.'' Dagan glared at the point above his head. ''I *know* it's possible, but it's also difficult and unreliable—and *I don't trust you.*''

The officer's jaw tensed. ''It's all right. You can trust me—''

''I will *not* go in there!'' Dagan growled. ''I don't know how much of it's escaped. You drop any part of me, let even a crumb of me touch its soil, and it'll absorb me like silt.''

''Whoa, calm down,'' the officer said. ''Nobody's going to do anything to anybody. . . .''

''You're right, you're right,'' Dagan muttered. ''For Gillian.'' He threw back his head, squeezing his eyes shut. And froze, his body hardening to dull, reddish stone.

The officer choked on a shout. Gillian took another step back.

With a pop, the stone spirit shattered, its surface a web of tiny cracks. Sand seeped from the rifts like blood. Then the spirit began to shimmy. A deep rumble resonated from within, erupting in a nerve-splintering boom. Dagan crumbled to dust.

The officer gaped at the mound of fine dirt. He shook his head, his lips moving wordlessly.

A gust of wind whipped the pile of dust into a reddish funnel. The funnel twisted and stretched until it towered over the fence. A face formed, Canace's face, and flowed into the contours of her body. Molded entirely of swirling red dirt, she gazed down at the police officer with flat, lusterless eyes. She raised her arm and pointed at him—

He ran.

The accusing spirit melted into a funnel again. Swarming through and over the fence, it drifted inches above the ground, circled the steps of the Seraphim, then returned to settle beside Gillian. The soil pulled away from the seething wind and formed Dagan. The whirling air became Canace.

Canace brushed off the sleeves of her overcoat. "Can you believe that guy? I've never had to go that far to get rid of someone."

"He was probably in a state of shock." Gillian arched her shoulders to release the tension. "If it makes you feel any better, you almost got rid of me."

Dagan looked hurt. "But Gillian, you *know* us."

Canace snorted. "All the more reason."

Dagan glared at her. "What is that supposed to mean?"

Canace ignored him. She reached into the right pocket of the overcoat and pulled out the angel's hand. She offered it to Gillian. "Dagan said you wanted this."

Gillian took the hand. It was heavier than she expected. She turned it over, examined each dimpled knuckle, then stroked the curve of the thumb. A feather wedged between the ring and middle fingers. A touch of the Wind or the Ocean?

Gillian smiled. "Thank you."

"I JUST HOPE EARTH LISTENS TO DAGAN," CANACE SAID as she and Gillian turned onto their street. Canace sniffed. "Of course, the way he explains things . . . ."

Two quick sprinkles freckled Gillian's nose. She looked up at the dark belly of the clouds.

Nothing. Not another drop.

Gillian sighed.

"You all right?" Canace said.

"I thought I felt rain."

"God, I hope not. That's all we need—" Canace stopped, a frown furrowing her brow. "What's going on over there?"

Gillian followed Canace's gaze to the small knot of people gathered between the water tanker and the barbecues. KC and Hiram flanked Mrs. Timako, both men leaning forward, ready to lunge. Lily pressed against a table, Denny crouched at her feet. To the side of the barbecues, Ms. Jansen anchored Beth Ellen to her chest, hand clamped over the girl's mouth. Jake Rubio swayed forward, then froze.

Gillian craned her neck. "Canace, can you see—oh, my God!"

Dorcas Kretski stood near the tanker, guarding a caravan of three red wagons, each overburdened with ten-gallon water jugs. A rifle hung from her shoulder. Reg Kretski stood between her and the crowd, his rifle aimed at Mrs. Timako.

TWENTY-THREE

"WE DON'T WANT TO HURT ANYBODY," REG KRETSKI said, his gaze darting rapidly over the crowd. "We just want our due."

Hiram inched away from Mrs. Timako in an obvious ploy to attract Reg's attention. "Just take a few jugs and come back when you need more," Hiram said, his voice high and strained. "Like the rest of us. If you fill all of those now, we could run out in a day or two. Who knows when the National Guard'll bring in another tanker."

Gillian winced. Of all the things for Hiram to say. . . .

"Then we're definitely filling them all," Dorcas said. She held a jug to the spigot.

"Survival," Reg said, sighting down the barrel at Mrs. Timako. "Darwin."

KC eased to the left, slow as a drifting feather. "You," Reg shouted, and swung the rifle toward KC. "Stay right where you are."

Gillian leaned closer to Canace. "Can you deflect bullets?" she whispered.

Canace frowned. "Can I—?" She smiled suddenly. "Yes. But not like this."

She evaporated like steam.

Gillian steeled herself. Having the Wind on her side might not be enough, not against two rifles. She squared her shoulders and strode toward the barbecue area, stopping well outside and to the right of her neighbors. "Darwin, huh?" she said. "I don't think people like you are what he had in mind."

The rifle swung toward her. Gillian's heart pounded. "Survival of the fittest," Reg Kretski said.

Dorcas sneered. "It's her, hon. The one who was spying on us, trying to steal our food."

"Having a gun makes you the fittest?" Gillian said. "Pretty sad. A real tragedy for the gene pool if social misfits like you have the guns."

Reg glared at her. "If I've got the intelligence to use one—"

"Don't listen to her," Dorcas said, capping the third jug and reaching for a fourth. "She's just trying to get your goat, hon. Keep an eye on all of them."

Reg tipped his head with the slightest of nods. He scanned the crowd quickly, then snapped the barrel toward KC. "Didn't I tell you not to move?" he said.

KC froze.

"You sure you want to shoot *him*, Reg?" Gillian said. She caught KC's anxious gaze, pleaded with a glance: *Trust me.* KC's eyes narrowed. He thought for a split second, then gave her a grim, thin-lipped smile.

Gillian tilted her chin. "You'll only get one shot before the rest of us are all over you and Dorcas. Why waste it on the tall guy? He doesn't know where you live."

The rifle swung back to Gillian.

"Dang it, Reg," Dorcas said, setting the fourth jug down. "Don't you see what she's trying to do? She's one of those sacrifice-the-one-for-the-many types. Even if you did shoot her, none of these folks're gonna rush us. They'll be too afraid we'd take out somebody else." She scowled at the crowd. "We will, too."

Gillian gritted her teeth. *Damn you, Dorcas.* "You've got four of those ten-gallon jugs filled," Gillian said. "That'll last you days, weeks. If you run us out of water, what the hell are we—"

"Watch your tongue there, missy," Reg growled.

"Gillian, please," Mrs. Timako said. "You're only antagonizing him."

Gillian wet her lips. Although KC's gaze fixed on Reg, it flickered her way every few seconds as if seeking reassurance.

"You better listen to her, missy," Reg said. He blinked and wiped at his cheek. "Don't antagonize me."

"You can't antagonize an asshole with an IQ lower than the calories in a fucking diet cola," Jake said.

Reg snarled and aimed the rifle at Jake. "Watch your language, you stupid moron."

Gillian straightened. Swearing. That was the way to light Reg's fuse. Gillian whispered a quick prayer to Canace, then swaggered forward.

"This is stupid, all of us being held hostage by this shithead," she said. She brushed a bead of moisture from her nose. "We should overpower them and go to their fucking house. You wouldn't believe the food they have stashed away. Cases and cases, lining their entire living-room wall. We could feed everyone here for at least a fucking month—"

Reg cocked the trigger. "Listen, missy—"

"Ignore her, hon," Dorcas said. "She's just trying to—"

"It's that two-story blue house on Tinker Loop," Gillian said. "Their name is right on the fucking door. It's—"

Gillian felt the concussion before she heard the shot. She had no idea where the bullet went. She imagined it caught between Canace's thumb and forefinger. Gillian locked her knees, fighting the giddy relief that threatened to topple her.

Everyone hung in dazed suspension until the echo ricocheting off the houses faded. Then KC shouted, "Get them!"

Everyone blurred into movement. Enough of a blur for Dagan to materialize behind Reg Kretski without anyone noticing.

Caught between KC and Dagan, Reg Kretski hesitated

a second too long before swinging the rifle like a club. KC caught it easily and jerked it away. He handed it to Lily. She held it carefully pointed at the ground and jogged toward the maples. Mrs. Timako and Denny lunged for Dorcas, who'd had the presence of mind to kneel behind the wagons. She raised the rifle into position. Jake and Hiram sneaked toward her from the sides. After thrusting Beth Ellen under the nearest picnic table, Ms. Jansen advanced on Dorcas, an angry gleam in her eye.

Gillian's scalp prickled at the steadiness of Dorcas's rifle . . . which was aimed at Gillian. Jake reached for the barrel—

A loud crack boomed, silencing the jumbled shouts. Something wet splashed over Gillian's face and shoulders, gumming her lashes shut. She forced her eyes open and scanned the crowd, frantic to figure out who was missing. She swiped at her damp cheek.

A flash kindled the distant sky. Within seconds another rumbling boom shattered the quiet.

"It's raining!" Denny shouted. "Finally! Something's going *right*!"

Cheers rose like startled pheasants.

A breeze tickled Gillian's cheek. "I pleaded with Fresh Water," Canace whispered. "I'm sorry, Gillian."

Gillian frowned, confused. Why was Canace apologizing? She'd caught the bullet—

Gillian stiffened as panic swept through her. The gun— where was Dorcas's gun? She lunged toward the Kretskis—

KC caught her arm and reeled her back. "Let them go, Gilly. They're harmless."

Gillian struggled. "KC, they're killers—"

"They're survivalists," he said. "They were just trying to get what they felt they needed."

"But Dorcas's rifle—"

KC pointed. "Jake's got it."

Grinning like a split mango, Jake raised the rifle over his head.

Ms. Jansen raced past them, dragging Beth Ellen behind

her. "When we get to the house," Ms. Jansen said, "I want you to get that old bucket—"

"Everybody, go home and get any pots, pans, casseroles, anything," Mrs. Timako said. "It's probably just a sprinkle, but we want to catch as much as we can. Lily, Denny—go door-to-door and tell whoever's not here."

"You want us to bring the stuff here?" Denny said, already edging away.

"It's more open here," Hiram said. "There'll be less chance of shingles and things falling into 'em."

Denny spun without looking and nearly ran into Dagan. Dagan stared up into the clouds, a stricken look on his face.

Gillian turned. The Kretskis crawled toward each other, the rain turning the dirt ground into their clothes to mud. They helped each other to their feet and looked around, shaken and bewildered. Reg muttered something to Dorcas. She shook her head. They trudged across the park, the little wagon train of water jugs forgotten by the tanker.

Jake hooted. "Hey! Reggie, Dorcas—you forgot your water!"

Reg's shoulders rode up. He flipped Jake off without turning around. Dorcas lifted her head and turned, glaring at Jake with the scorn of the righteous. "We don't need your tainted, chemical-saturated government water now," she said. She spat, then aimed her finger at Gillian. "You come anywhere near our house, missy," she said, "and I'll swear it was self-defense."

Acid burned in Gillian's throat. She swallowed.

Jake smiled and waved. "Have a nice day!"

Dorcas flinched as if she'd been struck. She elbowed Reg. They limped home.

As soon as the Kretskis turned the corner, Gillian's knees gave out. KC caught her.

"Thanks," she murmured.

A third hand grasped her shoulder. Gillian started.

"I'm sorry," Dagan said.

TWENTY-FOUR

RAIN BEADED GILLIAN'S LASHES AND TRICKLED DOWN HER nose. "Sorry?" she said. "For what? For getting rid of those monsters?"

Dagan shook his head. "Gillian—"

"You folks still here?" Hiram shouted. He clattered toward them, his southwester and yellow slicker shiny as oiled skin, a stack of copper bottom sauce pans clutched to his chest. "We need pots! Who knows how long this will last? We need to catch every blessed drop!"

"One minute," Gillian said, turning to Dagan.

He was backing away, skin mottled with rain. His gaze held hers. "Speak well of Fresh Water," he said. "She's in pain and no more responsible for Her actions than the Earth."

Gillian sucked the clean, sweet water from her upper lip. "Dagan—"

"I've got a roaster," Mrs. Timako said, joining them. She struggled, trying to pry the two halves apart. "I don't know how long it's been since I've used this. Gillian, be a dear and set it on the table?"

Gillian reached for the roaster. KC reached around her and took it. "I'll do it," he said. "See to your friend."

Gillian glanced at him, expecting jealousy or sarcasm,

but KC's eyes reflected only concern. She nodded and stepped back.

Dagan was gone.

Jake jostled her, loaded down with a wooden box of skillets and soup kettles. "Sorry," he said.

Gillian stared at him. "Why is everyone sorry?"

"Gillian, KC," Hiram said, "hurry! Before the rain stops!"

Gillian shook herself. "Right," she said.

She darted after KC, following him across the sticky lawn. His footsteps lifted patches of mud, revealing the parched soil underneath.

GILLIAN STOOD IN THE ENTRY, TRANSFIXED BY THE PAT-ter of rain. Her ears ached with a smile. How long since she'd heard such beautiful music? Five years? The sharp staccato tapped across the roof while a softer, stringlike *thwap* rustled the plastic that covered the windows. Trickling water droned.

She bent down and picked up the bottle of shampoo on the doorstep. She smiled at the rain again, taking guilty pleasure in the sheer abundance of it. The rain *would* slow repairs. PG&E would have a fit. And the phone company— well, the phone was hardly a priority right now. Food, water, shelter—those were priorities. And power. Power would be nice. She splashed down the front steps and onto the lawn.

Tipping her face to the sky, Gillian let the rain sluice over her. It tugged at her waterlogged jacket and coursed down her jeans. The faint stench of grease, smoke, and mud flared her nostrils: dirty hair. She touched her head, wrinkling her nose when her fingers met damp, oily cloth. She ripped the scarf from her head and shook her hair free.

She squeezed shampoo into her cupped palm. Leaning over, she worked the thick, pear-scented liquid through her hair. White froth plashed onto the cement walk.

"Sometimes you have to take care of yourself," Canace said, "before you can take care of everyone else."

Still bent over, Gillian cocked her head and looked up

into Canace's drawn face. A kindliness tempered the urgency in her gray eyes. Gillian scrubbed at her scalp, hurrying the shampoo from her hair. "I'll only be a minute," she said. "Where did you go? I've been looking for you."

"Take your time," Canace said. Stiffened by the rain, her short, dark hair stuck out like quills. "This may be your last chance to pamper yourself for a long time."

Gillian squeezed the excess moisture from her hair. "What do you mean?"

"I can't promise you a week. The others—" Canace scowled. "Gillian, you need to find the other metaphors. Soon. Before another member of the Four lashes out."

Gillian straightened. "Canace, I can't find metaphors when I'm actively looking for them—"

"I know, I know. I know. Unless they surprise and delight you, they ring false—especially to the Four. But, Gillian, be open."

"That's like saying, 'Pick a rose without looking at it, but don't get pricked by the thorns.' "

Canace smiled crookedly. "I know." She sobered. "I can't promise you it won't be the Wind that lashes out next."

Gillian wrapped her sodden arms around herself. Water oozed from her jacket. "How long do you think?" she said, searching Canace's eyes.

"Four more days. Maybe less."

Gillian squeezed herself tighter. "I'll find them."

Canace held her gaze a half minute longer, then nodded. "Get inside, Gillian," she said gently. "Get warm. Lorna's boy has a cold. So do two other kids—and Pablo Guzman, the man who lives next door to Lily. Nick Trestle is running a fever. With all the trauma and this wet chill, it won't be long before a lot more people get sick."

Canace turned and walked toward the street.

"Where are you going?" Gillian called.

Canace waved without looking back. "To help Lorna with Nick. And to get out of your way."

Gillian hovered like a feather over a vent, then slogged next door to KC's. After a quick rap, she turned to watch

Canace cross the park. Rain swirled around Canace, dogging her every step.

The door opened. Gillian swung to face KC.

"I was just coming to get you," he said, ushering her in. "I'm heating up some soup. I thought you and Canace might like to join me for dinner."

Gillian glanced at Canace one last time. "Canace is busy," she said, "but I'd love to."

RAIN LASHED AT THE PLASTIC TACKED OVER KC'S WINDOWS. Three white tapers illuminated a small circle in the middle of the living room, the light barely touching the boxes and furniture lining the walls. At Gillian's request, a huge baking sheet stretched beneath the candles to catch any drips—or falling wicks. Zipped into sleeping bags, Gillian and KC leaned against the back of the sofa, as far from the erratic flickering as possible.

KC's silence gnawed at Gillian. He'd asked a few questions, but had said nothing to indicate whether or not he believed a word of what she'd told him. She had to admit the whole thing sounded like a demented bedtime story: *And then the angry Earth said, "Starve me and I'll cast your houses to the ground!"*

"How are the Four going to 'use' you?" KC asked.

"I don't know." Gillian tilted her head back, peering at the candles from under her lashes. "Canace has been pretty vague—"

Gillian tensed as the middle taper flared suddenly. She imagined Mom and Dad gazing mournfully at her from the candle's halo. She slid deeper into her bag.

KC shifted beside her. "You believe all this?"

There it was, the skepticism she'd expected. Gillian pulled away. "Yes, I do. I've seen what the Earth can do—"

"Hey," KC said. "I'm not doubting you. It's just—" He tugged gently at the cord on her sleeping bag. "Gilly, from the sounds of it, if *you* don't believe, you could get hurt—"

"Killed."

KC inhaled with a hiss.

Gillian stared at the tapers. The middle one flickered again, the flame bending in an unfelt draft. Gillian sat up suddenly and stared. The flame twisted around itself, winking at the dark, shimmying. To either side, the other two candles burned steadily, but this middle one wriggled and reached for the Wind. . . .

They spoke at once:

"I want to—"

"Can I—"

"—help you."

"—have that candle?"

KC blinked. "The candle? Sure."

Gillian shrugged her shoulders free of the bag and crawled toward the tapers. She balked, then reached for the middle one. The flame leaped and pirouetted, dancing like an autumn leaf spun by the Wind. Gillian blew it out. Smoke twisted and rose. The stiff, black wick spiked like Canace's hair.

The wax taper was smooth to the touch. Gillian couldn't decide whether it reminded her of stone or ice. It hardly mattered. She didn't have to understand the metaphor all at once.

GILLIAN PUSHED OPEN HER FRONT DOOR AND STEPPED IN-side. She combed the water from her hair with her fingers, then turned and leaned against the door frame. Swollen gray light suffused the early morning, as solid as clouds. Raindrops skittered and hopped across the street, gamboled along the sidewalks, hammered at the soil.

Gillian inhaled, savoring a wet, clean breath. A few more hours of this and Rio Santo would have plenty of water—assuming everyone took advantage of it. Across the street, pots, soup kettles, bowls, and pans dotted Linnet Park like some vineless pumpkin patch. Gillian smiled.

Canace padded into the entry, arms folded over her chest. "You were at KC's?"

"Yeah." Gillian reached into her pocket and pulled out the candle.

Canace raised her eyebrows. "The Wind?"

Gillian nodded.

Canace's smile broadened. "I like it. Fresh Water . . . ?"

"Not yet." Gillian put the candle back in her pocket. "How's Nick?"

"Not good. He keeps complaining he can't swallow. Lorna's afraid he's got strep."

Gillian touched her throat. "Canace, if that spreads—"

"Tell me about it. We've got him confined to his bedroom. Marjorie—his wife—refuses to stay away from him, but we convinced her to send the kids over to Lorna's." Canace shook her head. "We may have to take him to the hospital or an emergency clinic."

"Why haven't you?"

Canace gritted her teeth. "Those places have got to be a zoo. With everything else going on, who knows when a doctor would get a chance to even look at him? Besides, this way, we can keep him isolated."

The slosh and splash of booted feet tramped toward them. Hiram hailed them from under a maroon umbrella. "Hey, Gillian, Canace."

Mrs. Timako peered at them through the clear plastic sides of a bell umbrella. "Since we can't use the barbecues while it's raining, we're organizing indoor meals. Do you have a camp stove?"

"Not a thing," Gillian said.

Mrs. Timako poked Hiram. "There, you see?" she said, then looked up at Gillian and Canace. "You girls will be coming over to my house. Lunch at eleven, dinner at four?"

"Sounds good," Canace said.

Gillian nodded. "Perfect. Do we need to bring anything? Plates or flatware?"

"No, dear," Mrs. Timako said. "Just yourselves. See you at eleven."

Hiram waved. He and Mrs. Timako picked their way carefully over the fingers of mud clutching the sidewalk. "I can handle one more," Mrs. Timako told Hiram, "but that's it. Gloria's got room for at least three and I think the Guzmans can handle a few. Do you think the Leeds . . . ?''

Canace sighed. She lifted her jacket from its peg. "Well, I better get over to Lorna's. Keep your eyes open, Gillian."

Gillian watched her go, each step as quick and graceful as a dancer's. Or the flame of a candle.

THE FLASHLIGHT BEAM STRAYED FROM THE MOLDING TO the stack of books beside her bed. Gillian yelped as a fat brown spider raced across the light, diving for shadow.

Gillian clicked off the flashlight. An embarrassed laugh escaped her. "I am *not* afraid of spiders," she muttered.

Good thing, too. The rain had driven dozens of them indoors. She'd already found six or seven while wandering room to room, hoping some metaphor for Fresh Water would catch her eye.

This was the first spider that ran.

"Startle reflex," Gillian said. She clicked the flashlight back on. At lunch, everyone had checked in: Canace was tending the ill, KC was helping with repairs, Mrs. Timako and Hiram were feeding the hungry, Lily was watching Lorna's children—and she was sweeping her walls and floors with a flashlight, looking for metaphors.

Canace had told the others Gillian had been doing an inventory of Melanie's herbs.

Gillian chased shadows with the yellow beam.

Light winked at her, glimmering off of a plastic bottle. Like sun on water? Gillian groaned. She slid the light along the wall. A stubby, short-legged spider clung to a crack in the plaster.

What was the worst a spider could do, anyway? she mused. It *could* bite her. Fall into her mouth while she was asleep, get tangled in her hair—

Gillian shook herself. "These aren't my fears," she said.

They were Trevor's. . . .

Trevor'd shrieked, shoving himself from the table, and

immediately· began tossing his red hair with his fingers.
"Get it off!" the first grader had screamed. "Get it off!"

Lucinda frowned at the spider crouched on the storyboard. "It'th only a daddy longlegth. Him won't hurt
you."

Even the mortification of being comforted by a kindergartner couldn't stifle Trevor's terror. "Kill it! Kill it! Before it gets us!" he'd wailed. . . .

Gillian imagined Trevor's terror now, magnified by
hoards of spiders fleeing the rain—especially in the mountains where he lived. And her other students, which of their
fears were stalking them through the devastation of Rio
Santo? Rafael and Amanda cowered in the dark, David
fought for breath, Lucinda shivered with cold—

Lucinda was always cold. She rarely shivered—only her
pigtails. They waved like wind-tossed banners. She must
be freezing right now, with no gas or electricity to warm
her.

And no doubt Tess, who feared everything, was praying
for them all—

Unless she lay beneath that wooden marker on Jamarillo. . . .

Gillian stumbled from the room. She had to find the
fourth metaphor. There could be no more earthquakes, no
more threats by the Ocean or the Wind. She ran down the
hall, banking off the walls with her hands. At least Fresh
Water had offered some relief. . . .

Yanking her overcoat from its peg, Gillian darted out
into the rain.

TWENTY-FIVE

GILLIAN STOOD ON THE TOP STEP JUST OUT OF THE RAIN'S reach. Another cloud-blanketed, wet morning. Drawing a breath across her teeth, Gillian surveyed the changes that had taken place during the night.

The street had all but disappeared. A lake now lapped both curbs, its surface a mosaic of droplets, leaves, and grass. An island of oily asphalt split the lake like a spine. Mud streamed across the sidewalks to feed the rippling waters. Up and down the street, cars waited beside the curbs, the water swirling along the bottom of their doors. A green Acura parked in front of KC's seemed to bob a little like a moored boat. A red ball and a huge knot of persimmon leaves jostled the car's bumper.

The length of the block, trees had been stripped of every last leaf.

At the corner, a dam of sticks, mud, and debris clogged the storm drain. Jake, KC, and Denny prodded the tangled mass with crowbars and shovels, trying to reopen the drain and bleed the street. Waders glistening, Jake stepped off the curb. He sank up to his knees in the murky water. KC leaned over and lifted a copper saucepan from the drain's mouth.

Gillian turned toward the park.

Water seeped between the pots and pans carefully lined

up along the edge of the sidewalk. Floes of mud and rain nudged at the pots, urging them forward. At any time the cookware could slide to the street and float away, setting a course for the storm drain.

Gillian slapped down the steps. At least she could rescue the pots. Last night at dinner, while everyone talked about what they had done to ensure the neighborhood's survival, she'd sat quietly, chasing her beans around her plate. Mrs. Timako and Hiram had watched her, not with disapproval but with concern. "She's not pulling her own, poor dear," Gillian imagined Mrs. Timako saying over the camp stove. Canace and KC covered for her, asking her how the patrol had gone. Lily, who had seen her slogging through the streets on her search, exclaimed, "Oh, *that's* what you were doing!" Mrs. Timako and Hiram warmed immediately, but Gillian still felt like a slacker.

Especially since the only thing she'd seen that reminded her of Fresh Water was water. . . .

Gillian stopped at the curb to study the choppy lake. She backed up, then ran and leaped, touching down on the island and springing across the second arm of the lake. She landed on the sidewalk with a skid, flailing her arms to catch her balance.

Silt sucked at the soles of her shoes. Gillian scraped them on a crack in the sidewalk. She'd been over the house two, three times and hadn't seen her rubber boots once. She'd look for them after lunch. Canace couldn't begrudge her that.

Gillian flinched, remembering the growing apprehension in Canace's eyes. Whenever other people were around, Canace maintained a determined, almost cheerful demeanor. The pretense faded when the two of them were alone. Canace's shoulders fell like a glider hitting dead air. A haunted look settled over her features, while her mouth tightened with resistance.

Gillian shivered and bent over the pots and pans. Water dribbled over the metal lips. She squatted and picked up the nearest pot. She stood, then headed across the molten lawn for the picnic tables.

She stopped. Something bright and round sparkled among the lawn's white stubble. Her pulse quickened. Was this the last metaphor? Trembling, she knelt to look. The mud bubble exploded with a pop. Gillian sagged, setting the pot down. She lowered her head into her hands.

Her mind filled with Canace's expectant face. "Have you found it?" Canace asked whenever they saw each other. Her second question went unasked. It swelled between them: *Why aren't you out looking for it?*

Gillian lowered her hands. Picking up the pot, she lurched to her feet. "I promise you, Canace," she whispered. "I *am* looking. Every time I open my eyes."

Shouts rose above the stutter of the rain. Footsteps burbled and smacked at the mud, splashing toward her. Gillian turned. Beth Ellen and Bibbie galloped across the park, laughing and waving their arms. Their hair, uniformly dark, clung to their heads and the shoulders of their slickers. Suddenly Bibbie's feet shot out from under her. She slammed onto her bottom. Beth Ellen circled back and helped her to her feet.

Gillian hurried to join them. "Are you all right?"

Bibbie wiped the mud from her coat and pants. "Yeah. Wish I had cleats."

Beth Ellen lifted a shoe to show Gillian the spiked sole. Gillian whistled. "Nice. What are you two doing out here?"

"We're bored," Beth Ellen said. "We want to help you."

Bibbie nodded.

Beth Ellen frowned. "What are you doing?"

"I'm trying to keep the pots and pans from sailing away," Gillian said. "Still want to help?"

"Sure!" the girls chorused. They darted across the park.

Gillian smiled, a surge of affection warming her. She carried her pot to the nearest picnic table and set it down. Most of the soup kettles and pans sitting on the tables and benches were half to three quarters full. A lot of rain, Gillian thought, looking up at the clouds. And no end in sight.

The girls sloshed over to her. Each carried a small

saucepan as if it were filled with scalding soup.

"They're pretty full," Beth Ellen said. "What if we fill the Demonic Duo's bottles?"

Gillian stared at her. "Say it again?"

"Demonic Duo's," Bibbie said, pointing to the Kretskis' wagon train of ten-gallon jugs.

Beth Ellen shrugged. "That's what Mom calls them."

"Has she got *them* pegged," Gillian said. She wiped a pinstripe of mud from Beth Ellen's cheek with her finger. "Great idea, Beth Ellen. And once we get the jugs filled, we'll take them to Hiram."

GILLIAN PICKED HER WAY ACROSS THE OOZING PARK, carefully planting each foot. Her feet sucked and smacked with every step, the mud more and more reluctant to let go. Rivulets of sand eeled from the volleyball pits. A patch of gravel wrenched her from her feet when it refused to give. She plopped down heavily, mud splattering her jacket and face.

Gillian rubbed her right cheek against her shoulder, then struggled to her feet. The clouds shrunk the last of the afternoon to dusk. It had to be almost four. Thank God the girls had decided to go to Bibbie's to play dress-up an hour ago while there was still light. She shuffled to the curb.

A sheen of water rippled over the asphalt island. Looking down at her shoes, Gillian sighed. The leather uppers had darkened from buff to walnut—at this point they held more water than they repelled. Traction was nonexistent. Gillian removed her shoes, rolled up her pant legs, and waded into the street.

The water was surprisingly warm.

Gillian glided on. A plastic garden stake drifted past her. She squinted at it: begonia. Several broken pickets torpedoed by. Tendrils of ivy clung to one plank.

Gillian sloshed toward the far curb.

KC walked to the edge of the lake. "Hey!"

Gillian smiled. "Hey, yourself."

"How'd it go?" he said. "Any luck?"

She shook her head. "None. Got the jugs filled, though. The girls came back after lunch."

KC sighed. He offered her a hand. She took it. He hoisted her from the water. "You're soaked," he said. "What am I going to do with you?"

Gillian shook back her hair. "Take me to dinner."

"After you get out of those."

"Sure thing, Dad."

KC grinned crookedly. "Touché. Come on."

Gillian started to follow, then turned. A red Power Ranger floated by with his arms lifted toward her. The current spun him for a second so that his painted eyes seemed to search for hers before the water swept him away. Another Power Ranger, a yellow one, drifted past, one arm raised above her head, the other parallel to her side as if she were doing the backstroke. Before she swirled away, a black Power Ranger swept past, facedown. Dead man's float.

A chill expanded in Gillian's chest.

She turned away.

THE HURRICANE LAMP DRAPED THE SIX DINERS WITH A cloak of light. The rest of Mrs. Timako's dining room receded into shadows on shadow—an empty china cabinet, bare walls with nails, books stacked in the corner.

Gillian wrapped spaghetti around her fork. Canace questioned her with a look. Gillian shook her head.

"What else did the radio say?" Lily asked.

"Mud slides have closed all the mountain roads," Hiram said, poking at his spaghetti. His white bow tie reflected his fork. "Two National Guard supply trucks got caught. One of them was buried."

Lily set down her fork. "Dearest God!"

KC sucked his lower lip. "With that chunk of highway missing up north . . ." He clicked his teeth. "What about the south coast road?"

Mrs. Timako and Hiram exchanged a look. Mrs. Timako cleared her throat. "The bridge washed out at Primavera Creek this afternoon."

"Snapped like a rotten rubber band," Hiram said.

Gillian pushed herself away from the table. Her gaze locked Canace's.

"We're completely cut off," Lily murmured.

Canace offered the barest shrug. Strain hollowed her cheeks. "I'm trying," she whispered.

"What else?" Lily said, resolve firming her voice. "We might as well hear it all."

"They're evacuating the mountains," Mrs. Timako said.

Hiram fidgeted with his fork. "Slides are taking down trees and houses. Smashing them. There've been . . . several families are presumed dead."

Gillian's lower lip trembled. Trevor—

"They don't know yet," Mrs. Timako added quickly. "A few houses slipped down the hill. The searchers won't know anything until they get a chance to go in there."

Gillian pressed her lips together to stop the trembling, but her whole jaw quivered. *Not Trevor. Please, not Trevor. Send him spiders, not mud slides. Let him be afraid, not dead. . . .*

KC's hand cupped her knee. She placed a damp hand over his. If the mountains were dissolving with all this rain, the river must be—

"The river," Gillian said. "Have they—has the downtown been evacuated?"

"Yesterday," Mrs. Timako said.

Gillian's chest constricted. Lucinda lived there, and Tess . . . most of her students. Yesterday. They were safe, they had to be. The street here hadn't become a canal until this morning. . . .

No one said anything for several minutes. Fear spun Gillian's mind, sucking her into its center like a whirlpool. She fought its pull. She could stop this destruction, she had to—

"It's not a hard rain," Hiram said. "There's just a lot of it."

"Too much," Canace said quietly.

• • •

ON THE WALK HOME, CANACE SPLASHED AHEAD, HUGGING herself. Gillian and KC trotted to keep up with her. KC tried to shine the flashlight beam just ahead of Canace, but she walked too quickly, driving through the rain like a wedge.

KC squeezed Gillian's hand. "Do you want to look through my things?"

Thick, silted water churned over Gillian's feet. "No, thanks."

Canace spun to face Gillian. "Why not? It's worth a try."

"I think that's the problem," Gillian said. "I *am* trying, maybe too hard."

Canace's shoulders hunched, then fell. "You're probably right," she said, turning. "I'm just—I'm having a hard time convincing the Wind not to strike out. I—I don't know how much longer I can resist Her myself."

Gillian touched Canace's arm. "I'm sorry. I don't know why this one's so hard."

"Because you've never met a Fresh Water spirit," KC said.

Gillian stopped and stared at him.

"It's true," Canace said, grasping Gillian's arms. "You've met the Wind, the Earth, and the Ocean, but not Fresh Water. How can you expect to find a metaphor for something you've never seen?"

"Why didn't I . . . ?" Excitement bubbled through Gillian. "Can you talk to Fresh Water? Ask one of the spirits to come to me?"

Canace took a deep breath. "I'll see what I can do . . . but that doesn't mean stop looking."

"No, of course not." Gillian slipped her arm around KC's waist, causing the flashlight beam to bob wildly. "KC, you're a genius—" She froze. "Hold the light steady. Over there."

Canace eased in beside her. "What is it?"

"I thought I saw something," Gillian said, stepping forward. Mud gave under her foot. "KC, do a sweep along the curb here."

KC raked the street with the flashlight beam. In the dark there was no curb, no gutter—nothing but the ripple of black water as it oozed over the sidewalk.

"Damn," Gillian said.

Canace tilted her head to one side. "Seen enough?"

"For now," Gillian said.

KC slid the beam back to the sidewalk. Something glinted, then disappeared. Gillian caught his arm. "Shine it over there," she said. "I'm sure I saw something."

"Is it . . . ?" Canace whispered.

Gillian frowned. "I don't know. . . ." She took KC's flashlight-wielding arm and moved it slightly so that it shone a little beyond the submerged curb. Something sparkled just below the water. "There," she said.

Without disturbing the silt, she glided to the curb. She crouched. Something sparkled beneath the surface. It looked like a silver ring with a large glass stone. She reached for it. Her fingers closed on a cold, stiff hand.

Gillian's throat nearly closed.

A *small,* stiff hand.

"KC, Canace, help me," she said, dragging the body onto the sidewalk.

"Sweet God," KC murmured. Shoving the flashlight at Canace, he grabbed the corpse's shoulder and helped Gillian reel it onto the sidewalk. Canace shone the light on the face. Gillian covered her mouth with her hand, choking back bile.

Bibbie.

TWENTY-SIX

GILLIAN PEELED BACK THE PLASTIC FROM THE LOWER-
right-hand corner of her bedroom window. Propping her
elbows on the sill, she rested her chin in her hands and
stared out into the darkness. Rain shot by, shimmering
black streaks against the matte-black night. Strange how
even without streetlights or stars the rain still glittered.
Like metal.

Like bullets.

Gillian squeezed her eyes shut.

Bibbie's face swam to the surface of her mind, lips
parted in shock, eyes dull and sightless. Mom, her hair and
clothing aflame, slipped an arm around Bibbie's shoulders.
Bibbie's eyes blinked into focus at Mom's touch. Mom
hugged her, then looked at Gillian. "Don't worry, Pumpkin," she said. "I'll warm her."

Dad drifted to Bibbie's other side. He slid his flaming
arm around the girl's waist. "*We'll* warm her," he said.

Bibbie relaxed into the cradle of their arms, an infant in
death. Bibbie's eyes pleaded. "Scared," she said.

Gillian gasped and opened her eyes. The images vanished.

She scraped the tears from her cheeks. If only she had
collected the Power Rangers as they floated by. If only she
had taken them to Bibbie, then Bibbie wouldn't have gone

looking for them. If only she hadn't been so caught up in her search for the fourth object—

An image jagged across Gillian's mind like lightning: Ms. Leeds clutching Bibbie's body, her fingers digging at the cold wrist, trying to massage the pulse back to life. . . .

The bedroom door creaked open. "Are you all right?" Canace asked.

Gillian nodded. "Better than the Leeds."

Canace crossed the room and laid a hand on Gillian's shoulder. "You need to get some sleep."

Gillian shrugged off Canace's hand. "Did you know her real name was Raquel? Her little brother couldn't pronounce it."

Canace's voice softened. "How did he get Bibbie out of Raquel?"

"He didn't. She wore bibs, he called her Bibbie." Gillian rested her chin on the sill. "She was eight, Canace. Only eight years old."

Canace's hand settled on Gillian's shoulder again.

"Have you talked to Fresh Water?" Gillian said.

An exasperated hiss escaped Canace. "I tried."

"And?"

"Sometimes I think Fresh Water is crazier than the Earth. More bullheaded, at any rate."

Gillian raised her eyebrows. "You need a common language."

Canace patted her shoulder. "We have one. We just need to use her."

Gillian stared out into the rain. Anger welled up inside her. She gritted her teeth. "So far there's been earthquake, drought, *and* flood. Marea is making veiled threats about tidal waves. What about you, Canace? What are you holding back?"

Canace's voice was barely audible. "Hurricane."

Gillian stood very still. She waited till her heartbeat slowed, then said, "You don't have a choice, do you? You're only part of the Wind."

"A small part," Canace said. "Just like the spirit who

finally comes to you from Fresh Water will be only a small part. Be open, Gillian. Be welcoming.''

"I don't know if I can," Gillian said. "I keep seeing Bibbie's face and I feel so helpless . . . and guilty. If I'd had the fourth metaphor, she might not have died. Who else will die because I can't find it? What else can't I stop?"

"It's not your fault—"

"No? And what if Nick is contagious? My students— are they all right? What about Nora and Debbie? Who's dead that I don't know about? Who's going to be next?" Gillian pressed her fists against the windowsill. "Sometimes, Canace, I wish my mind would go blank for a while so I didn't have to face any of it."

Canace tilted Gillian's face to hers. "Don't turn away," she said. "It'll just be waiting when you turn around again."

"I need a sign of hope, Canace," Gillian said. "Until I can find it in myself."

Canace stepped back. "I don't know your students, but I do know Nora. Where does she live?"

"Two-oh-one McKenna."

"I'll find her." Canace smiled sadly. "Try to get some rest. You need your strength."

Gillian looked away. "Thanks."

The door opened and shut. Gillian peered out into the storm. "It's not a hard rain," she said, quoting Hiram. "There's just a lot of it."

A draft riffled the hair along her temples. "Nora is fine," it whispered. "So is Debbie. Nora misses you."

Relief tempered the ache in Gillian's heart. "Thank you," she said.

The breeze died.

Outside the world echoed with the hollow sound of water on water as streets became canals and yards became lakes. Even solid ground grew treacherous under its mantle of mud.

Gillian rested her cheek against the side of the window. "I'm sorry, Bibbie," she said.

"A branch knocked her down," someone said.

Gillian's shoulders folded inward. "Dagan?"

"No, not Dagan." The voice rippled and rushed as it drew nearer. "Beck."

Just beyond the eaves, a flurry of raindrops swirled into a cascade. The torrent curved and flowed, molding itself into the thin, silver silhouette of a man. Hardening like ice, the silhouette absorbed color from the night. Gillian held her breath. With a shake of his short, wet hair, the man stepped toward her, the tails of his flannel shirt clinging to his muscular, denim-clad legs.

He stepped under the eaves. "Beck," he repeated. "My name is Beck."

Gillian exhaled. "You're a Fresh Water spirit."

He nodded once, then gazed steadily at her.

Gillian pulled herself closer to the windowsill. The spirit's features and body were as lean as a falling raindrop. Like Marea's, his skin shimmered with a beading of water. Gillian stared into his wide-set eyes, searching their depths. She guessed they were blue. Right now they were as dark as night.

Behind him, rain continued to fall.

Gillian's jaw tightened. "Why did you do this?"

A raindrop trailed his cheek like a tear. "You wanted water, didn't you?"

"We did," she said. "But not this much. Not all at once."

He shrugged. "No pleasing some people."

Gillian gritted her teeth. "Pleasing? People are *dying*. You've got to stop this—"

"Why?" Beck's eyes narrowed to icy slits. "For six years She warned you with a drought. You ignored Her. Well, She got your attention this time, didn't She? And now you want *Her* to stop because *you* can't handle it?"

"Leave her alone, Beck," Dagan said, stepping under the eaves.

The Fresh Water spirit sneered. "Leave her alone? Because the settled don't understand? Because they don't know how to pay attention?"

"The drought got our attention," Gillian said. "And the earthquakes."

"Ah, the earthquakes," Beck said. Wistful appreciation flowed through his words. "They did seem to bring you around. But what good did that do?" His voice hardened like hail. "We're still waiting."

Dagan's eyes narrowed. "Why don't you try waiting just a few more days, Beck? Fresh Water could stand to learn a little patience."

"Seven years, Dagan," Beck said. "And how patient is the Earth? Some of those mud slides required very little coaxing."

Gillian gripped the sill. "Dagan . . . ?"

He ducked his head, avoiding her gaze. "I'm only part."

Only part. . . .

Gillian held herself very still, trying to relax. She stared at the Fresh Water spirit. He smiled, a slow, mocking smile.

Sudden rage pumped through her, warming her for the first time in days. After all she'd been through, after all she'd tried to do, to be sent someone who would rather punish than rebuild. . . .

"And there are other parts to Fresh Water, too," she said. "I want to talk to one of them. Someone who can communicate Her needs and help me understand them without hiding behind threats and bullying. Someone who wants to reach out to the other members of the Four and foster some kind of understanding, not point his finger in ridicule and blame."

Dagan paled, making a short cutting motion with his hand. Beck simply regarded her from beneath those dewy lashes. "Someone you can work with," he said.

"Yes," Gillian said. "Someone who's willing to listen as well as spout accusations. You're right, She has been neglected—so have the others. But She needs to understand why. She needs an intermediary who knows how to listen."

"Gillian . . ." Dagan said.

"Don't 'Gillian' me," she said. "Rio Santo is being ripped apart by droughts, earthquakes, and floods. The city is crumbling, people are dying—and why? Because the Four can't get along! They need a common language, someone to teach them how to communicate. And guess what? I'm it. And I don't know anything about this... role, except that somehow the Four are going to 'use' me. *Use* me, to save the people I love. So I have to trust a handful of spirits, even though one of them had no qualms asking me to do things that might have got me killed and another one wants to destroy everything in sight!"

Beck blinked. "I don't want to destroy everything."

"Don't you?" Gillian said. "You talk about waiting seven years. Well, I'm real sorry about that, but did anyone start looking for another language right away? Not that I've heard. Oh, I know. Languages are rare. Well, *I'm* a language, and *I'm* willing to teach the four how to communicate, but I just got here." She paused a half second to catch her breath. "I've had five days to find the metaphors I'll need. I've found three. You know how hard that was when all I was told was, 'Look, but don't look or you'll never find them'? Then Fresh Water sends *you*."

"Careful, Gillian," Dagan said.

"Careful, nothing," Gillian said. "I don't even know what kind of metaphor I need for Fresh Water." She snorted. "Or maybe I do—now. Something cold and stiff and unyielding—how about my sister? She'd make a great metaphor for Fresh Water."

"Your sister?" Beck said.

Gillian's lip curled. "Nora's about as willing to listen and understand as you are."

"I'm willing," Beck said softly.

"She's—" Gillian blinked. "What?"

Beck nodded earnestly, the challenge in his eyes rinsed away. "I'll work with you. I'd be happy to work with you."

With a sigh of relief, Dagan melted and disappeared.

Gillian's rage died. "Just like that?"

"I trust you," Beck said. He smiled. "I like your sense of humor."

Gillian laughed nervously. "What sense of humor?"

"Your sister as a metaphor for Fresh Water." His smile broadened. "Too bad you can't use her."

Gillian bit her lower lip. "I'll keep looking, thanks."

Beck leaned closer and took her hands. His skin was warm and damp. "You'll find something. Soon. Get some rest, Gillian. We need you."

He released her hands, then stepped back, dissolving into the rain. Splash and patter filled the night.

Gillian clung to the windowsill. Despite the calm growing inside her, she trembled with the violence of her spent anger. She reached for the plastic, lowering it back into place. She raised it again at the sound of approaching voices.

"You said you wanted to help her," Dagan said.

KC sputtered. "I do, but where—how did you know—?"

"The Earth beneath your feet," Dagan said. "You need to stay with her tonight."

Gillian smiled.

"She told me she wanted to be alone," KC said.

"Ask her again." Dagan stopped five feet from the window. "Gillian!"

She leaned out the window. "Yes, Dagan? Hi, KC."

Dagan frowned. "That was dangerous, trying to get Fresh Water to send someone besides Beck."

Gillian's smile faded. "Why?"

"The other Fresh Water spirits," Dagan said. "They're worse."

TWENTY-SEVEN

WATER RUMBLED AND SPAT AS IF THE HOUSE HAD BEEN swallowed by a waterfall. Morning barely penetrated the plastic-covered window, casting a feeble, watery light across Gillian's bedroom. KC sat on the edge of Gillian's bed, tugging on his jacket. "You're sure you want to do this?" he said.

"I want Dagan to meet Debbie. Besides, a metaphor is as likely to show up on the way to Nora's as anywhere." Gillian scoured the closet with the flashlight. "They aren't here. I must have left them in the other closet."

KC zipped up his jacket. "I have an extra pair of boots you can borrow."

Gillian squinted at KC's feet. At least four sizes larger than hers. "I'll check the entry closet," she said.

The boots weren't there. Gillian grimaced, picking up her damp, stiff shoes. She sat on the floor and shoved them on. Moisture invaded her wool socks. She held out a hand to KC.

He pulled her to her feet. "Are you sure you don't want me to get those boots?"

Gillian wiggled her toes. "Positive."

She opened the door and stepped outside. KC followed. Rain poured from the eaves in sheets.

"Your gutter's clogged," KC said. "I'll clear it when we get back."

Gillian lifted the hood of her overcoat. "Are you sure they aren't going to need you here?"

KC took her hand. "Gloria can help Jake and Denny with the storm drains. So can Hiram. They may have to patch a few leaks, things like that. You, on the other hand, don't know what you're going to run into. You may need help lifting branches or climbing over things."

Gillian nodded. "The brawn factor."

"Gilly, I can't help you with anything else," he said. "Let me do this."

She squeezed his hand. "Don't knock moral support, KC. Let's go."

They darted through the curtain of water and down the steps. The lake now extended from a small rise in the park to the baseboards of the houses. Gillian braced herself and stepped into the murky sludge. Her shoe sank to the top of its laces.

The mud was warm. Gillian murmured low in her throat, grateful for any small comfort, then trudged toward the sidewalk.

KC squished along beside her. "When are you going to call Dagan?" he said.

"When we get closer to Nora's."

GILLIAN PEEKED AT THE SKY FROM UNDER HER HOOD, BUT drips blinded her. She lowered her head and forded the flooded street, using KC's hand for balance. Sticks and planks twisted together into dense, half-submerged nets, snatching mangled tricycles, lawn furniture, and fencing from the flow. Shards of broken flower pots and birdbaths rose like shark fins from the muck. Gillian skirted a dismantled porch railing, tripping on a tangle of clothing. She pitched forward. KC grabbed her, steadying her.

Gillian stopped and grasped the bill of the hood. Holding it still, she tilted her head back so that she could see ahead without being blinded. Porches and steps made up the banks of the slough just as they had on her street. Trees listed toward the street, their branches trolling the slime. A slender maple had toppled completely. Quick pruning jobs had been done on some trees, limbs and trunks hacked to splinters to prevent them from falling on houses and sheds.

Turning slowly, Gillian tried to get her bearings. The street signs jutted parallel to the road: Waxwing and Red Willow. "Two blocks from Nora's," she said. She cupped her hands around her mouth. "Dagan!"

KC joined her. "Dagan!"

They called several times, then Gillian raised her hand for silence. She listened to the plash and chatter of the rain. "Maybe the other Earth spirits will tell him," she said. "Let's keep moving."

KC nodded, sloshing ahead.

The mud grew thick and treacherous with snares—lost shoes, a bowling ball, a truck muffler, uprooted shrubs. With a yelp, KC dropped to his knees after stepping on the bowling ball. Gillian yanked him upright and they trudged on. They developed a shuffle so that they'd kick objects before they tripped over them.

"Dagan!" Gillian called.

"I'll see if I can find him," a breeze whispered.

"Thanks," Gillian said. She tugged at KC's sleeve. "Canace is looking for him. Let's keep going. We're almost there."

The water got deeper, swirling around Gillian's calves. A stick scraped her knee, catching her rolled-up pant leg before spurting out of the water. It darted away.

Water bubbled and churned behind them. "I'm here," Dagan said.

Gillian turned. Rounded and slightly swollen, Dagan looked as if he'd absorbed too much water. He waded toward them, the mud sucking at his legs like skin around a syringe. "You wanted to see me?" he said.

"I want you to meet someone," Gillian said. "As insurance. In case something happens to me."

Dagan's cheeks hollowed. "Another language?"

"No," Gillian said. She hugged herself. "You'll see."

KC draped an arm around her shoulder.

Dagan's eyes sparkled, the swirls of blue and green more vivid in his excitement. "Have you found . . . ?"

"I don't want to tell you what I've found," Gillian said. "I want you to tell me."

A fierce hunger sharpened Dagan's features. Gillian's stomach knotted. Did Debbie really deserve this?

Gillian's mind returned to the altar at Briar Hollow, to the trellis of carved roses. A half circle of Earth spirits closed in on her like an aftershock. The white-haired spirit, Petra, shouted, "Kill her!"

Kill her.

Melanie stretched across the altar. She smiled. "Hey, it's all right, Gillian," she said. "You want this instead?"

Gillian's mind wrenched back to the flooded street. Broken houses slumped, their chimneys heaped beside them, fences and shrubbery peeled away. Unlike the vision, this destruction did not fade.

"Nora's house is just around the corner," Gillian said. She hurried ahead, climbing out of the muddy waters onto a ridge of buckled sidewalk. Head lowered, she led man and spirit out into the street, past the gate folded around the beige Volvo, up the bubbling slope of Nora's driveway.

"My God," KC said.

Gillian looked up. The house still stood, shouldering the storm with weary perseverance, but the front porch had disappeared. The only reminders that the porch had ever existed were a few frayed boards and a front door that opened four feet above the mud.

The rain gutter sagging along the front overhang ripped free with a shriek of metal on wood.

"Oh, Nora," Gillian murmured. She stumbled back a step, then ran to the back gate.

Tugging at the clasp, Gillian shoved against the gate's sodden planks. It refused to give. Grasping the top of the gate, she shook it, rattling the fence. KC joined her, working the catch while she pulled.

The back door banged open. "Stop where you are," Nora called. "I have a gun. Who's there?"

"It's Gillian," Gillian shouted, "and you do not."

Footsteps splashed to the gate. "Gilly!" Nora said. "Are you all right? Wait a minute. We propped a log against the gate. Debbie, help me."

After several grunts and muffled curses, the gate swung open. A torrent of mud gushed from the backyard. Nora stepped through, followed by Debbie.

Nora reached for Gillian. "Gillian, I'm sorry I said anything about you and—" She stopped, her face suddenly crimson. "Uh, hi, KC."

She recovered and pulled both KC and Gillian into an awkward hug. "Thank God, you're okay."

KC wriggled free. Nora's arms enfolded Gillian. "Debbie and I have been listening to the radio," Nora said. "I've been so worried about you."

Gillian burrowed into Nora's embrace. "I've been worried about you, too. Your porch—"

"Sometime last night," Nora said. She leaned back, still clutching Gillian's shoulders. "How about your place?" Her eyes widened, focusing on something beyond Gillian. "Who are you? What do you want?"

Gillian turned, breaking Nora's grip. Dagan waited a few feet away, his gaze locked on Debbie. "It's okay," Gillian said. "He's a friend of mine. Nora, Debbie, this is Dagan."

Debbie drifted toward the spirit as if unable to see anything but him. Dagan yearned toward her, his eyes alive with hope.

Chafing her arms, Nora studied them, apparently fascinated and unnerved by the attraction between the two. "Why did you bring him here?" she said.

Gillian watched Debbie and Dagan. It was an odd attraction, not at all sensual or romantic. "I wanted to be sure you were all right," Gillian said. "He . . . asked if he could come along."

Debbie offered Dagan her hand. He shook it.

"Why?" Nora said.

"He's . . . ." Gillian glanced at Dagan. "He's . . . a ge-
ologist. He specializes in soil erosion. I told him about a
talk I had with Debbie and he wanted to meet her."

Debbie frowned. "You don't interfere, do you?" she
said. "Not while She's reshaping and recreating Herself?"

"No, I wouldn't dream of it," Dagan said, the excitement in his voice dammed behind forced calm.

Nora walked toward them. "Debbie . . . ."

Debbie fluttered her hands. "The Earth needs to shift
and rearrange now and then. It's Her way of stretching. If
we get in Her way, She just gets all tense and knotted up."

A smile touched Dagan's lips. "You're perfect."

Nora faltered to a stop. "Deb?"

Debbie shook her head. "No, no. *Listen.* It's like that
forest fire in Yellowstone. The forest *needs* fires to re-
energize the soil. But everyone had to freak out. They
nearly ruined everything."

Dagan's smile grew. "Yes, exactly."

KC nudged Gillian. "A meeting of the minds."

"Of intent, anyway," Gillian said.

Nora pulled Gillian out of Dagan and Debbie's hearing.
"Why did you bring him here?" she said in a low voice.

"He wanted . . ." Gillian's words trailed off.

Disaster heaped on disaster had tattered Nora's confi-
dence. Nora squared her shoulders. "Yes?"

"They have certain ideas in common—"

"I can see that." Nora's features hardened. "Is this your
way of showing your disapproval? Setting her up with
someone else?"

"Dagan's about as sexual as a rock—"

Fear flickered in Nora's eyes.

Gillian backpedaled. "Nora, I'd never do that. I don't
care who you love. I want you to be happy—"

"So why introduce them? Why now?"

Gillian glanced past KC, Dagan, and Debbie at the
street. A gust of wind whipped the surface of the water
into whitecaps. Gillian sucked her lower lip. It tasted
faintly salty, like the sea. *I may never see you again, Nora,*

she thought. *I don't want our last time together to be like this.*

She turned back to Nora. "He needs her help."

"Now?" Nora said, head cocked.

"I had to introduce them now," Gillian said. "I may never get another chance—"

"Finally going to run away from Rio Santo?" Nora said. "Does KC know?"

Gillian flinched. "Nora, don't do this. . . ."

"Damn me." Nora massaged her temples. "I'm sorry, Gilly. I don't know why I keep pushing you away."

Gillian brushed Nora's sleeve with her fingers. "We'll work through it. We will." *If I live.* "I have to go now. I want you to know, whatever happens, I love you."

Nora's cheeks hollowed. "Whatever happens—?"

Gillian backed away. There was no time to explain. "I've got to go. KC, you ready? I need to find Canace—"

Gillian stopped and stared at a slim, crystal handle twitching against the house two or three feet beyond Dagan. She hurried past him, showers of grit and water exploding with each step. The handle clacked against the house, caught by a web of twigs and exposed roots.

Gillian lifted a Waterford punch cup from the swirling waters. Despite the crack splitting its lip, she recognized it. Nora had bought the cup the summer the two of them went to Ireland. Gillian turned it over in her hands. Light flowed along the cup's facets in glossy currents until she held it still, then the crystal glowed like ice.

Like Beck.

Gillian imagined the Fresh Water spirit laughing. She *had* found his metaphor through her sister. . . .

"I'll get you another one," Gillian said, raising the cup to Nora. "KC, Dagan, let's go."

Nora frowned, confused. "You don't need to replace— what do you want with a broken cup?"

Dagan jerked away from Debbie. "Fresh Water?"

Gillian nodded.

KC and Dagan swooped down on her, each hooking an

elbow. As they rushed her down the driveway and out into the street, Dagan murmured, "At last, at last, at last." KC said nothing. Gillian glanced up at him. Determination and dread warred in his eyes. His eyebrows knotted above the bridge of his nose. Her own fear and relief hammered through her veins like hail.

Laughter rose in Gillian's throat. She swallowed it, afraid its bubbling hysteria would sweep her away.

TWENTY-EIGHT

THE OVERBURDENED POCKETS DRAGGED AT THE OVER-
coat, making it difficult to zip. Gillian fumbled with the
zipper. The angel's hand dug at her left hip, the Waterford
cup and sea stone bounced against her right. She slipped
one of Dera's fronds into the breast pocket and grasped
the zipper again. She yanked the pull to her chin.

Canace paced the entry, cradling a plastic vegetable bag
to her chest. The candle and matchbox were barely visible
beneath the green store logo. "Ready? Did you put the oil
on?"

Gillian felt along the bottom of the closet for her rubber
boots—again. "Yes, behind my ears. We can't leave yet.
We have to wait for KC."

"KC? Why?"

"Moral support." Gillian straightened. The angel's
hand smacked her hip. "Canace, will you stop pacing?
You're making me nervous. More nervous."

"Sorry." Canace stood still—for five seconds. Like a
horse champing its bit, she began pacing again.

The front door swung open. Rain gusted around KC's
broad shoulders as he stepped inside. He handed Gillian a
pair of black rubber boots. "Put them on over your
shoes," he said. He combed the water from his hair with
his fingers. "I ran into Mrs. Timako. Had a hell of a time

getting away from her. She's worried because we missed lunch. She doesn't want us to get sick.''

"Right, right," Canace muttered. "Can we go?"

Gillian pulled the hood over her head. She eyed Canace. "You're really fighting Her, aren't you?"

Canace nodded.

Fear scalded Gillian's throat. If Canace was fighting this hard to hold back the Wind, what about the others?

If Canace was this frightened. . . .

"Let's go," Gillian said. She slipped between Canace and KC and out the door. Slush stung her face like a cloud of hornets. She glanced back at the house, wondering if she'd ever see it again.

"You will," Canace said.

Gillian's lower lip trembled. She hurried down the stairs, sinking to her ankles in the cloudy water that lapped the bottom step. If the water rose three more steps, it would ooze over the threshold and into the house. Forcing the thought from her mind, Gillian stepped into the turgid swamp that had replaced her lawn.

Mud licked within an inch of the tops of her boots.

Beck glided toward them from the branches of the rosemary. Rain and tiny green leaves studded his hair and clothes. "Finally," he said.

Canace glared at him. "Leave her alone."

Beck's bottomless blue eyes narrowed.

"We don't have time for this," Dagan said, rising from the mud at Beck's feet. He grasped Beck's elbow, guiding him away from Canace. "We need to get to the wall."

"To the wall?" KC whispered to Gillian.

She took his hand and pulled him toward the street. "The seawall. To meet the Ocean. She can't go beyond reach of Her element. During a storm, that reach extends to the seawall."

Head lowered, Gillian splashed toward the sidewalk. Wind flapped her hood, wheezing over her ears. Beneath the water that raged over the buckled concrete, a slick of mud shimmied under her feet. Gillian picked her way through the bog until a string of Christmas lights wrapped around her ankles. She tripped, slamming into the green Acura before KC and Canace could tug her back to her feet.

Submerged to its doors, the car rocked under her weight. Gillian shook herself. "I'm all right," she said.

Canace released her shoulder. KC clung to her hand. A small blue saucepan rode the rapids, swirling over the curb. The pan's twig and leaf passengers jostled and tumbled over its sides. Gillian nudged KC and pointed. "Isn't that one of yours?"

KC shook back his hair. "I was wondering where that went."

"You left it in the park," Dagan said.

Gillian started to smile, then sobered as the pan clanged into the back of Jake Rubio's shovel. The pan swept around Jake and moored itself against the dike of tree limbs, poles, shingles, and other refuse damming the storm drain.

Backs bent, Gloria Hidalgo and Denny hacked at the debris with crowbar and hatchet. Jake scooped up the scraps and tossed them toward one of the Kretskis' wagons. Perched at the top of Gloria's sloping lawn, the wagon was already piled high. A splintered skateboard leaned against its rubber wheels.

"Over here," Jake said, probing with the shovel. "Got something huge over here."

Denny grunted and swung the hatchet to the right of the shovel's blade. A loud pop erupted.

Jake jumped.

"Calm down, babe," Gloria said. "It's just a ball."

"Get that shit out of there before it fills up again," Denny said. "Yo, KC! Grab a shovel."

"Later," KC said. "Gillian and I have to help some people."

"Yeah? What about your friends?" Jake said, nodding at Dagan and Beck.

"Those are the people," Gillian said.

Gloria swung the crowbar at a warp of branches. It exploded into twigs and sticks. She glanced at Canace. "You going to the Red Cross? I heard Lorna took the Trestles there this morning.''

Canace frowned. ''The Red Cross? Where are they set up?''

''Bunch of places,'' Jake said, prodding at a mangled window screen. ''Closest is Lowen Elementary. Denny, see if you can get this thing.''

Gillian imagined her speech room filled with cots and moaning people. The wind howled, the rain hammered, the ground shook. Red Cross volunteers in bloodied, disheveled rags carried more patients into the already crowded room—

''We've got to go,'' Gillian said. She lurched forward, fighting against the flow of water and fear that threatened to sweep her from her feet.

GILLIAN RETREATED FARTHER INTO HER HOOD. HAIL stung her neck and back. The wind keened and wrapped itself around her, invading her overcoat, bleeding her of warmth. A shiver beneath her feet quieted before it became a tremor. Gillian plunged her hands deeper into her pockets, only partially reassured by the angel's fingers and the cup's facets. The sea stone clicked against crystal.

The hail pummeled her, then abruptly softened. Softened . . . to snow? Gillian peeked from under her hood. A heavy mist shrouded the ravaged streets. Gillian pushed the hood back a little. Beck waded beside a withdrawn Canace, his eyes feverish, his cheekbones taut. He gritted his teeth, then shuddered. The mist swelled to a driving rain.

Gillian looked down at her feet. A baby doll stared up at her, its leg caught in a bicycle chain. The image of Bibbie's face crackled like static across Gillian's mind.

Gillian looked away, stumbling forward.

KC's booted feet sloshed beside her. Gillian's chest constricted. Her moral support . . . would the Four respect that? Or would They destroy him as if he were part of the landscape? If the pain of the three spirits gathered around her was any indication, the Four were growing more impatient and less inclined to listen.

Would They listen to her?

Gillian faltered a step. How would They use her?

You won't be taken over, Canace had said. *You're more than a voice. You're a language. Language is alive, it shapes the speaker's thoughts and understanding.*

Gillian bit her lower lip. *You won't be taken over.* Despite Canace's promises, it still sounded like possession. Each of the Four would enter her and—what? Manipulate her like a puppet? Force her to do and say things? What kinds of things?

Canace's words echoed inside her like a death knell: *You're the words and tones and gestures we use to open up to each other.* Words could heal. They could also fester, crippling the heart and mind like an infection. So could gestures and tones. But they could also devastate the person uttering them. . . .

Gillian's pulse hammered in her ears. Why did They need her? Why not just rail and lash out at each other?

Because we can't destroy each other . . .

Gillian clasped the angel's hand. *How did Jamison die?* she wanted to ask. *Did the Four kill him by using him?*

"How—" she whispered. She cleared her throat. "How long did the Four use Jamison?"

Canace's voice was clipped. "Twenty-six years."

Gillian flinched. *And then someone accidentally—*

KC slipped his hand into her pocket and twined his fingers through hers. "Gilly, I keep thinking about what Nora said. *Are* you planning to run away from Rio Santo?"

Gillian swung to look at him. He gazed at her thoughtfully, a hint of concern warming his eyes. "I don't know," she said. "I guess it's always in the back of my mind. I've never felt at home here. I've never felt like there's been anything to keep me. Since Mom and Dad died, I've felt so . . . homeless. Unattached." She frowned. "Why are you asking me this now?"

The shadow of a lie crossed KC's face, then disappeared. He grinned crookedly. "To distract you. And me."

Gillian stared at him. "What?"

He shrugged. "You looked scared."

"I am. Are you?"

"Shitless. I don't know what—"

Light exploded across the sky. KC fell silent. A second later thunder ricocheted between a row of crumbled villas. "No," Canace murmured. "We're almost there. Please."

Gillian edged closer to KC, twisting to look at the decimated landscape around them. A street sign jutted at an angle, pointing toward the ruins of the Mediterranean hovels. Its metal finger read MADRUGA AVENUE. The villas had collapsed into heaps, palm fronds clinging to the remains like geckos.

Less than a block away, the seawall separated the brown waters of the flood from the gray-green waters of the sea.

Shock numbed Gillian. She lurched toward the sea, removing KC's hand from her pocket. A wave raced across the last inches of sand and slammed the seawall, sending an explosion of foam and spray into the air. Wind whipped the shattered wave to a froth.

Canace moaned. Lines carved her face as if the effort of harnessing her own patience and anger had scored her. Gaze fixed on the wind-tossed foam, Canace handed Gillian the plastic bag with the candle and matches. "Take it," she said in a hoarse voice. "Take it now."

Gillian clutched the bag to her chest. She glanced at Beck and Dagan. Beck glided through the churning waters, his eyes feverish above an expectant smile. Dagan clasped himself as if holding himself together. His teeth chattered.

"KC, stay with me," Gillian said. She held out her hand.

KC grasped it, pulling himself to her side.

Spume flowed over the seawall and became Marea. The Ocean spirit paced before the tattered bricks, her head bowed slightly, her hair and lavender sheath flapping in the wind. She lifted her head and stared straight at Gillian.

Her eyes shone with madness.

Gillian shrank back. "Canace, what if I—"

Canace's wail pierced the storm.

Gillian's cheekbones ached. Gusts of wind raked across her head and shoulders, ripping back her hood. The rain strafed her eyes. Her hair cycloned around her face, blinding her.

KC's grip tightened, anchoring her.

Another squall swept the hair from Gillian's face. Along the edge of the beach, a wave rose three stories high and rushed the seawall. It slapped the stones, engulfing Marea, then retreated. Marea walked from its grasp, stepping through a gap in the wall. Another wave rose behind her.

Gillian braced herself. The ground shuddered with the wave's impact. One of the villas groaned and shattered, collapsing in on itself.

A tremor nearly drove Gillian and KC to their knees.

The Earth stilled. Temples pounding, Gillian swung toward Dagan. "Tell Her to stop it—stop it now!" Gillian shouted. She turned on Beck, grasping the front of his shirt. "Tell *all* of Them. I'm *here*. What more do They want? To kill me? *Before* They use me?"

"No," Beck said. "That's not—no."

The rain shrank to a mist, the wind's keening to a sigh. The waves retreated, exposing a strip of flooded sand.

Gillian released Beck. She took a deep breath, fighting her own anger and panic. "All right," she said. "All right."

She searched each of the spirits' eyes for some glimmer of sanity. She met Canace's steady gaze. "What do I do?" she said.

TWENTY-NINE

THE WIND GREW STILL. CANACE SEPARATED GILLIAN AND KC's hands. "Let him go," she said, "or you'll kill him."

"*We* will kill him," Beck said.

Gillian jerked her hand away. KC stepped back reluctantly. Canace glared at Beck, then took Gillian's hand. Pressing Gillian's palm, she led her to the Ocean spirit. "Marea's power is greatest here," she said.

Calm resurfaced in Marea's eyes. She smiled. "You're good for us, Gillian. You are what a language should be. Clear and direct."

"Most languages are," Gillian said. "If they're not abused."

Marea's smile twitched wider. The waves behind her broke in shallow gasps. "Remind us often. We forget so easily."

With a nod to Canace, Marea reached for Gillian's hand. Canace passed it to the Ocean spirit as if it was a chalice. Marea led Gillian to the seawall. "Place the metaphors here so that we may look at them," she said.

Rain swelled into fat drops then dissolved back into mist. "Hurry," Beck said, his voice taut. "She's appeased now, but I don't know much longer that will last."

Gillian glanced at KC. With his pale face and his controlled stillness, he looked small against the backdrop of boiling skies and shattered buildings. Small, and yet he embodied all the fears and hopes of Rio Santo.

Gillian squared her shoulders and faced the wall. She wedged the plastic bag into a gap in the weathered stones to keep the candle from rolling. Reaching into her left pocket, she pulled out the angel's hand and set it on the wall. Then she reached into her right pocket for the stone and cup. "There," she said.

The four spirits drew closer. Canace and Beck brushed against Gillian, one with a feather's touch, the other with a damp chafe.

Gillian looked at the four objects on display, trying to imagine them as the four spirits saw them. The angel's hand seemed worn and sad, the crystal cup shabby. Encased in its vegetable bag, the candle looked crass and commercial. Only the stone seemed perfect. Gillian scratched the bridge of her nose.

Canace placed a hand on Gillian's shoulder. "You need to explain your metaphors so that we can begin to understand you. What do these symbols mean?"

Gillian's shoulders sagged. "They seem so foolish now."

Beck snorted. "Great."

Gillian leaned away from him, the stones of the seawall rasping against her overcoat.

"Leave her alone," Dagan said in a low, gravelly voice.

"If these mean nothing to *her,* how are we going to use them to understand each other?" Beck said.

Canace hissed. "Damn you, give her a chance!"

Beck's voice hardened to ice. "We need symbols—meanings—not chance."

Marea pulled Gillian close and whispered in her ear. "You're giving in to our frustration. Do that, and each of us will define you. You are the language, you need to define *us.*"

Gillian wet her lips.

Marea's voice caressed her like the sea. "Tell us about these metaphors as if you were just discovering them."

Canace cupped Gillian with her body. "Teach us their importance. Teach yourself."

Gillian leaned into Canace. "And if someone refuses to accept my metaphor?"

"If someone doesn't hear you," Canace said, stepping away, "Rio Santo will suffer. We'll all suffer."

A murmur caught in Gillian's throat. *Make them hear you,* she thought. She reached toward the metaphors.

Her hand hovered over each in turn. It was too soon, too frightening to explain Fresh Water. Remembering Dagan's fear of the Seraphim, she decided against the Earth. The Ocean had shaped the stone . . . but it was the Wind, it was Canace she felt safest and most comfortable with. She picked up the plastic bag and unwrapped the candle.

"This candle reminded me of the Wind," Gillian said, then stopped, a chill spreading through her. *Reminded me: is like.* A simile, not a metaphor. The whole time she'd been gathering her tools, her symbols, she'd been thinking in similes. In a metaphor, something *is* the object it's compared to, it isn't *like* it. If her purpose as a language was clarity and understanding, she needed to be precise.

A metaphor, Canace had said, a physical metaphor.

Gillian looked down at the candle in her hand. It succeeded as a simile. Would it succeed as a metaphor?

Her hand shook as she took out a match and lit the candle. "When lit, this candle is the Wind. It darts and flickers, playing with the light and air around it. It bends and wriggles, becomes still, then bends again."

She glanced at Canace. Canace nodded, lips curved slightly.

The encouragement buoyed Gillian. "This candle is also Canace," she continued. "When I am wise enough to use it, it lights my way—but only so far. It teaches me both to use the light and to trust the darkness."

Canace fought a smile. "Fair enough," she said. "Yes, I see the Wind there."

Gillian's pulse quickened. She dripped melted wax onto the wall, then planted the candle. The flame burned steady, as if sheltered by an invisible screen. Gillian picked up the smooth, round stone and turned to Marea.

"This stone is the Ocean," she said. "It curls around itself in a wave of rock, its surface unbroken as it flows into itself. It has changed over the years and will continue to change—at times it has been and will be smooth and calm. Other times it has been and will be rough and ragged. The first time I picked it up, it was warm. Today it was cold. It changes. But somehow the feel of it in my hand calms me, like Marea."

Marea took Gillian's hand and folded Gillian's fingers over the stone. "I am this stone," she said.

Gillian set the stone beside the candle. She reached for the angel's hand, then hesitated. She glanced at Dagan.

Fear darkened his eyes.

Reaching beyond the angel's hand, Gillian picked up the crystal cup. She squared her shoulders and faced Beck.

The Fresh Water spirit eyed the cup with disappointment. A sneer threatened to curl his upper lip.

Don't give in to his frustration, Gilly, she told herself. *Don't let him define you.*

But his frustration clung to her like fog.

"This," Gillian said, heart pounding, "was my sister's."

Beck blinked, his face frozen for an instant, then smiled like sun rippling across water. "I do like your sense of humor," he said.

Gillian raised the cup between them as if toasting. Rainwater pooled in its bottom. "This is Fresh Water," she said. "Clear and hard, it is also delicate and easily broken, like the balance between too much rain and too little. It . . . ."

Gillian blanched. Not a simile, how could she be so careless? She searched Beck's face. He studied the cup, his eyes alive with interest. She breathed a sigh of relief.

"It is ice and it is water," she said, swirling the contents of the cup as she offered it to him. "Its facets cut one minute and cast rainbows the next."

Beck touched the cup without taking it. He stepped

closer to Gillian. Tipping the cup to his lips, he left the weight of it in her hands, forcing her to hold it. He sipped, then pressed the cup to her lips. He rocked it so that a trickle of sweet, chilled water coursed down her throat. They lowered the cup together, then Beck removed his hands.

"Thank your sister for me," he said.

Gillian nodded. "I will."

She set the cup down, glancing at Dagan before picking up the angel's hand. His breathing was ragged and shallow. Fear chiseled his reddish features.

Put him at ease, Gillian told herself.

She caressed the angel's palm. The feather had been torn from the stone fingers. "I've always loved the Seraphim—"

Dagan flinched.

"Especially the angels," Gillian said. "They carried the weight of that building on their shoulders and in their hands. This is one of the Earth's hands."

Dagan relaxed enough to moan.

Gillian turned the stone hand over. "The Earth holds the weight of us all. She holds Ocean, Fresh Water, plants, animals, and people. Her hand is strong and firm, but hands can tire." She caught Dagan's gaze and held it. "When She does, the Earth reaches out—to help and be helped. As She has through Dagan."

Dagan chafed his lips together. "The spirit is still insane."

"So is the Earth," Gillian said. "And She always will be, just a little, now that people have built so many buildings and other obstacles between Her and themselves."

Dagan hesitated, then nodded. He took Gillian and the angel's hands and kissed the angel's palm. He then kissed the corner of Gillian's mouth. His fingers trailed from her cheek to her chin. "I was right to trust you," he said.

Gillian smiled. She set down the angel's hand, looking over each metaphor again. They had all been accepted, but something didn't feel right. Something was missing. What?

Four objects—one for the Wind, one for the Ocean, one for Fresh Water, and one for the Earth—

"We begin," Marea said.

Gillian buried her misgivings and looked up.

The four spirits boxed her in, Canace and Marea nearest the seawall, Dagan and Beck between her and Rio Santo. A breeze fingered Gillian's hair, lifting it from her face. Mist settled on her skin and overcoat like dew. The promenade along the wall was firm beneath her feet.

Beyond the four spirits, the storm raged, angrier and stronger than ever. Hail and lightning slashed and stung, gales howled. Palm trees and devastated buildings quivered under the assault of Fresh Water, Wind, and Earth while around them the soil bubbled and spat. To the right and left of Gillian the Ocean hurled Herself at the seawall, spilling over the bricks and gurgling between the chinks, reaching for Rio Santo.

Gillian pushed Dagan gently aside so that she could see around him. KC knelt in the intersection, shoulders hunched against the storm. Mud licked at his calves and thighs.

Gillian faced Beck. "You're protecting me."

"Yes, we are," Canace said.

"Then allow KC to join me and protect him, too," Gillian said, turning to Canace.

Canace frowned. "Gillian—"

"Please, Canace," Gillian said in a low voice. "Something's missing. Something's not right. It might be KC."

Canace scraped her lower lip with her teeth. She nodded. "Let him in," she said.

"What?" Beck said.

Gillian swung toward him. She met Dagan's gaze.

Marea sputtered. "We don't have the power—"

"Do it," Dagan said, gaze locked on Gillian.

Marea hesitated, then stepped away from the wall. "KC," she said. "Come here."

Beck stiffened. "But—"

"Not a word, Beck," Marea said. "KC, come."

Tension lifted Gillian to her toes. Her misgivings grew,

threatening to overpower her. What if KC wasn't what was missing?

Then at least he'd be safe.

And her—was she safe?

KC lurched to his feet and stumbled toward her. Beck drew back with a sneer, but Dagan touched KC's shoulder. KC stood an arm's length from Gillian. She motioned for him to come no closer. Marea eased back against the seawall.

Gillian's throat cinched shut. *Oh, God. It's not KC.*

"Well?" Canace said.

The sky roiled with rain and wind. Gillian tried to infuse herself with calm. "I don't know," she said. "Let's just do it."

Canace nodded. "All right."

Gillian glanced back at the Wind spirit, searching for reassurance. She gasped.

Beyond Canace and Marea, spirits stepped from the surf and gathered along the rim of the sand. Flurries of wind stirred the foam and grit, solidifying into more spirits. Gillian turned toward Beck and Dagan. Rain wept into more spirits and the ground oozed upward into still more.

Gillian's heart beat faster. There, among the Earth spirits, stood Petra, her white hair rippling down her back. She glared at Gillian, her eyes narrowed to fissures.

Panic swarmed in Gillian. Something, something was missing. . . .

"Gillian," KC said, reaching for her.

Gillian shrank from his outstretched fingers. "No, KC. Don't try to save me. I have to do this alone."

"Bravo, Gillian," Marea said. Compassion filled her eyes just as it had that day with Dera—

Gillian fumbled in her breast pocket and removed the redwood frond. She laid it across the stone. "Return in your time," she whispered.

Peace touched her, then withdrew. Something was still missing, something important—

"Begin!" someone shouted.

Other spirits took up the cry. "Begin! Begin!"

Gillian looked out over the crowd. Wind whipped their hair. The storm swept over them in javelins of hail. A distant rumbling stopped Gillian's heart. Aftershock.

"Look!" Petra cried. "She falters! She is not the one!"

Gillian's heart hammered to life. She rushed to the wall. Raking her hair away from her face, she pored over the metaphors. Wind, Earth, Ocean, Fresh Water, plants—

"Gillian, what's wrong?" Canace shouted over the rising cacophony of wind, storm, and sea.

"You've got to do something," Beck said. "We can't hold them back much longer."

Marea staggered forward under the concussion of a wave. "Gillian, what is it?"

Gillian shook her head. "There's something missing—an object—"

"There are four objects!" Beck cried. His breath warmed her cheek as he leaned into her. "One for each of us—"

"And one for Dera," Canace said.

The candle's flame winked out. Gillian grabbed the box of matches and struggled to light one. A breeze whistled between Marea and Canace, extinguishing each spark.

"Tell Her to stop!" Gillian said, scraping a match along the side of the box. Hail hammered along her spine. "Tell Them all to stop!"

"Gillian," Marea said, "you've got to try."

"Leave the candle," Canace said. "It's all right."

Hands shaking, Gillian lowered the match. "Are you sure everything's here?"

"Everything," Dagan said.

"All that Jamison had," Beck said. He glanced at KC. "And more."

Gillian braced herself, lifting her chin. "All right. Use me."

"Marea," Canace said, "you and Beck go first. Start with something minor—"

Marea snorted. Beck rolled his eyes.

"Something easy to resolve," Canace said. "Quickly!"

Marea stepped toward Gillian, the edges of her body

shimmering like sea spray. She handed Gillian the stone, then stepped into Gillian.

A roar filled Gillian's ears, as if she stood at the very heart of a wave. Her own heart matched the ebb and flow of the Ocean. She struggled a little, then relaxed, letting herself drift. She turned toward the seawall. A legion of Ocean spirits poured over the stones. The first one reached her, shattered into spray and entered her.

Surf rolled through her, tossing her like a bobble of kelp within herself. She clung to a splinter of calm, trying to float, but each invading spirit deepened the Ocean within her.

The Ocean seethed inside her until all she saw were sheets of foam-laced green water closing over her. The waves grew stronger, each pulling her deeper beneath the surface. Battered and helpless, she tumbled and scraped the bottom of the sea. The sand ground away the edges of *her,* of Gillian. Soon there would be nothing left—

Panic sparked Gillian. She thrashed against the tumult of the Ocean, gasping and floundering for the surface. She closed her eyes against the burning salt. The tide flung her as another wave closed over her, knocking the breath out of her. Salt water filled her mouth and lungs. She kicked and flailed, straining for the surface. Another wave tumbled her, as if she were the sea stone. . . .

The stone, her metaphor for the sea. She was lost inside the metaphor, being carved and smoothed to nothing. Soon she would become part of the Ocean. Soon there would be no Gillian left, just the Ocean surging inside a soulless body—because there was no metaphor for her.

A metaphor for her, that's what was missing. And she knew just what and where one was.

She had to break away, had to free herself of the Ocean's grip and get the metaphor for herself so that she could anchor herself against the deluge of spirits.

She let the next wave smash her against the sandy floor. Tucking herself, she pushed off the floor and shot toward the surface. If she could break through—

She rocketed into the salt-drenched air. Opening her

eyes, she saw a hand reaching for her. She gritted her teeth and swam away from it. If she accepted this person's help now, her struggle would drown them both.

A wave rushed toward her. She eased herself into it, caught it, so that its momentum skimmed her along the surface instead of rumbling over the top of her. She rode the wave to shore. It sanded her across the grit. Crawling from the foam, she sat back on her haunches and gasped for breath.

And suddenly felt the mud-slick sidewalk in front of the seawall beneath her hands and knees, felt the patter of rain on her back. She vomited seawater.

"What happened?" Canace said. "What did you do to her?"

"I have no idea what happened." Marea's voice shook. "She was drowning. I couldn't save her. Then suddenly she cast us out."

Gillian coughed up another lungful of seawater. "I know," she panted, "I know . . . what's missing."

KC knelt beside her. He draped an arm around her shoulder and drew her close. He folded his other hand over hers. Gillian stared. It was KC who had tried to pull her from the waves. . . .

"Gillian," Canace said, crouching beside them. "What is it? What's missing?"

"A metaphor, for me," Gillian said. "I need to get it. So I won't get lost in any of you."

Canace paled. "Do you have to—do you know what it is?"

Gillian nodded. She lifted her arms. KC and Canace helped her to her feet.

"How long will it take you to get it?" Beck said.

Gillian sucked in another lungful of air. "As long as it takes me to get home and—"

KC pulled her close. "Oh, my God!"

"What—?" Gillian turned and froze.

A mountain of water rushed the shore, its summit a rising crest of foam and spray.

THIRTY

THE WAVE TOWERED ABOVE THEM, A FORTY-FOOT CLIFF about to crumble. Gillian's back bowed, anticipating the avalanche of water. Dagan, Beck, and Canace scrambled into a protective triangle.

"Marea," Canace begged.

"I'm trying!" Marea shouted.

The wave curled and broke with a deafening crash. Water churned around Gillian and KC as if they stood on an island at the bottom of a funnel. Ropes of kelp wrapped around the four spirits as water rose to their shoulders. Flecks of foam sprayed Gillian's face. KC sputtered and stumbled closer to her. She took his hand and squeezed it, hard.

The wave retreated with a garbled suck. The mud-drenched streets reappeared behind Dagan and Beck, then the seawall and a strip of sand behind Canace and Marea. The other spirits had vanished beneath the crush of seawater.

Gillian lifted her face to the clouds. For a few, brief seconds the rain forgot to fall and the wind to blow. The ground lay quiet beneath her feet. Then, slowly, the Four swelled into motion.

"Why, Marea?" Canace said, pulling bits of kelp from her hair. "Why attack now?"

"She felt rejected by the language," Marea said. "Cast out."

Canace flung away scraps of seaweed. "That's ridiculous—"

"It's true," Gillian said. "Without a metaphor for me, I'll be absorbed by the first to use me." She looked at Marea. "I'd be defined."

Marea closed her eyes. She wavered like water at a distance, then solidified again. She opened her eyes. "She understands, but She asks that you hurry."

"Just as soon as I can get home and get back," Gillian said.

"Do you have a metaphor?" Canace said.

"A Zuni altar doll."

"The one from Nora's shop," KC said.

Gillian nodded. "I rescued it during salvage."

Beck touched Gillian's elbow. "How long will it take you to get back?"

Gillian clicked her teeth together. *A conservative guess is always best,* Mom once said. "About two and half, three hours."

"Three hours, Beck," Canace said. "Fresh Water will agree to that. They all will. They have to."

"She's beyond patience," Beck said. He closed his eyes, fading as Marea had done. He solidified, eyes open. "Two hours, not a minute more."

"Dagan," Canace pleaded.

"Two, no more," the Earth spirit said.

Canace turned to the Ocean spirit. "Marea?"

Marea shook her head. "However long it takes. I'll stay with the metaphors."

"The rest of us will go with Gillian," Dagan said.

Beck frowned at him. Dagan grabbed his arm and swung him toward the street. "We might be able to convince Fresh Water and Earth to part the water and the mud," Dagan said. "Come on. The sooner we get there and back, the better."

• • •

THE STREET SIGN FOR TINKER LOOP BENT AT A FORTY-five-degree angle. Gillian hunched deeper into her over-coat, dreading any sign of the Kretskis. With luck, the Demonic Duo had barricaded themselves in their house behind a wall of baked beans.

Gillian stepped over a twisted chaise longue. The sludge nearly sucked the boot from her foot. KC and Canace waited while she wrestled it free. Up ahead Dagan and Beck forded the intersection, Dagan muttering curses. The rain misted around them, the breeze barely ruffled their hair, but the streets still gushed mud. The Earth spirits refused to cooperate.

Gillian sighed.

"What?" KC said.

Gillian started and looked over at him. "Say it again?"

KC skirted a trellis embedded in a corner lawn. "I can hear your mind working. What are you thinking about? And don't say, 'Nothing.' "

Gillian flexed her hand. "KC . . . ."

Canace dropped behind.

"KC," Gillian said, "I don't want you to go back with me."

KC combed water from his beard. "You want to tell me why?"

"I don't want you to get hurt. It's too dangerous. If one of the Four decides to lash out . . . ." She shivered. "The spirits will protect me. They'll try. But they might not protect you again, even for me."

"Gilly, it's a risk I'm willing to take."

She took his hand. "I'm not. I don't want to lose you."

"I don't want to lose you, either." KC kicked at a rubber ball. "Gilly, you nearly drowned—*out* of water. If something like that happens again, I want to be there to pull you back—"

"KC, if you'd touched me," Gillian said slowly, "we'd both have drowned."

He stopped and stared at her.

"That's why I don't want you there," she said.

They walked toward their street.

"I won't touch you," KC said. "I won't interfere in any way. Gilly, you can't stop me from coming."

"No," she said. "But I can ask you."

At the corner, leaves, branches, and boards gorged the storm drain. Denny looked up and waved. Jake and Gloria tugged at a car fender wedged between two boards.

Denny trotted toward them, shovel in hand. "Man, is it good to see you! We had the damn thing cleared and then the squall from hell drove us all inside. If that storm kicks into gear again, we're sunk."

"Water reached the front steps," Jake said. "We don't clear this shit, we're dead meat. Gloria, what'd you do with the other crowbar?"

Gloria let go of the fender and wiped her brow. "It's in the house, babe."

Jake waved her off. "Go get it! We got us another body."

"I don't know how long—" KC began.

"What do you need?" Canace said. "We've only got a few minutes, but if there's anything we can do to help . . ."

Denny handed her his shovel. He bent over the fender. "You guys want to give me a hand with this?"

Dagan grasped one of the boards. "Come on, Beck."

"Beck, huh?" Jake said. "Like the guitar player or the singer?"

Beck stared at him blankly.

Canace scooped up a shovelful of soggy leaves. She raised her eyebrows at Gillian. "Well?"

"I'll be right back," Gillian said. She spun on the ball of her foot and ran home.

The front door stood open. No surprise there, Gillian thought. Mud striped the steps like the foam in an empty Guinness glass. A gritty rime clung to the top step.

Gillian slipped out of KC's boots before stepping inside. Her shoes squeaked on the damp tiles. Someone sniffled behind her. Gillian turned.

Beth Ellen sat on the floor under the coat pegs, shoulders folded inward. She wiped her nose with the back of her hand. "Hi," she whispered. Her voice was raw with tears.

Gillian dropped to a crouch. Beth Ellen blinked at her, eyes red and swollen. Tears striped her cheeks. Gillian touched her chin. "Beth Ellen," she said.

Beth Ellen threw herself into Gillian's arms. Sobs quaked through her rigid body. "She's my buh-best friend. It isn't true. It cuh-can't be!"

"Oh, Beth Ellen," Gillian said. She held the girl close, stroking Beth Ellen's greasy hair. "Oh, honey. I wish it wasn't. God, how I wish it wasn't."

A spasm jerked Beth Ellen. She crumpled against Gillian, kneading the back of her overcoat. She whimpered into the damp fabric.

Gillian's heart shattered. Each facet reflected her own ghosts—Bibbie, Mom, Dad, Melanie, Tess—each clothed in breath-stopping pain. A grief more powerful than the Ocean struggled to suck her under, submerge her beneath its numbing surface. It would be so much easier to feel nothing, to forget to care . . . to avoid the anguish in Beth Ellen's eyes.

How did she answer that anguish? What words could she possibly use to mute the pain and make it bearable?

"There are no words," Gillian whispered, resting her cheek against Beth Ellen's head. She fought against pulling the girl closer, afraid she'd hurt her by squeezing too tight.

Footsteps slapped along the sidewalk. "Beth Ellen? *Beth Ellen!*"

Gillian lifted the girl to her feet and carried her to the door. "Ms. Jansen!" she called. "She's here!"

Beth Ellen's mother pounded up the steps. She dug Beth Ellen out of Gillian's arms. "Oh, thank God! Oh, Beth Ellen, sweetie. I've been looking everywhere for you."

Beth Ellen wriggled, peeking at Gillian from over her mother's arm. Gillian searched Beth Ellen's face, as if it might inspire some wise, healing words. She brushed the hair from Beth Ellen's forehead. "It hurts," she said. "It hurts a lot. It's okay to be hurt and angry and sad. It's okay to miss her. I miss her."

Beth Ellen sniffed. "I suh-still have her Buh-buh-buh-buh." She pressed her lips together. "Her duh-doll clothes."

Gillian smiled. "That's okay, too."

GILLIAN SQUATTED IN FRONT OF HER BEDROOM CLOSET and felt around for the scrap box. The altar doll had to be in the pocket of those old jeans, the ones she had worn the day of the salvage. Her fingers folded over cardboard. She pulled the box out of the closet.

Stirring the box's contents, Gillian tossed aside towels and pillowcases until her fingers brushed denim. She grasped the jeans by a leg and hauled them from the box. She slipped her hand into one front pocket, then the other. Her fingers slid through tattered holes.

Beth Ellen's tear-stained face loomed in the back of her mind. She plunged both hands into the box, throwing everything at her bed. Her fingernails scraped cardboard. Nothing.

The altar doll could be anywhere—buried beneath the rubble of The Happy Wanderer, lost behind the fences barricading the downtown, hidden under a table at the Action Café. It *might* be in Nora's little trailer. . . .

Gillian rose slowly to her feet. She couldn't go back to the Four empty-handed. And she couldn't get back late. How much time had already passed? How much time had she spent with Beth Ellen?

"Not enough," she muttered.

She gritted her teeth until they ached, trying to imagine another metaphor. Her mind kept returning to the altar doll. She had an odd feeling, a hunch, that the doll was nearby. She frowned, trying to remember: what else had she been wearing that day? Hard hat, sweatshirt—boots.

Rubber boots with fleece lining.

But where were they? She'd already scoured her own and the entry closet for the boots. If they'd been in the garage, she'd have tripped over them. She'd searched every room but Canace's—

She ran to Canace's room and flung open the closet.

Empty. Gillian sniffed. What had she expected? Espadrilles? Satin pumps? Clothes?

Gillian leaned against the wall. *Try to remember everything that happened after you got back from The Happy Wanderer,* she thought. *The boots were sweaty and uncomfortable. Where did you take them off? You came in the front door and—*

She straightened, then raced to the living room. Dropping to her knees in front of the last standing bookshelf, she began wrenching boxes aside. The right boot toppled against her knee.

Gillian grabbed the boot and thrust her hand inside. Her fingers closed around two inches of something small and cool and cylindrical. Laughter rose in her throat.

She pulled the doll from the boot.

The altar doll stared at her, its little circle mouth more an O of surprise than a song. Its coral arms held out its offering of crumbled turquoise and kernel-shaped stone.

Like me, Gillian thought, *offering the Four a way to hear and be heard.*

GILLIAN HIT THE SIDEWALK AT A RUN. BACKS TO HER, THE people clearing the drain had stopped working. "I've got it!" she shouted. "Let's go!"

Without turning, Beck made a cutting motion with his hand.

Gillian slowed.

"Go?" Reg Kretski said, stepping between Denny and Jake. He aimed his rifle at Gillian. "But Dorcas and I just got here."

Dorcas Kretski chuckled. She trained her revolver on the others. "And you, missy," she said, "are the one we came to see."

THIRTY-ONE

CANACE STEPPED TO THE SIDE, AWAY FROM THE OTHERS.
Like a mirror image, Beck eased away on the other side.
"What do you want her for?" Canace said.

"She's the one lured us here in the first place," Dorcas
said. "All that talk about water. Just so you creeps could
steal our rifles and wagons and stuff."

"Pretty slick," Reg Kretski said, sighting down the rifle
at Gillian. "But not slick enough."

Gillian inched toward Canace. Of the three spirits, Canace seemed the surest protector. She'd deflected the bullet
last time.

Beck edged farther away. "What are you going to do
with her?"

"Hold still," Dorcas said. She aimed the revolver at
Beck. "None of your dang business."

Gillian imagined her skin tacked to the Kretskis' wall
next to Frankie's. She leaned closer to Canace.

"But it is my business." Beck took another step. "I
need her, too."

"Stop moving!" Reg shouted.

"Sure," Beck said. He folded his arms across his chest.

Dagan dissolved behind KC. KC shifted a little, covering the spirit's sudden disappearance.

"You, mountain man," Dorcas said, pointing the revolver at KC. "Stay right where you are. Enough of this chitchat. Missy here is going with us, soon as we get our—"

Beck charged Dorcas. She swung and fired.

Beck rippled. The bullet passed through him like a stone skipping through water.

Before the gun's report echoed off the houses, Dagan materialized behind Dorcas. He bear-hugged her, pinning her arms and knocking the breath out of her. Canace evaporated. KC dived for Gillian just as Jake, Gloria, and Denny rushed Reg.

Reg fired.

KC screamed, collapsed with the bullet's impact. Blood erupted from his collarbone, a bubbling red spring. Canace solidified in time to catch him. She lowered him to the mud gently, cradling his head in her lap. Gillian dropped to her knees beside them, ripping open KC's jacket and shirt.

Canace pushed Gillian's hand away before she could explore the wound. "Let me," she said.

Gillian moved aside. She cupped KC's bearded chin with her palm. He managed a weak smile. "Be careful what you wish," he whispered. "Guess I won't be going with you after all."

Gillian rubbed the side of her nose. She wanted to laugh and to slap him at the same time. She stroked his beard instead.

Canace's fingers dissolved into KC's shoulder. She pulled her fingerless hand back. The digits solidified. "Lodged against the bone," she said.

Gillian's stomach twisted. "We've got to get him to the hospital—"

"You commie fag!" Reg shouted. Staked to the ground by three pairs of arms, he bucked and writhed. "Get your hands off her! Dorcas!"

Dagan's eyes narrowed. He slowly squeezed Dorcas until she gasped, then squeezed her harder. Her eyes bulged in their sockets, her tongue dripping over her lower lip.

Easing up a little, Dagan questioned Reg with raised eyebrows. "More?" he asked.

Reg went limp.

"Beck, get their guns," Jake said.

Gloria snarled down at Reg. "I'll get them. Beck, come and hold this prick."

Beck pinned Reg's wrists, freeing Gloria. She staggered to her feet and snatched up the guns, then headed for her house.

"Where you going?" Denny called.

Gloria trudged up her driveway. "I got three sets of cuffs in the cookie jar on the fridge. That should hold them."

"Handcuffs?" Beck said.

"Her ex is a cop," Jake said. "Guess he forgot a few things when he moved out. Gillian, how's KC?"

Gillian looked down into KC's clammy face. His attempted wink turned into a wince.

"Not good," Gillian said. "We need to get him to the hospital."

"With the roads so screwed up, the hospital's a long shot," Denny said. He grimaced. "Shit. We got to get him to Lowen—quick."

"Canace," Gillian said, "can you take him to Lorna?"

Canace's lips set in a grim line. "Gillian," she said in a low voice. "We don't have much time."

"She's right," KC said.

Gillian looked up at the sky. Black clouds curdled overhead. Beneath her, the ground quivered as if waking up.

She fisted her fingers through KC's hair. "We can't leave him here. He'll die—"

"We'll get him there," Jake said. "Soon as we get rid of these assholes."

Gloria stomped down the driveway, handcuffs jangling from her fist. She bent over Dorcas. "You're first, babe."

Dagan knocked the breath out of Dorcas one more time, then turned her over to Gloria. Gloria snapped the cuffs in place.

"Gilly," KC whispered. "You've got to go. Trust them."

Gillian's cheeks flushed. "Damn it, KC. I want to be sure you get help."

"So I won't die?" KC chuckled mirthlessly. "Gilly, if *you* take me to Lowen, I'll die for sure. Me *and* Rio Santo."

Gillian jerked as if she'd been slapped. "You're right," she said. "I got so caught up in . . . Canace, how much time do we have?"

"Maybe an hour," Canace said. "Probably less."

Gillian turned to the others.

Gloria cuffed Reg. He didn't resist, just shivered, his eyelids fluttering. With his blue pallor, he looked like he was freezing. The shadow of a smile curved Beck's lips.

"There," Gloria said, rising. "Come on. We'll put them in the garage."

Gloria stomped on ahead. Jake and Denny herded the Kretskis up the driveway.

Beck and Dagan knelt beside Canace. Beck nudged her. She transferred KC's head to his lap. "You need to get going," Beck said to Gillian. "I'll stay here until Denny and Jake can take him to the Red Cross."

"I'll stay, too," Dagan said. "We'll catch up."

"Do it, Gilly," KC said.

Gillian swallowed. She bent over and kissed KC's cheek, then rose. "Come on," she said, tugging Canace's sleeve.

They hurried off at a slow trot. Gillian resisted the urge to look back. Dipping her hand into her overcoat pocket, she clasped the altar doll.

ANOTHER DEAD GOPHER FLOATED BY. GILLIAN AVOIDED it.

Rain lashed her back. She pulled the hood lower, trying to protect her face from the whiplike drops. The ground shimmied like Jell-O under her feet.

Canace trudged ahead, forging a path through fallen trees and sheared boards, often leading Gillian along the

edges of porches and front steps to avoid the growing
marshlands. They had already had to retrace their steps
once because two pines and a sycamore had fallen, crushing the houses on either side of the block and barricading
the end of the street. They'd lost a lot of time—

Canace stopped four houses from the intersection. Gillian caught up to her. An old refrigerator and a car door
wedged together, blocking the storm drain. The small lake
lapped porches and front steps.

"I wish those two would hurry," Canace muttered. She
stepped into the dark, rippled water. Her leg disappeared
to the knee.

Gillian braced herself and followed. The overcoat
fanned across the surface of the water.

The rain turned to sleet.

They were within a yard of shore when Canace cried
out and sprawled forward. Gillian resisted the urge to rush
to her side. Instead, she shuffled carefully to Canace, her
shin bumping up against something hard. Momentarily
freed, a tricycle broke the surface then sank again without
a trace.

Gillian grasped Canace's arm and pulled her to her feet.
Canace squeegeed the slime from her legs, cursing under
her breath. "Damn them," she said. "If even one of them
showed up, I could go ahead and look for obstacles."

"Why don't you?" Gillian said. "The rest of this street
looks fairly clear. I shouldn't have any problems."

Canace pursed her lips. "It might save time. . . ."

"Then do it," Gillian said, plowing ahead. She waded
from the bog and picked her way along a ridge of sidewalk.

Canace jogged up beside her. "It would mean leaving
you unprotected for a minute or two."

Gillian lowered her head against the sleet. "I'll be fine."

The Wind spirit vanished.

Gillian struggled on. A breeze swirled around her, licking the hem of the sodden overcoat. The breeze swelled
and grew until the coat flapped like a toothless mouth. A

sudden gust blasted the hood to her shoulders, sanding her face with hail.

Grasping the hood, she tugged it over her head. It billowed around her face. Hail peppered her shoulders and chest. Wind cycloned around her, a wall of air stopping her in her tracks. She leaned into it, straining against it. It forced her back a few steps, then hit her from behind. She pitched forward, smacking her knees against fractured concrete. The storm shrieked and swiped at her.

Pushing herself to her hands and knees, Gillian crawled toward the corner.

Someone lifted her to her feet. "What are you doing?" Canace shouted. "Leave her alone!"

A chill blast slapped at them, then died down. The hail warmed to rain. Gillian broke free of Canace and stumbled on. "How's the next street?" she asked.

GOLDFISH SWAM BETWEEN GILLIAN'S CALVES, WRIGGLING toward a plastic bucket beached against an overturned trailer. A few of the fish stopped to snap at the raindrops striking the surface.

Gillian pulled herself along the side of the trailer. "Canace, why are the Four fighting me?"

Canace swung toward her. "They're not fighting you."

"Oh, really? Why set a deadline and then do everything They can to keep me from meeting it?" A splash erupted under Gillian's foot as she stepped into shallow waters. "How much time do I have left?"

"I don't know. Ten, fifteen minutes." Canace flinched under a barrage of hail. "Where's Beck? I can't believe it's taken them this long."

Red blossomed through Gillian's mind, a torrent gushing from KC's shoulder. His blood spilled over Rio Santo, rising to cover the roofs of the city. . . .

Wind whistled through the drumming rain. A rumble growled in the distance—thunder or aftershock?

"They're not trying to keep you from meeting the deadline," Canace said. "They're angry and confused. They're frustrated with each other and with the settled, so They're reaching out in the only way They know how."

"By destroying everything?"

"By asking to be heard."

Gillian shook her head. "Canace—"

"No one's heard Them, Gillian. Unless there's a language, no one ever hears Them until They're forced to raise Their voices."

"Sometimes a whisper gets more attention," Gillian said.

"And did you pay attention to the drought? Aside from buying bottled water and not flushing your toilet?"

Gillian took a deep breath. Salt mixed with the scent of water-churned soil. "So They've all gone crazy. . . ."

She stopped and looked around. The sign at the corner read MADRUGA AVENUE. Less than a block away, the Mediterranean villas bowed to the flooded streets. "Canace, we're almost there!" Gillian shouted, rushing forward. "We made it!"

She plashed along the slick street, her hood whipping back. The rain ripped at her cheeks, the wind keened in her ears. She blundered on, gaze fixed on the far corner. The ground sloped upward, a gradual incline that helped her see a little farther. Once she made that intersection, she'd be on Beach and Playa, within sight of the seawall—

"Gillian, look out!" Canace yelled.

Gillian turned just as she stepped into nothing.

THIRTY-TWO

GILLIAN TUMBLED BACKWARD, HER FEET SKIDDING OUT from under her. She tensed, expecting to slam into the pavement, but nothing broke her fall. A layered cliff face grew above her, weathered and straight like the cliffs at Briar Hollow.

She cried out, then struggled to relax. She stood a better chance of surviving the fall if she hit the bottom like a rag. The sky receded quickly, now only a jagged gray smile in the dark.

Gillian closed her eyes. *I'm falling into the center of the Earth,* she thought.

She smacked into something firm but giving. It held her, encasing her in a shifting, gritty warmth. She inhaled deeply, the damp, mildewed scent of turned soil filling her lungs. Beneath her, the ground turned to stone. Opening her eyes in the near dark, she felt with her hands, shifting slightly. Her right foot jutted out into nothing. A rock skidded into the chasm and pinged against the wall. She strained to hear the rock hit.

Silence.

She curled up on her ledge, deeper into the soil that blanketed her.

"It's all right, Gillian," Dagan said. "I've got you."

Gillian laughed, relieved. "Thank God!"

A breeze ruffled Gillian's hair. "So how do we get her out?" Canace said. "Can you convince the spirit of this place to help her?"

Dagan sighed. "The spirit is completely mad. It's split itself in two. There's no reasoning with it."

"Any chance it'll decide to close the fissure?" Canace said.

"Maybe," Dagan said.

Gillian scooted back until her shoulders scraped the cliff. The wall felt stable—for now. "How real and how soon is that a possibility?"

"The spirit is insane," Dagan said.

The opening above flared white. Lightning.

"The spirit might be, but the Four aren't," Gillian said. "I don't have much time left. Dagan, can you make me a stairway?"

"This isn't my land," Dagan said. "There's not enough of me to get you to the top and still protect you with a ledge in case you slip."

A warm fog kissed Gillian's cheeks.

"But we can," Beck said.

Canace hissed. "A stairway of water? Be serious, Beck."

"Of ice," Beck said.

Gillian rose to her knees. "Who's 'we,' Beck?"

"I've convinced a few other Fresh Water spirits to help."

"But *ice*?" Canace said. "She'll slip—"

"Not if I sprinkle gravel on each step," Gillian said. "That is, if the spirits will let me. I think I can chip some from these walls."

"Use me," Dagan said. "If Fresh Water will allow."

"We'll allow," Beck said.

Gillian bit the corner of her lip. "Dagan, what will that do to you?"

"Never mind that," he said. "Far worse will happen to me—to all of us—if the Four don't use you." Lightning flashed. "Soon," he added.

Gillian hesitated, then scooped a handful of dirt. "Thank you," she whispered.

"I'll be right behind you, as a shelf," Dagan said. "Whenever you need more, take more."

Gillian nodded, then took a deep breath. "Ready, Beck?"

"Ready."

Gillian tested the darkness in front of her with her foot. She stubbed her toe on a step. Leaning over, she sprinkled it with dirt, then stepped on it and sprinkled the next. Slowly, she began climbing out of the fissure.

GRAY LIGHT ILLUMINATED THE CHASM'S WIDENING mouth. Gillian still had another eight, nine feet to go. She scattered grit on the next two stairs, then stepped on the first one. Her foot shot from under her.

She flailed toward the chasm. There wasn't enough of Dagan to catch her this time—

A wall of air pinned Gillian to the cliff face. "I'm going to ease away," Canace said. "Don't overcompensate."

"Got it," Gillian said. She regained her balance, then sprinkled more dirt on the step.

Within steps of the top, Gillian grasped the fissure's lip and pulled herself to safety. She felt in her pocket for the altar doll, then crawled to her feet. The corner of Beach and Playa was a good block and a half, two blocks away. She took several deep breaths, her shoulder blades wincing as she waited for hail to batter her spine. Then she sprinted for the corner, slamming her feet down like jackhammers to keep from sliding.

The iced mud crunched beneath her feet.

She skidded around the corner, her breath escaping in billows of steam. Wind howled around her and whipped her breath away, but sleet and hail were mercifully absent. At the end of the street, Marea stood by the seawall, shouting and signaling wildly with her arms. Snow whirled around the Ocean spirit, dusting her with powdery white flakes.

Gillian stumbled to a stop. The blizzard shrieked around

her, snow tumbling in drifts from the sky. Gillian's chest ached, the air icing her lungs. Snow froze to her hair and lashes. "No," she murmured, breaking into a run. "No!"

Beyond the seawall, a wave rushed the shore, rising higher and higher until it towered over the beach, shrinking the sky. At least seventy feet high, Gillian thought, much taller than the last great wave. Snow and foam melded into a turbulent froth.

"Gillian!" Marea shouted. "Hurry!"

Gillian pounded across the street and onto the sidewalk. Throwing her arms around Gillian, Marea pulled her into a crouch. Gillian's metaphors lay at Marea's feet. Canace materialized in front of Gillian, covering Gillian's face with her hands. A torrent of water and mud flowed from the sky and became Beck and Dagan. Dagan seemed smaller. They positioned themselves on either side of Gillian, Beck freezing into a wall of ice, Dagan into a wall of stone. Together they sheltered her.

The wave curled above them, then broke. "Breathe," Canace said. Gillian inhaled Canace's hands as a crush of green water roared over her cave of rock and ice.

Geysers of foam exploded, drenching her. The wave retreated.

Dagan and Beck thawed and took human form. Canace stood, her hands solidifying into fists. "She's here!" Canace shouted.

"Quickly," Marea said, helping Gillian to her feet. "You must begin *now*."

Marea collected the metaphors and placed them on the wall. The redwood frond was long gone. Gillian brushed each metaphor with her fingers, then took the altar doll from her pocket.

Gillian held the doll high above her head. A breeze swept the melting snow from the doll's face. "This is me," Gillian said. "This is me, offering You the gift of language. My arms cradle the gifts I bring, my mouth opens to allow You to speak through me. Take whatever words and understandings You need, but remember that I

am the language and I must exist separate from each of
You, or there can be no communication."

Snow drifted into Fresh Water spirits. With whistling
moans, the Wind spirits spun themselves from the chill air.
At the edge of the sand, the sea slapped the shore, releasing
a host of Ocean spirits. Mud and dirt heaved into spirit
forms. Petra shook her long white hair, a challenge gleam-
ing in her eye.

Gillian lowered the doll, then picked up the sea-polished
stone and the crystal cup. She held the stone and the altar
doll in one hand. Marea and Beck glided toward her, nodded to each other, then entered Gillian.

Gillian gasped, closing her eyes as water bubbled up
inside her.

At her very heart, a wild, gushing river met the tumble
and roar of the sea. Both pulled at her, tossed her back
and forth like a riptide. Gillian floundered, sucked beneath
the surface of the waters. She thrashed and sputtered,
clutching at phrases and sounds that floated through her
mind:

Touch your tongue to your upper teeth.
Yesterday, today, tomorrow.
Thuh-thuh—try that—thuh-thuh.
That's it—now do it again.

The altar doll waded toward her and stopped. Taller than
Gillian, as tall as KC, it waited for her, its waist belted by
the flow of the waters. Rivulets streamed from its shoulders. Dew beaded its turquoise offerings. Mouth circled to
form an O, it sang, its voice clear and sweet and wordless
above the bubbling rumble of Fresh Water and Ocean. Gillian swam to the doll. Shuffling its burdens, it opened its
arms and held her. Gillian and the altar doll became one.
The soaring, wordless song became Gillian's.

And she understood. She understood the frustrations,
hopes, and joys of the Ocean and of Fresh Water as they
mingled inside her. Jumbled images—disappointments and
desires—flowed through the currents surging around her:

Rivers gushed toward the reaching sea, the river trickling to nothing before the two could join.

Fog shrouded the redwoods, moistening their roots with its faintly salted breath, then evaporating before it could soothe the trees when Fresh Water withdrew too soon.

Rain dimpled the surface of the sea. . . .

R-r-r-r-r-r. That's it. R-r-r-r-r-r-r.

Fresh Water withdrew and the Wind gusted through Gillian, shattering the whitecaps. The Wind whipped the Ocean into dancing sprays that arced like shooting stars. Gillian squared her shoulders against the pull and push of the Wind.

Fog strained for the redwoods, then settled yards from the trees' rough bark as the wind quieted, stranding it. The fog boiled away.

A breeze snipped at the whitecaps, cutting free tatters of foam—

Gillian gasped. Images raged through her too fast to hold.

The Ocean ebbed. For a few seconds she hung suspended in the cyclone's core, then the Earth settled beneath her feet. Dust devils waltzed around her, chafing her with grit. Madness tinged the dirt a deep, angry red. Petra's manic shouts rode the wind, her accusations and threats reverberating like an echo inside Gillian. *She is not the right one!* Petra shrieked. *Kill her!*

Gillian shrank from the Earth's insanity, then opened herself. The Four had to communicate freely, however crazed and angry. She welcomed the Earth. The grit softened to a fine dust. Petra's voice faded.

Gillian bowed slightly under the weight of Earth and Wind. Images battered her—topsoil swept away, breezes caged between ridges and cliffs—as if they were the words of someone speaking so fast that although she understood, only the feeling was conveyed—

The Wind withdrew and Fresh Water rushed in and then the Ocean again and through it all Gillian sang and sang and sang, offering everything but her physical essence, her anchor to the everyday world, KC's world. She lost track of who filled her, filling herself with her own song, swelling with it, with Them—

She collapsed, suddenly emptied of all but a faint, warming breeze.

With a hiss, the breeze withdrew.

Gillian stood still. Her body shrank to fit her and only her. She opened her eyes. . . .

She held the candle's last inch and the altar doll. The other metaphors lay in a half circle at her feet. The late-afternoon sun warmed her shoulders and reflected off the glassy surfaces of the puddles. The sea rolled and hissed across the sand. The ground was still. Gillian murmured. How long since the world had looked so . . . peaceful? Someone touched her shoulder and she turned. Canace.

They were alone, she and Canace, amid the devastation—the flattened villas, the shattered seawall, the broken and twisted trees. Gillian shaded her eyes. Kelp and driftwood crisscrossed the beach, netting gulls, fish, scraps of metal and plastic.

Gillian placed her hand over Canace's. "I—I'm glad you stayed to say good-bye," she said. "I'll miss you."

Canace smiled. "I'm not gone yet."

THIRTY-THREE

CANACE HANDED GILLIAN THE CRYSTAL CUP AND THE stone. Gillian slipped them into her overcoat pockets, then reached for the angel's hand and the candle nub.

"Leave the candle," Canace said. "You can get another one."

Gillian nodded, then looked at the nub. She put it in her pocket. "To remind me," she said.

She nestled the altar doll in her breast pocket.

"We'd better get going if we want to get home by dark," Canace said.

Gillian touched Canace's elbow. "I'd like to go to Lowen, see how KC is."

Canace smiled. "Lead on."

They shuffled through a rich stew of bloated fish, sludge, and kelp. The mud-covered remains of the villas looked like a jumbled display of truffles. The palm trees drooped. Three had fallen and now stretched across the street. An octopus tangled around the base of the Beach and Playa street sign as if it had tried to anchor itself. Gillian shuddered and walked toward Madruga.

At the corner, a fishing trawler slumped against an unrecognizable pile of rubble, its hull pierced by a spine of masonry. Gillian swung to look back. A sailboat wedged against the jagged seawall a quarter mile down the beach.

A half block away, another trawler folded into a brick-and-plank-strewn foundation, its name still legible: *Jenny-B-Good*.

"Canace," Gillian said. "Did we save Rio Santo? Is the entire town like this?"

Canace slipped an arm around Gillian's waist. "*You* saved Rio Santo, Gillian. This is the worst of it. The Ocean can only reach so far."

"But the snow—"

"It didn't last long enough to do real damage."

Gillian inhaled through her teeth. All around them, clothing and streamers of seaweed twisted together like distraught hands. The people were evacuated, she reminded herself, days ago. The people are safe. Some are with friends and families, others with the Red Cross at places like Lowen. . . .

Gillian turned to Canace. "Canace, can you go to Lowen and be sure KC's all right?"

Canace hugged her, then faded into a whistling gust of wind. "Sure," she whispered. "I'll be back in a minute."

Gillian trudged on. Toilets and sinks rose like buoys from the still waters. Refrigerator doors, car doors, freezer doors, screen doors—every kind of door imaginable drifted along the streets or lodged in dams of siding, trees, and tires. A numbness grew in Gillian, born of despair. Lucinda had lived around here, and Tess . . . who knew how many of her students. Now the homes they'd known and treasured were gone. And how many of them as well? How many had sneaked back, refusing to leave their worlds behind?

If she had acted sooner, would this have happened?

Gillian clothed herself in guilt and followed the ravaged street into the heart of Rio Santo.

SUNLIGHT FADED FROM A BRIGHT, COOL BLUE TO CRISP yellow. Gillian hunched her shoulders against the deepening chill. Judging by the light, it had been at least half an hour since Canace left. Gillian's chest tightened. *Please, KC,* she prayed. *You've got to pull through.*

She detoured around a plastic sign pinned beneath a motorcycle. QUI, it read.

QuikStop.

Gillian looked up. Lowen was only a mile, mile and a half from here. She surveyed the houses. Shingles scattered like leaflets across lawns and driveways, while water streamed along walkways, little rivers rich with plastic toys, broken vases, books, toothbrushes, and clothes. Despite all this, these buildings had survived with nothing more devastating than a few missing porches and collapsed rooms. Chimneys had fallen, every window had broken, but these houses could be shifted back onto their foundations and rebuilt. A curious elation bubbled through Gillian. She smiled.

The smile and the elation evaporated. A few feet away an arm dangled from under a crush of brick.

Flames flickered higher as the house shuddered and fell. Bricks and fiery planks burying Dad. . . .

Gillian jerked away and stumbled on.

"I'm sorry," a breeze whispered against her cheek. Canace appeared beside her. "He's not at Lowen. I've searched for him everywhere. I can't find him."

Gillian wrapped her arms around herself, trying to hold herself together. "What do you mean, you can't find him?"

Canace tried to embrace her. Gillian twisted away. "What do you mean, Canace? What about—" She swallowed the tears brewing in her throat. "Not even his body?"

Canace hesitated. "Nothing, Gillian. I've looked everywhere. I even went to Nora's. She and Debbie are fine—they're worried about you. But KC . . . ." She shook her head. "I asked the other Wind spirits to help. Gillian, if KC were drawing breath, we'd have found him."

Gillian stared at the mud-streaked ground.

"Gillian, I'm sorry," Canace said.

Gillian murmured, then walked on.

Canace fell in step beside her. "Gillian, where are you going?"

"To Lowen," Gillian said. "To find out where they sent his body."

GILLIAN SAT ON A MILK CRATE AND GAZED ACROSS THE dimly lit cafeteria. Kerosene perfumed the air like cheap incense. Cots stretched from one end of the cafeteria to the other, rumpled clothes and stuffed animals peeking from beneath thick blankets. People snuggled down under the covers or gathered together, chatting and playing cards. A few read by lantern light. A mother played Pogs on the floor with her daughter and son.

The mug in Gillian's hands thawed her fingers. She held it to her face, letting the steam dampen her cheeks. She inhaled the fragrant licorice tea, then sipped, careful not to dislodge the thick wool blanket draped over her shoulders. The tea warmed her. She closed her eyes. She'd forgotten what warmth was.

"Ms. Wheatley?" someone said.

Gillian opened her eyes. A Red Cross volunteer squatted in front of her. "Ms. Wheatley," he said, "I've gone through all the logs and talked to everyone. I'm sorry, but KC Brennan never made it here."

Gillian squeezed the cup. "He never . . . ?"

"I'm sorry," the man said. He studied her carefully. "Are you all right? Is there anything I can do for you?"

Gillian stared into the cup. The dark tea steamed like lost blood. "No. Thanks."

The man patted her knee, then rose and walked away.

She set the mug between her feet. *Didn't even make it. . . .*

Canace sat down on the crate beside her. "Any word?"

"None," Gillian said. "You?"

"Gillian! Mama, it'th her! Her'th here!"

Gillian nudged the mug out of the way and stood. Clutching her stuffed bunny, Lucinda dodged between the maze of cots. "Gillian! Gillian! Do you lothe your houthe, too?"

Gillian scooped up the girl and hugged her fiercely. "Thank God, thank God," she murmured into Lucinda's neck. "Oh, Lucinda, it's so good to see you. And Bunny."

Lucinda wriggled a little and Gillian set her down. Although thin and a little dirty, Lucinda looked wonderful. Five braids sprouted from her scalp, each bound by a neon barrette.

Lucinda squeezed the stuffed rabbit. "I telled Bunny itth okay. Thee, Bunny? Here'th her, all thafe!"

Gillian touched Lucinda's cheek. "How long have you been here?"

"Oh," Lucinda said, twisting her mouth to one side. "Thinthe tomorrow."

Lucinda's mother walked up. "Hello, Ms. Wheatley. Lucinda, come on, honey. It's time to get ready for bed."

Lucinda pouted. "No! Teth ithn't in bed."

Gillian's pulse raced. "Tess? She's here?"

Lucinda's mom nodded. "Monday, same as us. Sorry to scoot, but it's this gal's bedtime. Now, I don't want any sass," she said as she hefted the kindergartner onto her hip. "What'd I tell you? I'm not Tess's mama. . . ."

Relief swept through Gillian. Tess and Lucinda, both alive—Gillian sat down and leaned against the wall, staring at the ceiling. She exhaled, long and slow.

"I found Nick and Marjorie Trestle," Canace said. "There's a whole classroom with nothing but strep cases—"

"Gillian?"

Gillian lowered her gaze. "Jenna!"

Jenna Pelligrini crouched beside her. "Gillian—what are you doing here? Don't you live near Linnet Park? I thought that neighborhood was safe."

"Our house is fine," Gillian said. "Canace, Jenna. Jenna teaches first."

Canace hollowed her cheeks. "Do you live near the river?"

Jenna's face sagged, weighted with care. "In the mountains. *Lived.*"

Gillian clasped Jenna's chapped hand. "Jenna, I'm sorry."

Jenna combed a stray hair from her face. "Don't be.

Del and I were lucky. The radio told us to stay put, but when the house started creaking, we just looked at each other and ran. We barely made it to Timber Valley Road when we heard this—this sound. This wave of mud shattered our house like it was made of cards. There were these trees . . . surfing . . . the edge of the slide . . .''

Jenna closed her eyes and covered her hand with her mouth.

Gillian's throat tightened. "Jenna—"

"No," Jenna said, wiping her cheek with the back of her hand. "No, don't be sorry. We're alive, me and Del. Some people weren't so—weren't so lucky." The forced cheeriness in her voice cracked. "Oh God, Gillian. Trevor MacLean . . . .''

Gillian doubled over as if struck. Expecting it didn't take away the sting. She remembered Trevor being brave for Lucinda, trying to coax her out from under the table—

"His—his whole family," Jenna said. "Swept down the ravine . . . .''

Gillian shivered. She rolled and unrolled the hem of her jacket. "Who else? Have you heard about anyone else?"

"Amanda Kleiber," Jenna whispered. "A—a bookshelf crushed her." She stared into her cupped hands. "They took David Hawk to the hospital. His asthma . . .''

Canace squeezed Gillian's arm. Gillian's heart shrank beyond reach of pain. She probed her dry mouth with her tongue, wanting to know but afraid to ask about Rafael and the others. She cleared her throat—

An explosion echoed through the night, followed rapidly by another.

Everyone froze. Silence filled the cafeteria like smoke. Then someone laughed, a high, nervous peal. Children began to cry. Several people rushed for the door, darting outside. Gillian grasped Canace's hand.

Rising slowly, Jenna backed a few steps, glancing right and left. "Del?" she said. "Del!"

"Jenna?" a man called. "Jenna, where are you?"

Jenna squeezed Gillian's hand once, then slid hers away. "Over here, Del!" she said. She hurried toward his voice.

"What now, Canace?" Gillian said. "Haven't we been through enough?"

One of the doors slammed open. The curious plodded back in, stunned and trembling. The door swung closed, then opened again. Dagan stepped inside.

Even from this distance, Dagan looked worn and harried. Gillian held her breath.

His eyes widened as he spotted her. He snaked between the cots.

Gillian stood. The blanket fell from her shoulders. Panic broke through the numbness, hammering with her heart.

"Gillian," Dagan said, lurching to a halt in front of her. "Gillian, the Seraphim is down. The spirit is free."

THIRTY-FOUR

DAGAN PACED IN FRONT OF GILLIAN, SANDING HIS PALMS
against each other. "I was with Debbie when it happened.
She's on her way to the Seraphim now. She may be able
to nourish the land on her own, but I'd feel better if you
were there, too."

Dagan's pacing pierced Gillian's exhaustion. "Dagan,"
she said, "I offered the Earth peace. She accepted. I could
feel that while She was using me. Why doesn't She stop
this spirit?"

"It's part of Her," he said. "Its anger is part of Her."

"But She was at peace," Gillian said, stepping into his
path.

He stopped pacing. "This spirit won't accept peace."

Canace stood. Her eyes narrowed. "What *will* it accept?"

Dagan's voice trailed off. "Nourishment, worship . . . ."

Gillian reached for her overcoat. "Let's go."

"Gillian," Canace said, "after all you've been
through—"

A sigh hollowed Gillian. "After all I've been through—
after all I've lost—I will not let some deranged spirit destroy Rio Santo."

"Not just any spirit," Dagan warned. "This one's crazier than all the rest of the Earth spirits put together."

Canace held Gillian's gaze. "But we talked about this, outside Briar Hollow. The Earth needs someone to nourish Her as She nourishes humans. She needs someone to complete the circle, someone born *of* Her. Debbie completes that circle—"

"I'm going," Gillian said.

Canace shook her head. "Then I'm going with you."

Dagan hurried toward the doors. "I'll meet you there."

"Where are *you* going?" Canace said.

"To talk to Debbie," he said. "She needs to know what she's up against."

"What about Gillian?" Canace said.

Gillian followed Dagan outside. "I already know. I just don't know if I'll be facing the Virgin Mary or some Ohlone god."

The downtown glowed orange, an eerie dawn straining to break.

CANACE AND GILLIAN CLIMBED THROUGH A MAZE OF overturned cars and orphaned porches and walls. An awning spanned one street, bracing a canopy of uprooted trees. Gillian dropped to her knees and motioned to Canace. They crawled under poles and limbs, popping free two blocks from the Seraphim. They pushed themselves to their feet without stopping.

Ash drifted over them like snow. Somewhere a siren wailed, unable to get closer. It screamed and screamed, receding as Gillian and Canace drew nearer the Seraphim.

Flames tickled the night, jabbing and prodding the dark from between heaps of stones and bricks. Smoke engulfed the moon and stars, recreating the horizon. Heat swept over Gillian in waves.

"Why fire, Canace?" Gillian said, stepping over a fallen bicycle rack. "Why not another earthquake?"

"It needed to destroy the foundation," Canace said. "With the Seraphim that badly damaged, all the spirit had to do was break a gas main."

"Like Dagan," Gillian said.

Canace shook her head. "Dagan didn't bring that house

down. The Earth did. She knew he was one of the few
spirits She could trust. Maybe the only one that wasn't
completely insane.''

An involuntary shudder quirked through Gillian. What
a disaster it would have been had the Earth sent Petra to
find someone to replace Melanie. . . .

Gillian stiffened. If Melanie hadn't run away, she'd be
facing the spirit, not Debbie and Gillian. The responsibility
threatened to crush Gillian. What if Debbie wasn't ready
for this?

Gillian squared her shoulders and led Canace across the
parking lot toward the Seraphim. A stretch of the Cyclone
fence had fallen just in front of the old theater like dis-
carded chain mail.

Sweat bathed Gillian's face. She shucked off the overcoat, wiping the back of her neck with her hand. After
removing the altar doll from her pocket, she draped the
coat over her arm.

Canace touched Gillian's shoulder. "This is close
enough," she said. "Let's wait for Dagan here."

Gillian nodded. She stared into the flames, imagining
Mom and Dad staring back.

Gillian averted her face, searching the rubble-choked
streets for Dagan and Debbie. Across the parking lot and
the street, two fence posts leaned into each other in a broken cross. *A sacred symbol,* Gillian thought. *Which sacred
person will the spirit choose this time?*

Someone with contemporary significance. In this day
and age, that could be any of a number of figures. The
spirit might appear as Jesus, Buddha, Muhammad, Isis, the
Green Man . . . or as a rock musician, a film star, an ath-
lete. But which one? If she had some idea, she could brace
herself for the encounter.

Her mind lingered over the image of a fallen angel, its
eyes glowing red and its leathery wings spread wide. It
leered at her, its lips curling back in scorn.

Gillian gritted her teeth. "Sacred," she muttered, "not
profane."

Canace started. "What?"

"Nothing," Gillian said. She scanned the streets again, then turned to the Wind spirit. "Canace, how did Jamison handle things like this?"

"He didn't," Canace said. "Nothing like this happened while he was the language."

"Gillian!" someone screamed.

Gillian and Canace jerked toward the Seraphim. A lone figure raced across the cleared lot beside the old theater, glancing over his shoulder at the burning building. The ground under the Seraphim quivered and swelled, smashing the retaining wall that circled the adjacent lot.

"An Earth spirit," Canace said. "The Seraphim is trying to absorb him—"

A wave of rock and grit rumbled toward the fleeing spirit. He screamed as the wave broke over him, slamming him to the ground. Writhing and flailing, he melted into the dirt.

Another figure sprang from the Earth on the far side of the retaining wall, her white hair reflecting the oranges and golds of the flames. "Eben!" she cried.

Gillian pointed. "Canace, it's Petra."

The retaining wall rattled and shook.

"It's going after her, too," Canace said.

Petra backed away, her body curled for attack like a cornered animal. "Leave me alone," she shouted. "I will not be part of you. Stay away from me!"

Petra strove for an air of defiance, lifting her chin, but the curl of her shoulders betrayed her. Gillian's mind rang with Petra's remembered threats and taunts: *She is not right! Kill her!* A sense of poetic justice steeped in Gillian, smug and bittersweet. It evaporated with the thought of Petra's lust for vengeance wedded to the Seraphim spirit's anger.

Gillian dropped the overcoat and sprinted toward the Cyclone fence. Cinders seared her lungs. She stopped, coughing and gasping for breath. "Petra," she said, beckoning with her hand. "Petra, hurry!"

Petra shook her head. "Whether I stay or go, it will

claim my land and me. Get away from here before it tries to absorb *you*.''

A shiver crept along Gillian's spine. "Let me help you. What can I do to help you?"

"It's too late," Dagan said, grasping Gillian's arm.

She tried to shake him off, but his grip was rock firm. "It's not too late," Gillian said. "Not until the wall crumbles."

With a grinding crack, the wall split apart.

Petra danced in place as if uncertain whether to flee or attack the Seraphim spirit. She pivoted toward Gillian and ran. "Gillian!" she screamed. "Please!"

Gillian struggled against Dagan. "Petra!"

The wall exploded. One of the stones struck Petra behind the knee, toppling her. The dirt absorbed her like quicksand.

Gillian leaned into Dagan. He held her, as much for his own support as hers. "Until you and Debbie stop the spirit," he said, "it's going to destroy everything and claim every Earth spirit within reach."

"And if we can't stop it?" Gillian said.

"It'll claim us all," Dagan said.

Gillian swallowed. All that madness, all that power, bent on the destruction of Rio Santo. "How far is it to Frigate?"

"My street?" he said. "Not far enough."

Gillian straightened. "Where's Debbie? We've got to get started."

"Here," Debbie said, joining them.

Canace hung back, eyes closed, face tilted to the sky. She dissolved.

Debbie watched calmly.

"Did Dagan explain everything to you?" Gillian said. Debbie nodded.

Gillian turned to Dagan. "Did you?"

"Yes," he said.

Gillian studied him for several seconds, then glanced at the Seraphim. The flames slowly sputtered and winked out. The rubble shook as if bristling with anger. The tremor traveled toward the plots on either side of the building.

"Dagan, you need to tell us exactly what we're doing here," Gillian said. "Are we nourishing this spirit, helping it communicate, worshiping it? You need to tell us the *essence* of what we're supposed to do."

"The spirit needs to be nourished," Dagan said. "And worshiped. The wandering people had a rite—"

"Your rites nearly got me killed in Briar Hollow," Gillian said. "Your *incomplete* rites. No, the spirit approached the coastal people as one of their gods. Then it approached the Spanish settlers as the Virgin Mary. You can't tell me the coastal people and the Spaniards had the same rites—"

Movement drew Gillian's attention. The office building next to Petra's plot vibrated. From the heart of the old Seraphim, the ground rolled in waves, slamming at the office building's foundation. Shored up with scaffolding on three sides, the building shimmied until the braces started to snap, one by one. The structure swayed drunkenly, groaning and shrieking. It reeled with each blow.

The building burst and fell.

A huge cloud of dust rose, mingling with smoke into a dense tule fog of plaster and ash. A head poked tentatively above a fragment of wall, haloed by dust. With a startled scream, the little figure flung its arms over its head and disappeared in a blur.

Gillian's pulse pounded in her ears. Beside her, Debbie murmured wordlessly, twisting the hem of her shirt.

Dagan stumbled back a few steps. "It's getting stronger."

"What do—what do we need to give it?" Debbie said. "Besides nourishment?"

"Awe." Dagan's voice was dry with fear. "You need to make it an offering . . . of your hearts and hopes."

Dagan's terror leached into Gillian's bones. She shivered. Awe was easy enough, but how could she find it in her heart to adore and worship anything as destructive and desperate as this spirit?

She glanced at Debbie. Debbie caught her lip between her teeth and stared at the heap of plaster and wood. Any adoration on her part would have to break through the terror reflected in her eyes.

But maybe all Debbie had to do was nourish the spirit.

Which left the offering of heart and hopes to Gillian.

"Well," Gillian said quietly. "Debbie? Are you ready?"

Debbie took Gillian's hand.

"Stay on the pavement," Dagan said. "If you set foot on bare soil, the spirit will kill you."

Debbie's hand tightened around Gillian's. Gillian squared her shoulders. "Come on," she said. She led Debbie toward the edge of the parking lot and the fallen fence.

A figure rose amid the rubble, a silhouette in the dust. Gillian and Debbie halted abruptly, still five feet from the dirt. The figure held its arms out. "Dagan," it called. Its voice resonated with a guttural rumble. "Come! Join me. Don't wait for me to find you. Come to me now and help me undo the harm done by the settled."

"No." Dagan stepped back. "I won't help you destroy them. You don't really want that either. You're hurt and angry, but you need them as badly as the rest of us."

"Hurt?" The spirit sneered. "Angry? For over a hundred years, the settled bound me—me, the Holy Ground— and turned their backs on me. I, who have it in my power to give them so much."

Debbie trembled. "What can you give us?"

"Visions, child," the spirit said, its voice seductive and gentle. "And peace. I can provide the center that binds your dreams and I can lead you to those dreams. Or—" It snarled. "Or I can poison your dreams and your every thought, casting your soul into madness, as you have done mine."

Debbie drew closer to Gillian.

Once more the spirit turned its attention on Dagan. "Join me. Help me reclaim this land and get rid of the settled."

"I don't want to get rid of them," Dagan said. "I like the touch of their hands as they plant and the press of their feet as they walk. I like the hopes and dreams that seep from them and enrich my soil.''

"Even though they trap you, holding you prisoner in your own land?" the spirit said.

Dagan flinched and turned away.

Gillian cleared her throat, took a deep breath, cleared her throat again. "But we can offer you peace, just as you offer it to us. Let us heal your pain—"

The spirit laughed. "Ah, Dagan! A new language? What, did it take a while to find another after I silenced the last one?"

Gillian's heart stopped. "Dagan—?"

Dagan wet his lips. "Jamison was the custodian. At the Seraphim. He was—he was crushed—"

"While cleaning the boiler room," the spirit said. "The foundation shifted and fell on him. Pity. It wasn't enough to free me. Not immediately."

"You . . . planned this?" Gillian said. "This whole disaster?"

"I set events in motion," the spirit said. "And hoped. And waited."

"Dagan, why didn't you . . . ?" Gillian looked around wildly. "Canace? Why didn't any of you tell me?"

A hot, dry breeze brushed Gillian's cheek. Canace appeared beside her. "I had—we had no idea Jamison's death wasn't an accident," Canace said. "Believe me. . . ."

The hair stood on Gillian's neck. "This spirit doesn't want peace," she said. "It wants sacrifice."

THIRTY-FIVE

CANACE AND DAGAN STARED AT GILLIAN. DEBBIE CLOSED her eyes.

"What kind of sacrifice?" Canace said in a low voice.

"I'm . . . not sure," Gillian said. She avoided the answer looming in the back of her mind.

"Dagan?" Canace said.

Dagan shrugged.

Debbie murmured a quick prayer, then opened her eyes. Fear bleached her face. "Whatever it is, I'm ready. If it wants my life in exchange for Rio Santo, well, that's the way it's got to be. You can only die once."

She attempted a smile.

Gillian tried and failed to imagine Debbie as the giggly woman she'd had tea with less than a month ago—before Debbie moved in with Nora. And before she met Dagan. It seemed Nora's love centered her while Dagan's need focused her. Her newfound calm fortified Gillian.

Wrapping her arm around Debbie's waist, Gillian hugged her. "If we were earthworms, we'd have seven hearts," she said. "The spirit would have to kill us seven times."

Debbie's smile recovered. "I'm glad we're not earthworms."

"Me, too," Gillian said.

Debbie squeezed Gillian's hand. They walked to within a foot of the asphalt and stopped.

The spirit stepped from the protective shroud of dust. Gillian shook her head in disbelief. Walking toward them was a living altar doll, turquoise eyes vivid against antler-white skin. Pale umber shot the hair around her broad face and trimmed her flowing ivory sheath. She opened her arms wide to welcome them, her coral sleeves whipped by the breeze. Her footsteps followed her, each impression filled with semiprecious stones—turquoise, jasper, and rose quartz. She, too, stopped before she reached the asphalt.

Unlike Gillian's altar doll, the spirit had a small, delicate nose. Her mouth was closed rather than open in song.

Gillian marveled at the doll come to life. She tried to remember anything Nora had said about the altar doll when it first arrived at the Happy Wanderer. She drew a blank. She wondered what significance the doll had to the Zuni, what its spiritual role was. A benevolent guide, surely, one that helped the Zuni on their spiritual journey.

But how would this living altar doll approach them? How would she expect to be approached?

Gillian looked into the doll's eyes. There were often two sides to spiritual beings. In The Old Testament, God was both loving and vengeful. The Roman and Greek gods both helped and hindered mortals. What was the altar doll's other side?

Debbie moaned, pulling away from Gillian. Gillian tore her gaze from the spirit's and turned. Debbie's lips moved, but all she could manage was a soft hiss. Her eyes brimmed with terror.

Gillian frowned. Debbie knew the altar doll. While working in the shop, she'd probably dusted it and moved it from display to display many times. How could the altar doll inspire such fear?

Gillian glanced at the altar doll, then back at Debbie. A thought occurred to her: what if Debbie wasn't seeing the altar doll?

What if she saw someone else?

"Debbie," Gillian said, "who do you see?"

Debbie's lower lip trembled. "The apostle Paul."

Gillian blinked. "The apostle Paul?"

Debbie nodded. "My father—"

Gillian turned. The altar doll stood at the edge of the asphalt, her arms farther outstretched. "Where is this peace you offered me?" the spirit said. "This healing? Come closer so that I may receive these gifts from you."

Without shifting her gaze from the altar doll, Gillian whispered, "What did Paul say?"

"Peace," Debbie mumbled. "Healing. Come closer."

Gillian took a deep breath. At least they heard the same words. Was the spirit modeling Paul or the altar doll?

"Why are you so afraid of Paul?" Gillian said.

"Sunday school." Debbie's voice grew fainter. "My father . . . he said Paul hated women. . . ."

Gillian frowned. If the spirit chose someone so embedded in Debbie's psyche . . . why had it plucked the altar doll from her own? She'd only embraced it as a spiritual guide when she chose it as a metaphor for herself—

The only spiritual guide she'd embraced in years. . . .

The spirit drew a line in the dirt with its toe. Turquoise and rose quartz filled the gash in the soil. "Here," it said, gesturing to the semiprecious stones at its feet. "I have all this to offer you, and yet you come to me empty-handed?"

Debbie screamed. Gillian held her fast, unsure whether Debbie would bolt or collapse if she let go. "What?" Gillian said. "Debbie, what do you see?"

"The woman," Debbie said, her voice rising. "Didn't you see what he did? He stoned her! Broke her neck—"

Debbie shook with sobs. Rocking her gently, Gillian stroked Debbie's hair. She studied the spirit. It seemed to be trying to communicate with them using images they were familiar with: who it was mattered less than what it said. And perhaps, by extension, what it felt.

It hardly mattered what a Zuni altar doll represented. The spirit was itself and only itself.

That alone might prove deadly enough.

The asphalt at Gillian and Debbie's feet ruptured into

tiny fissures. "What do you bring me?" the spirit said.

"Peace and healing," Gillian said. "Visions."

The altar doll spat. "What good are these things? Where are your sacred objects?"

Gillian gently pushed Debbie aside and stepped closer to the spirit. "In here," she said, touching her chest. "The people I love."

"People?" the spirit scoffed. "What kind of sacred objects are those?"

"The most sacred," Gillian said. "Without my love for them, they cannot be sacred. *I* make them sacred."

Debbie clutched Gillian's elbow and pulled herself forward. Her hand was damp but steady.

"Then without your love, these people have no meaning," the spirit said.

"They have worth," Gillian said, "but my love for them makes them sacred to *me*."

The altar doll paced the lip of asphalt like a caged lion. "And you plan to use these sacred objects to make your offering? What is your sacrifice?"

"I'm . . . willing to die for them," she said.

Debbie's fingers dug into Gillian's arm. "Gillian," Debbie whispered, "you can't—"

The altar doll stood still. Its eyes gleamed with hunger and madness. "You are not enough," it said. It pointed at Debbie. "I want her, too."

Gillian wrenched out of Debbie's grasp. "No!"

Debbie pressed her lips together to contain her fear. She squared her shoulders. "Sure," she said in a thin, tight voice. "Okay."

Gillian drew Debbie aside. "And if we both die, what will Nora do?"

"Survive," Debbie said. "If she dies, she can't do that."

Debbie nodded to the spirit. She set one foot firmly on the line of asphalt and dirt.

"No!" Dagan shouted. "Don't set foot on its land—"

A tremor silenced Dagan. Gillian shuddered.

Unperturbed, the altar doll held out a hand to Debbie

and Gillian. Debbie balked, then tensed and slowly reached for its hand.

A rush of warmth filled Gillian—and inspiration. She placed a hand on Debbie's rising arm and lowered it, then stepped in front of Debbie. A cry escaped Dagan as the ash-crusted soil billowed under Gillian's feet. With the last of her strength, Gillian took both of the altar doll's hands. "She's one of my sacred objects," Gillian said. She brought the altar doll's right hand to her chest. "She's *here*. There's no need for you to take her. Let her go."

The altar doll gazed into Gillian's eyes. A smile touched its lips. "I can feel her." It turned to Debbie. "Go. Now. This one will be enough."

Gillian locked her knees to keep from collapsing. "You—you heard the spirit," she said. "Go."

Debbie's voice quavered. "I can't leave you—"

"You have to," Gillian said. "Nora needs you. And the Earth. You're needed *there*." Gillian looked into the eyes of the spirit. "I'm needed *here*."

Seconds passed. Finally Debbie's footsteps shuffled away, then broke into a short run. Canace murmured. Voice thick with tears, Debbie sobbed, "I'm all right, I'm all right."

Relief dulled the edge of Gillian's fear. Debbie, Nora, Beth Ellen, Lucinda . . . this much—more—of Rio Santo was safe.

Gillian bowed her head. "I'm ready."

The altar doll led her across the churned and fractured earth to the heart of holy ground.

The broken steps of the Seraphim lay scattered around them. *Like children's blocks*, Gillian thought, *like my students' blocks*. The Seraphim itself lay in a confused heap of stone, concrete, and ash, savaged with such rage and force Gillian could only stare—and wonder. Once freed, the spirit could easily have stripped away the asphalt under her and Debbie's feet. It could have opened a chasm and sucked them underground, grinding and suffocating them in the closing fissure. Why hadn't it?

What did it want from her?

The altar doll pulled her into an embrace. "Show me these sacred objects," it said.

The arid heat of sunbaked earth enveloped Gillian. She writhed, eyes shut tight, trying to shrink from the altar doll's radiant touch. It wound its arms around her. Gillian's skin dried and cracked. The sour, metallic stench of scorched cotton stung her nostrils as her clothing singed and burned. Gillian gritted her teeth. Constellations of sharper, more intense pain blistered here and there along her arms and back as if bits of liquid ore had mixed with the dirt of the altar doll's skin.

Gillian cried out.

The altar doll shook her. "Show me!"

Gillian forced herself to focus on Rio Santo. Her mind tumbled through the town's human faces, polishing and smoothing them like the semiprecious stones at the altar doll's feet. Each memory spun past her, crystallized in some bright moment:

Nora, nervous and expectant, sitting behind the counter of The Happy Wanderer on opening day. "Okay, Gilly. It's ten. Let the hordes in."

Lucinda's dark eyes bright, her braids bobbling. "I thaid it! I thaid a eth!"

Mrs. Timako crooning to Frankie, Hiram strolling the neighborhood with his crowbar, checking each gas main. Beth Ellen counting the cherries in the fruit cocktail, before turning triumphantly to Bibbie—

Gillian choked on the hard knot in her throat. Bibbie's still, blue face . . . Trevor, Amanda, Melanie, David—

KC.

KC, hands encased in thick gardening gloves, pawing through the glass and ceramic strewn across the floor of The Happy Wanderer—

KC crouching beside her as the light filtered in through her plastic-covered windows. His kiss, sweet and warm—

KC holding her, whispering into her hair as he tried to fill the echo of Bibbie's loss . . .

Who would fill the echo left by KC?

Gillian withdrew, fleeing her grief. Dad called to her,

his voice chasing her deeper into herself. Mom appeared. She shook her head. "You can't run away, Pumpkin," she said.

Gillian filled her mind with a bright, colorless sky—

"No!" the altar doll shouted. It placed its hand on her cheek and turned her face toward its own. A small, sharp pain blazed just under her right ear. With a gasp, Gillian opened her eyes. The altar doll glared at her, its anger tempered by pain and loneliness.

It bared its teeth, seething with wounded rage. "This is nothing, this gift of yours. You offer me comfort and peace, then you thrust me away. I don't want your distance."

Distance, Gillian thought. *The same gift I've offered KC all these years. . . .*

"I'm sorry," Gillian whispered. She wound her arms around the altar doll and clasped it to her. "Forget the sacred objects. This is what I give you."

Gillian closed her eyes again. She exiled every face from her mind and focused on the love beneath. It swelled inside her until she wondered how her body could hold it all.

She pressed into the altar doll, its molten body yielding to hers. Its arms flowed around her, encasing her in a brittle shell. Cocooned in rock, Gillian expanded to fill the altar doll's cracks and hollows. Without pulling away, she recalled one face, that of the little altar doll she'd used with the Four. She recalled, too, the face of the spirit with its bone-white skin and turquoise eyes. She blended the two, creating one face, much as she herself had merged with the smaller altar doll.

"We are one," she said.

The spirit melted into her.

The ground opened up around her, swallowing her whole. It cupped her gently, as a parent holds a robin's egg so that a small child may see. Waves of loneliness swept over Gillian, whitecapped with baffled anger—year upon year of hurt and rage. Gillian dribbled back all the love and hopes she'd known, the shore casting grains of sand into the hungry mouth of the sea.

And the sea tumbled the sand back, replenishing the hollowed footprints of Gillian's own flawed affections. Distance vanished with each footstep until KC stood beside her. Gillian reached for him, pulled him into the circle of her and the spirit's embrace. Behind KC, her parents smiled at her, no longer haloed by flame or scarred by her grief. They were whole again, a memory of life rather than death. Gillian and the spirit opened their combined hearts wider—

Nora approached, a dissonant chord prickling along Gillian's spine. Tone by tone, the dissonance fell away, revealing the one pure note beneath all the argument and the pettiness. Gillian let herself vibrate with that one note, the love she and her sister shared. Another voice built upon that one note, its song full and sure.

The spirit is singing, Gillian thought. *We are singing.*

Peace touched Gillian. She reached out with both hands to the darkness pressing against her, her fingernails clawing at the rock and dirt, her skin scraped by jagged stone. Her chest collapsed under the weight of that darkness, her lips parting to release the song. Earth filled her mouth, rich and musty and warm.

THIRTY-SIX

A SMALL TREMOR WOKE HER. HOW LONG, HOW MANY years had she slept in this midnight world? She'd been absorbed, recast in stone . . . so this was how the Earth spirits were formed. She had imagined them simply existing, like the Earth itself, or the Wind, or the Ocean, or Fresh Water, called into being by whatever forces created the planet. An older spirit claimed a sacrifice and a new spirit melded with it and became part of it—

Another tremor jostled her, accompanied by a low rumbling. Was this a call to extricate herself from the land? She tried to turn her head, struggling to break free of the press of the soil. She dangled in time, suspended in stone. Perhaps the Earth wasn't calling to her. Perhaps it was just her newly awakened awareness sensing the Earth around her. She tried to feel the Seraphim spirit, but touched nothing.

Perhaps the plot had been divided again. That might explain her solitude. How big was her plot? She tried to spread her fingers. They couldn't move even a fraction of an inch. Her plot must be small. Small and weak.

Her body hurt all over.

The soil around her shifted and shook. She moaned. Every bone, every inch of her ached. If she could just dissolve into dirt and flow to the surface. . . .

She reached out toward the quiet rumble. Someone clasped her hands, squeezing them. The rumble grew louder as the ground quivered. Someone was helping her . . . the Seraphim spirit? The Seraphim spirit . . . the spirit without a name. Dagan didn't really have a name, nor did Canace. Not until they took on a body and an identity. She had no name. When she finally broke free, she would choose one. She would choose a body—male or female? Did it matter?

The rumble became words. "Help me. Help me, I've got her arms."

Hands clasped her wrists.

"Don't pull. You'll rip her in two."

"Don't just stand there. Help us."

"She must free herself without my help."

"Free herself! She can't even move! At least loosen the dirt."

"I think I've got her elbows."

Hands slid from her forearms to her biceps, then disappeared. Fingers shifted and probed the dirt around her face.

"Dagan, do something! All that weight—I don't know how much longer I can keep breathing for her."

"Here's her head!"

"Will you help us, *please*?"

Fingers chipped the dirt away from her face. Thumbs gently dusted her eyelids. She opened her eyes. Dagan leaned over her, his smile highlighted by the first glimmer of dawn. He loosened the dirt and gravel packed around her head, while someone behind her dug to her shoulder blades.

She choked and spat. Dagan opened her mouth and cleared it of mud and gravel with his finger. "Is that better?" he said.

She nodded gratefully.

Canace's voice warmed her ear. "Why don't you get Earth to help you?"

"An earthquake right now would crush her," Dagan

said. He caressed her cheek. "We're going to try to lift you out. Ready?"

She nodded, not trusting her voice. The nerves along her neck screamed.

Dagan looked at someone above her. Hands slid under her arms. Dagan grasped her around the biceps. "Ready, set," Dagan said. "Now!"

Dagan grunted, then rocked back. He and the other person tugged her a few inches from her rock cocoon. Two sets of hands crept down her torso and gripped her around the upper ribs. She cried out. The person behind let go. Dagan shimmied his hands to her waist. Eyes screwed shut, jaw clenched, he slowly, carefully twisted her, finally tugging her free.

She clung to him, her entire body shaking with pain and fatigue. The breath squeezed suddenly from her lungs. She gasped, collapsing against his chest. She sipped at the air, then sipped a bit more. She panted and sucked for breath until her lungs filled. Canace materialized beside her and began massaging her shoulders. The person behind her worked the kinks from her spine.

She blinked, staring at the destruction around her. Ragged stone blocks and shattered angels littered the ground before her. The altar doll sat on a chunk of concrete, its brow knitted in concern.

She sniffed. So she wasn't part of the Seraphim spirit. She turned her head slowly toward Petra's plot, flinching when one of her vertebrae popped. Petra's plot stretched empty and smooth, just as it had since the bulldozers knocked down its building after the first earthquake.

Her heart sank. After all they'd been through, the people of Rio Santo had decided not to rebuild. . . .

"Can you stand?" Dagan said.

She shifted her weight out of his arms and onto her feet. And fell.

Dagan and Canace caught her. Dagan held her upright. "Her legs might be broken," he said.

"It might be cramps," Canace said.

The person behind her began massaging her calves.

Gillian winced, grinding her teeth. "Is it always this hard? Will it be easier next time?"

Dagan stared at her. "Next time?"

She tried to raise her hand to her face, but her hand was too heavy. "What do I call myself now?" she said. "What am I?"

Dagan brushed a fleck of dirt from her nose with his finger. "Gillian," he said. "Who else would you be?"

Gillian tried to stand again. Her legs folded under her and she found herself dangling between Canace and Dagan.

The altar doll jumped to its feet and ran to her. "How is she?" it said, reaching out to take her from Dagan and Canace.

Canace eased between Gillian and the altar doll. "All right, no thanks to you," Canace said. "Debbie, can you get her coat? It's over by the fence."

"Sure," Debbie said from behind Gillian. The hands stopped kneading Gillian's calves.

"She's freezing," Canace said, chafing the chill bumps on Gillian's arms. "Debbie, hurry or we'll lose her!"

"Lose me?" Gillian said through chattering teeth. "Then I'm not a spirit?"

"Not even close," Canace said.

THE MORNING FADED FROM GRAY TO CRISP BLUE. GILLIAN sat on a broken step beside a fallen angel, hunching her shoulders so that the overcoat draped her entire body. Exhausted, she dozed in and out, catching occasional snippets of conversation.

"—can't walk—"

"—should be here—"

"I can carry—"

Gillian woke at one point to find her head in someone's lap. She struggled to sit, but strong hands eased her down. "Rest, child," the altar doll said. "I'll wake you when they reach a decision."

Gillian looked up into the altar doll's face. The spirit's

eyes no longer burned with anger and madness. Its smile curved with a gentle warmth.

"You didn't kill me," Gillian said.

The altar doll brushed the hair from Gillian's forehead. "Your willingness to die was enough."

"That was my sacrifice?"

"Oh, no. I have claimed one of your sacred objects."

A twist of fear wrenched Gillian's stomach. "Who?"

"Gillian?" Debbie said.

Gillian turned. Debbie stood five feet away, her gaze shifting warily between Gillian and the altar doll. Gillian struggled to her feet. She managed three steps before her legs folded.

Debbie caught her. "I'm sorry," she said. "I didn't mean for you to come to me. I just wanted to tell you I'm going to get Nora. We'll meet you at the hospital."

Gillian frowned, confused. "Nora?"

"Nora," Debbie said. "Your sister."

A sister? Gillian rifled her memories but could find no face or emotions that bore the name Nora. She glanced at the altar doll. The altar doll nodded.

"Gillian," Debbie said. "Are you all right?"

"I'm just . . . ." Gillian rubbed the side of her face. "I'm dazed, I guess."

A numbness seeped through her. Had she loved this sister?

The altar doll's voice touched her mind: *Enough to offer your life for hers*.

Gillian waited for a sense of loss, but there was none. "I did it for all of Rio Santo," she said.

The altar doll nodded.

Debbie touched her arm. "Gillian, I need to go. I'll see you later, okay?"

Gillian murmured. Maybe when she saw Nora with Debbie, she'd know her. The emptiness of the name warned her she wouldn't.

CANACE LED THE WAY AS DAGAN CARRIED GILLIAN through the streets of Rio Santo.

The city cowered like a battered dog. Porches and sidings embedded the mud-gorged streets. Yards flowed one into the next, slick expanses of silt decorated here and there with tires, shredded bushes, and mangled car parts. Two utility poles, their wires unraveling around them, sprawled across one street as if waiting for loggers to claim them. Toys peeked from beneath tarps of leaves and mud.

"She blamed herself for what happened to you," Canace said, stepping over a hump of sidewalk. "The whole time we were digging you out, she kept saying that if she'd only stayed with you, the spirit might not have buried you."

Gillian lifted her head from Dagan's shoulder. "Did she explain why she was so terrified?" she asked.

"When she was a kid, her father used to quote the apostle Paul," Dagan said. "He told her that Paul was right, women were soulless, profane creatures, not fit for human society."

Canace shook her head. "When she was five, he told her that Paul waited at the gates of heaven so he could cast all the women into hell." She nudged Dagan. "Wasn't that when Debbie's mom divorced him?"

Dagan shrugged, then tightened his grip on Gillian. He stepped over a red fender. "When Debbie told him she was a lesbian, he begged her not to sully herself with women, that she would be doubly damned."

Gillian shuddered. Had the spirit's version of Paul looked like Debbie's father? She shook her head, then started. This sister—this Nora—was she Debbie's lover? Is that how she and Debbie met? No, she'd met Debbie at The Happy Wanderer. She smiled. She'd gone there with KC. . . .

Her throat constricted. *Not yet,* she thought. *I'm not ready to face that yet.*

She focused on the broken, violated streets.

Not a footprint or a whisper betrayed human life. For as far as she could see, Rio Santo had been deserted.

Her waking fear returned: devastated and lost, the people of Rio Santo had drifted away, leaving the city to crumble under the weight of their absence and the press of time. . . .

A strange hum droned in Gillian's ears. Voices textured the silence, snagging the quiet. Gillian swiveled her head. She slid a little in Dagan's arms. Two men and a woman stood on the corner dressed in blankets, sweats, knit caps, and ski boots, staring up at the sky.

"Not a one," said a man in a yellow cap. He lowered his gaze and smiled. "Hello, there! Where you folks headed?"

Canace slogged toward them. "Hospital," she said.

Dagan followed, hefting Gillian a little higher. "What are you looking for?"

"Clouds," the woman said. Her blanket slid off one shoulder. "Want to be sure this storm's over before we get started."

"Get started?" Dagan said.

The second man shook his head slowly. "Evie, I think we should wait till the aftershocks knock off—"

"And do what?" the woman said. "Scratch our butts? No way. I'm getting as much mud out of my house as I can. Then I'm going to start putting everything back together, pronto."

"I'm with Evie," said the man in the yellow cap. He tipped his chin at Dagan. "You folks need a hand?"

The relief rising in Gillian escaped as a laugh. Rebuilding! "We'll be fine," she said. "Don't let us keep you."

THE HOSPITAL HAD SUSTAINED LITTLE DAMAGE. GILLIAN stared at the labyrinthine, many-legged structure crouched low to the ground. Surrounded by a dark sea of asphalt, the building was beyond threat of mud slides or falling trees. It was also new enough, Gillian remembered reading once, to be heavily reinforced with steel bars.

Dagan carried her along the walk, Canace trailing behind this time. Gillian frowned. There was something odd about the hospital windows. . . .

"What's that yellow stuff reflecting off the glass?" Dagan said.

"My God," Gillian said, "they still have panes. And electricity."

"But that's impossible," Canace said, ducking ahead of them to open the door. "The whole city was knocked out days ago—"

"Emergency generators," Gillian said.

Cots filled the square, white lobby and lined the short piece of visible hallway like dominoes. People huddled under blankets. Some slept while others stared at the ceiling. Nurses and orderlies wandered among them with trays and clipboards. The air smelled tired and old.

Canace's eyes grew wide. "Do they recirculate air?"

Gillian shrugged. "I don't know. They might."

"I'll be right back," Canace said. She rushed out of the lobby, vaulting several cots. She disappeared as she turned the corner.

"But—" Gillian sank back in Dagan's arms. "You might as well put me down—"

A nurse with flushed cheeks approached them. Eyes banded with exhaustion, she still managed a calm, professional smile. "And what can we do for you?" she said.

Fruit cocktail, Gillian almost blurted out.

She bit her lip and kept silent.

"She was buried by a rock slide," Dagan said. "She seems to be all right, but we wanted to be sure there were no broken bones or internal damage—"

"He's here!" Canace materialized as she sprinted around the corner. "KC's here!"

Gillian struggled from Dagan's arms. He set her down gently. She took a step toward Canace and crumpled.

Dagan and the nurse helped her sit up. Canace crouched in front of her and took her hands. Canace laughed. *"He's alive!"*

Gillian stared at her, afraid to hope. "But you said if he was breathing—"

Canace shook her head. "Recirculated air. No Wind. No Earth or Fresh Water. A person enters one of these buildings and just disappears."

"Like Melanie," Dagan said. "That's how she hid from us. Why didn't I think of that?"

Gillian began to shake. Tears dampened her cheeks.

WHEELCHAIR NUDGING THE BED, GILLIAN PROPPED HER elbows on KC's mattress. Nestling her chin in one hand, she reached out and traced KC's arm from elbow to wrist. He took her hand, playing with her fingers. He looked . . . okay. A cast and brace immobilized his collarbone. His face was almost as pale as the plaster.

He lifted her hand to his lips and kissed it. "I'm so glad to see you. I was worried about you."

Gillian smiled. "And I thought you were dead."

"It's not that easy to get rid of me." KC chuckled. "After all these years, I figured you knew that."

"Yeah, but the Kretskis didn't." Gillian pressed his hand with the little strength she had left. "Promise me it'll never be that easy."

"Promise." He turned her arm gently, examining the bruises and star-shaped blisters. "Nothing's broken? They're sure?"

"Doctor said I'm suffering from bruises, muscle strain, and fatigue. Canace added hunger and bought me a Power Bar. Hospital's out of fruit cocktail." Gillian raised her eyebrows. "She promised me a little time with you, then she and Dagan are taking me home."

"She'll stay with you?"

"For a little while." Gillian looked away. "Now that it's over, she won't be able to stay long. She needs to return to the air. I'm going to miss her."

"But you'll see her—"

"Once in a while, when the Wind doesn't need her. But it'll never be the same as living with her."

KC caressed her thumb. "What about Dagan?"

"Depends how soon a new foundation is laid." Gillian laughed halfheartedly. "Funny, now that I finally feel at home in Rio Santo, I'm losing three of the people that make it home. Including a sister I can't remember."

KC kissed her hand again. She looked up.

"I can help you with Nora," he said. "I've heard all the stories—from both of you."

"You know her pretty well?" Gillian said.

"Real well."

"Will I like her?"

KC hesitated. "I can't promise you that. She's a good person—strong, good sense of humor, creative. She loves you very much. But she's also a little . . . self-centered. She tends to push you a lot to get her way."

Gillian sighed. "I think you and I better have a debriefing when I'm not so tired."

"You got it," KC said.

A woman's voice carried down the hallway. "Why would I want to buy a piece of property and not build on it? Especially on Frigate Street?"

"Nora," whispered KC.

Gillian sat up and turned toward the door. "What do I do? How do I act?"

"It's good land," Debbie said. "You could do a lot with it. You could turn it into a community garden or—or a garden for the homeless."

Nora's voice was sure and impatient. "I don't know, Debbie. . . ."

"Just be yourself," KC said. "That's who she loves."

Canace stepped into the doorway. "In here."

Gillian took a deep breath. *I wish I had seven hearts,* she thought. *Then maybe Nora would still be in one of them.*

Debbie and a strange woman in a teal mackintosh followed Canace into the room. The woman looked a lot like Mom.

"There you are!" the woman said, rushing to Gillian's side. She flung her arms around Gillian's neck. It took Gillian a few seconds to remember to hug this stranger back. The effort exhausted her. Her arms trembled as she lowered them to her lap. The woman released her and stepped back.

Gillian glanced at her hands before looking up at the woman. Except for the woman's uncanny resemblance to

Mom, there was nothing familiar about her. Gillian looked into Nora's eyes.

And met fear, hurt, and a fierce love, all directed at her. The woman's eyes were red as if she'd been crying. "Gilly," Nora said, "are you all right?"

A bitter ache filled Gillian, tearing at her. For the first time she could see—and feel—the sacrifice she'd made.

She tried a smile. "I'm okay. I'm so exhausted I can't think, that's all. KC's doing better than I am on that one."

"I'm just doped to the gills, that's all," KC said.

Nora turned to him, seeing him for the first time. Her jaw dropped. "My God, what happened to you?"

"I got shot," he said.

Nora stood there, clearly unsure what to do. The corners of her mouth twitched nervously.

"I'm fine, Nora," KC said. "I got a bed. All Gillian got was a chair."

"Yeah, but I get to go home," Gillian said.

KC pretended to be wounded. "Oh, thanks, rub it in."

Nora's precarious grin swelled into a smile. She crouched beside Gillian's wheelchair. "Gilly, I'm—when Debbie told me you were in the hospital—" She shuddered. "I'm sorry I've been such a jerk lately. With everything that's been going on . . . ." She reached into her coat pocket and removed a can. She set it in Gillian's lap. "I brought you something."

Gillian turned the can so that its label faced her. She smiled.

Fruit cocktail.